THE ARMAGEDDON PROJECT

^{THE}ARMAGEDDON PROJECT

Tom Sancton

Other Press • New York

Production Editor: Robert D. Hack

Text design: Jeremy Diamond

This book was set in 11.1 pt Janson Text by Alpha Graphics of Pittsfield, NH.

10 9 8 7 6 5 4 3 2 1

Library of Congress Cataloging-in-Publication Data

Sancton, Tom.
   The armageddon project / Tom Sancton.
     p. cm.
   ISBN-13: 978-1-59051-252-4
   ISBN-10: 1-59051-252-9
  1. Journalists–France–Paris–Fiction. 2. Arabs–France–Fiction.
3. Terrorism–Fiction. 4. Political fiction. I. Title.
   PS3619.A523A8 2007
   813'.6–dc22
                        2006012190

For Julian and Sandy

CHAPTER

1

THE BOMB THAT EXPLODED in St. Jean de Patmos Church at midnight scattered its entrails all over the Rue Galande. The head of the patron saint, with its gilded halo, lodged against a tree trunk in the adjacent park. The hands, still clasped in prayer, crashed into a doorway across the narrow street. Loose pages from hymnals and prayer books littered the area like confetti after a wedding. On the bloody sidewalk in front of the church, a police photographer stepped over charred timbers and snapped pictures of four mutilated bodies—two British tourists and a young Parisian couple who had the bad luck to walk by at the wrong time.

Sam Preston stood behind a police barricade, along with a dozen other journalists.

"It's obviously Al-Qaeda," said a reporter from *Le Figaro*.

"How do you know?" asked the *Le Monde* correspondent.

"Simple logic, *cher ami*. New York, Madrid, London. Paris was next in line."

Sam wasn't so sure. His French colleagues were often quick on the draw with theories and suppositions—and just as quick to reverse themselves when the facts contradicted them.

At 2:15 a.m., after the bodies were removed and the last glowing embers extinguished, the Paris police prefect approached the knot of reporters huddled at the barricades. Normally, it would be the duty of the police spokesman to brief the press. But the prefect, Jacques-Marie

Trigani, had political ambitions and gravitated to the spotlight as often as he could.

"The bomb was a military-type high-explosive device set off by a remote-controlled detonator," he declared in the self-assured cadences of a senior civil servant. "It was placed directly under the altar. The victims—two British males, one French male, and one French female—were in all likelihood chance passersby and not intentional targets."

"Any idea who did it?" asked the *Le Monde* correspondent.

"In the absence of a credible claim of responsibility or forensic evidence linking the attack to a particular individual or group, any comment on that point would be pure speculation."

Père Joseph pulled onto the Boulevard Périphérique and glanced at the clock on the dashboard. Nearly 2:30. He had hoped to spend a peaceful weekend at the farmhouse near Seaulieu, in Burgundy, where the church held its semiannual retreats. His assistant had offered to officiate at Mass during his brief absence. But Père Joseph had not been away more than three hours when he got the dreadful phone call from his concierge. St. Jean de Patmos, the magnificent little Assyrian Christian church that had been the center of his life and labors for ten years, was a smoldering ruin.

He exited the ring road at the Porte d'Orléans and headed north toward the center of Paris. Traffic was light that time of night. Within a few minutes, his old Citroën BX had reached the Seine and turned onto the Quai St. Michel. As he approached the Rue Galande, he could see flashing red and blue lights from the emergency vehicles. He had half hoped that it was all a mistake, that he would find the Byzantine facade and gilded dome still intact. Now he had to accept the terrible truth.

He parked on the sidewalk and approached the police barricade. Behind it, what was left of St. Jean de Patmos—the burnt beams, charred pews, shattered stained glass, and broken statuary—was obscenely illuminated by police searchlights. A dozen officers with flashlights, gloves, and plastic bags were poking through the ruins of his beloved church. White chalk marks on the sidewalk and street still showed the position of the bodies. Mercifully, the fire hoses had washed the blood away.

Sam watched the cleric from a park bench across the street. He had filed an initial story from an Internet café on the Boulevard St. Michel. It was well past two when he finished, but he had decided to return to the bomb scene and glean some more details for a follow-up article the next day. A terrorist attack in Paris was a big story and he wanted to be on top of it. The other journalists had scattered as soon as Trigani finished his cursory briefing.

Sam wondered who the gaunt, gray-haired figure could be. The man, dressed all in black, was talking animatedly to a policeman behind the barrier, waving what looked like a passport or ID card in one hand. The officer stepped aside for a moment and spoke into a walkie-talkie. Then he turned back to the man and shook his head.

"I'm sorry, Father," said the cop. "It's a crime scene and it's still dangerous. We'll escort you inside when we have finished our work."

"But, officer," said the man. "You don't understand. It's my . . . my church. I belong there."

"Those are the orders, Father. We'll take you in as soon as possible."

The officer turned briskly and moved away, leaving the distraught supplicant alone at the barricade. He gazed at the dark, smoldering shell and mumbled silently to himself. As Sam drew closer, he saw that the priest's eyes were glazed and his hands, resting limply on the cold metal, were shaking.

"Father?"

Père Joseph turned to see a tall, bespectacled man in a denim jacket, holding a spiral notebook in his hand. He assumed it was a plainclothes policeman or perhaps an Interior Ministry official gathering information for his report.

"Sam Preston of the *Chronicle*. Could I ask you a few questions?"

Ah, yes. The press. This would be all over the newspapers in the morning. Ghoulish photos of his eviscerated church splashed on front pages all around the world. That is just what they wanted, those who did this. But there was no help for it.

"I am Père Joseph, rector of St. Jean," he said in slightly accented French as he shook the journalist's hand. "It is a terrible tragedy. Our

3

people have been through so much. Massacres. Centuries of tribulation. Then the latest turmoil over there . . ."

"Over there?"

"In Iraq. We Assyrians come from Iraq—don't you know? We were among the first inhabitants of ancient Mesopotamia. And the first to convert to Christianity. We are now a tiny island in a surging Islamic sea. Many of our people have fled over the years. This little church was a beacon for the Assyrian diaspora. And now, you see what they have done to it?"

"Who do you think might have done it?"

"The same people who have tortured and tormented us over centuries—the Kurds, the Sunnites, the Shiites. Our very existence is intolerable to our Muslim neighbors."

"But Father, those groups are all opposed to one another. They can't all be responsible for this."

"If they agree on one thing, they and Saddam's Baathist brigands, it is their opposition to a Christian enclave in their midst. They will never accept us. In their minds, we are associated with the 'infidels.' We are a fifth column for the Crusaders. And, if I may say so, Mr. Preston, your president did not help matters by sending his troops into Iraq and stirring up the hornet's nest. Now we are getting stung along with you."

"I never thought the invasion was a good idea, Father. But I'm only a reporter, not an agent of the U.S. government."

"And what does a reporter do that is so different? You are writing down every word I say."

"We write news stories to inform the public, not secret reports."

"And you tell the truth?"

"We try to."

The priest studied Sam for a moment. His black, Levantine eyes burned like coals under bushy white eyebrows. "Very well," he said, nodding slowly. "Then you must meet Rafat Ganjibar."

"Who is that?"

"He is the leader of our movement. He will tell you our story. And you can tell it to the world."

CHAPTER

2

"NICE STORY, PRESTON."

Sam glanced up from his computer screen to see Clive Woodridge standing in the doorway. Clive was the *Chronicle*'s Paris bureau chief. A New Zealander by birth, he was educated at Eton and tried to pass himself off as a Brit. His affected Oxbridge accent and gold cufflinks gave an impression of opinionated brilliance that was not always backed up by his journalistic prowess. But Woodridge understood the intricacies of office politics far better than Sam. That's why he was the bureau chief and Sam was number two.

"Thanks, Clive. I guess bombs and bodies will always make the front page. It's pretty hard to mess up a story like that."

"Quite." Woodridge hoisted up his impeccably pressed trousers and took a seat on Sam's couch. "If I may say so, I rather liked the first version better than the second. The new lead with the priest crying at the barricades sort of thing—I found that just a tad, well, operatic, don't you think?"

Sam shrugged. "I thought they'd use the interview as a sidebar in the late edition. But New York decided to lead the main story with the priest. That's what we have editors for."

"Ah, yes, editors," said Woodridge. "What would we do without them?"

He stood up, stretched, cocked his arms back and executed a mock golf drive. Apparently in no hurry to get back to work on this Monday afternoon, Woodridge studied the titles on Sam's bookshelf. He pulled out a thick blue clothbound volume. "What's this?"

"If you must know, Clive, that is the A.A. manual."

"A.A.?"

"Alcoholics Anonymous."

"Good God, man! You haven't quit drinking, have you?"

"I'm trying."

Sam remembered more than one dinner when he and Woodridge had wound up three sheets to the wind after two bottles of Bordeaux and a couple of cognacs. One night, they had gotten so rowdy that an elderly member of Clive's club told them to pipe down and mind their language. Those were the early days, when they were the best of buddies. Sam was learning to be more cautious now.

"What a pity," said Woodridge with a shake of the head. "Imagine being a correspondent in Paris and not drinking the wine! That's what they sent us here for, isn't it?"

"Maybe I've already drunk enough for one tour of duty."

"Nonsense, dear boy! You'll get over all that next time we go to dinner. I'll see to it."

Sam leaned back in his chair and folded his arms across his chest.

"Yes, umm, speaking of dinner," Woodridge continued, "I have to go to a British Embassy banquet tonight. Prince Charles is hosting a little reception. Awful bore, but I really must be there. Show the flag sort of thing."

Sam raised his eyebrows. "And?"

"Yes, well, you see, I was hoping you could do the late duty tonight. I know it's my turn, but it really wouldn't do to snub Prince Charles, would it?"

"Fuck Prince Charles. I've worked late every night this week. I promised to take Sandra to dinner. I'm not married to this bureau, you know."

Woodridge frowned and rubbed his chin. "Yes, I know, it's an awful nuisance. But it looks like somebody's going to get stood up tonight and—well, to put it bluntly, old boy—it won't be Prince Charles."

Woodridge turned on his heels and walked out.

It was nearly seven o'clock when Clive left the bureau. Sam was about to call his wife and offer a rain check for their dinner date when a TV news flash caught his attention. A scrolling banner at the bottom of the screen announced: "Islamic group claims Paris terror strike." CNN's Paris correspondent, Jim Enderman, was doing a live shot in front of the burned-out church. Sam grabbed the remote control and turned up the volume.

"Richard, an unknown group claiming responsibility for the bombing last Saturday that killed four pedestrians in front of Paris's St. Jean de Patmos Church. In a message posted on an Islamist Web site, a group styling itself 'The Avenging Scimitar of Allah the Omnipotent' said it had carried out the bombing as a warning to the so-called 'Crusaders and their puppets who are defiling the holy land of Mesopotamia.' Mesopotamia, of course, the ancient name for Iraq. Richard?"

"Jim," said the anchorman, "any idea why France was targeted, and why this particular church?"

"Richard, French investigators offering no firm conclusions as yet, but they do note that this church is connected with Iraq's Assyrian Christian minority, which is currently pressing for more autonomy from the country's Muslim regions. Richard?"

"Thank you, Jim. That was CNN's Jim Enderman in Paris. And now for the latest international weather picture . . ."

Sam hit the mute button and turned back to his computer. He had just launched a Google search on the Assyrian Christians when the phone rang. Probably Sandra checking to see if he'd made the dinner reservations, Sam thought. But when he picked up the receiver, he heard a man's voice on the line.

"Mr. Preston, this is Père Joseph."

"Oh, hello, Father. I was meaning to call you. Seems some Islamic group has claimed responsibility?"

"We know nothing about this group. But we have a pretty good idea of what is behind the attack. Our political leader, Mr. Ganjibar, has agreed to see you if you are interested in learning more."

"Of course, Father, of course I am interested." Sam grabbed a pen and notebook. "When and where can I meet him?"

"Next Monday, June 19th, at four." The priest gave him an address in Boulogne, in the southwestern suburbs of Paris.

The phone rang again, only this time it was the mobile. That wouldn't be Sandra. She always called first on the office line.

"Tête de patate!" said the caller. He instantly recognized the mocking voice of Charles Dumond, diplomatic correspondent of the weekly *Actualités*.

The two had first met on the press plane during a French presidential visit to Washington a couple of years earlier. Dumond, an indefatigable reporter who had written a few books about American politics and society, instantly latched onto Sam as an interesting specimen. Sam was a big drinker in those days, given to boisterous eruptions of exuberance or rage, forever on the lookout for great yarns but not always prudent in pursuing them. The American was intrigued by Dumond's stories about the civil war in Lebanon, where he had been taken hostage and lived in a rat-infested basement for six months. True, Dumond tended to dine out rather shamelessly on that old experience—every time a French hostage was taken in Iraq, the local TV stations would trot him out as a talking head—but he was a shrewd observer of international politics and Sam valued his cool, analytical mind.

"What's up, Frogface?" said Sam.

"Meet me in the lobby of the Claridge on the Champs Elysées in fifteen minutes. This is important. I'm onto a great story."

"What's it about?"

"I don't want to talk about it on the phone. You know the D.S.T. hears every word you say—even when you talk dirty to your girlfriend. I've heard the tapes myself. Shocking."

"Oh yeah? You should see their videos of you at the Pigalle

live shows." He could hear Dumond's high-pitched giggle on the phone.

"Be there in fifteen minutes, potato brain. It won't take long."

Sam looked at his watch. It was just after eight.

"I can't leave the bureau just like that. I have late duty tonight."

"Just be there. Trust me."

CHAPTER

3

As soon as Sam walked through the Claridge's revolving door, he spotted Dumond sitting in an armchair, reading a newspaper and nervously running a hand through his thinning black hair. Sam was never sure whether his friend did that to straighten his unruly locks or check on how much was left.

Dumond waved the American to an adjacent chair. "Listen, man," he whispered. "This story could make us the next Woodward and Bernstein. But I'm warning you, it could be dangerous. Are you up for this?"

"First of all, tell me what it's about."

"Not yet. I have to know if you are ready to work with me on this story, give it everything you've got, follow it wherever it leads."

Sam took off his glasses and wiped them with his handkerchief. He and Dumond had shared ideas, tips, and tidbits before, but it was quite a different matter to team up on a major investigation. "How can we do this together, Charles? We work for different newspapers."

"We can publish it simultaneously as a joint *Chronicle–Actualités* exclusive."

"My editors would never go for that."

"Then we publish it as a book. Guaranteed best seller. Trust me."

"If this story is so hot—and you're onto it already—why don't you do it by yourself?"

Dumond smiled. "Sammy boy, you're my best friend. I just want to cut you in on the story of a lifetime."

"Don't bullshit me, Charles."

"Okay, I need to do it with an American."

"Why?"

"You'll see. Are you in or out? Otherwise I'll go talk to Rick Swift at *Newsweek*."

"Swift? Oh yeah, your other best friend."

"Don't get jealous, Sammy. In or out?

Sam looked intently into Dumond's black eyes. This time the Frenchman was not smiling.

"In."

Sam followed Dumond up the elevator to the third floor and down a long corridor. Dumond stopped at the end of the hall and knocked. The door opened a crack. A swarthy face in wraparound Ray-Bans peered out from behind the brass chain.

"Hi, Niko," said Dumond.

The man put a finger to his lips.

He pulled the journalists inside, then closed and double-locked the door behind them. He was short, muscular, and very tanned, like someone who spends a lot of time under a UV lamp at the local gym.

"Who's this?" he said, pointing at Sam.

"My friend Sam. He's with the *New York Chronicle*. Sam, this is Nikola."

"The *Chronicle*?" the man repeated with a frown. "Why not the *Times* or the *Washington Post*?"

"Tired old matrons, living on their reputations. The *Chronicle*'s brassy, edgy, lean, and mean. And Sam here"—he tapped the American between the shoulder blades—"happens to be the best investigative reporter in the business."

"We don't need a good reporter. We need someone with a fat checkbook."

Sam glared at Dumond. The Frenchman shrugged.

"We have to talk this over with Michel," said Nikola.

He opened a door and led the pair into an adjoining sitting room, where they found another man ensconced in an armchair. His denim workshirt was undone to the third snap, exposing a hairy chest and a heavy gold neck chain.

Nikola made a hasty introduction and Michel pointed to a couch. He leaned forward and picked up a manila envelope from the coffee table. "What's in here," he said in a thick Marseille accent, "is dynamite. It could bring down the French government. But you won't get it for free."

"Sorry, the *Chronicle*'s not into checkbook journalism. We're wasting our time here." Sam started to get up, but Dumond pushed him back down on the sofa.

"Cool it, Sammy," the Frenchman scolded. "Wait till you hear what it's about."

Sam sat back down and folded his arms.

Michel leaned forward and looked Sam in the eyes. "It's about arms sales. We're not talking about the kind of crap they sell the Africans, the cheap Chinese-made AK-47s and World War II hand grenades. This is high-tech stuff I'm talking about. Sophisticated weapons, powerful weapons, controlled weapons."

"What, for example?" asked Sam.

"I'm not going to give it to you for free. You think I'm stupid?"

"Where do the arms come from?"

"Everywhere. Brazil, ex-Soviet Union, France, South Africa, China, Czecho, Israel."

"WMD's?"

Michel shook his head. "All conventional. But high-end conventional. The kind of stuff that can do serious damage."

"Give me just one example," said Sam.

"TOW missiles—tube-launched, wire-guided anti-tank weapons. Turn a tank into toast from 4 kilometers away."

"What else?"

Michel smiled. "Not until you pay for it."

Sam looked over at Dumond. "This is getting nowhere, Charles. I really want to go."

"Sammy, you're asking all the wrong questions. The important thing is who is selling it and where it is going."

Sam turned back to Michel. "Well?"

"It's going," said Michel, with a smirk, "to your enemies. It's going to the resistance forces fighting the U.S. in Iraq, for example, and to the Iranians who are hunkering down to defend their nuclear facilities, and to their allies in Hezbollah."

"You see, Sammy? I told you this was dynamite."

"What about Qaeda?" Sam asked.

Michel laughed. "Qaeda's a bunch of suicide bombers and head-choppers. They wouldn't know what to do with a TOW missile. Of course, the Stingers might interest them."

"Stingers?"

Michel nodded.

"Tell Sam who's selling it," said Dumond. "That's the really juicy part."

A faint smile flickered across Michel's thin lips. He glanced over at Nikola. The Greek was cracking his knuckles and tensing his bodybuilder biceps. He gave Michel a nod.

"Roland Peccaldi."

"Roland Peccaldi?" said Sam. "The old Gaullist politician?"

Michel nodded.

"That's ridiculous," said Sam. "Peccaldi's a senator, a former foreign minister, a member of the president's political family."

"They fell out a while back," said Michel, "in case you hadn't noticed."

"I'm well aware of that," said Sam. "Still, a man of Peccaldi's stature, an ex-cabinet minister, he couldn't be involved in something like this unless the government knew about it."

"Who said they don't?"

"If that's true, this story could destroy the French president, divide the NATO alliance, and cause a major international flap."

"That's not my problem," said Michel.

Sam shook his head. "This all sounds like bullshit to me."

Michel took a half-inch thick stack of papers out of the envelope and ruffled the edges with his thumb like a card dealer. He pulled a page out, apparently at random. "Take a look."

Sam took the paper and perused its contents. It was a financial document, but the Swiss bank's name on the letterhead was blacked out with a marking pen. It was addressed to a bank in Monte Carlo (name also blacked out). "Dear Sirs," it said,

> Please notify Armexco, 23 Avenue de la Princesse Grace, Monte Carlo, that we open in their favor our credit, to the extent of U.S. $73,600,000 (Seventy-Three Million, Six Hundred Thousand Dollars and No Cents). Their drafts are to be paid immediately upon presentation of documents evidencing current shipment to [company name blacked out], Istanbul, of the goods described on the attached invoice, No. 557/66/9/B.

"This is bank gobbledygook," said Sam, handing back the paper. "It doesn't say what was shipped by whom or to whom. It could be toilet seats, for all I know."

"Seventy-four million bucks for toilet seats?" said Michel with a malevolent chuckle. "Only the U.S. Air Force would pay prices like that. You want to know what it's for? Check this out."

Michel handed over another page, whose reference number matched the previous one. It was from Armexco, Inc., addressed to a company in Istanbul whose name was blacked out:

INVOICE No. 557/66/9/B

QTY	DESCRIPTION	UNIT PRICE	TOTAL
5	Cobra AH1-PS Helicopters	$3,000,000	$15,000,000
10	T-80 Tanks	$4,000,000	$40,000,000
10	Stinger Missiles	$100,000	$1,000,000
25	Matra Otomat Mark-I missiles	$300,000	$7,500,000
200	Gallil assault rifles	$500	$100,000
20	TOW 2A missiles	$500,000	$10,000,000
		TOTAL DUE:	$73,600,000

Shipment: Maritime freight to Istanbul
Terms of Payment: Letter of Credit

Signed: Miguel Carvallo,
President, Armexco, Inc.

Sam held the document out to Dumond. The Frenchman shook his head. "I've already seen it," he said. "Pretty interesting, no?"

Sam ran his fingers through his wavy brown hair. "I'm not convinced. Anybody could have typed that on their computer. The bank names are blotted out. There are no phone numbers, no way to doublecheck. What could a serious journalist do with that kind of crap?"

"Look," said Michel, raising his voice, "I intentionally blacked out some stuff on those sample photocopies, okay? I'm not stupid enough to open the whole kimono. All the information you need, un-adulterated and totally verifiable, is in this envelope. But you won't get it for free. If you don't want it, *tant pis*, we'll sell it to somebody else."

"How much?"

"Make a reasonable offer."

"We're just wasting our time here," said Sam, rising to his feet. "I couldn't offer you anything without clearance from New York. And they don't pay for real documents—much less outright fakes."

Michel slid the papers back into the envelope and stood up. "These aren't fakes, my friend. When you're ready to get serious, you can see the rest of them. Think it over."

"That won't take long," said Sam, turning to Dumond. "Let's go, Charles."

Michel took a step toward Sam and waved a finger in his face. "Have it your own way. But understand this well: no money, you forget every-thing we told you."

Sam wanted to head back to the bureau immediately, but Dumond in-sisted that they have a quick drink in his favorite bar, a trendy place on the Rue Balzac, just off the Champs Elysées.

Dumond slid into a corner booth and ordered a Chardonnay. Sam ordered a Perrier with lemon.

"What do you think?" asked Dumond.

"Two-bit con men. The whole thing stinks."

"C'mon, man, you saw those documents."

"Charles, anybody with a computer can manufacture documents like that."

"I'm telling you, man, this is for real. This is a huge story."

"And who are those guys?"

"Nikola is a Greek hustler, informer, and petty drug dealer. I met him a couple of years ago in Ibiza. He tried to sell me some documents about the sale of French missile components to the Chinese."

"You actually bought documents from that creep?"

"No, but I used his information to track down the story. It checked out. But I never published it."

"Why?"

"Use your head! You know my newspaper belongs to a big arms and aerospace conglomerate, the Larcher Group. My editor said the story would get us both fired, so he spiked it."

"That's French press freedom for you. I love it! And just what makes you think your paper will publish a story about an illegal arms deal that could destroy a powerful Gaullist politician and maybe even bring down the French government?"

Dumond grinned and patted Sam on the shoulder. "That's what I need you for, buddy. If an American paper exposes this story, the French press will have to follow suit."

"Oh, I get it—follow me, you first."

"You catch on fast," said Dumond with a high-pitched cackle.

"What about the other guy, the one with the gold neck chain and the cheap cologne?"

Dumond finished his Chardonnay and lit a cigarette. "Michel is more serious—and more dangerous. He works for Peccaldi. He has access to sensitive information."

"He works for Peccaldi?"

Charles put a finger to his lips and looked around the room. "Keep your voice down. The old guy doesn't fuck around. If his name leaks at this point, we could both wind up at the bottom of the Seine. I'm serious."

"I don't like this story."

"You're afraid?"

"No. I just think the whole thing is bullshit."

Dumond grabbed the American's wrist and gave it a hard squeeze. "Don't you tell me this story is bullshit. It's for real."

"What makes you so sure?"

"Let's just say I know more than those guys told you."

Sam looked at his watch. "Jesus, it's 9:30 already. I gotta get back to the bureau. I'll call you tomorrow."

"Don't forget, Sammy," Dumond called out as Sam bounded toward the door, "you said you were in."

Sam grabbed for his cell phone as he headed down the Champs Elysées. He had forgotten to turn it back on after leaving the Claridge. As soon as the screen lit up, the phone emitted a high-pitched beep. There were seven messages from the news desk in New York. Something about a break in the French bombing investigation. New York needed him to file a story immediately. The last message made him wince. "Stand down, Preston. Kemp is on the case."

Bradley Kemp had arrived in the bureau a couple of months earlier. He was only twenty-eight, but everybody said he was a young man on the move. Kemp was boyish and affable, but he was like a little machine that never stopped. "The Energizer bunny" is what people called him behind his back.

When Sam entered his office, he found Kemp sitting at his computer. "Hi, Sam. My machine crashed so I'm using yours. Hope you don't mind. Actually, I didn't think you were coming back."

"What's this story about?" Sam took off his jacket and threw it on the couch. Bradley's pinstriped coat occupied the hook behind the door.

"The St. Jean bombing. The French investigators discovered that the explosive was identical to the one used by the London Metro bombers. Scotland Yard is sending a team over to work with the French."

"The St. Jean bombing is my story."

"Oh I know that, Sam—terrific piece, by the way. I wouldn't dream of big-footing on your turf. It's just that you weren't around and New York asked me to jump in. Don't worry. This is just a short item."

Bradley went back to the keyboard. With his French cuffs, bow tie, and suspenders, he looked to Sam like a carbon copy of Clive Woodridge. Except that Kemp had a thick head of immaculately brushed auburn hair, while Woodridge was going thin on top and gray on the sides. Kemp was also a head taller than the bureau chief. But then so were most people.

Sam's office phone rang. He leaned over to pick it up, but Bradley grabbed it first. "I'm expecting a call back from the Interior Ministry," he whispered, then barked into the mouthpiece: "*Chronicle*. Kemp speaking."

Bradley looked disappointed and handed the receiver to Sam. "It's for you."

"Not surprising, Bradley. It's my office. Hello . . ."

"Sam, where have you been? I was so worried."

"Oh, Jesus, Sandra, I'm sorry. Clive asked me to stay and do the late duty. I meant to call you."

"But Sam, you weren't in the office. I called ten times. I called your cell phone, too, but there was no answer. I was really worried about you."

"I had to check out a story. I'll explain it all to you over dinner. The Brasserie du Théâtre is open till midnight. It's only ten o'clock now."

"Dinner? You must be joking, Sam. I'm going to bed."

CHAPTER

4

C LIVE WOODRIDGE SAT IN a heavy leather armchair, picking salted almonds and hazelnuts out of a crystal bowl and leaving the peanuts. He quaffed down the remains of his first whiskey-and-ice and slid the glass to the side of the table. A waiter appeared almost instantly with a fresh drink and a paper napkin that bore the red logo of Fouquet's bar.

Woodridge glanced at his Rolex, then unfolded his *Financial Times* and read the headline: "Oil hits $75 in London." He muttered an obscenity under his breath. Should have bought those oil futures at $50 when I had the chance, he thought. But who'd have imagined it could go any higher? He shook his head and flipped to the inside pages to check on his stocks.

He looked at his watch again. Then he saw Sam crossing the Champs Elysées. He was tall enough to stand out in a crowd. And that lazy, loping gait of his, well, only a Yank could walk like that. Woodridge buried his nose in his FT and pretended to read.

"Hi, Clive," said Sam, settling into an armchair and grabbing a handful of nuts.

Woodridge looked up and slowly took off his reading glasses. "Preston, how good of you to come. Didn't anyone ever tell you that punctuality is the courtesy of kings?"

"Last time I checked, neither of us was royalty."

"Very perceptive, dear boy," said Woodridge with his crooked smile. "Waiter! I'll have another Chivas and water. What are you having?"

"Diet Coke."

"Still not drinking? No more vices of the flesh or spirit?"

"I still eat," said Sam, patting his belly. He wasn't fat, but his once lanky frame had filled out since he'd arrived in Paris four years earlier. French cuisine was hard to resist—especially on an expense account. Sam looked absently at the menu. There was no food on it, just cocktails.

The waiter brought their drinks and a fresh bowl of mixed nuts. Woodridge took a large gulp of whiskey and cleared his throat.

"Right. Let's cut to the chase, shall we?" said the bureau chief, wiping his moist lower lip with a paper napkin. "About that unpleasantness last Monday. I believe I did mention, didn't I, that I wanted you to do the late duty while I went to the Embassy. Am I right?"

"Of course."

"But you seem to have gone AWOL."

"Somebody called me with a tip about a story. I went to check it out. I was only gone an hour. I'm sorry, okay?"

Woodridge took another quaff of whiskey and carried on. "As bureau chief, I took the flak for your negligence. Fair enough. The bureau chief always has to be a lightning rod. But he also conducts heat. So you should know, old boy, that whenever I get called to book for your cock-ups, you will feel the heat. Am I making myself clear?"

"I said I'm sorry. It won't happen again."

Woodridge stared silently at Sam. His eyes were getting dull and his lower lip was sagging. "I've always liked you, Preston. You're a good man. Just don't blot your copybook. The *Chronicle*'s not just a newspaper, it's a big corporate team. We've all got to play by the rules."

Woodridge flagged a passing waiter and pointed to his empty glass. "So tell me about your holiday plans. Surely you're not going to Dover again?"

"Actually, we might spend a week or so there. Sandra's mother is getting up in years. We have to check on her once in a while."

"Sandra's got a brother in Dover, doesn't she? Why don't you let him look after the old girl?"

"Nigel? He's always off traipsing around Europe in his camping-car."

"I see. One of those working-class gypsies in their grotty little caravans. Speaking of holidays, I'm off on July 15 for a month. Jill and I have rented a villa in the South of France. Swimming pool, olive groves, fig trees, and a nice local red wine. Doesn't travel, mind you, but it goes down quite nicely around the pool. You and Sandra should come visit us down there."

Sam looked puzzled. "You know we can't take vacation at the same time. I have to man the bureau as usual."

"Actually, you'll have plenty of time. Kemp's going to be in charge while I'm gone."

"Kemp? He just got here. How can you put him in charge?"

"Not my idea, old boy. New York wants it that way. They're grooming him. Up the greasy pole sort of thing. They only sent him to Paris to punch his ticket as a foreign correspondent."

"But Bradley's ten years younger than me. He hardly speaks French. He doesn't know anybody. How the hell can he run the Paris bureau?"

"Don't be naive, Sam. This isn't the civil service. It's not seniority that moves you up the ladder. It's not even journalistic talent. It's all about politics, relationships, networking. If the powers that be like the cut of your jib, you'll move up. If not, you'll keep pedaling with the rest of the pack no matter how good a reporter you are. You've never understood that, Sam. You've always been a bit of an odd duck. Personally, I find that endearing. But, face it, you're no Bradley Kemp."

Sam folded and refolded his straw until it looked like a plastic accordion. "Ten years at the *Chronicle*, two Overseas Press Club awards, one Pulitzer nomination, and I'm going to have to take orders from Bradley Kemp?"

"Let's not get histrionic about it, old boy. You won't really have to 'take orders' from him. It's just an administrative thing really, paper shuffling, budgets, signing stringer forms. You don't want to do that anyway. You'll be free to do what you're really good at—reporting."

"Oh, that's wonderful. I hadn't thought of it that way."

"That's another thing that keeps you down. You can't hold your tongue. You're a whiner."

"You're wrong, Clive. I'm just somebody who squeals when he gets fucked up the ass. You public school boys should understand that."

CHAPTER

5

QUENTIN RITTER WAS GETTING up in years—he'd turn eighty in September—but he remained remarkably active. The son of a Boston Brahmin family, fourth-generation Harvard man, decorated veteran of World War II and Korea, he'd made a fortune in the oil business and served six terms in the U.S. Senate, where he had been one of the most influential Republicans on Capitol Hill. The one thing he had not done, though, despite two failed attempts, was get himself elected to the White House. No, it took his wisecracking, fraternity-boy, born-again son to achieve that.

The old man had embraced Jack on election night, and shed proud tears over the honor that the American voters—well, nearly half of them—had bestowed on his patrician family. He wasn't so sure how well suited Jack was for the job, however, so he made sure his old friend Bill Cordman would be right at his side every step of the way. And he himself resolved to do whatever he could to help the boy. He knew Jack detested his phone calls and advice. His most effective role was to act as his son's personal, secret envoy to the movers and shakers of the world. In this way, he quietly lined up Saudi investments, Taiwanese orders for warships and fighter planes, Chinese purchases of Boeing jetliners, and British backing for his son's dubious foreign adventures.

Now his globetrotting mission had brought him to Bogotá, where he sat in an antechamber waiting to see President Chico Martinez, elected to office six months earlier with discreet American backing and money. The financing of a foreign election campaign was illegal and unofficial, of course, but Quentin Ritter had collected a tidy sum from the well-heeled corporate contacts that filled the pages of his address book. Now it was payback time.

The ornate double doors to the presidential office opened, and Chico Martinez rushed out to greet his distinguished visitor. The Colombian, who smelled strongly of after-shave and cigar smoke, wrapped his arms around Ritter and hugged him tightly. The old man had always disliked physical contact of any kind, but he managed a symbolic pat on the shoulder as he stepped back from the president's sweaty, macho embrace.

"Quentin, *viejo amigo*, it is so wonderful to see you again. How is Susan?"

"She's slowing down a bit, but still feisty as ever. Doesn't let me get away with anything."

Martinez laughed loudly and shook his head. He escorted his guest into the presidential office and closed the doors. "In my country, it is the men who wear the pants. It is much better that way."

"Don't tell Susan Ritter that, or she'll bite your head off."

Martinez sat down and waved the American to a wooden armchair whose high, elaborately carved back dug painfully into the old man's spine.

"And how is your boy?"

"He's fine, Chico. But he needs your help."

Martinez grinned. "I was expecting that. What can I do for him?"

"He needs money. A lot of money."

The Colombian raised his eyebrows. "The president of the richest country in the world needs money from a poor lawyer from Bogotá?"

"You may have been a poor lawyer before we found you—and you were not so poor at that—but you're now president of one of the richest countries in Latin America."

"But, Quentin, Colombia is not rich. Our GDP is not one-fortieth of yours."

"I'm not talking about GDP, trade figures, indebtedness. Save all that for the World Bank and the IMF. I'm talking about all the money that is actually floating around in this country."

Martinez smiled and cocked his head slightly to one side. "I do not know what you mean."

"You know exactly what I mean, Chico. I'm talking about your country's biggest export."

The Colombian slowly drew a cigar from his breast pocket and lit it with a gold lighter. He held out the leather cigar-holder. Ritter waved it away.

"I am not a coca farmer, Quentin. I am merely a public servant."

Ritter blew his nose into a monogrammed handkerchief. "Chico, I worked and traveled all over Latin America when I was in the oil business," he said. "In the Senate, I headed special committees that investigated these matters quite thoroughly. I have access to intelligence information that leaves no doubt about the relationship between occult money and political power in this part of the world. So let's cut the cow doo-doo."

The Colombian stroked the corners of his thick black mustache. His eyes moved slowly around the room, then back to Ritter. "How much does he need?"

"Five billion dollars."

Martinez's eyes widened, then he burst out laughing and coughing, expelling a thick cloud of cigar smoke. "You are joking."

"I never joke, Chico. It's not my style. My style is loyalty, friendship, and respect for gentlemen's agreements. You could not have imagined that our help came with no strings attached."

Martinez stood up and paced around the room. "You want me to fork over five billion just like that?"

"Nobody's talking about forking anything over. We're offering you a good investment opportunity—a ten-year loan, fully guaranteed by a syndicate of private investors, with a five percent commission in the form of a balloon payment at the end of the term."

"Ten percent."

"Seven and a half."

"Done."

Martinez smiled grandly and gave the old man a firm handshake. Ritter stood up slowly, rubbed his back, and followed the Colombian to the door.

"We'll be in touch about the technical details, Chico. The president thanks you for your loyalty."

"Please give him my warmest regards, Quentin. And also to Susan."

"I shall."

Quentin Ritter was a most effective, and persuasive, advocate. By the end of his two-week tour of friendly Latin American capitals, followed by a swing through Riyadh, Kuwait, Dubai, Bahrain, Seoul, and Taiwan, he had amassed a total of $25 billion. Once the money had transited through a kaleidoscope of cutout companies and offshore institutions, it found its way into five numbered accounts in a private Swiss bank on the shores of Lake Lugano. All that had happened six months earlier. In the meantime, someone had started putting the money to good use.

CHAPTER

6

RAFAT GANJIBAR SAT IN THE BACK seat of his black Audi SUV and perused the business section of that Monday's *Herald Tribune*. A sedan would have been a more appropriate vehicle for a man in his position. But Ganjibar's 350-pound frame could not fit easily into a normal-sized car. Not that his Audi lacked elegance. The seats were custom upholstered in cream-colored leather, the FM-CD console featured wraparound sound, the computer terminal in the rear compartment kept him in constant touch with the Internet and doubled as a TV with a built-in DVD player. Just now, the screen featured a sweating black woman who was singing and pounding on a tambourine. Ganjibar glanced occasionally at the image, but he had muted the sound.

His cell phone—a gift from some American friends—chimed out the first two measures of "Jesus Loves Me, Yes I Know." He fished the device out of his jacket pocket and answered in a loud, flat voice that rose steadily in volume as he spoke.

"Yes? . . . Yes I know. . . . Tell him I am stuck in traffic."

Ganjibar's chauffeur glanced at him in the rearview mirror. The Audi was speeding through the Bois de Boulogne at sixty mph.

Ganjibar snapped the phone shut and went back to his newspaper.

The Audi emerged from the wooded park and proceeded across the St. Cloud bridge. The chauffeur signaled a right turn, but Ganjibar tapped him roughly on the shoulder.

"Straight ahead, then turn left at the second stop light," he barked.

"Oui, Monsieur le Président," said the chauffeur, "but that will take us out of our way."

"Do as I tell you, Dominique."

"Oui, Monsieur le Président."

The chauffeur drove on, then executed the left turn onto a narrow one-way street.

"Stop here!"

"But, Monsieur le Président, there is no place to park and there are cars behind me."

"Do as you are told, you idiot. Go into that patisserie and get me three chocolate éclairs and three lemon tarts."

"Oui, Monsieur le Président." Dominique pulled on the hand brake and stepped out of the car. As he took his place in the waiting line, the street began to reverberate with honking horns. An irate driver got out of his car and attempted to jerk open the rear door of the Audi. Ganjibar, who had locked the doors from his rear control panel, gazed impassively at the other man through the tinted window then turned on the radio to drown out his shouts.

Five minutes later, Dominique returned, sweating and red-faced, and handed a package to Ganjibar. It was gift-wrapped in flowered paper with a red ribbon and bow. Ganjibar ripped off the paper and stuffed half an éclair into his mouth. He mumbled something unintelligible as the Audi pulled away, leaving the other driver shaking his fist in a cloud of hot exhaust.

"Sorry, Monsieur le Président. What did you say?"

Ganjibar finished the other half and wiped his mouth with the wrapping paper. "I said, the dogs may bark, but the caravan passes."

Sam sat on a leather couch in the reception area wishing that he had not skipped lunch. The receptionist, a young Parisienne with a revealing décolleté, glanced at him a couple of times and smiled when her eyes met his.

"The president should be here any minute now."

Sam nodded and looked around the spacious foyer. A bronze crucifix hung on the wall behind the receptionist. To the right of her desk was a heavy mahogany door with a brass plaque that read: "Provisional Assyrian Republic—Office of the President." A flag hung on the far wall, a large white cross on a burgundy field. It looked suspiciously like the Swiss flag—except for the interlaced sword and palm tree in the upper left quadrant.

An owlish-looking man with a gray crew cut and round horn-rimmed glasses suddenly emerged from a corridor and approached the journalist with an outstretched hand.

"Sam Preston?" he said. "I'm Hal Carpenter, special assistant to the president. He tells me he's caught in traffic and running a little late. Sends his apologies and all that. Why don't you step into my office and I can fill you in on our movement."

As Sam followed him down the hallway, Carpenter jerked his head in the direction of the reception desk.

"Sweet, huh?" he said with a wink.

"What's that?"

"Monique, the president's private secretary. She's got a pair to die for. Look but don't touch, know what I mean?"

"Yeah, listen," said Sam, "maybe I can come back another time, or talk to Mr. Ganjibar on the phone."

"No, no, no. He won't be but a minute. I'll tell you all the background, so you'll be right up to speed when you talk to Rafat. Here take a seat."

Sam sat on a folding wooden chair. It was too small for him, and uncomfortably hard, but it was the only one in the room besides Carpenter's desk chair.

Carpenter tapped on the keyboard of his portable computer. "Just give me a second, here, Sam. I was working on something."

Sam could see the computer screen dimly reflected in the office window. It was a game of solitaire. Carpenter dealt himself a card and paused the game.

"Okay, done!" Carpenter said, and swiveled his chair in Sam's direction. "Say, you want a candy bar or something? Your stomach's growlin' like a herd of cattle headed for the slaughterhouse."

"No, it's all right."

Carpenter smiled, opened his desk drawer and slid a Milky Way over to Sam. "I eat these things all the time. Got a real sweet tooth from workin' in the Middle East. I never gain an ounce, though. See, I've got sleep issues. I lie awake all night worryin' about when I'll fall asleep. That burns off the calories. Better than exercise."

Sam tore off the wrapper and bit into the candy bar. "What's this Provisional Assyrian Republic all about?"

"Well, first off, you need to understand where Rafat is coming from. See, his family were prominent members of the Christian community in northwestern Iraq. His father was a wealthy businessman, and had a lot of political influence in the region. But he ran afoul of Saddam Hussein and had to flee the country in the late seventies. So he moved his family to Beirut and continued his activities there."

"What kind of activities?"

"He bought and sold stuff—oriental rugs, jewelry, oil, commodities, machinery, you name it. He also kept up his political ties to the Assyrian community. He was kind of revered as an elder statesman, see? Rafat was his only son. When the old man died, Rafat inherited his fortune, and his political influence. He was only twenty then, but he has built on that legacy. Today, he is considered the de facto leader of the whole community—inside and outside Iraq. He has also turned his father's business into a major industrial group—the Ganjibar Corporation."

"What does it do?"

"Rafat's into everything—construction, real estate, transportation, high-tech, medicine. He's the largest importer of pharmaceuticals in the Middle East. That's how I got involved in his operation."

"You're in the pharmaceutical business?"

Carpenter chuckled. "Naw, not directly. See, I'm a doctor. I met Rafat at a medical services convention in London ten years ago. We hit it off right away and he recruited me to run his pharmaceutical division. I didn't know didley squat about the business, but all he really needed was a doctor to run around the Middle East and help him sell drugs. He offered me a hell of a lot more than I was making as a GP back in Alabama, so I joined his company, moved to Beirut, and never looked back."

"What are you doing in France?"

Carpenter peered at Sam over the top of his glasses. "Well, you see, Rafat runs all his business out of Paris these days—including the political stuff. Once he started working on the Assyrian Republic project, he decided it would be better to set up his headquarters outside the Middle East. That way it would be easier to deal with Western supporters and donors."

"What donors?"

"I better let Rafat talk to you about the fund-raising issues. He'll explain it better than me."

"So you're not involved in his political activities?"

"Oh, I am. Don't quote me on this, Sam, but I'm gonna be the minister of health and human services once we're up and running. We're planning to set up a complex of state-of-the-art hospitals and clinics, and draw high-end patients from all over the Middle East. We're gonna be real big on plastic surgery. Rafat says he wants me to run all that."

"But what do you do now?"

"Well, I really shouldn't talk about this, but I kind of trust you, 'cause you're a fellow American and all. Fact is, I'm Rafat's unofficial link to the American Evangelical community. See, my uncle is a very well-known TV preacher—I can't tell you his name, but you'd know it. We're working hard on building up Rafat's contacts and support among American Christians."

Suddenly the door cracked open and an elderly man poked his head into the office. The first thing Sam noticed was the hair—sparse on top, close-cropped on the sides, gray at the roots, with a very poor brownish-orange dye job. The second thing he noticed was the lisp.

"Mister Preston? I am Professor Daniel Rappola, Collège de France. I am a faithful reader of your newspaper, and I just wanted to introduce myself."

Sam stood up and shook the man's hand. It was cold and moist. "Pleased to meet you, Professor. You work with Mr. Carpenter here?"

"Oh, him," said Rappola, with a nod in Carpenter's direction. "I don't know how much work *he* does. I am a senior advisor to the president. In fact—and this is for your information only—I'm sure you will appreciate that a certain amount of discretion is advisable—indeed, necessary—at this point in time, no?—I will serve as minister of education and culture once the republic is operational."

"I see. Will there be any actual Assyrians in this government?"

Rappola laughed. "Alas, yes. There will be plenty of portfolios to go around."

"Yeah," said Carpenter. "Rafat likes to have a lot of people around him."

"You mean the president," Rappola corrected, then turned to Sam. "Well, I won't keep you any longer, Mr. Preston. I expect we'll be meeting again. Great things are under way, things that will surely be of interest to a famous journalist like yourself."

"I'm hardly famous," said Sam.

"If you stick with this story, perhaps you will be."

As soon as Rappola had closed the door behind him, Carpenter shook his head. "Sad," he muttered.

"Excuse me?"

"Rappola. He's just a doddering fool—old fuss and feathers, I call him. Pay no attention to him."

"But he said he's going to be a cabinet minister."

Carpenter clicked his tongue. "Rafat tells a lot of people a lot of things. Fact is, Rappola is useful to him in building up his contacts in France, especially with the Jewish community. Rappola's very active in, you know, those kind of organizations. But the old fart's right about one thing."

"Which is?"

"If you stick with us, you'll have a hell of a story. Rafat never talks to the press, but he really liked the article you did. He's giving you this interview as an exclusive. And if you play ball with us, you'll have the inside track once this thing hits the headlines. Like we say back in Alabama, 'You dance with the one that brung ya.'"

Carpenter's phone rang.

"Yes, sir. . . . Yes, he's here with me. . . . I'm sorry, I didn't realize that. . . . Yes, sir, I'll bring him right in."

He hung up and rolled his eyes. "Rafat's off on one of his tirades. Says he wanted to be the only one to talk to you. C'mon, I'll take you in there."

Carpenter led Sam back down the hall to Ganjibar's office and knocked softly on the door.

"Are you the stupid?" shouted a booming voice inside. "You know I am expecting you."

Carpenter opened the door. "Mr. President," he said, "this is Sam Preston of the *Chronicle*."

"I know who it is. I have appointment with him, don't I?" Ganjibar advanced toward Sam and flashed a broad smile. On top of his gargantuan body sat a round, jowly face with all the features—beady black eyes, aquiline nose, and sensual lips—grouped in the center.

"Welcome, Mr. Preston," he said, shaking the journalist's hand and patting him on the shoulder. "Please forgive me. Traffic was very bad in Paris. Bumper by bumper, you know."

"No problem. Mr. Carpenter here gave me some useful background."

"I give you background, not him." He scowled at Carpenter. "Leave us, please."

"Sure thing," said Carpenter. "I'll be in my office if you need me."

Ganjibar closed the door. "You know what Lenin say about useful idiots? He is useful idiot. Here is my real right-hand man, Maître Tikhani. He is my lawyer, advisor, and I would say also father confessor—except he is Jewish."

"So was Jesus," said Tikhani, a tall, slender man with a hawklike face, dressed in an elegant gray suit and a collarless black shirt. "Robert Tikhani. Pleased to meet you."

Ganjibar invited his guest to take a seat next to Tikhani on a leather couch.

"First of all, Mr. Preston, I want to thank you for your article in the *Chronicle*. You write with heart. The way you talk about Père Joseph, quote his words, make the people understand how this is terrible tragedy for whole Assyrian community. You are a great, great journalist."

"Thank you," Sam said. "I was sorry to see that beautiful church destroyed."

"Yes, we Assyrians are very attached to our church," said Ganjibar. "But we will rebuild just like before. I will pay for it myself. Most important thing is what this attack says about our position in Iraq today. You know story of Assyrian people?"

"I've researched it a bit on the Internet," said Sam.

"Forget Internet. Too many idiots writing garbage on Internet. I tell you the real history. We trace our roots back to great Assyrian Empire, 5000 BC, with capital city in Nineveh. Today is called Mosul. In Bible times, the prophet Jonah come to Nineveh and preach repentance to Assyrians. After Jesus die, Assyrians become first people to convert to Christianity. But later we suffer centuries of persecution from Muslims, Kurds, Ottoman Empire, everybody. And our enemies, they try to kill us like Hitler kill the Jews. In 1918, we lose nearly two-thirds of our people at the hands of Kurds and Muslims. This is Assyrian Holocaust, terrible tragedy. That make many Assyrians flee to other countries. And Saddam Hussein, he persecute us, too, and more people leave. Today, Assyrian diaspora is more than six million people. But more than two million are still in Iraq, mostly in the northwest. And they are persecuted even more today than under Saddam and Baathist Party."

"How can it be worse than it was under a bloodthirsty tyrant?"

"Because Saddam, he hate all religion. He keep us down, but he keep down Muslims, too. Today, Muslim guerrillas and terrorists are running wild all over the country. They say we are spies for the Crusaders, because we are Christians. They blow up our churches, our homes. They are the ones who destroy our church in Paris. They give us two choices: convert to Islam, or leave Iraq. But we will make third choice—we build independent Assyrian Christian Republic."

"How can a small minority like yours hope to ever become an independent state? Even a large ethnic bloc like the Kurds have had trouble obtaining an autonomous region."

"League of Nations promise us a state in 1928. Nothing happen. You know why? Because international community don't care about us then. Today, we will show the world we are key to peace and prosperity in the region. You shake your head?"

"I understand your desire for an independent homeland. It is a beautiful dream. But in the current context, it just doesn't seem realistic."

"You want to talk about realistic? I show you realistic."

Ganjibar stood up slowly, putting his hands on the desk top to maintain his balance while he extracted his rear end from the chair. "Come! Come!" he said, leading Sam into an adjacent office.

In the center of the room, mounted on a large wooden pedestal, stood a detailed architect's model of a thriving metropolis, complete with high-rise office buildings, hotels, luxury apartment complexes, plazas, fountains, parks, tree-lined avenues, a gold-domed cathedral, and an artificial lake with an island in the middle bearing what appeared to be an outsized statue of Jesus stretching out his arms in benediction.

"This is our future capital, Assyria. We build brand-new city right on the desert sands. And this"—Ganjibar pointed to an architect's drawing mounted on the wood-paneled wall—"this will be our international airport. We will build big duty-free mall, bigger than Dubai. People come from all over the world to shop there. You are still not believing me?"

Sam let out a deep breath. "That kind of infrastructure will cost billions. Where will you get the funds?"

"Assyrian diaspora contains many wealthy people. Plus we will get help from our friends."

"Who are your friends?"

"People who share our values and want to see Christian democracy thrive in the Middle East. Believe me, Mr. Preston, we have many powerful friends. Just look at my photographs."

Ganjibar walked Sam around the room and pointed to the dozens of photos of him gripping and grinning with famous people: the U.S. president, the British prime minister, Jerry Falwell, Pat Robertson, Billy Graham, and the Israeli prime minister. One picture showed Henry Kissinger shaking hands with Ganjibar right there in his Boulogne office. Sam pointed to it and asked, "What was he doing here?"

"Kissinger will advise anyone who pay him. But, in fact, his advice was lousy. He say we should cut a deal with the Kurds—split the oil revenue with them and become self-governing enclave within their autonomous region. No good! We will never accept anything short of full statehood—like United States of America become independent of British king. We want to be like America. Land of the free, home of the brave."

"What oil revenues?"

"*Attention!*" Tikhani, standing next to Ganjibar, raised his hand. "I think the president was perhaps a bit premature in speaking of oil revenues at this point. The fact is that there are some indications of possible deep oil reserves within the territory claimed by the Assyrian community. But it will require much more exploration before the actual presence of oil is confirmed. I would appreciate your not mentioning anything about this in your article."

"A big oil strike would be a windfall for your movement," said Sam.

Ganjibar smiled.

"And a major bone of contention between you and the other Iraqi communities."

"We are well prepared to defend our interests and our existence, Mr. Preston," said Ganjibar. "Let me show you something."

Ganjibar led Sam back into his office and pushed a button on a wall panel. A movie screen slowly descended. Another button activated a projector mounted on the ceiling.

"This is a rough version of DVD we are preparing for our friends in United States."

Over a soundtrack of "Onward Christian Soldiers," a title appeared on the screen: "The Assyrian Liberation Force—God's Army in Iraq." The camera panned across a long row of battle-ready troops standing smartly at attention with automatic rifles at their sides. They wore burgundy berets emblazoned with little gold crosses. Then the camera cut to a parade of military hardware rumbling down a desert track—armored personnel carriers, Humvees, mobile artillery pieces, rocket launchers. Helicopters flew low over the advancing column, bristling with rocket pods and gun turrets.

"More than two thousand years ago, Jesus died to make the world safe for Christian values," intoned an off-camera narrator. "The U.S. Army is defending those values in Iraq today. And the valiant Assyrian

Christians are preparing to take a stand for God, freedom, and democracy. Won't you take a stand for them? Please send your donations to the Assyrian Christian Support Center, P.O. Box 4759, Rockefeller Center, New York, NY, 10020. Help advance God's work in Iraq, and keep His army on the march."

As the theme music continued softly in the background, the image of Rafat Ganjibar appeared on the screen, framed by the American and Assyrian flags, with the map of the Assyrian Autonomous Region behind him. "My fellow Christians," he said, reading slowly and hesitantly from a prepared text, "as provisional president of the future Assyrian Republic, I want to thank you from the bottom of my heart for your prayers and donations. Our brave Christian community has survived for many centuries in the face of hostile neighbors. Today, we want to do more than survive. We want to turn our territory into an independent Republic, and become a model of freedom, justice, and Godliness for the whole Middle East. But we cannot do this on our own. We need your help. So, please, continue to send your generous donations. And, please, write to your senators and congressmen and ask that they extend official recognition and funding to our movement. With your help, and God's grace, and the love of our Lord Jesus Christ, we can and will succeed together. Thank you, and may God bless you!"

"This is shit!" Ganjibar growled at Tikhani. "We must redo my statement. That white shirt makes me look fat. And we got to put the church bombing in there, to show everybody how we are persecuted." Then, turning back to Sam, he flashed a broad smile. "Like I say, this is work in progress. Once we get it right, we send it to all the Christian TV stations and churches in America. They will put so much pressure on your president, he have to recognize us."

"Are you in touch with the administration?"

"You saw the picture of me and the president? He is my good friend. I even stay at his ranch. But he is afraid to say so in public."

"Actually," Tikhani added, "the official American position is to observe a strict neutrality among the different Iraqi groups. But I can tell you unofficially, and on deep background, that the president is very favorable to the idea of Assyrian autonomy. Whether Congress will support him on this is another matter, but our people in Washington are working on that."

"And the Israelis?"

"I cannot speak for the Israeli government, of course, but my firm has an office in Tel Aviv and I do a lot of business there, so I am familiar with their thinking. How shall I put it? You know the expression, 'The enemy of my enemy is my friend'?"

"Of course,"

"Well, an anti-Muslim Christian enclave in the Arab world can only be seen as an objective ally of Israel. Israel supported the Christian Phalangists during the Lebanese civil war for the same reasons. But in the current Middle East context, Israel would be doing no favors to a Christian group if it voiced overt support."

Ganjibar folded his pudgy hands behind his head and leaned back in his chair, causing the springs to groan. "The Israelis are our friends, just like Americans," he said. "When we have our own state, the first thing we do, we sign peace treaty with Israel and form economic and trade union with them, just like European common market. We will do good business with Israel. Then the other Arab countries, they see how good it works, they all want to join our union. We let them in, but on our terms."

"What terms?"

"They recognize Israel, sign peace, crack down on terrorists, and be friends with America. You will see, this is beginning of golden era in the Middle East. And you know why? Because God want it that way. We do God's work. That's why your president love us."

CHAPTER

7

B ACK IN THE *CHRONICLE* BUREAU on Monday evening, Sam hunched down over his notebook and underlined the best zingers from the Ganjibar interview. The guy may be nuts, but this was great copy. Once he topped off the story with the latest updating on the St. Jean bombing investigation, he would segue into a profile-cum-interview with Ganjibar. A colleague in the Beirut bureau was checking on his bio details and business activities there. Somebody in the Washington bureau was supposed to touch base with the White House and State Department to get their reading on Ganjibar and his movement. A more specialized correspondent would see if he could wheedle any information out of the C.I.A. As colorful a character as Ganjibar was, Sam did not want to run a story on him until it was thoroughly checked out.

Sam grabbed his desk phone. He figured it was Beirut, since they were in the same time zone. Instead, he heard the voice of Charles Dumond, trying, as usual, to affect a hip American accent, and not quite making it.

"Hey, man, when you're gonna get off your ass and follow up on this arms sale story?"

"I'm on deadline. I'll call you back."

"Don't you dare hang up!"

"Charles, I told you I'm on deadline. Besides, I think that whole thing is a two-bit hustle."

"And I told *you* it's for real. Listen, Sammy, whatever you're working on is a pile of shit compared to this. You have to meet me tonight so I can give you a key piece of the puzzle."

"For Christ sake, just tell me on the phone. I don't have time for this right now."

"Not on the phone. I was only half joking before when I said French intelligence was listening to your calls. It's always possible. You know, they keep their eye on journalists—especially foreign journalists."

"I'll call you when I turn in my story."

As soon as Sam hung up, another call came in on his second line.

"Hi, stranger," said a woman's voice. "You never call, you never write."

"Lisa," Sam replied. "It's been a long time."

"Too long for my taste."

"Things are different now."

"I know, I know, you're married," she said, with the exaggerated inflections and rasp-edged voice typical of American women. "I suppose I'll get over it somehow."

"I hope so—for both of our sakes."

"Don't worry about my sake, sweetheart. I've got my job to keep me warm. Speaking of which . . . I've got some information for you."

"On Ganjibar?"

"Precisely. State says he's a self-promoting charlatan. He hasn't even set foot in Iraq since his childhood. He's been involved in some shady business dealings in Lebanon. State looks on his so-called independence movement, such as it is, as an irritant that could feed ethnic frictions and complicate the transition toward a unified, democratic Iraq."

"And the White House?"

"Well, there, the story is very different." Sam heard the sound of Lisa's breathing as she shuffled the pages of her notebook. "The spokespeople will make no official comment on Ganjibar and his movement. But one of my best sources there tells me, on deep background, that the president is quite taken with Ganjibar. The Christian right sees him as a heroic Crusader, and the neocons believe a pro-Western democratic enclave in Iraq could be a catalyst for their Greater Middle East policy. But no one at the White House will go on record in support of Ganjibar."

"And the C.I.A.?"

"Langley's a black hole on this. We can't get anything out of them."

"Kind of a murky picture. This won't be an easy story to write."

"I'm not here to make your life easier, Sam. But I could make it interesting."

"Good night, Lisa."

CHAPTER

8

IT WAS AFTER TEN when the Beirut stringer finally called to give Sam the background on Ganjibar's activities in Lebanon. It was not a pretty picture: he had been convicted of fraudulent bankruptcy, double billing on government contracts, underpayment on taxes, and was under investigation for laundering money through a casino in which he owned a part interest. All that jibed with the information Lisa had gotten from State.

"This guy didn't move to Paris for business reasons," said the stringer. "He basically fled the country to stay out of jail."

"And he's still supported by the Assyrian Christian community?"

"By the vast majority of them, yes. He's convinced his followers that he is being persecuted by their enemies for political reasons. He claims the charges against him are all part of an Islamist plot to run the Christians out of Iraq."

Sam decided the story needed more reporting before he could run it. It was a hell of a good yarn, but he could not profile this guy in the *New York Chronicle* until he was sure he was more than a self-promoting con man.

Sam checked his watch. It was nearly eleven, too late to meet Charles. He decided to head home and call him in the morning. He took the elevator down five flights and emerged into the ground-floor foyer. They turned off the lighting after office hours and the hallway was dark. Sam was about to press the front door buzzer to let himself out when someone grabbed his shoulder from behind.

He wheeled around to see the gleeful face of Charles Dumond.

"You asshole! Why did you scare me like that?"

"To keep you on your toes, Sammy boy. I told you this was a dangerous story."

"Don't joke all the time. You almost gave me a heart attack."

"C'mon, I'll buy you a beer."

"I don't drink beer."

Charles crossed the street and entered a café-tabac that was pulsing with loud techno music.

They sat in a booth in the back of the room. Dumond lit a cigarette and picked a tobacco crumb off his lower lip. "I've got something for you."

He removed a folded sheet of paper from his wallet and slid it across the table. It contained a telephone and fax number.

"What's this?"

"It's the satellite phone numbers for Miguel Carvallo, president of Armexco—the guy who signed the invoices we saw over at the Claridge. He's a Brazilian arms merchant."

"Where'd you get this?"

"I have connections."

Sam put the paper in his hip pocket. "Why didn't you call him yourself?"

"He knows my byline and he knows my paper's, how shall I put it, affiliation with the French arms industry. He'd never talk to me."

"But he'll talk to an American?"

"Maybe," Dumond shrugged. "You'll never know if you don't call him."

"He's in Monaco, right? Armexco had a Monte Carlo address if I remember correctly."

"That's just a letter-drop address. Carvallo works out of a yacht out in the Mediterranean. A yacht with a very big cargo hold full of you-know-what. So don't light any matches when you meet him."

CHAPTER

9

A T 11 A.M. ON WEDNESDAY, June 21, Sam stood on a dock in the port of Imperia, a low-rent resort town on the Italian Riviera. He had flown to Nice that morning and drove here in a rented car.

Sam was amazed that Carvallo had agreed to meet him. Once over the initial surprise of his call, in fact, Carvallo had seemed quite eager to see the American and tell his story—unless, as Dumond had jokingly suggested, he really intended to throw him to the sharks that abounded in the deep waters of the Mediterranean.

He saw the motor launch enter the harbor and head toward the appointed rendezvous, a concrete quay just behind the hotel Croce di Malta. The sleek white craft reversed its engines twenty yards out and chugged in toward the dock in a cloud of white, eye-stinging smoke.

"You are Preston?" shouted the man at the wheel.

"Yes."

The man reached up and shook Sam's hand, then gripped his forearm and helped him over the side of the gently rocking boat.

"I am Sergei," he said with a smile that wrinkled his tanned face. His eyes were pale blue, almost white, like a Siberian husky.

Sergei powered up the twin engines, turned the craft around, and headed out to open sea. Sam sat near the stern and let the wind and salt spray blow across his face.

Twenty minutes out from Imperia, he saw a white yacht looming off in the distance.

"That's the *Empress*," Sergei shouted over the roar of the engines.

Sam nodded. As they got closer, he could see that the superstructure of the ship bristled with antennae and satellite dishes. She rode low in the water and flew a Maltese flag.

Carvallo was waiting at the top of the ladder when Sam stepped over the gunwale. He was a middle-aged man with skin the color of a pecan shell, a pencil-thin mustache, and a bald but well-shaped head. In his Bermuda shorts, sandals, and red-and-green flowered shirt, he looked more like a tourist than a master of arms.

"Welcome aboard the *Empress*, Senhor Prescott," he said, with a warm smile and handshake.

"Thank you, sir."

"Please, call me Miguel," he said, leading Sam along the upper portside deck. "Nice boat, eh? I bought it from George Mavros, the Greek shipping magnate. Now whenever the son of a bitch sees me coming into port in Monte Carlo, he moves his own yacht out. He knows what I have on board."

"Which is what, exactly."

"I will show you, come."

Carvallo led the journalist down a narrow stairway into a large cargo hold. It was stacked high with rows of wooden crates, hundreds of them, perhaps a thousand or more.

"What's in the boxes, Mr. Carvallo?" said Sam.

"It's Miguel, amigo, just Miguel. Here, you can read the labels for yourself—'automobile parts,' 'canned tomatoes,' 'machine tools,' 'tractor engines,' 'bicycle tires.' As you can see, we carry a wide variety of merchandise."

Carvallo patted the top of a box and smiled at the journalist. "I just keep a little part of our stock on board to fill emergency orders."

"Where is the rest of it?"

"It's all over the world."

"I see." Sam walked along a row of crates and studied the labels that were stapled on them. "What's really in the boxes?"

Carvallo laughed and wagged a finger in Sam's face. "You nosy journalists. You live by the written word, yet you don't want to believe what is written on my labels. Well, you are right."

He picked up a crowbar and pried the top off the closest box. He reached in and pulled out a hand grenade. "The HG85, also known as the 'little Pearl.' Filled with three-millimeter steel balls. This little beauty can cut through a steel plate at five meters, and has a kill radius of thirty meters. Lightweight, easy to carry. Very popular item."

Carvallo opened another box. "Claymore M-18A1 land mines. Spews steel balls over a casualty radius of one hundred meters. Widely banned, but your president considers them legal. That's excellent for my business."

Still another box. Sam peered inside and saw six long, pointy metal cylinders. "Stinger missiles," Carvallo said proudly. "Shoulder fired. Shoot down an airplane from two miles away. Easy to use, too. Any kid can do it after a ten-minute lesson. If you were authorized to buy of these babies legally, it would cost you $10,000. I sell them for 100K apiece."

Carvallo walked Sam through row after row of boxes. "Mortar shells, machine gun rounds, M-16s, Uzis, Kalashnikovs, TOW missiles, anti-aircraft guns, high-explosive tank rounds, training rounds, combat helicopter parts—we've got it all, Sam."

Sam stopped and faced the arms merchant. "Miguel, why are you showing me all this?"

"Why? To protect myself and my business. Come, it is time for lunch."

Carvallo's private dining room was fitted out with teak paneling, polished brass portholes, and a rather incongruous cut-glass chandelier from Murano. Baccarat wineglasses, Limoges plates, Tiffany silverware, hand-embroidered damascene tablecloth. It all exuded money and power, if not necessarily good taste.

Carvallo and Sam sat face to face. Sergei served them fresh baked Mediterranean sea bass with fennel and *tomates à la Provençale*. He filled their glasses with a dry white Bordeaux that Sam politely held to his lips but did not drink, though it smelled delightful.

"I think you'll enjoy the meal," said Carvallo, drinking deeply from his wineglass. "I stole my chef from Ducasse. Used to work at the Hotel de Paris in Monte Carlo. He's the one who did all the work in the kitchen."

"It's delicious," said Sam, savoring his first flaky bite of sea bass. "You should keep him."

"Where else can he go?" Carvallo laughed. "He's on a fucking boat. That's what's so beautiful about living on the high seas. My people can't leave, and all the other bastards can't get at me."

"You must have a lot of enemies."

"No enemies. You see, we don't take sides. We are strictly neutral. I will sell arms to one buyer, and also to the people he's fighting. I made a fortune during the Iran–Iraq war selling to both sides. Everybody did that—the French, the Americans, the Germans. Then there was the civil war in Angola: Moscow backed the Marxist government, Washington backed Savimbi's rebels—and I sold arms to both of them. There are many, many of us playing this game. I am just a small cog in a huge machine."

"Don't you ever have any qualms about what you do?"

He tore off a piece of bread and chewed it. "Who am I to tell right from wrong? I am not God. Tell me who's right and who's wrong in Palestine. The Jews took the Arabs' land, the Arabs kill the Jews with bombs, the Jews destroy the Arabs' villages with bulldozers and kill their leaders with exploding cell phones. It goes on and on. Right and wrong? Who can say? But for business, it is all good."

"Do you have family?"

"My wife is dead," Carvallo said, and took another sip of wine. "My son despises me for dealing in death, as he puts it. But he took my money when I sent him to Stanford and set him up in his law practice. You see, at the end of the day, Sam, money has no color and no odor. It's just money."

"Where do you get the arms from?"

"Everywhere—United States, France, Brazil, India, Israel, China, Turkey, South Africa. We are an equal-opportunity business. Whoever has what we sell, we buy it from them. And whoever wants what we offer, we sell it to them—Sierra Leone, Angola, Sudan, Iran, Syria, North Korea, Pakistan . . ."

"And to terrorists?"

Carvallo shook his head. "No, not to terrorists. Never. But to liberation movements, yes. Over the years, we have sold to PLO, Hezbollah,

ETA, the Corsicans, the Bosno-Serbs, the Chechens, the Polisario Front. Now we sell to Iraqi Resistance, to the Sunni, the Shiites, the Kurds, and also to militias that support the U.S. Like I told you, Sam, we don't take sides."

"How can you get clandestine arms into Iraq? The Americans are all over the country."

"All over? Don't make me laugh. They are afraid to leave their barracks. There are pockets of Americans here and there, but vast areas are in control of local militias. Iraq leaks like a sieve. We get arms in through Turkey, through Syria, through Iran. And, I'll tell you a little secret, the Americans actually help us move arms into certain areas."

"The Americans work with you?"

"Not directly with me, but they move the stuff, or let it move, to the people they are supporting."

"Who?"

Carvallo smiled. "I don't wish to go into detail, Sam. I am doing very good business with certain groups now and I will say nothing that might compromise that. And you, amigo, you must say nothing."

"Nothing?"

"Nothing. Nothing at all. All that you saw here is strictly off the record. You know the business I am in, and you know, or you can imagine, the kinds of friends I have. Do not write anything about me or my operation."

"Then why did you invite me here? Why did you show me all this?"

"Because I know where you got your information. I knew it from your first phone call, as soon as you described the invoice you saw. I know exactly where your documents came from. I don't like to be betrayed. And I don't let anybody fuck with me. Especially people I do business with."

Carvallo finished his wine and refilled the glass.

"You know, Sam. We Latins are not like gringos. We don't forgive and forget so easily. We're macho. You do wrong to a Latin, it will sit there eating at him like a worm. You understand what I'm saying?"

"Americans don't like getting fucked over either."

"Maybe, but you have short memories. We forget nothing. Once, when I was young, I went to the beach with some friends. We were driving back to town, all full of beer. We passed an old rattletrap pickup truck. One of my friends had a .45 pistol on him. Just for fun, he took a potshot at the truck's radiator as we drove past. The truck swerved off the road and ran into a ditch. We laughed our asses off."

The Brazilian chuckled to himself. He swirled his wineglass and took another drink.

"And then one day, more than a year later, I was eating at a restaurant on the beach in São Paolo with the same bunch of friends. I saw a man in work clothes walk in with a paper bag in his hand. The guy glared at us like a bull about to charge. We all dived under the table just as he pulled a gun out of the bag and started shooting. There were bullet holes all over the wall where we had been sitting. The son of a bitch had recognized our car. You see, Sam? That's the way Latins are. A wrong eats at us. It might take a while, but one day we do something about it."

Sam nodded.

Carvallo put down his empty glass. "So I want you to take a message to Monsieur Roland Peccaldi. You tell him to stop fucking with Miguel Carvallo. Stop cheating me on commissions, stop stealing my customers, and, most of all, stop talking about my business to nosy motherfuckers like you."

He stood up, wiped his mouth with his napkin, then threw it on the table. "Remember what I told you. Sergei will take you back now."

CHAPTER
10

ON FRIDAY AFTERNOON, Charles Dumond sat alone in his favorite Chinese restaurant near the Pont d'Issy. He worked in a gleaming white office building nearby, but he spent so much time in this hole-in-the-wall that he called it his "Asian annex." That's where he'd told Sam to meet him the day after he returned from his Mediterranean rendezvous.

"About time you got here," he said when the American arrived and slipped into the booth beside him.

Sam filled him in on what he had learned from Carvallo. "You were right," he said. "This thing is for real, and Peccaldi is in it up to his eyeballs."

"I told you so," said Dumond, with a triumphant nod. "Peccaldi's the guy I told you would send us to the bottom of the Seine if we started sniffing around this. Remember?"

Sam poured himself a cup of cold tea. "Only too well."

"So this is good news and bad news. The good news is that it confirms what Michel told us about the deal. The bad news is Peccaldi."

"What's so special about Peccaldi? He's just another corrupt French politician, right?"

"Wrong. Let me tell you about Peccaldi. First of all, he's a Corsican, which means he was born with a stiletto between his teeth and isn't afraid to use it. When he was sixteen, he volunteered for the Resistance in the

South of France. He was so good with a knife that they used him to slit the throats of German sentinels at night so they could go in and blow up their outposts. After the war, he made a fortune smuggling cigarettes and booze into the port of Marseille, and sent more than one rival down to feed the fish in the Mediterranean. Then he got involved in Gaullist politics and helped organize the general's secret security force, the Service d'Action Civique, which was famous for bashing the supporters of rival candidates during electoral meetings. When De Gaulle decided to support Algerian independence, the S.A.C. hunted down and eliminated the Algérie Française diehards who were plotting to kill him. They say Peccaldi personally interrogated dozens of suspected Algérie Française leaders. They nicknamed him *Roland-la-cuillière* because of his penchant for popping people's eyes out with spoons."

"Holy shit. I knew he had a shady background, but I thought it was just the usual bribery and kickbacks kind of thing."

"He did that, too. When the general died, Peccaldi threw his allegiance to the mayor of Lyons—none other than Georges Carnac—and ran the secret fund-raising operations for his presidential campaign. He raised millions for Carnac's war chest—and millions for himself. When Carnac was elected the first time, he rewarded Peccaldi with the Foreign Ministry."

"I know that part of the story. I was here when Peccaldi fell out with Carnac and ran against him when he was up for reelection. He was crazy to think he could beat a sitting president."

"He never thought he could win. It was just a chance to raise campaign funds for himself, and stash them offshore. He went around promising the African presidents all sorts of French concessions, and they sent millions into his Swiss bank accounts. It's the same old game: hit up *les rois nègres* for tribute. Now he's doing the same thing with illegal arms sales to Sierra Leone, Liberia, Angola, you name it. Peccaldi ran the Gaullists' African networks for 40 years."

Sam picked up a fortune cookie left over from Dumond's solitary lunch and took a bite. "So where do we go from here?"

"You've got to talk to Peccaldi."

"Why me?"

"Because he hates me and he hates my newspaper. He'd be more likely to talk to you. He likes Americans. He's from the war generation that was liberated by the G.I.'s."

"So I'm supposed to walk in there like, 'We saved your butts in 1945, so tell me all about the arms sales.'"

"No, turd-brain. Tell him you're doing a big historic piece on the Gaullist movement. He'll go for that. Then you kind of work the conversation around to arms deals and see what he says."

"And tip him off to what we know? That's crazy—and dangerous."

"If you want to see the queen bee's knickers, you have to kick the beehive."

CHAPTER
11

S AM ACCOMPANIED DUMOND BACK to his office, where he spent a couple of hours reading clippings from Peccaldi's bio file in the *Actualités* archives. At 6 o'clock he caught the Metro at Mairie d'Issy, the first leg of his long trek back to Le Vésinet. It was a Friday afternoon and the train was jammed, as usual, with Parisians dashing home from work to prepare for the weekend. Weekends are a big deal in France.

Sam got off at Etoile to catch the suburban RER train. The corridors of the bustling station were patrolled by soldiers in camouflage fatigues and dark blue berets who held their automatic rifles at the ready. Their deployment was part of *Opération Vigipirate*, an antiterrorism plan launched after a murderous Metro bombing several years earlier and reinforced following the attack on St. Jean de Patmos Church. The presence of armed troops was supposed to dissuade terrorists, but the main effect was to remind the passengers that they were living under the constant threat of being blown up by some lunatic with a backpack full of explosives and a heart full of hate.

These were terrifying times for everyone. But for Sam, embarked on an investigation that was leading him into murky and sinister waters, the sense of imminent peril was palpable. What he felt was not so much fear as a kind of vulnerability. When Charles had asked if he was in or out, there was only one possible answer. Not because he was a brave man or a hero, but because he was immersed in danger regardless of what he did. That was the curse that bedeviled everyone in this fanaticized age.

His thoughts turned to Sandra. He would have to tell her about his arms investigation. He had been vague about his trip to Nice, not wanting to frighten her by saying he was headed to a rendezvous on a floating arsenal. But now, after his encounter with Carvallo, he felt he was being drawn into a labyrinth from which he could not turn back. He had to let Sandra know, so she would understand what he was getting into. She would worry, of course. Which wasn't necessarily a bad thing. In the old days, back in Washington, Lisa was always egging him on to take risks, go after the big story no matter where it led him. Sandra was a better counterweight; she provided the stability and practicality that he often lacked.

It was nearly seven when the RER pulled into the station at Le Vésinet-Centre. Sam headed home on foot. As he turned onto the Rue Henri-Cloppet, he saw his aged Peugeot 205 parked on the street. That was odd. Usually Sandra left it in the driveway, behind the metal grille. But the drive was occupied by an enormous camping-car. The boxy white vehicle was gargantuan—some 10 feet high and 8 feet wide. Its roof was covered with strapped-on surfboards and spoked wheels and rolled-up nylon sails. A rack attached to the rear panel held a dirt bike, a mountain bike, and a racing bike. The blue and white Chelsea bumper sticker and the GB plates left no doubt.

"Oh shit," Sam muttered to himself.

As soon as he opened the gate, an unspeakable brown mongrel charged in his direction, barking furiously and sending gravel flying in every direction. The beast leapt up and smeared Sam's khakis with mud from Sandra's flowerbeds.

"Nina!" Sam's brother-in-law sat up in his chaise longue and glared menacingly at the dog. "Mind the gravel, you bloody cur. You'll scratch the paint on the camping-car."

Sandra emerged from the kitchen door, drying her hands with a dish towel. "Look darling, Nigel and Glennys have dropped in for the weekend. Isn't that a lovely surprise?"

"Lovely," Sam repeated.

"Yeh," said Nigel, looking up from his comic book and shading his eyes from the late afternoon sun with his right hand. "We're on the way to Spain and thought we'd pop in for a visit. 'Aven't seen you and Sis for ages."

Not long enough, Sam thought as he shook Nigel's callused hand. He'd put on even more weight since the last visit and his hair, which he had worn Beatles style since the seventies, had gone a bit grayer. His hairy legs and arms were tanned and his large nose was red and peeling.

Glennys greeted Sam with a peck on the cheek. Her loose shorts and baggy T-shirt did little to hide her corpulence. Sam always thought she looked like a mud slide about to happen.

Nina was jumping up on Sam, drooling and sniffing his crotch.

"Nina!" Glennys shouted, pounding the mongrel repeatedly with the flat of her hand. "Lie down. Lie down!" The dog shrieked and rolled over on its back, legs splayed out in abject submission.

"Where's Alfie?" Sam asked.

"I locked him in the basement," said Sandra. "They had a go at each other as soon as Nina arrived, so I thought it best to separate them."

Sam could hear faint whimpers coming from the basement as he lay his shoulder bag on the grass and settled into a teak lawn chair.

Nigel worked as a garage mechanic in Maxton, a suburb of Dover. Threatened with a layoff after twenty-five years on the job, he had negotiated a part-time schedule that lowered his pay but allowed him to save up vacation weeks. The result was that he and Glennys, a part-time secretary with the local town council, were on holiday some three months out of the year. That put them on an equal footing with the average French worker, but very few Brits enjoyed such leisure-time largesse.

Nigel and Glennys understood nothing about Sam's world—nor did they care to. They knew he was some kind of Yank writer, but they'd never read any of his articles and could never remember the name of the paper he worked for. As for Sandra, Nigel's kid sister, they thought she was a tad snobbish, with her high-falutin' accent and her artsy-fartsy pretensions. She claimed to be an artist, always puttering around with brushes and turpentine in her studio, but as far as they knew, she had never sold a canvas. For that matter, they wouldn't hang one of them in their own home because her paintings didn't look like anything recognizable. Still, they all got on reasonably well together, as long as there was enough beer and wine to drink. There was little danger of running out, in fact: Nigel never traveled anywhere without a few cases of his favorite Newcastle Brown Ale in tow.

Nigel was an amiable enough fellow, but he was not much for conversation. He would sit quietly for hours at a time, sipping his ale and reading comic books or, if he felt intellectually industrious, the occasional detective novel. The one thing that could get him verbally animated was talking about the amenities on his camping-car—built-in toilet, fridge, freezer, hi-fi, air-conditioner, TV, shower, stove, three beds, and a folding dining-room table—or commenting on the photo album of his latest vacation.

"You know, Sam," Nigel said, settling back in his chaise longue, "there's a whole philosophy that goes with the camping-car lifestyle. It's all about freedom and individualism. See, when you and Sis go on holiday, you go to hotels. Always sleeping in a strange place, strangers making your bed and fixing your breakfast—and it costs you a bundle of money to boot. When Glennys and I go on holiday, it's like we take our own home with us. We can stop anywhere we bloody well like. You drive down the road, see a nice sunset along the seashore, you can stop right there and have dinner. That's the ultimate freedom. See what I mean?"

"What about the freedom of other people to see the same sunset without a great bloody camper blocking their view?" said Sandra, shooting a glance in Sam's direction.

"Yeh, well, some blokes aren't considerate. That's a fact."

"Doesn't that thing consume a lot of gas?" Sam asked.

"No more than an SUV. Besides it's a question of priorities. If you choose the camping-car lifestyle, you have to pay a price for it. I'd rather spend my money on petrol than give it to the bloody Club Med. Right Glenn?"

Glennys didn't hear him. She was in the kitchen, pulling dishes out of the washer and stacking them on the table.

"Oh, don't bother with that, Glennys," said Sandra. "I'll do it when I fix dinner."

Glennys shook her head violently. "No, no, no! You're not fixing dinner for us. We don't want to impose. We have frozen dinners in the camper."

"You are not going to eat frozen dinners in my house," said Sandra. "In France, mealtimes are special and you are our guests."

Glennys was homely at the best of times. When she started to sulk, her flabby face bordered on the grotesque. "Frozen dinners are special enough for us. We didn't come here to eat your fancy French food."

"I've got a great idea," Sam called from the garden. "We'll do a barbecue. Put a chicken on the grill, make a salad. Nothing fancy about it."

Glennys frowned and busied herself stacking dishes.

"We're out of charcoal, Sam," said Sandra.

"No problem," Nigel chimed in from the garden. "I've got a whole bag in the camper."

"Oh, what luck," said Sandra, who had always disliked cookouts as much as her husband enjoyed them.

Nigel fetched the charcoal and poured a large mound of briquettes into Sam's barbeque pit. Then he doused it with lighter fluid and struck a match. It caught quickly and burned with a blue flame for a minute or so, then started to flicker out.

"We had a bit of rain in Brittany yesterday," Nigel grunted. "Maybe it's still wet."

He poured more lighter fluid on it, but again the flame began to sputter.

"Bloody hell," said Nigel. "Reckon I know how to make the damn stuff catch."

He disappeared into his camper and emerged with a red jerry can.

"Gasoline?" said Sam. "Isn't that dangerous?"

"Bollocks. I do it all the time." With a violent jerk of his hand, he splashed gasoline all over the coals. He struck a match and threw it into the pit. An orange fireball exploded over the coals with a loud "WHOOOOF," singeing Nigel's eyebrows and Beatle bangs and setting the brick chimney on fire. The chicken, which had also been sprinkled with gasoline, was soon engulfed in the inferno.

Sam turned on the garden hose full blast and doused the flames. The force of the water knocked over the plate, and what was left of the chicken rolled a few feet across the lawn. Nina sniffed it, licked it once, then ran off in the other direction.

Sam turned off the hose and everyone stared silently at the smoldering mass of muck. Nigel ran his fingers over his singed hair and brows trying to assess the damage.

"Umm," said Sandra, "I'm afraid we haven't anything else to eat. The chicken was all we had."

"Right, then." Glennys cleared her throat. "I could offer you some frozen dinners—if that's not too ordinary for you lot."

"What do you have?" said Sam.

"Macaroni and Spam."

CHAPTER
12

SANDRA USUALLY SLEPT IN on Saturday mornings, but today she was up at seven. She threw on a polo shirt and cotton skirt, and attached her luxuriant auburn hair in a ponytail. Sam, half asleep, watched her dress.

"I'm going to buy fresh bread and milk," she said, with a pat on Sam's cheek. "Why don't you get up so we can have a nice breakfast with Nigel and Glennys, and make up for last night's unpleasantness."

Sam turned over and put a pillow on his head. He had to talk to her about his story, but when would he get a chance with these bothersome in-laws squatting at their house?

As soon as Sandra emerged into the garden, she saw Nigel and Glennys sitting at a folding table next to their camping-car. Nigel was spreading Borvil on a piece of sliced white bread. Glennys poured tea from a pot commemorating the Queen's Silver Jubilee.

"What are you two doing out here?" said Sandra. "I was going to make breakfast for everyone. I'm just headed to the shop for bread and milk."

"Don't bother," said Glennys. "We brought frozen bread and powdered milk from England. It's much cheaper. And we don't want to put you out any more than we already have."

Nigel sipped his tea and stared straight ahead. Sandra knew that look all too well. He was feeling sorry for himself and angry at the world.

"Nonsense," said Sandra. "Why don't you come in the kitchen? I'll make a proper English breakfast—scrambled eggs, sausages, grilled tomato. Then we can go into town. It's market day."

Nigel shook his head. "We're off as soon as we've washed up and put the table away. Gotta get to Spain before evening. Can't stand to drive at night."

Sam was still brushing his teeth when he heard Nigel rev up the camping-car. He looked out the bathroom window just in time to see the lumbering vehicle back out the gravel drive and into the street. Sandra stood at the gate and waved as the camper turned the corner and disappeared from sight.

When Sam got downstairs, he found Sandra sitting alone at the kitchen table sipping coffee. She wiped her eye with the back of her hand.

"What's up with Nigel? Why did they leave like that?"

"He's pouting. Whenever Nigel's not feeling right, he tries to make everyone around him miserable."

Sam put a hand on her shoulder. "If you come back upstairs with me, I'll make you feel better."

She smiled and patted his hand. "Give me a rain check on that. I'm afraid I'm not in the mood."

The market was in full sway when they arrived at around ten. Outside, shaded from the summer sun by lime trees and rows of parasols, greengrocers and flower sellers hawked their wares. The covered market housed the fishmongers, butchers, poultrymen, cheese sellers, and more greengrocers. Whole tuna, codfish, squid, live crabs, and shrimp lay on beds of shaved ice. Rabbits, some still enrobed in fur, hung by their feet, alongside quail, ducks, and guinea hens. At the pork butchers, dozens of suspended sausages dangled over bowls of pâté, hogshead cheese, and *mousse de foie*. There were open vats of olives, crates full of mushrooms, nuts, dried beans and peas, salt cod, fragrant cheeses of every type and provenance.

Sam held Alfie on a short leash. But the rambunctious bulldog, excited by the smell of all the red meat and raw fish, pulled in every direction and managed to pee on a few stacked vegetable crates before Sam could yank him back.

"I'd better go wait for you in the café while you shop," he said, and jerked Alfie, drooling and yelping, away from a smaller female dog that he was trying to sniff.

"Pick up some bread on your way, will you?" said Sandra.

Sam tied Alfie to a lamppost in front of the bakery. He emerged five minutes later with a baguette that was still steaming from the oven, tore off a crunchy end and popped it into his mouth. Then he picked up a *Herald Tribune* from the newsstand next door.

Le Méditerrannée was a typical French café, with tile floors and large wooden tables. On market days, it got very crowded around lunchtime, but it was still early. Sam had no trouble finding a table near the door with plenty of room for Alfie to settle down and lick his private parts.

He ordered a café crème and looked out the window just in time to see a man pull up on his bike. The seat was too high and he nearly fell over when he dismounted. It was Jacques Danton, his next-door neighbor. Danton entered the café and walked right past Sam. Following his usual habit, he went straight to the bar and ordered a beer.

Sam studied him from behind. Danton had always seemed a bit weird, with his shiny black nylon shorts held up with a draw-string and leather sandals over high-topped white crew socks. But then, Danton was a scientist, so being geeky was normal for him.

He suddenly spotted Sam, waved and brought his beer over to the table.

"Did you see this?" he said, pointing to a headline in Sam's *Herald Tribune*: "OIL HEADING FOR $80 A BARREL."

"All this hyperventilation over oil prices is completely ridiculous," he said. "Oil has no place in the energy future of the planet."

"Really? I don't see a lot of windmills or solar panels around here."

"Forget about all those silly green gadgets," said Danton, with a boyish grin that belied the professorial effect of his thick gold-rimmed glasses. "I can tell you the energy future in one word: hydrogen."

"Hydrogen? As in hydrogen bombs?"

"No. Hydrogen as in fuel cells. My lab is doing a lot of research on this now, and we are near a breakthrough. In the future, all our motor vehicles will be powered by fuel cells that run on hydrogen and give off pure water vapor as their only emission. All the buses in Iceland are already running on hydrogen."

"I've read about that. But I seem to remember there was some problem with fuel cells."

"Well, to be sure, it's not a silver bullet. You see, the hydrogen is derived through electrolysis—running an electric current through water to separate the hydrogen and oxygen atoms. But the electricity needed to do that has to come from somewhere else."

"Right! That was the problem. You still have to burn fossil fuels to generate the electricity. Or use nuclear energy, which everybody's afraid of since Chernobyl. So what's the answer, professor?"

Danton flashed an impish grin that revealed a gap between his front teeth. "Hydrogen."

"You're just going in circles now."

"Not at all. Hydrogen is also the central element in the process of fusion, the inexhaustible energy source of the sun and stars. Instead of splitting atoms, as in a conventional nuclear reaction, fusion works by combining light elements like deuterium and tritium to form hydrogen, with a huge release of energy. Researchers have been doing that for years on an experimental scale. Now the race is on to perfect a fusion reactor for commercial use. Everybody's working on that—the Americans, the Japanese, the Russians, the Chinese, the Europeans. It's maybe 20 years off, but that would be just in time."

"In time for what?"

"In time to replace hydrocarbons. At the current rate of consumption, all our oil reserves will be used up in twenty years or so. Whoever can tame fusion energy by then will be the real master of the universe. No telling who it will be at this point. But I can tell you one thing—oil, the Arabs, and the Middle East won't matter more than a rabbit's fart when that happens."

"I'll have to look into that. Sounds like a good story."

"A *big* story. I'll send you some articles if you want to pursue it. Of course, you'll have to interview me and put my picture on the front page of the *Chronicle*."

Sam was never sure if Danton was kidding or not. He had a great deadpan.

When they got back home, Sandra started putting away the things she had bought at the market. Then she set a pot of water on the stove, threw in a handful of rock salt, some bay leaf, ground pepper, a slice of lemon, a couple of quartered onions, and, finally, a whole codfish, head and all. "I thought some fresh *cabillaud* would make up for the macaroni and Spam last night," she said with a little laugh.

Sam sat at the kitchen table and watched her while she worked. Her brown eyes were large, catlike, under arched brows; the auburn hair was long and curly to the roots. Sandra felt his eyes on her and looked back. She had always been proud of her husband's looks. He was tall and broad-shouldered, with wavy, light brown hair and deep-set hazel eyes. He was no matinee idol, but his little imperfections—the slight overbite and that pert, turned-up nose—gave him a boyish, sensitive look that contrasted nicely with the mannishness of his frame. He had put on a little too much weight over the past year or two, but nothing that a little jogging and dieting wouldn't burn off. She thought that perhaps he was subconsciously overeating to compensate for his cold-turkey kicking of alcohol. And for the sake of his sobriety, she was more than willing to put up with a little extra padding.

She took a bottle of Chablis from the fridge and poured herself a glass. "Do you want a Coke, Sam?" she asked.

"No thanks. I'll have a fake beer."

She took out a Buckler, twisted off the top, and poured it into a half-pint beer mug that Sam had stolen from a London pub in his drinking days. The golden brew with the foamy white head brought back a lot of memories, though there were things about that time that he preferred not to remember, and indeed things that he could not remember.

She held up her wineglass and clinked it against the beer mug. "Here's to being alone at last," she said.

"I'll drink to that." Sam took a deep gulp of the cold, stinging brew. It tasted a lot like real beer, though he knew it would not leave that tingling sensation in his head that he used to crave—and now feared like a poison. The first delicious swallow of beer had always led to another, and another. Now he was free of all that.

After lunch, Sandra repaired to the converted garage that served as her studio. She put on a paint-spattered apron and removed the plastic covering over a clay figure on her worktable. The room was awash with summer light that filtered in through the sliding glass doors. The white plasterboard walls were covered with images—a poster for a Matisse show at the Grand Palais, a postcard-sized photo of Picasso, a Bonnard reproduction, curling photos of rock formations that she intended to use as models for her own painting and sculpture.

But there were none of her own paintings on the wall. She stacked them in the attic almost as soon as they were dry. Sam often asked why she did not hang them in her studio, or in the house. Was she ashamed of them? "Not at all," she'd say. "It's just that when I've done something, I've done it. I don't want to be influenced by what I have already done. I always want to push ahead. Discover something new."

There was something so uncompromisingly idealistic about Sandra's work that Sam had to admire her for it. What motivated Sandra was art for art's sake. His own work, he thought, was different. He had a hunger, a passion perhaps, for chasing after big stories, but it was never completely detached from the idea of reward: praise of his peers and bosses, promotions, prizes. But in fact, the really big stories were few and far between. Much of what he did these days was routine, repetitive, predictable. That's why he was so drawn to this arms sale investigation, in spite of the dangers it might involve.

Sam watched his wife through the sliding glass door. She had her back to him, kneading and pounding on the gray mound of clay on the table in front of her. As she leaned over the nascent form, he could see the muscles in her tanned legs tighten, her well-toned neck and shoulders taut with effort, damp with perspiration.

He entered quietly and put his hand on her shoulder. She turned and smiled. "What do you think?" she asked.

The mass of clay had little identifiable shape as yet, but he could see the vague outlines of a woman's body—round, fleshy buttocks, massive breasts, a protruding belly, a prominent pudendum. Yet there was only the most rudimentary suggestion of a head, arms, or legs.

"It's a good start," he said, and sat down on a stool next to her.

"Start?" she laughed. "It's almost finished. What's here is the pure essence of womanhood. The rest is just anecdotal. Don't you see what I mean, Sam?"

Sam ran his hand lightly over the clay breasts and buttocks. "It is very womanly," he said.

"You see? Faces aren't important. That's just portraiture. Faces are okay in a painting, but sculpture is about fundamentals. Anyway, that's how I feel it."

"Sandra," Sam said, "there's something I have to tell you."

She turned and looked at him.

"It's about this story I'm working on. The one that took me to Nice the other day."

"That thing on the new director of the Nice Opera?"

"No. I lied. I didn't want you to worry. I actually went down there to meet an arms dealer."

"An arms dealer? Are you out of your mind?"

"Sandra, it's a big story. It involves some important people, powerful politicians, people selling weapons willy-nilly to whoever can pay for them, including some very unsavory groups."

"And you want to get caught in the middle of all that?"

"It's what I do, Sandra."

"But what if they threaten you, or try to harm you? What would I do if something happened to you?"

"Nothing's going to happen to me, Sandra. Nobody's going to attack a journalist in a civilized country like France. The people who have to worry are the ones who are doing bad things."

"And you think you're going to stop them with a newspaper story?"

"Look at Watergate—two guys exposed some criminal activities at the highest levels of American power and brought down a corrupt president. I have no idea where my own story is leading. But if it can make a difference, I have to have the courage to pursue it. It's almost like a test of manhood."

"That sounds a bit boy-scoutish to me," she said softly. "But if you want to prove your manhood, I can think of better ways." She ran her fingernail up the inseam of Sam's jeans.

He pulled her close to him and put his arms around her. His hands caressed her bottom. He could feel through her thin cotton dress that she was nude underneath.

"Naughty girl," he said. "You're not wearing any knickers."

She laughed mischievously. "I was wondering how long you'd take to discover that."

CHAPTER

13

GÉRARD CHEVALIER'S MONDAY MORNING phone call had caught Sam by surprise. Chevalier had been one of Sam's best police sources until his retirement a year earlier. He had even invited the American to his farewell party at the legendary headquarters of the *police judiciaire*, 36 Quai des Orfèvres—a rare honor for a journalist and a foreigner. After thirty-five years on the job, they sent the ace detective off with a buffet of canned pâté sandwiches, potato chips, and cheap red wine. Jacques-Marie Trigani, the police prefect, had drawn a few tepid laughs when he lauded Chevalier's "penetrating" interrogation techniques. The deputy interior minister declared that "God broke the mold when he made Gérard Chevalier." And his immediate superior, a tough-as-nails woman whose father and grandfather had been cops, personally unveiled his retirement present with great fanfare: a clock radio that doubled as a digital calculator.

Chevalier, single and childless, choked up a little when he thanked everyone for the memories and assured one and all that they were his "best and only family." The guests—mostly fellow cops in jeans and leather jackets, or ministry officials and magistrates in suits and ties—munched on the greasy sandwiches and told old war stories until the crowd dwindled down to a half-dozen die-hards around the last keg of wine. Chevalier had invited them all to his favorite watering hole for a nightcap, and more stories. It was a café called Le Soleil d'Or, just down the street from police headquarters. Sam had been among the stragglers.

He was still drinking in those days and had only a foggy memory of how the evening wound up—except for the parting scene when Chevalier gave him a teary fraternal hug and thanked him for sticking by him till the end.

More than a year later, Chevalier called Sam and invited him to Le Soleil d'Or to "catch up" over a drink.

Sam found him in his usual place—a wooden table by the front window, where he could bask in the sun and watch the girls walk by along the Boulevard du Palais. When Sam walked in, Chevalier was throwing dice with three off-duty cops to see who would pay for the next round of beer. He lost and gestured to the barman to fill up the glasses.

"Tough luck, Commandant," said Sam as he leaned over the table to shake the detective's hand. Chevalier introduced him around.

"This guy is a great reporter," Chevalier told his friends. "Works for the *New York Chronicle*."

"That's great," said a lanky guy in leather motorcycle pants. "Only I can't read English."

"You can't read, period," Chevalier snickered and winked at Sam. "He's from the Action Service. They don't have to think."

"That's what we have you desk guys for. We do the dirty work and you write the reports."

"And we save your ass, sometimes."

The lanky guy laughed and sipped his beer.

When the glasses were empty, the other cops stood up and said it was time to get back to work. Two of them left on foot. The third one zipped on a leather jacket and roared off on a BMW motorcycle.

"You see that guy?" said Chevalier, lighting a Marlboro and flicking the match into an overflowing ashtray. "He led the commando that shot Martino."

"Who's that?" said Sam.

"Jacques Martino, one of the most famous gangsters in French history. Our guys finally caught up to him at a traffic circle at the Porte d'Aubervilliers in 1979 and filled him full of holes. I saved their butts on that one."

"How's that?"

"They shot him in cold blood. No warning, nothing. Poor bastard still had his seatbelt on. By the time I finished writing up the report, it was a classic case of self-defense. I was good at that. Always had a way with words. I'd have made a good journalist."

"Not really. We have to stick to the facts."

Chevalier grinned. Short of stature with a ruddy complexion, he had a youthful-looking face when he smiled—in spite of his two-day stubble and graying hair. Sam guessed he had spent much of his life trying to prove himself, prove he was as big and tough as the next cop, talking constantly about his own exploits. There was a vulnerability behind the bravado that Sam had always found touching.

"Well, maybe not a journalist. But a writer. I should write detective novels with all the stuff I've seen. God, the stories I could tell."

"Try it."

Chevalier shrugged. "We'll see. I have to do something, for Christ sake. I can't stand sitting around, you know, just being retired—whatever the hell that means."

"Must be a wrench."

"Thirty-five years on the force, cracked all the toughest cases, made my bosses look good, and what happens? As soon as I hit fifty-five, they give me a cheap alarm clock and a boot in the tail."

"Pretty shabby."

Chevalier bit his lower lip and looked out at the facade of his old headquarters across the boulevard. "You know, Sam. I really was one of the best. Nobody could beat me as an interrogator. I had style and finesse. None of this crude, vulgar stuff like your people did at Guantanamo and Abu Ghraib."

"Oh really? I've heard some pretty hairy stories about the Algerian War."

"That was military. I'm talking about criminal investigations. There was one case where I spent twelve hours. I gave the guy whiskey and hashish provided by the narcotics squad. It went on all night—question, answer, whiskey, question, answer, hash. Eventually, the guy let his guard down, started to contradict himself. When he finally cracked, he cried like a baby. I told my colleagues that not even Claudia Schiffer, naked, from behind, could have given me as much satisfaction. It's almost like rape. But these young guys today—they don't know how to do it."

Chevalier emptied his glass. "Well, enough of that. I saw your article on the St. Jean bombing. Nice piece."

"Thanks."

"You want to kick some butt on this story?"

"Sure."

"I still have good contacts with some of my old buddies over there. I've been talking to them about this thing and reading all the transcripts."

"What do they make of it?"

"They're pretty pissed off. Trigani's putting a lot of pressure on them to wrap up the investigation quickly. He's the one who invited the Scotland Yard guys over here to help speed things along. The Brits think it's the same Al-Qaeda–linked bunch that did their Metro bombings, because it's the same kind of explosive. But they're full of shit."

"It's not the same?"

"That's the only thing that is the same. Everything else is different—different detonator, different modus operandi, and different motive. Nothing to do with the Paki network that hit London."

"How come you're so sure? Couldn't they have been outsourced to do this?"

"I'm telling you there's no connection. This was not a clumsy suicide bombing. It was a sophisticated device placed under the church altar. It was a remote-controlled, military-type explosive—the kind the Americans are using in Iraq now—not one of those jerry-rigged cell phone contraptions."

Sam pulled out his notebook and started writing. Chevalier took no notice. He knew the journalist would never quote him by name. Those were their standing ground rules.

"Judge Bouvard, the investigating magistrate, also thinks the Brits are on the wrong track. But he's got his own theory. He thinks it's a band of young French-born Arabs who learned the jihad methods and ideology as volunteers with the Iraqi resistance. Now they're coming back to wreak anti-Western havoc at home."

"That's plausible, isn't it?"

"Look at the target here. It wasn't the Americans, it wasn't the French, it wasn't even Western. It was a church with direct links to the Christian minority in Iraq. I'm telling you, Sam, this is not about jihad. It's all about the political power struggle in Iraq."

"Then who did it?"

"I have my own idea," said Chevalier. "But I won't tell you until I have more information."

"Damn it, Gérard. You can't just drop me like this."

"Save it for the next lesson," said Chevalier, crushing out his Marlboro and blowing a last cloud of smoke toward the ceiling. "Oh, by the way, my sunglasses have a nasty chip on the edge, you see that?"

"Yeah. So what?"

Chevalier reached in his pocket and handed Sam a folded piece of paper. It was a color printout from the Gucci Web site with circles around two models of luxury eyewear. Their prices: $250 and $295, respectively.

CHAPTER

14

"FIND PRINCESS TAWANA!"

Sam drew a blank. "Princess who?"

"Princess Tawana."

Sam's assignment editor could be a bit cryptic on the phone. "Sorry, Ed. I don't know who you're talking about."

"You've been in Paris too long. Don't you read the U.S. press anymore?"

Sam let the remark pass.

"Princess Tawana—listen, Sam, I'm really amazed you've never heard of her—Princess Tawana is a Gospel singer from Georgia who has the number one hit in the U.S. these days."

"So why are you calling the Paris bureau?"

"Because Princess Tawana happens to live in Paris. She recorded the tune with a French jazz band for some obscure local label called Fleur-de-Lys. They shipped some copies to the U.S. a few months ago and it caught on like wildfire. The Christian radio stations are playing the hell out of it and the stores can't keep it in stock. Now an Evangelical label has reissued it and they've already sold 10 million copies."

"For a Gospel tune? That is pretty amazing. What's it called?"

"'The Battle of Armageddon.' Look, Sam, I don't have time to educate you on the phone. Check her out on the Internet, track her down. We want you to do a big feature on Tawana and the Froggy band she plays with. Go hang with them, find out how she wound up in France, how she met up with these cheese-monkey jazz guys, what her future plans are. You know, big profile kind of thing. We might make it the cover of the Sunday mag."

"Sounds like fun."

"Sam, you're not supposed to have fun on this job. You're supposed to bleed, sweat, and suffer for the *New York Chronicle*."

Sam laughed. "In that case, you shouldn't have sent me to Paris."

No sooner had he hung up the phone than Sam had Princess Tawana's Web site up on his computer screen. The home page displayed the photo of a round-faced black woman in a red sequined gown, arms stretched apart, eyes shut and mouth wide open in song. The logo was a seven-pointed purple crown encircled by the words "Princess Tawana—the Gospel Diva."

Sam dialed the number of her French booking agent and soon had a certain Marie Caledoni on the line.

"I'm Sam Preston of the *New York Chronicle*," he told her. "I was hoping you could set me up for an interview with Princess Tawana."

"You'll have to wait in line," said Caledoni. She had the voice of a three-pack-a-day smoker. "Ever since 'Armageddon' took off in the States, everybody wants to interview the Princess. How much time do you need?"

"A lot. We're not just talking about a quickie Q & A, but a substantial profile. I need face time with her, access to the guys in her band, her French record company. The big picture."

"And what's the circulation of the *Chronicle*?" asked Caledoni.

"Around a million copies a day. Right behind the *New York Times*."

"Hmm. Let me check her schedule." Sam heard computer keys clicking, then a long silence.

"I don't see any slot for a sit-down interview before mid-July," Caledoni finally said. "Unless . . ."

"Unless?"

"Unless you can make it to Orly by 3 p.m. The band is flying off to a jazz festival in Latvia. I'll reserve an extra seat on the plane if you can get there in time."

There was no mistaking Princess Tawana at the check-in line for Balt Air flight 3703. Dressed in a multicolored African tunic with designer sunglasses, a black feathered boa, and a large rhinestone-studded crucifix necklace, she would have stood out in any crowd. The half-dozen guys clustered around her were no less conspicuous. They wore identical black and gold T-shirts emblazoned with the words "Les Jambalayas" and a large fleur-de-lys emblem. Their suit bags, backpacks, and musical instrument cases sprawled out in every direction, causing disgruntled, muttering passengers to step over them on their way to the counter. Chattering loudly in French, laughing and gesturing extravagantly, whistling at all the young girls who passed by, they seemed oblivious to the nuisance they were causing. An aura of stale sweat, cigarettes, and beer hung over the boisterous group.

"I take it you're Tawana," said Sam.

"Princess Tawana," she corrected, offering him her hand palm down. He wasn't sure at first whether to shake it or kiss her ring. He shook it.

"You must be the reporter Marie told me about. She reserved a seat for you, right next to me. We can talk all the way to—hey, Jean-Pierre, what's the name of that place we flying to?"

"Riga," said one of the Frenchmen, a tall, swarthy-faced guy with graying temples and a salt-and-pepper mustache, "I'm Jean-Pierre Robichaux, trombone player and band leader, at your service."

Sam smiled and shook his hand. "Sam Preston of the *New York Chronicle*. I'm going to make you guys famous."

"Honey, we already famous," the Princess chuckled. "We doin' *you* a favor."

The cabin was cramped—Balt Air still flew vintage Tupolevs left over from the Soviet days. Sam took a seat next to Princess Tawana and buckled up. She checked her makeup in a compact mirror and touched up her ruby lipstick as the plane pulled slowly away from the terminal. The lumbering craft turned and began to roar down the runway, bumping, shaking, and creaking until the landing gear finally cleared the ground.

Sam looked over at the Princess. She was muttering silently to herself, eyes shut and hands clasped tightly on her lap. Then she whispered, "Amen," and opened her eyes.

Sam took a notebook from his jacket pocket and flipped it open. But it was the Princess who asked the first question.

"So where you from, Sam?"

"I was born in Connecticut."

"Good. I was afraid they'd send me another one of those mushmouth southern boys like the last guy that interviewed me. If there's one thing I can't stand, it's a redneck. That's all they had in Georgia when I was growin' up. Main reason I moved to Paris was to get away from 'em."

"I guess Paris is about as far as you can get from Georgia rednecks."

"Don't you believe it, Sam. This country is full of racists. Looka here—soon as I walk on this plane, one of those French guys sittin' behind us start singing, 'Oh, Mammy, Mammy Blue.' I'm the only one looks like Aunt Jemimah on the whole damn plane. So who you think he's talkin' about with that 'mammy, mammy' shit?"

Sam looked up from his notebook. "I'm not so sure about that . . ."

"Don't try to tell me what's goin' on, baby. I know. 'Mammy, mammy!' What's that shit supposed to mean?"

Sam unbuckled his safety belt and slowly leaned back in his seat.

"You don't believe me, do you?" she said.

"Sure I believe you. I mean, I believe you see it that way. But, you know, 'Mammy Blue' was a big pop hit in France in the 70s. Everybody knows it. I don't think it has anything to do with race."

"Then why he start singing it soon's I walk on the plane? I'm tellin' you, the guy is a racist asshole."

"Maybe he just spent all night in a disco and has the tune spinning around in his head."

"Don't tell me that, Sam. Don't go there. Why is it white people can never understand?"

The ninety-minute flight was half over before Sam got the Princess to settle down and tell him her story. She was born in Athens, Georgia, in 1965. Daughter of the Rev. Alton Pickens, pastor of the Zion Hill

Pentacostal Church, she started singing in the choir at age ten. Everybody said she had a gift, and by age fourteen she was singing all the lead parts. When she was sixteen, a producer from Atlantic Records "discovered" her and promised to make her "the next Aretha Franklin."

"They flew me up to New York to do a test pressing. But, see, they want me to sing soul music like Aretha. I told 'em the only soul I was interested in was the one the Lord gave me. I never sing anything but religious music. So Atlantic dropped me like a hot potato."

But her renown as a Gospel singer continued to grow. At eighteen, she toured Europe with the Zion Hill choir and fell in love with a French sound man. They were soon married, and quickly divorced. She stayed on in Paris, teaching voice lessons and giving occasional church recitals. Then she met the Jambalayas. "They were a real wild, rag-tag bunch, into all that old-style traditional jazz—old New Orleans stuff, you know. But they asked me to do a couple of concerts with them and we just hit it off. Wherever we play the folks really love us. We get 'em jumpin' up and down and clappin' their hands. They don't understand a word I'm singin' half the time, but that Gospel music just gets to 'em."

"Why is that?"

"You have to hear us yourself before I can answer that."

It was just after eight o'clock on that Tuesday evening when the band went onstage under a red and white banner reading "Riga Jazz Festival." Ten thousand Latvians jammed the town square and cheered lustily as the musicians took their places. Huge screens on either side of the stage relayed their outsized images across the vast sea of people.

Sam had given up a privileged spot in the wings in order to immerse himself in the crowd and pick up the vibes. The people were mostly young, dressed in jeans, T-shirts, and crop-tops like kids at an American rock concert. Sam had never seen so many beautiful young girls in one place—blonde, high cheek-bones, fresh skin, almond-shaped eyes.

When Princess Tawana appeared in the central spotlight in a skintight gold lamé gown and her trademark boa, a roar went up from the crowd. "Yeah!" she shouted, her white teeth dazzling under the lights.

"Yeah, I *like* that. We gonna get the spirit on us *tonight*, y'all. Can't you feel it?"

"Yah," came the response from ten thousand fans.

"Can y'all feel the *spirit*?"

"Yah!"

"Y'all ready to get *down*?"

"Yaaaaah!"

"Well, let's go then!" She started to beat a steady cadence on her tambourine, alone at first, then the banjo, bass, and the drums kicked in. The horns laid down a funky riff, the trumpet punched out a simple melodic line, the clarinet and trombone answered with a syncopated counter-rhythm. Princess Tawana stood in the spotlight with her eyes closed, pounding the tambourine and moving her hips in a circular motion that sent whoops and whistles up from the crowd. Finally, she put her ruby lips up to the microphone and started to sing: "Will the circle be unbroken . . . by and by Lord, by and by . . ."

The crowd picked up the beat, clapping their hands over their heads in time with the tambourine. Sam was mesmerized by the pulse and flow of the music and soon found himself clapping along with the others. Tawana's bluesy slurs and quarter tones and uncanny timing soon whipped the crowd into a state of ecstasy, enhanced no doubt by the pungent cloud of marijuana smoke that floated over the square.

It went on like that, number after number. Then, just when Sam thought the frenzy had peaked, the Princess, her face glistening with sweat, stepped up to the microphone and announced the last tune. "This here is a very special song, brothers and sisters. It tells a story about the glorious future that is awaiting us all if we just have faith. And the way everybody's movin' out there, I *know* y'all got the faith. Y'all got the faith?"

"Yaaaaaah!"

"Well, listen real good, I'm fixin' to tell you the greatest story on earth. And I want y'all to sing along and clap your hands, 'cause this is your story, too."

The stage lights went dark except for the central spot that bathed the singer in its silver beam. She stood still for a moment, head down, eyes closed. An eerie hush fell over the crowd. Then she began singing a slow minor-key melody with no accompaniment but her tambourine.

We gonna win the battle of Arma-ged-don,
Arma-ged-don, Arma-ged-don,
We gonna win the battle of Arma-ged-don,
On that glorious Judgment Day . . .

The other musicians joined in, the horn players clapping and singing the responses, the rhythm section laying down a relentless beat that reverberated through the central square of Riga.

The righteous gonna triumph at Arma-ged-don,
Arma-ged-don, Arma-ged-don,
The righteous gonna triumph at Arma-ged-don
And the sinners be swept away . . .

The crowd picked up the cadence and ten thousand voices echoed the refrain. Sam sang and clapped along with the rest of them, forgetting momentarily who he was and why he was there. He had been sucked into the collective trance.

As the band played an ensemble chorus, the Princess swung her hips, rolled her eyes heavenward and shook her head wildly, sending droplets of sweat flying in every direction like a boxer who has just received a hard blow to the jaw. Multicolored stage lights swept back and forth over the band, strobing and morphing and pulsing to the beat. Smoke machines began to bathe the musicians in a celestial cloud. At the rear of the stage, high over the band, a huge neon crucifix suddenly lit up and turned the smoke blood-red with its intense glow. The Princess shouted out the final stanzas in her powerful contralto:

Well you can keep your Iwo Jima,
And forget about Waterloo,
It's gonna be bigger than Viet-Nam,
And badder than World War Two.

Oh, Jesus gonna lead us at Arma-ged-don,
Arma-ged-don, Arma-ged-don,
Jesus gonna lead us at Arma-ged-don,
So you better kneel down and pray . . .

Yes, you better kneel down and pray . . .
Yes, you better kneel down and pray . . .
You better kneel down and pray . . .

At the end of the last chorus, the whole square erupted. Deafening applause went on for ten minutes. The Princess and the band came back onstage two or three times to bow and blow kisses, but the repeated shouts of "Encore! Encore!" went unheeded. "Can't do no encore after 'Armageddon,'" the Princess said into the mike. "That's the end of everything! Brothers and sisters, thank you, God bless y'all, and keep the faith."

Sam felt like a wrung-out sponge in the hot, humid night air. As the crowd began slowly to disperse, he picked his way toward the stage. He flashed his press badge at a security guard and entered through a rear door. A raucous party was going on backstage. The musicians were gobbling Latvian sausages and canapés and washing them down with liter-sized steins of beer. A bevy of local girls was fluttering around them, giggling, drinking beer, laughing at their French accents. One of the younger musicians, the bass player, had his arm around a blonde girl with wavy Botticelli-Venus hair who couldn't have been more than sixteen. The trumpeter had a petite redhead on his lap and was nibbling the brass stud in her left earlobe. The older players looked on the scene with wry smiles.

Robichaux, the leader and trombone man, spotted Sam and invited him over to the buffet table.

"Great show," said Sam, grabbing two canapés and stuffing them into his mouth. "Where's the Princess?"

"In her dressing room."

Sam walked down the corridor and rapped on her door. He wanted to talk to her while the concert vibes were still fresh.

"Come in," said a soft voice inside.

He pushed open the door and found the Gospel diva sitting at her dressing table, surrounded by a mountain of flowers. She was wearing jeans and a T-shirt that proclaimed "Jesus is my Main Man." The nails on her bare feet were painted the same ruby red as her lipstick. Her gold lamé gown, soaked through with perspiration, hung on a clothes rack. The tight space smelled of sweat and perfume and female flesh.

"Hello, Princess," said Sam.

"Hi, Sam," she said with a smile as she sat before the mirror and pulled pins out of her hair. "You can call me Tawana. That Princess stuff is just show business."

"The concert was amazing. I've never seen anything like that in my life."

"Then you must not have spent a lot of time in church, honey."

"Not in your kind of church."

"See, that's the problem." She swiveled around on her stool and faced her visitor. "All these people, they get into the music, but they don't get into the *religion*. That's what it's all about. I want to help save these people, get everybody ready for the final days. That's why I wrote that song."

"*You* wrote 'Armageddon'?"

"Sure did. I mean, I took the melody from *Joshua Fit the Battle of Jericho*, okay? But, see, that song talks all about the past, old Bible times and all that. I wrote new lyrics 'cause I wanted to sing about the future—the final battle between good and evil."

"You really believe in that?"

"Oh, yeah, honey. And you better believe it too. It's written right there in the Book of Revelations. The Apocalypse, you know? Jesus gonna lead the righteous in a final battle against evil. That's how the world's gonna end. And anybody who ain't right with God on Judgment Day, that's his ass. He gonna burn in Hell till the end of time. You better get yourself ready Sam, 'cause it's comin'. It's comin' real soon."

"So, to you, 'Armageddon' is the literal truth."

"Not the literal truth. The *only* truth. That's why it's such a big hit in America. The Evangelicals know I'm singin' the truth. The president knows it, too. They tell me he plays my record in the White House. He even sent copies to every member of Congress."

"And all those French guys in your band, they believe in that, too?"

Tawana let out a sigh. "You better ask them that yourself, honey. But if you want my opinion, I think they don't believe in nothin' but liquor and pussy. I keep tellin' 'em to get themselves right with God, but there's just something about men. When their gland get hard, their brain get soft, you know what I mean?"

Someone knocked loudly on the door and burst in without waiting for a reply. It was a skinny, pasty-faced man in a brown double-knit suit.

"Oh, be joyful in the Lord all you lands," he bellowed. "Serve the Lord with gladness, and come before His presence with a song."

"Hello, Chris. This is Sam Preston of the *New York Chronicle*. Sam, Chris Blassingame."

The intruder turned to see Sam, half-hidden behind the door. "Oh I beg your pardon," he said, "I didn't know the Princess had company."

"Pleased to meet you," said Sam.

"Actually, we've already crossed paths. I was in Mr. Ganjibar's waiting room when you came out of your interview the other day. I'm a friend of Hal Carpenter's, grew up with him in Alabama."

"I see," said Sam, studying the man's stiff-looking straw-colored hair and wondering whether it was a toupee. "And what were you doing at Ganjibar's?"

"I'm helping Hal promote the Assyrian movement among the Evangelicals. I work with a Washington-based group called the National Christian Council. That's what brings me here in fact. I'm writing an article about the Princess for our on-line newsletter. She's a hot item among the Evangelicals."

"Honey," she said, sliding a cigarette between her lips and striking a match on her fingernail. "I'm a hot item, period. Y'all seen all them people out there tonight?"

"Princess, that's nothing compared to what you're going to get on your U.S. tour. Your concerts are already sold out from coast to coast. Every Christian in America wants to hear you sing about Armageddon."

Sam watched the man's head bob up and down, and decided it was definitely a hairpiece. "Mr. Blassingame . . ."

"Chris!"

"What's so special about that song? Why are Evangelicals going bonkers over it?"

"Because it announces the final battle we've all been waiting for— the triumph of good over evil. In fact the first skirmishes are underway right now. We're heading straight into the End Times, my friend."

"How's that?"

"Look at what's happening in the Middle East, in Iraq, Israel, Lebanon, Palestine. There's strife and conflict breaking out all over, just like the Bible says. It's all laid out in black and white, Sam: Israel consolidates its dominion over the Holy Land, the forces of God band together to fight the infidels, and finally, Jesus returns with his mighty sword to smite the evil-doers and reward the Righteous."

"Including the Jews?"

"The Jews are our greatest allies. In fact, we Evangelicals are fervent Zionists, because Israel must prevail before Jesus comes."

Sam balanced his notebook on one knee and jotted down Blassingame's words. "And what happens to the Jews after Armageddon?"

"Well, unfortunately, most of them will be killed in the battle. The survivors will have to convert to Christianity."

"And those that don't?"

"You're not a Jew are you?" Blassingame asked.

"No, I'm not, but . . ."

"Then you got nothing to worry about. Rejoice, Sam. Praise the Lord and rejoice!" Blassingame threw open his arms and burst into a tremulous baritone: "*Fling out the banner, let it float, skyward and seaward, high and wide . . .*"

The Princess puffed on her cigarette and slowly shook her head. "Don't quit your day job, Chris."

When Sam emerged from the dressing room, the backstage party had dwindled down to Robichaux and the drummer, a short, toad-shaped man whose belt seemed to pass just under his armpits. Robichaux had abandoned the beer and was sipping whiskey from a pocket flask. He held it out to Sam.

"No thanks," said the journalist. "Where'd everybody go?"

"Ha! The youngsters took the girls back to their hotel."

"All the girls?"

"Yeah. And two bottles of vodka. They're probably in the middle of a wild orgy by now."

"Why don't you join them?"

Robichaux rubbed his bloodshot eyes and yawned. "At our age, all we can do is drink."

"Speak for yourself," said the drummer.

Sam looked around for something to eat. All that was left was one cold sausage coated in congealed fat. He wiped the grease off with a paper napkin, dipped the end in mustard and took a large bite. He'd tasted worse.

"Tell me something, Jean-Pierre," he said between chews. "Do you guys buy into that religious stuff, the Apocalypse and all that?"

"Me? You must be joking! I'm a life member of the French Communist Party. The only final struggle I believe in is the Revolution. *C'est la lutte finale, groupons-nous et demain, l'Internationale sera le genre humain . . .*"

"Then how can you go onstage with a born-again Gospel singer?"

Robichaux scratched his belly and emitted a loud belch. "Religion is the opiate of the people, right? Tawana is a child of the oppressed black proletariat. Religion is their solace, their call for help, *le cri du peuple, quoi.* Her revolt takes a different form from mine, but it's the same combat—the oppressed against the oppressors."

"*Merde!*" said the bass player. "I'm only in this for the money."

Robichaux shrugged. "There's that, too."

Sam's profile of Princess Tawana practically wrote itself. His editor loved it—"I can see you had fun with this piece, Sam"—and said the photos from Riga were terrific. New York planned to put it on the cover of the *Chronicle*'s prestigious weekend magazine the following Sunday.

Bradley Kemp stuck his head in Sam's office and gave him a thumbs up. "Way to go, Sam. I just read your Tawana piece on the computer.

You ought to do more features like that. That's where your real talent lies."

"You mean I'm a fluff writer, Brad?"

"No, no, not at all." Kemp placed his hand on his chest and laughed. "I just mean you have such a talent as a writer, such a flair for color and style, it's a shame you spend your time on all that investigative stuff. I mean, any hack can do that. But not everybody can write like you. You have such a gift."

"Thank you, Bradley. I suppose I should take that as a compliment."

"That's what it is. Keep up the good work, old boy."

Sam eyed the back of Kemp's white Oxford shirt as he walked out and closed the door behind him. *Old boy!* He was already picking up Woodridge's mannerisms in preparation for taking over the bureau.

CHAPTER

15

JACK RITTER LOOSENED THE KNOT on his baby-blue power tie and undid the top button on his starched white shirt. On his ranch back in New Mexico, he favored work shirts and blue jeans, but that wouldn't do in Washington. Especially for the president of the United States.

The man across the table from him, William Cordman, looked much more comfortable in a business suit. After all, he had been the CEO of a major oil-services company, the Bullington Group, before Ritter had tapped him as his running mate in a tightly contested election. The fact that their ticket had won by a paper-thin margin in no way diminished their sense of entitlement as holders of supreme power, or their determination to reshape the world in the image of the U.S.

Cordman was the older of the two, a former senator and cabinet member who was much more experienced in the ways of Washington. Cordman had one of the world's great poker faces—dark brown eyes that peered out impassively under his white brows, and thin reptilian lips that curled into a permanent sneer. Compared to Cordman, with his white hair and pot-bellied gravitas, Ritter looked almost juvenile. But though the president stayed trim with his daily workouts in the White House gym, the burdens of high office had turned his temples gray and etched deep lines on his forehead.

As usual, Cordman did much of the talking at their regular Friday morning tête-à-tête breakfast. As soon as the waiter laid down a chafing dish of scrambled eggs and sausage and closed the door behind him, Cordman put down his coffee cup and wiped his mouth with a starched napkin.

"Jack, we may have a problem with Ganjibar."

"What kind of problem?"

"He might be moving off the reservation. The folks at Langley tell me he's getting headstrong. He's happy to get the funding and technical support from the agency, but he wants to call the shots himself. We still need him on board for now. He has a lot of clout with his community. But once we get operational over there, he might have to go."

Ritter speared a pork-link sausage. "Rafat's a good man. A real God-fearing Christian. You should have heard him say Grace when he stayed at the ranch. Almost brought tears to my eyes. And he knows how to run a business. I wish I'd a known how to make that much money when I was in the private sector."

"Jack, you bankrupted three companies. You weren't cut out for the business world." Cordman's perpetual sneer broadened into a grin. He always enjoyed reminding the younger man that he had run one of America's biggest industrial groups and still had the multimillion dollar stock options to prove it. Of course, Jack Ritter had also made money along the way; his political friends had always made sure of that. But when it came to running a company—or a government, for that matter—Cordman was the top dog. Or so he liked to think.

"Listen, Bill. Rafat's our guy over there. He cares about what we care about. He believes in what we believe in. No other leader in Iraq embraces both American-style democracy and Jesus Christ. He's made for us. His whole movement is founded on the Gospel."

"With all due respect, Jack, I don't care a rat's ass about the Gospel. But I do care about American power. As long as Ganjibar can advance our interests in the region, I'll support him. As soon as he becomes an obstacle to that, I say he's got to go."

Ritter spread a dollop of mayhaw jelly on a buttered biscuit and pondered the vice president's words. "Come on, Bill, what's he done that's so bad?"

"You think he cares about liberty and democracy? He's like dozens of tinpot dictators we've supported over the years. They talk the talk until they're in power, then they stuff their faces and their pockets until somebody overthrows them and does the same thing. You know what he really cares about? Duty-free malls, luxury health-care clinics, import and export monopolies, and, most of all, oil revenues."

"Well, we all care about that, don't we?"

"Mr. President, I don't think we'd be having this discussion if we didn't. The question is, who controls it? Who pumps it? Who sells it?"

"Are we really sure there's any oil there?"

Cordman opened his briefcase and pulled out a manila folder. He pushed it across the table.

"This is a prospecting report from my former colleagues at Bullington. Potential reserves of 100 billion barrels. That would give this little enclave the world's fourth highest oil holdings."

The president placed a pair of half-height reading glasses on the bridge of his small, simian nose. His lips moved slightly as he perused the document. "Who else knows about this?"

"Nobody. Bullington's in there on a top-secret no-bid contract. The whole perimeter is controlled by U.S. Special Forces embedded with Ganji's so-called liberation army. Nobody else can get in there."

"Has Ganjibar seen this?"

"No way! He knows that there are potential reserves in that area, but he doesn't know the specifics. Bullington sent this report directly to my office in a sealed pouch. I have forwarded an encoded copy to Langley."

Ritter placed his knife and fork on his plate and crumpled up his napkin. "We've got to keep this quiet, Bill. If the extent of this discovery leaks out, it could screw up our whole plan."

Cordman nodded. "That's one reason I'm worried about Ganjibar. Even though he doesn't know the numbers, he's likely to shoot his mouth off about oil reserves. We've warned him to keep a low profile, but that's not in his nature. He's been talking to a reporter from the *Chronicle*."

"What's his name?"

"Sam Preston. Works in their Paris bureau."

"Never heard of him."

"Not surprising, Jack. You don't read the papers."

The president straightened his shoulders and leaned back in his chair. "Why should I read the papers? I get the summaries. I trust my own people to give me the news, not a bunch of liberal reporters."

"Well, this is a name you should remember. He could be a problem. I've asked our folks in the Paris embassy to keep an eye on him."

Ritter stood up and brushed some biscuit crumbs off his trousers. "Goddamn reporters," he muttered. "By the way, have we found out who bombed Ganjibar's church?"

"We're working on it."

CHAPTER

16

ON THIS MONDAY, JULY 3, Gérard Chevalier wasn't in his usual front seat by the window of Le Soleil d'Or. Sam was afraid he might have missed him, but the barman indicated with a nod that he was sitting alone at a rear table.

"Commandant," said Sam, pulling up a chair and shaking hands with the detective. "Are you hiding from an Islamic hit squad?"

"Shh!" Chevalier whispered. "Keep your voice down."

"Sorry. I was just expecting to find you presiding over the bar from your usual perch up front."

"Not this time. This is a matter that requires the utmost discretion."

Chevalier folded his arms and gazed silently at the journalist. Finally, he cleared his throat and pointed to his eyes.

"Oh, right, I nearly forgot." Sam opened his shoulder bag and removed a package wrapped in a brown paper bag. He slipped it to Chevalier under the table. The commandant looked around the room casually as he tore open the wrapping and opened the box inside. He removed a pair of Gucci sunglasses with tortoise-shell frames and examined the logo. "Not bad," he said with tight-lipped smile. "I would have preferred the titanium frames but these are not bad at all." He put them on and gazed contentedly around the room. "Perfect fit, too."

"At that price, I'm not surprised," said Sam.

"Everything has a price, my friend. The better the quality, the higher the price." Chevalier slid a manila envelope across the table. "Read this, but don't take any notes."

It was a deposition that Père Joseph had given to the Antiterrorist Brigade two days after the St. Jean church bombing:

Q. State your name, age, and profession.
A. Aaron Joseph, 62 years old, Clergyman, Rector of St. Jean de Patmos Church in Paris.

Q. Place of birth and nationality.
A. Mosul, Iraq. Dual Iraqi and French citizenship.

Q. Where were you shortly after midnight on the morning of Saturday June 10?
A. At a church retreat center known as "Divin Repos" near the town of Seaulieu.

Q. How did you first learn of the bombing of St. Jean Church?
A. I received a telephone call from Monsieur Rainette, concierge of the church and the adjoining presbytery. I drove back to Paris immediately and followed the news bulletins on my car radio.

Q. Exactly who has access to the church after hours?
A. I do, of course, along with my assistant, Père Zorba, and the concierge. The woman who changes the flowers and candles on the altar also has a key, but she never comes at night.

Q. When was the last time you were in the church?
A. The night before the explosion. I celebrated vespers.

Q. Who else was there?
A. Père Zorba, the concierge, and about a dozen worshipers.

Q. Did you know them?

A. Most of them, yes. The evening mass doesn't draw a big crowd. It is almost all regulars, mostly elderly women.

Q. Did you notice a suspicious object under the altar—a package about the size of a shoe box?
A. No.

Q. Did you look?
A. I am not in the habit of looking for bombs under the altar, inspector, but I would have seen it.

Q. How?
A. Because I kneel to kiss the altar at the end of the mass. Something that big would have attracted my attention.

Q. Were you the last one to leave the church that night?
A. No. My co-celebrant, Père Zorba, and the concierge were still there when I left. Normally the concierge sweeps up and leaves last. He locks the church and it remains locked until 7 A.M. mass the following morning.

Q. Could anyone have entered the church during the night?
A. Not without shattering the stained-glass windows, breaking down the main door, or picking the lock. Unless, of course, they had the key.

Q. I believe your apartments are right next to the church?
A. Yes. They are separated only by a wooden door behind the sanctuary.

Q. Lucky thing you weren't sleeping there the night of the bombing, wouldn't you say? You might have been killed.
A. Yes. I suppose the Lord was watching over me.

Q. And why did you choose that precise day to leave town, father?

A. Mr. Ganjibar had asked me to go air out the country house and prepare it for our summer retreat.

Q. Is he an official of the church?
A. No, but he donated the house to us and finances the upkeep.

Q. Thank you, father. We'll be back in touch with you if we need any
more information.
A. I am always at your disposal, Inspector.

Sam reread the document several times. Then he put it back in the
envelope and handed it to Chevalier.

"So you think Ganjibar knew about this ahead of time?"

Chevalier put his index finger over his lips. "You never saw this,
okay?"

CHAPTER

17

GENERAL RICHARD "RICK" RUNTER was a soldier who had seen it all and done it all. First in his class at West Point; Rhodes scholar with a degree in politics, philosophy, and economics; distinguished combat service in every American conflict since Vietnam; senior staffer with the Joint Chiefs in Washington; and currently head of special operations in Iraq. But the thing Rick Runter was proudest of was his special relationship with Jesus Christ. The son of a Baptist preacher from Montgomery, Alabama, Runter was a dyed-in-the-wool, born-again, Christian soldier.

"You know," he told the attendees at a Fourth of July prayer breakfast in suburban Washington, "some people try to tell me I don't have the right to stand up here and pray with you folks while I'm wearing this uniform. Well, let me tell you something, friends. If it wasn't for Jesus Christ, I wouldn't be wearing this uniform. In fact, I wouldn't be wearing anything but a shroud. Jesus is my guide in life and my best buddy in battle. He saved my neck in five wars—plus a few other operations I'm not at liberty to discuss. So anybody who tells me I can't be an officer in the U.S. Army and a soldier for Jesus is doing the devil's work."

The small private dining room erupted with applause. Runter brushed back the few wisps of gray hair that remained on the top of his perfectly round head and waited for the clapping to die down. The medals and rows of battle ribbons on his chest gleamed in the spotlight as he stepped back up to the lectern. "And anybody who thinks military science is not compatible with the Gospel just doesn't know what the hell he's talking about."

More applause.

"My friends, I've read every work on the art of war from Sun Tzu and Thucydides to Machiavelli and Clausewitz. But you know the greatest book ever written on the subject? The Holy Bible."

Still more applause.

"You can learn plenty about battle tactics in the Good Book," Runter went on. "But the main lesson you learn is this: no matter what the odds, no matter what the size of the armies arrayed against you, no matter what fearsome weapons they may wield, the side that fights in the name of the Lord will win every time. Every time."

Runter nodded sagely and took a sip of water. "Friends, we are now engaged in a great battle over there in Iraq. Our enemies are the enemies of the Lord. They fight for another god, a false god, an evil god. But let me tell you something: Jehovah can kick that other guy's butt any day of the week."

The whole gathering, some fifty or so men and women dressed in their Sunday best, rose to their feet and cheered.

"Now don't get me wrong, folks," the general continued, holding out his right hand, palm down, to calm his overheated listeners. "The other side can hurt us, oh yes. They can draw our righteous blood and smite some of our finest boys with their terrible swords. Satan has the power to do great harm. His armies are mighty. But ours are mightier. And you know why, my friends? You know why? Because Jesus Christ is the greatest soldier who ever lived. And He will come to lead us in that final, cataclysmic battle against the Antichrist that is foretold in the Book of Revelation."

Runter put on a pair of glasses and flipped the pages of the book in front of him. "This is the kind of soldier Jesus is, as described in Revelation 19: 'And I saw heaven opened, and behold a white horse; and he that sat upon him was called Faithful and True, and in righteousness he doth judge and make war. His eyes were as a flame of fire, and on his head were many crowns; and he had a name written, that no men knew, but he himself. And he was clothed with a vesture dipped in blood: and his name is called The Word of God. And the armies which were in heaven followed him upon white horses, clothed in fine linen, white and clean.'"

Runter looked around the hushed room and held up his right hand. The spotlight above the lecturn cast dark circles under his deep-set eyes. "Now listen very carefully, friends, just listen how Jesus deals with the followers of the Antichrist: 'And out of his mouth goeth a sharp sword, that with it he should smite the nations: and he shall rule them with a rod of iron: and he treadeth the winepress of the fierceness and wrath of Almighty God. And he hath on his vesture and on his thigh a name written, KING OF KINGS, AND LORD OF LORDS.'" Rapturous applause again filled the room.

"Friends, brothers and sisters, fellow Christians. I sincerely believe we are approaching the End Times described in Revelation. All the signs point to this. What is going on in Iraq today is a precursor of the return of Christ and the final, terrible battle of Armageddon. I fully expect to take part in that battle as a soldier, just as you will take part in it as followers of Christ. And when I say that, some people tell me, well, Rick, that's fine, but who is the Antichrist over there? I tell them that Satan is clever and devious, that he takes many forms. He inhabits a whole bunch of folks—Saddam Hussein, Osama bin Laden, and all the Islamofascists, Saddamists, Baathists, and other terrorists who are arrayed against us. But do not fear, my friends, and do not doubt for an instant: when that glorious day comes, their blood will fill bottomless rivers that will run from the Euphrates to the Mediterranean, from the Jordan to the Red Sea. Then peace will reign in heaven and earth for a thousand years. And there'll be no more need for an old soldier like me. But until that day, friends"—he held up his hand and brought his fingers together into a clenched fist—"until that day, I say, 'Bring 'em on!'"

After a closing prayer, Runter was mobbed by well-wishers who tapped him on the back, pumped his hand, and asked him to autograph his new book, *Jesus at War*, a runaway bestseller in Christian publishing circles. In the back of the room, Chris Blassingame balanced a legal pad on his knee and scribbled notes for his next article in the National Christian Council newsletter.

CHAPTER

18

BEFORE HIS RENEGADE RUN on the presidency, Roland Peccaldi had worked and lived in some of the grandest digs in Paris: the gilded foreign minister's residence on the Quai d'Orsay, the Gaullist party headquarters near the Palais Bourbon, a luxury apartment in Saint Germain-des-Prés, secretly purchased by a state-owned oil company and put at his disposal by the president himself. Now that perk was gone, and he lived in a somewhat more modest 150-square-meter apartment near the Parc Monceau.

Some people thought—indeed, hoped—that Peccaldi might wind up in the far humbler surroundings of the Santé prison. He was currently under investigation for several cases of bribery, embezzlement, and illegal arms sales. His former mistress, a leggy ex-model-turned-lobbyist, was doing time at that very moment for taking illegal commissions on government contracts that she had allegedly shared with Peccaldi. But the old man just laughed at all this: as a lifetime senator, he had immunity against prosecution. Besides, he knew where a lot of skeletons were buried, and he was convinced the president would never let him take a fall that might bring him down as well.

Peccaldi did not like dealing with the press, especially the French press that had reveled in splashing his legal problems all over the front pages. But he had agreed to see Sam because the American papers paid far less attention to his scandals—what did U.S. readers care about France, after all?—and because a historical piece on the Gaullist movement was likely to cast Peccaldi in a positive light as a faithful supporter of the General.

Peccaldi received the journalist on the afternoon of Wednesday, July 5, at his senate office in the Palais du Luxembourg. The palace, built for Queen Marie de Médicis, was an exquisite piece of seventeenth-century architecture bordering a sixty-acre park filled with statues and fountains and landscaped flowerbeds. The grandeur of this former royal domain was all out of proportion with the senate's limited prerogatives under the Fifth Republic. But Roland Peccaldi's powers were not institutional; they derived from his ability to pull strings, threaten and bully, blackmail and cajole.

Sam was escorted to Peccaldi's office by a senate usher in black tails. The old man stood up to welcome the American. He walked with a slight limp, the result of a wartime injury: he had been tortured by the Gestapo in Lyons before escaping and resuming his cutthroat resistance activities.

"Monsieur Preston, so nice to meet you," he said in his lilting Corsican accent and warmly shook Sam's hand. He wore a dark blue pinstriped suit, expensive-looking but of an old-fashioned cut. A red Légion d'Honneur ribbon graced his wide lapel. He had a shiny mane of silver hair, brushed straight back over his collar; the skin on his jowly face was flaccid and pale as parchment. But when Peccaldi spoke, his voice rang with a crisp military authority.

"Please make yourself comfortable," he said, waving Sam to a couch and settling into an armchair beside him. Peccaldi opened a humidor and pushed it across the coffee table. "Cigar?" Sam admired the double row of Cohiba coronas, but politely declined.

"I hope you don't mind if I indulge myself," said Peccaldi, clipping the end off a Cohiba with a gold cutter and lighting it with a long match. "I know you Americans are getting harder and harder on smokers, but I developed a taste for fine Havanas years ago, when I was in the tobacco business, and it remains one of my favorite vices. I have a few others, of course, but I'm not the sulfurous creature that the French press makes me out to be. I'm just a French patriot, a Gaullist of the old order."

"Well, that's just the subject that interests me," said Sam. "People are still talking about Gaullism, even though De Gaulle has been dead for more than three decades. What does it really mean today?"

Peccaldi nodded his head slowly and let a plume of smoke escape from the corner of his mouth. "To understand what it means today, Monsieur, you must go back to June 1940. France was defeated, crushed, humiliated. On the darkest hour of the darkest night, General De Gaulle held out a beacon of hope for the French people. He was one of those mythic figures, a saviour really, like Jeanne d'Arc and Charles Martel."

The old man took a long draw on his cigar and went on.

"I remember the eighteenth of June like it was yesterday. I was just a boy, sixteen years old. When I heard the general's appeal on the BBC, it was so thrilling my hair stood on end. I ran away from my parents' home in Ajaccio the next day and headed for the mainland with a friend in a stolen fishing boat. We wanted to go join De Gaulle in London, but the Resistance needed us in Marseilles, so we stayed in the South of France. I fought for my country from the age of sixteen and I am still fighting for it."

"When did you meet De Gaulle?"

"I didn't actually meet him until after the war, at a ceremony to honor the Resistance heroes. It was in the courtyard of the Elysée. He pinned a medal on my chest, and I was so moved I had tears in my eyes. And he said to me, I'll never forget this, he said, '*Allons, mon brave, pourquoi des larmes après tant de sang versé pour la République?*'—'Why shed tears after spilling so much blood for the Republic?' I vowed right then that I would follow the general to the ends of the earth, and do whatever it took to serve his cause."

"I have heard you and your comrades used, shall we say, muscular methods to serve the general?"

Peccaldi's watery blue eyes twinkled as he gazed at the American. "We used all kinds of methods, *cher ami*. We faced multiple enemies—Communists, syndicalists, saboteurs, revanchard collaborators, Algérie Française assassins. Under extraordinary circumstances, you must use extraordinary means. Just like your president is doing now in the face of the terrorist threat. And he's right."

"You think Ritter is right?"

"Of course he's right. I'm not shedding any tears for the terrorists at Abu Ghraib and Guantanamo. There are too many bleeding hearts in this country. And too much anti-Americanism."

"De Gaulle was not exactly pro-American."

"The general was pro-French. He had a *certaine idée de la France*, as he liked to put it. True, he refused to kowtow to Washington, or ostracize Moscow. But in a crisis, he was always on the side of the U.S. I was there when the G.I.'s landed in the South of France in 1944. We must never forget that debt."

"Your president seems to forget it sometimes, doesn't he?"

"You know, that's one major point of divergence between me and my old friend Georges Carnac. I bitterly disagreed with him when he refused to back the U.S. invasion of Iraq. We are all threatened by the terrorists and we must stick together in fighting them. By whatever means."

"Including illegal arms sales?"

Peccaldi exhaled a cloud of smoke and watched it rise toward the high, molded ceiling. "Just what do you know about arms sales, Monsieur?"

"Only what I read in the papers."

The old man frowned and leaned back in his armchair. His labored breathing sounded like fireplace bellows. "Monsieur Preston," he said at last, "I can assure you that whatever you may have read or heard linking me to illegal arms sales is based on slander and fabrication. There is nothing at all to the story. You would be very unwise to pursue it."

He rose slowly to his feet and pointed toward the door. "This interview is over, Monsieur. Good day."

CHAPTER
19

"SAM, IT'S ME. Don't say my name on the phone."
The gravelly voice of Nikola was unmistakable.

"What's up?"

"Meet me at Le Berkeley in five minutes. It's urgent!"

The Greek hung up without waiting for an answer.

Sam looked at his watch. He had to file a story on the latest French unemployment figures by five o'clock, two hours from now, and he still had a couple of phone calls to make. That didn't leave much time.

As Sam dashed out of his office, he almost bowled over Bradley Kemp, who had been standing just outside the door.

"Sorry, Brad," Sam said. "Didn't know you were there. Were you listening through the keyhole or something?"

"Very funny, Sam. I was just coming to ask you how you were doing on the unemployment story. They might need it sooner in New York. And by the way, it's Bradley."

Sam marched down the hallway with Kemp in his wake. "If New York needs it sooner, Brad, they can call me directly, or go through Clive."

Kemp jogged down the hall trying to keep up with Sam's rapid stride. "Clive is still at lunch, so they went over the story list with me. You know I'll be filling in for him in a few days."

"I know, Brad, believe me I know."

Sam stepped into the elevator and gave Kemp a little wink as the door closed.

He strode briskly down the Rue du Faubourg Saint-Honoré, past the American and British embassies and the Club Interallié, where Clive Woodridge spent most of his time lunching, drinking, and playing squash. When he got to the Elysée palace, official residence of the French president, a policeman made him cross the street and walk on the other side. The requirement always irritated him, since he knew he could walk right through the front gate with his press pass and had done so dozens of times. Still, he dutifully crossed over and walked past the Hotel Bristol and the Interior Ministry, with its tall, gilt-topped iron gate. One block further down, he turned left on the Avenue Matignon.

Sam spotted Nikola sitting under a green parasol at a sidewalk table, sipping a *pastis*—the closest thing France has to the Greeks' beloved *ouzo*. He was wearing his usual wraparound Ray-Bans, and his body-builder's biceps strained the sleeves of his black polo shirt. But his year-round tan had given way to pale grayish tint, as if all the blood had drained out of his face.

He grabbed Sam's wrist. "Keep your voice down. We might be watched."

Sam craned his neck and looked around. There were a few people milling about at a stamp collectors' market in the park across the street, but no one seemed to be paying the slightest attention to the Greek and his companion. "Don't be paranoid. What's the matter?"

"This is the matter," he whispered, pointing to the copy of *France Soir* that was folded on the table in front of him. The headline of the garish tabloid read: "LEFT BANK RUBOUT." Underneath it was a large grainy color photo of a body sprawled on the sidewalk in a pool of blood, next to an overturned chair. The face was not visible, but the caption identified the victim as "Michel Lanzatti, bodyguard and political operative of former Foreign Minister Roland Peccaldi, shot dead at a Place St. Michel café by an unidentified gunman on a motorcycle."

"They hit him last night," said Nikola, his voice hoarse and shaky. "And now they're looking for me."

"Who hit him?"

"Some S.A.C. goons."

"You mean De Gaulle's private army? I thought they were disbanded years ago."

"You don't know shit about France, do you? When De Gaulle died, Peccaldi put the remnants of the S.A.C. together with a bunch of African mercenaries and turned them into his own militia. Who cares what the fuck you call them? They are the most dangerous bastards in France —and they are after my ass."

"Why?"

Nikola yanked off his Ray-Bans and glared at the journalist. "Because of you, asshole! You sold us out. You asked Peccaldi about the arms sales."

"Don't give me any ethics lessons. You stole those papers from Peccaldi, didn't you?"

"Michel did it. How the hell could I get into Peccaldi's safe? Michel had been with him for ten years. Peccaldi trusted him. He loved him like a son."

"Then why was Michel stealing his documents?"

"He was burned because the old man passed him over. Peccaldi put another guy in charge of his African networks, 'cause Michel was doing too many drugs. Michel was furious. He thought he could get back at the old man, and make a shitload of money at the same time. He photocopied all the documents and put the originals back in the safe so Peccaldi wouldn't miss them. Then he brought me in to help him peddle the stuff to the press. Said we'd make a million dollars."

"Did anybody buy it?"

The Greek shook his head. "We didn't show them to anybody but you and Dumond. Michel said if we talked to too many reporters the story would leak out piecemeal. He was sure you would pay for it in the end."

"Bad guess. And how could you guys have been so stupid as to steal Peccaldi's documents when you know how ruthless he is?"

"I told you, Michel did a lot of drugs. He didn't always think straight."

"And you? Didn't you know the risk you were taking?"

"I just thought I'd zip in and out of this, get my cut, and blow the country."

Sam shook his head. "Sounds like a bad Mafia movie. The Godfather meets the Marx Brothers."

"Fuck you. I'm in trouble, man. You gotta help me."

"You got yourself into this, Niko. What the hell can I do for you?"

"Take the documents, Sam." Nikola plopped a manila envelope on the table. "All the arms sales stuff is in here, plus a lot more. What's in this envelope will give you the whole money trail behind the arms sales. Take a look."

Sam pulled out a few papers at random. Much of it was the kind of arms orders, invoices, and letters of credit that they had seen at the Claridge. But there were also documents on money transfers, Swiss bank accounts, offshore banks, mysterious coded wire instructions, and balance statements.

Nikola suddenly yanked it all back and stuffed it in the envelope. "I'm not gonna let you sit here all day and read this for free, Sam."

"I didn't think so."

"But you can have it all for a modest price."

"How much?"

"A plane ticket to Athens. First class."

The journalist didn't react.

"Don't fuck with me, Sam." Nikola squeezed the American's forearm hard. "I gotta get out of here. I'll give you one minute to make up your mind or I go somewhere else with this shit. It's too hot. Those bastards are gonna kill me. They could shoot me down right here any second now—and you with me."

Sam watched the stamp collectors in the park across the street and wondered how he could possibly justify putting a first-class ticket to Athens on his expenses. Woodridge might let it pass, but Kemp would go to the mat over it to prove he could run a tight ship.

"Thirty seconds," said Nikola, staring at the counterfeit Rolex on his hairy wrist.

Sam looked at the bar check, threw some coins on the table, and stood up. "Okay, Nikola," he said. "I'll meet you at the post office on the Champs Elysées in twenty minutes. I'll bring the ticket and you bring the envelope."

"Done."

"Wait," Sam put his hand on Nikola's shoulder. "I bet you kept a copy of all this stuff."

"For my own protection, Sam," said the Greek. "But I won't sell it to anyone else. Trust me."

There wasn't much of a line at the Air France office near the Arc de Triomphe. Sam took a waiting number and sat down. He picked up a copy of the Air France magazine and flipped through its slick pages. Photo after luscious photo of beaches, palm trees, and aquamarine waters—twenty different holiday destinations, and they all looked exactly alike.

A burly man in a tan linen suit and a Panama hat sat down next to him. Sam noticed he was carrying an umbrella, though it was a cloudless summer day.

"Going on holiday, are you?" the man said in a crisp British accent. "You should try the Seychelles. Gorgeous white powder beaches. The Bahamas are lovely, too. Charming old colonial hotels. Crystal clear water."

Sam looked up from his magazine. "Yes. I'm sure it's quite nice."

Sam's number was called. He walked to the sales counter and asked for a first-class one-way ticket to Athens.

"I need the passenger's name and passport number."

Sam pulled out the folded paper napkin on which Nikola had hastily scrawled this information.

"Date of departure?"

"Today, first available flight."

"Let's see. I can get him on flight 2332. It leaves at 6:25 this evening, Thursday, July 6, and arrives at Eleftherios Venizelos International in Athens at 10:40."

"That's perfect."

"Very good, sir." She tapped on her computer keyboard, waited, and tapped again. The printer behind her clicked and buzzed. She put the ticket in an Air France envelope and slid it over the counter.

"With the VAT and airport taxes, that comes to 925 euro and 20 centimes."

Sam handed over his American Express corporate card and signed the chit. Then he slipped the envelope in his breast pocket and headed for the door. The man in the Panama hat was gone.

The sidewalks were jammed with afternoon shoppers, and Sam had to fight and weave his way through the crowd. He was already a couple of minutes late for his rendezvous with Nikola. The Greek was so jumpy today, he might just take off instead of waiting. At least Sam could refund the ticket in that case.

And then he saw him. The chatty Brit was sitting on a bench right in front of the post office, reading the paper with the umbrella in his lap. Sam tried to hide in the crowd and slip past him. But just as he prepared to open the door, the man put down his paper and waved. "Oh hello there. Fancy seeing you again. Got your ticket, did you? Have a nice holiday."

Sam nodded curtly and entered the post office. He pushed past a group of long-haired Dutch backpackers and found Nikola pretending to study a Foreign Legion recruiting poster in the back corner. His forehead glistened and his graying hair was matted with sweat.

Without a word, the Greek handed over the envelope. Sam quickly checked the contents. Then he gave Nikola the ticket and shook his hand. "Bon voyage. And be careful—there's a fat guy on a bench out there with an umbrella. I think he may be watching us."

"I saw him," said Nikola. "He was sitting on the terrace of Le Berkeley when we were there."

"Oh, shit! Now he's waiting for us to come out. What will we do?"

"What do you mean 'we'? You've got the envelope now. *Ciao, bambino!*" With a mock salute, the Greek turned and disappeared into a crowd of tourists.

Sam took out a pen and scrawled the name and address of Charles Dumond on the envelope. He couldn't remember the home address, so he sent it to the office of *Actualités*. It was safer than sending it to his own home. He waited in line for what seemed like an eternity. When Sam's turn finally came, he paid for the stamps and watched the clerk throw the envelope in the hopper.

Once outside the post office, Sam looked up and down the busy avenue but saw no sign of the stalker. He felt relieved. Perhaps the man's ubiquitous presence had been a coincidence, after all. Perhaps not. But there was no turning back. Dumond had hooked him into this story and now he had to follow it through wherever it led. But he sensed he was now moving into the danger zone and did not intend to brave it alone.

Sam crossed the Champs Elysées and walked toward the Metro station near the Etoile. He pulled out his cell phone and dialed Dumond's number. There was no answer on the Frenchman's cell, so he left a message: "Charles, it's Sam. I sent an important package to your office address. Hold it for me. I'll explain when we meet. Call me."

For good measure, he called Charles's office. A secretary informed him that Monsieur Dumond had left on a reporting trip to the Middle East and would be away for several days.

"Damn!" Sam muttered to himself. No telling when he could get his hands on those documents. And if someone else at Dumond's office opened the envelope first, their scoop would be ruined. It was just like the little Frog to leave without saying anything. There were times when Sam wanted to strangle Charles Dumond.

CHAPTER

20

F ROM THE OUTSIDE, the glass and concrete structure at 1 Rue Nélaton resembles any other modern office building. Inside, it looks more like an overworked precinct station than the nerve center of the Direction de la Surveillance du Territoire, better known as the D.S.T., France's internal security service. The offices are small and cramped. The walls are lined with filing cabinets; the desks covered with coffee cups, overflowing ashtrays, stacks of papers, and file folders. The only visible sign of modernity is the computer terminals that link the inspectors to the vast store of intelligence data captured by every imaginable means, ranging from high-tech electronic surveillance to rifling through people's garbage and looking through keyholes.

The brown manila envelope that landed on Louis Brigatti's cluttered desk that Friday morning didn't look like anything special. The writing on the front was a hasty scrawl. The addressee was a journalist with *Actualités*. Nothing unusual about that; the D.S.T. routinely surveyed the activities of the foreign and domestic press to make sure they were not threatening national security with their meddlesome reporting.

Brigatti took a sip of black coffee and opened the envelope. The glue had been expertly steamed off by the technical services downstairs. He pulled out the thick sheaf of papers and began the meticulous line-by-line analysis, piecing together bits of data, cross-checking and comparing it with information in the D.S.T.'s vast database. Before the morning was through, Brigatti realized that there was nothing ordinary about the file. He scooped up the papers and put them back in the envelope. Then he took it down the dingy hallway to the office of his superior, Col. Jean-Michel Canettone, and closed the door behind him.

Forty-five minutes later, as Brigatti exited his office, Canettone called the director of the D.S.T., Roger Pénarre, and set up a hasty meeting upstairs. The director then called the interior minister, who called the chief of staff of the Elysée Palace. An emergency meeting of the president's national security team was called for the following morning.

Georges Carnac sat behind his Louis XV desk and tapped on his writing pad with a letter opener in the shape of a Napoleonic cavalry officer's sword—a gift from the prefect of Corsica. On his face was the same grave expression he always wore whenever some real-world crisis intruded on his ceremonial presidency. Arrayed in a semicircle before him, in high-backed satin armchairs, were the president's elegant, silver-haired chief of staff, Arnaud de la Bruyère; Interior Minister Edouard Pantin, a long-time political crony of the president's; Dominique Steinberg, the president's in-house diplomatic adviser; Antoine de Bornville, director of the D.G.S.E., France's external security service; and D.S.T. Director Pénarre.

"Messieurs," said Carnac, "it appears that our services have uncovered certain activities that are prejudicial to our national interests and security. I have called this emergency meeting to inform you of the situation and take your advice on how to deal with it. Edouard, can you summarize the facts?"

The interior minister, hierarchically in charge of the D.S.T., put on his glasses and read from a briefing paper. "Monsieur le Président, esteemed colleagues, our services have intercepted a set of documents that tell a story of deception, financial misdoings, and clandestine military activities that could have the gravest implications."

"Summarize, Pantin. I will make the speeches."

"Oui, Monsieur le Président. Starting about six months ago, large amounts of capital—several tens of billions of dollars—started moving out of various countries in Latin America, Asia, and the Middle East in the form of long-term loans. This money transited through several intermediaries using numbered offshore accounts. The bulk of it now resides in a discreet private bank in Lugano, Switzerland, the Banco Bersalino. The funds are in fact divided into several Bersalino accounts, the largest of which is controlled by Roland Peccaldi."

The room fell silent, except for the ticking of the antique brass clock on the mantelpiece.

The president frowned. "Are we sure it's Peccaldi?"

"Monsieur le Président, these documents were stolen from Peccaldi's own safe. They are his personal documents."

"We stole them?"

"No. They were taken by a Peccaldi confidant who was trying to sell them. The man was killed two days ago, apparently by Peccaldi's own people, and we intercepted the documents. In any case, Peccaldi's implication in this affair leaves no doubt."

"I find this difficult to believe," said Carnac, nervously tapping the letter opener on his desktop. "Peccaldi's already pumped millions out of the African networks. Why would he need to borrow billions more?"

"It appears, Monsieur le Président, that Peccaldi was merely acting as an agent for the real beneficiary of these funds—for a hefty commission, of course."

"Who is the real borrower?"

"With your permission, Monsieur le Président," said D.G.S.E. Director Bornville, "perhaps I can pick up the story from here. My services have long been surveying Peccaldi's foreign activities and contacts. As you know, he has been quite active in African arms sales, Iraqi oil-for-food vouchers, and diamond smuggling, among other things."

"A man's got to make a living," the president quipped, prompting some nervous chuckles among the others.

"In the past few months, though," Bornville continued, "he has had regular and repeated contacts with agents of the C.I.A. and the D.I.A., the Defense Department's in-house intelligence agency. The electronic intercepts we got were fragmentary, often encrypted. There have also been a number of face-to-face contacts. Recently, he has made several trips to Switzerland and met with them there. Now, thanks to the information from the intercepted dossier, we have assembled most of the puzzle."

Bornville took off his glasses and glanced up at the president.

"Monsieur le Président," said the spymaster, "it is difficult to avoid the conclusion that Peccaldi is himself acting as an American agent in this affair. Part of the money in the Lugano account is being used to finance secret arms sales that are going to the Assyrian Liberation Army in Iraq, which as we know, is virtually a creation of the C.I.A. Funds from that and other Swiss accounts are also being used to finance a vast construction project in western Iraq, on territory controlled by the Assyrian Christians. Most of it is underground, so our Helios 2A satellite can't see exactly what they are doing, but based on the number of trucks that leave the site with loads of dirt and sand, it seems like a substantial excavation."

"What the hell are they building in the middle of the desert?"

"Sir, our analysis suggests a vast underground military complex that could be used to house a whole array of armaments and weapons systems ranging from tanks and heavy artillery to antimissile installations, Tomahawk batteries, and possibly even nuclear missile silos."

"*Putain!*" said Carnac. "Is that all?"

"No, sir. There is also considerable oil exploration and drilling activity in that sector."

"How could there be any oil there? Elf and Total were all over in Iraq in the old days. They never found anything in that sector."

"Correction, Monsieur le Président," said Bornville. "They found indications of possible reserves at depths over of two thousand meters—depths that, at the time, were not exploitable. But high-pressure diamond core drilling technology now exists to access those depths. Based on the data Elf and Total compiled in the seventies and eighties, there could be considerable reserves there."

"All for the Americans," said Carnac.

Bornville nodded. "In fact, they seem to be betting very heavily on oil production in the Assyrian region."

"It's not enough for them to control the existing Iraqi oil fields?"

"Sir, the older Iraqi infrastructure was heavily damaged during the invasion and Bullington has botched the job of repairing a key pipeline nexus under the Tigris. Current Iraqi oil production is just a fraction of what it was in Saddam's heyday."

"So the Americans are trying to make up for the shortfall by developing these new fields?"

"That seems to be their objective, Monsieur le Président. They may even be planning to run an underground pipeline directly from the Assyrian fields into Turkey."

"Are you sure of that?"

"We can surmise it. We know the Americans are helping the Turks build a large oil export depot in the Mediterranean port of Iskenderun. That is far to the east of the existing pipeline that comes into Turkey from the Caspian region. Our analysts see no other explanation for this depot than to export oil from the new fields in northwestern Iraq."

Carnac stroked his prominent chin and glanced up at the official oil portrait of Charles De Gaulle on the opposite wall. What would the general do in a situation like this, Carnac wondered. Would he lie down and let the Yanks dictate the law and grab all the oil, or would he find a way to resist in the name of that *certaine idée de la France*? The answer seemed obvious. He made a mental note to confront the American president about this at the G8 summit, which would take place in Newport, Rhode Island, in two weeks.

"Who knows about this?" the president asked.

"The Americans, of course. And Peccaldi."

"Who else?"

"Rafat Ganjibar."

"Ganjibar? That fat-assed *boudin* who claims to lead the Assyrian Christians? We should never have given him political asylum here."

"And then, Monsieur le Président, there are the journalists."

"What journalists?"

"The ones who got ahold of the file that we intercepted."

"Who are they?"

Bornville turned to the D.S.T. Director Pénarre.

"There are two of them," said Pénarre. "One is an American, Sam Preston of the *New York Chronicle*. The other is Charles Dumond of *Actualités*. They are working together on an investigative piece."

"What do we know about them?" said Carnac.

"Preston is thirty-six years old, married, no children. He's been here for four years. Attends A.A. meetings at Sainte-Marguerite Church in Le Vésinet, has regular contacts with the C.I.A. station chief at the U.S. Embassy, appears to have Democratic leanings, writes articles that are often critical of the Ritter administration. Unlike most of his Anglo-Saxon colleagues, his reporting is not systematically hostile to France."

"And the Frenchman?"

"Charles Dumond, forty-one, son of a prominent Gaullist party member, now deceased, single, former hostage in Beirut, center-right political orientation, respected journalist."

"I should add, Monsieur le Président," said the D.G.S.E.'s Bornville, "that Dumond is an honorable correspondent, that is, he occasionally shares information with our service. This relationship dates back to the time of his liberation and exfiltration from Beirut by our agents. We consider him reliable."

"So what should we do about them?" the president asked.

The room was silent. The clock ticked like a time bomb working its way down to zero.

"Monsieur le Président," said Steinberg, the diplomatic advisor, "if I may be so bold, I think we should restore the file to the journalists. Preston will probably pursue his investigation and publish a story that will expose what the Americans are doing. That can only work to our advantage. But we must make sure that Dumond publishes nothing about this affair. It would look like a setup if it came out in the French press."

"That's easy enough to do," said Carnac. "I can call my friend Hervé Larcher and tell him that we will cancel the Vengeur fighter-bomber if he allows *Actualités* to publish anything about this."

"That is a brilliant plan," said Arnaud de la Bruyère, the president's mercurial chief of staff, "except for one thing. The central figure in this arms network is a former minister of the French Republic. As embarrassing as this story is for the Ritter administration, Peccaldi's role could also hurt us."

The president scowled at the mention of his rival's name. "Roland Peccaldi," he said, "in no way represents the French Republic or my government. He shamefully and publicly betrayed me, he stole money from the coffers of the Gaullist party, he is under multiple investigations for embezzlement, influence peddling, arms trafficking, and God knows what else. We will have no problem portraying him as a rogue mercenary working for the Americans. Peccaldi's involvement is far more embarrassing to Ritter than it is to us."

"There is another problem, Monsieur le Président," said the D.S.T.'s Pénarre. "The source of the file is a Greek national named Nikola Lefkosias. One of our agents saw him hand it off to Preston at the Champs Elysées post office. That's how we managed to intercept it."

"What is the problem?"

"The problem is that the Greek probably kept a photocopy of the file. If he manages to peddle it to the press, it could come out in some seedy publication, or leak out piecemeal, which would allow the Americans to denounce it as a fabrication. Unless it is published by a reputable U.S. paper like the *Chronicle*, it will not have the impact we are counting on."

"Where is this Greek character now?"

"In Athens."

Carnac toyed with the letter opener. "Send someone to Athens." Pénarre nodded.

"What should we do about Ganjibar?" said the interior minister.

"Put him under round-the-clock surveillance. I want to know what he's up to, who he's meeting, what he's plotting. And, Pénarre, check into all his business dealings, tax records, financial transactions. If he's broken any laws of the French Republic, we will expel him—or put his fat *derrière* in the Santé."

"And Peccaldi?"

"I don't want to know," said Carnac.

CHAPTER

21

M ARIE CALEDONI'S FRIDAY MORNING call caught Sam running out the door to meet a U.S. Embassy analyst for lunch.

"Sam Preston? This is Marie Caledoni. How are you doing today?"

"I'm doing great, Marie. What's up?"

"Listen, this is kind of short notice, but Princess Tawana would like to invite you to her command performance at the White House next Wednesday, July 12. She really appreciated that story you did in the magazine—I mean, we all did—it was just fabulous, fabulous. She'd really like you to be there. In fact, we've already put you on the guest list."

"That's very kind of you. But I doubt that the *Chronicle* will fly me over there for that. Budgets are tight these days and they already have a whole bureau full of correspondents in Washington."

"Oh, we'd pay your way over and put you up."

"Thanks, Marie, but we can't accept freebies. It's against company ethics policy. I could get in a shitload of trouble if anybody found out."

"Nobody will find out, Sam. You'll be back in twenty-four hours. I'll messenger you a ticket this afternoon."

Sam jogged down the Avenue Montaigne toward the Place de l'Alma. Jason Winthrop had invited him to lunch. Winthrop was listed on the U.S. Embassy staff roster as a political analyst, but Sam had always suspected that he was something more than that.

He found Winthrop sitting at a sidewalk table and sipping a glass of champagne in front of Chez Francis. It used to be a grand restaurant, with polished bird's-eye maple wall paneling and priceless art nouveau chandeliers. But the current owners had sold off most of the fittings and the place had been going downhill for years. The best thing it had going for it was a spectacular view of the Eiffel Tower, just across the Seine.

"Sorry I'm a bit late," Sam said, out of breath, as he took a seat next to Winthrop.

"No problem. I was just enjoying the scenery—and the champers. Want some?"

"No thanks. I'll have a Coke."

"There's a loyal American for you."

A waiter came to take their order. They both went with the *spécialité du jour*: beef bourguignon with parsleyed potatoes.

The two men lunched together from time to time to compare notes on the French political scene and, often, just to shoot the breeze. They had an easygoing relationship, but Sam always tried to remember that government and the press had to be as separate as church and state. They were both young Americans in Paris, and they both enjoyed the culture and the lifestyle that went with that, but they did not play on the same team. Reporters who entered into complicitous relationships with the officials they covered were easy prey for manipulation.

"I hear you're headed to Washington," Winthrop said.

"Who told you that?"

"Your name is on the guest list for a White House dinner next week. The State Department checked with us to find out if you're bona fide. Routine security thing. Sounds like a fun trip."

"I'm not doing it for fun. It will give me a chance to check in with some Washington sources for a story I'm working on."

"About Rafat Ganjibar?"

Sam glanced at the diplomat over the top of his glasses and saw that Winthrop was smiling. "Are you tapping my phone or something?"

"Don't be ridiculous," he laughed. "We have much better things to do. Besides, that would be illegal in France."

"The National Security Agency could do it from a satellite and the French wouldn't even know about it."

"Sam, you are being totally paranoid. I hardly need a satellite to know you've been reporting on Rafat Ganjibar. One of your colleagues was over at State asking about Ganjibar for a story out of Paris. I read your story on the St. Jean bombing, so I figured you were the one working on Ganjibar. Call it an educated guess."

Sam ripped off a piece of bread and dipped it in his sauce—another local habit he'd picked up in Paris. "Maybe I am getting a bit paranoid these days," he said, "but that doesn't mean I'm wrong. Like they say, even paranoids have enemies."

"Well I suppose that goes with the territory when you do investigative pieces. You're bound to step on somebody's toes. So you have to be careful. Very careful."

Sam cut into a piece of braised beef. "I know the business, Jason. I can take care of myself."

"Of course you can. You're a pretty shrewd journalist. But I really wouldn't pay too much attention to Ganjibar if I were you. He's just a self-aggrandizing blowhard. Makes up most of it as he goes along. For example, he likes to let on that he's sitting on a pool of oil, but it's total bullshit."

"You're telling me there's no oil there?"

"Oh, there may be a few pockets here and there, too far down to fool with, nothing to write home about. Look, every inch of Iraqi territory has been prospected. The French companies had privileged access to the Iraqi fields for years. Before relations soured with Saddam, our companies were in there, the Brits were in there. What you see is what you get. Iraq has a lot of oil, but the big fields are in the north and south, not in the northwestern territories where Ganjibar's people are. Ganjibar's a joke, actually. You shouldn't waste any more time on him. Nobody in the State Department takes him seriously."

CHAPTER

22

CHARLES DUMOND SETTLED INTO his business-class seat on El Al flight 325 from Paris to Tel Aviv. His magazine didn't pay for business class, but he had upgraded with frequent flyer miles. He thought it was a fine place to be on this sunny Friday morning. There were a lot of empty seats, plenty of room to stretch out, four and a half hours to read and think without the constant distraction of cell phones and editorial meetings. Plus free champagne.

"Can I give you a refill, sir?" The flight attendant, clad in her well-cut blue uniform, reminded Dumond of Angelina Jolie. She had the same full lips and high cheekbones. But her complexion was darker, a deep tan that enhanced the glow of her green eyes.

"Why not?" said Dumond, holding out his glass. "It's very good. Moët & Chandon?"

"It's Israeli champagne, sir. I think it's even better than Moët."

"Don't tell our president that," Dumond giggled. "He'll declare a trade embargo."

"Your president is hostile enough to Israel as it is."

Dumond quietly sipped his champagne. What could he answer to that? Georges Carnac believed in nothing but winning the next election. He had been all over the map during his fifty years in politics. But he had inherited France's long-standing Middle East policy, based on leveraging French influence in its former colonies and protectorates in the Arab world to form a counterweight to America's pro-Israel stance.

And Carnac had also presided over an alarming flare-up of anti-Semitic attacks in France—the work, he insisted, of the kids of Arab immigrants angered over Israel's oppression of the Palestinians. Maybe Carnac had a point: the same kids periodically rose up against their own neighbors and burned their cars in the bleak suburbs of Paris. But try explaining that to an employee of Israel's state airline. In Israeli eyes, Georges Carnac was hostile and anti-Semitic. And so, by extension, were all the French.

Dumond set the glass down on his tray table and unfolded a copy of *Le Monde*. It was full of the usual horrors that make life interesting for journalists: soaring oil prices, global warming, Hezbollah rocket attacks on Israel, Iran's attempts to build a nuke, suicide bombings in Baghdad, a Chechen terrorist attack in Moscow, a lobbying scandal in Washington. Dumond skimmed half a dozen articles, and decided that, apart from the details, he had read the same stories many times over. Maybe he'd been in the news business too long.

He folded up the paper and pulled a book out of his computer bag. It was Amos Oz's latest work: *How to Cure a Fanatic*. Dumond was halfway through it, and thought Israel would be better off if its political leadership had as much lucidity as the famous novelist and peace advocate. He was looking forward to interviewing Oz once he got to Tel Aviv. That was the main reason for his trip to Israel.

Two flight attendants pushed a serving cart down the aisle. The Angelina Jolie look-alike told him there was a choice between *pavé de boeuf* with mushroom sauce or poached salmon with chives, capers, and sour cream. He took the beef, accompanied by an Israeli Cabernet-Sauvignon that turned out to be quite drinkable—even if it was a bit heady with its fourteen percent alcohol content. Dumond sipped the ruby-colored wine and continued to read, stopping occasionally to underline a passage or make a marginal note.

When the cart came around again, he asked for coffee with cream.

"I can give you black coffee, sir, but no cream," said the flight attendant. "You had the beef. It's not kosher."

"But I'm not Jewish," Dumond protested.

"I'm sorry, sir, but it's the same rule for everyone. This is the Israeli national airline. The law says we have to keep kosher."

Dumond shrugged, then held out his cup and watched her fill it from a stainless steel thermos. At least it was hot.

The Boeing 767 landed at Ben Gurion International Airport shortly after 2 p.m. Dumond was among the first to deplane, but he ran into a delay when he reached passport control. Seeing that he was French, and a journalist at that, the Israeli security personnel invited him into a windowless side room, where they questioned him about his business in Israel, photographed and fingerprinted him, and went carefully through his bags. Routine harassment, Dumond thought. But it wasn't just the Israelis. He'd had worse treatment—including a body-cavity search—on arriving at JFK. Those were the things you had to put up with when you came from a proud, independent country that was not afraid to speak its mind.

By the time he emerged from the security area, all the other passengers from flight 325 had already gone through. Good thing he had only carry-on luggage, or he would lose more time looking for his baggage. The upside was that there were only a few people in the taxi line when he emerged from the terminal into the blazing afternoon sun.

"Hotel Yamit Park Plaza," he told the driver, as he settled into the backseat of an aging white Mercedes.

The driver, a dark-faced man with a thick mustache, looked at Dumond in the mirror as he pulled away from the curb.

"You are French?" he asked.

"Yes."

"Why your president hate us? Why your people burn synagogue and hit Jews on the head? Why your Le Pen, he love Hitler so much?"

Dumond pulled out his newspaper. "I like Israel," he said dryly. "That's why I chose to come here on vacation, not to talk politics."

"Vacation, business, it make no difference. Everything is politics."

Dumond shuffled his paper. But the driver's angry monologue lasted the whole twenty-five-minute drive to the seaside hotel.

When the taxi pulled up at the entrance, the journalist drew four crisp bills from his wallet. The driver handed one back. "I don't take no tip from Frenchman."

"*Tant pis pour toi, connard*," Dumond muttered as he picked up his bag and walked through the revolving door. The air-conditioning was a welcome relief from the searing Middle East heat outside.

He headed for the reception desk and saw that the crew from his El Al flight was checking in just ahead of him, pilots first then flight attendants. Dumond took his place in line behind the young woman who had served him in business class. She was a half head taller than him, which made her all the more attractive in his eyes. He'd always regarded tall women as good breeding stock.

Dumond watched carefully as she signed the register: Hannah Avner, room 413. When the receptionist handed her the room key, she turned around and looked at the journalist.

"Hello," he said.

"Oh, hello!" Avner smiled enticingly. "I see we're at the same hotel. The rooms aren't very big, but the Mediterranean view is lovely."

"In that case," he said, staring straight into her green eyes, "I'll ask for a room with a view. Unless you want to show me yours."

Avner's white teeth were dazzling. "Oh, no, Monsieur," she laughed. "You will have to get your own."

"I was just kidding. But perhaps you'll join me for a drink?"

"Not now," she said. "I must go for a swim first. But you can meet me at the pool if you like."

The pool at the Yamit was not the nicest Dumond had ever seen. It was small and narrow, wedged in between the rear of the hotel and a high security wall, with a limited view of the Mediterranean. But as soon as Hannah emerged from the glass door in her white bathrobe and designer sunglasses, he thought there was nowhere else in the world he'd rather be.

"Hello, there," she said with a smile, and put her bag on a yellow deck chair next to Dumond's. When she undid her belt and shed the bathrobe, the Frenchman's heart almost stopped. Hannah Avner was the most exquisite woman he had ever seen. Her statuesque body was perfectly sculpted. Her skin was like polished amber. Her muscles were taut and toned. And her skimpy black two-piece left little to the imagination.

Charles, out of shape and fifteen years her elder, kept his bathrobe over his shoulders. His face, arms, and belly glistened with the sunblock he had slathered on just before she arrived.

Hannah executed a perfect racing dive and swam three quick laps. Then she hung on the side of the pool near the journalist. Her brown hair dripped and glistened in the sunlight. "Aren't you coming in?" she asked.

"Oh, I'll come splash around a little, but I can't keep up with you."

"I know that," she laughed. "I used to be a junior Olympic champion—freestyle and butterfly. But you don't have to compete with me, you know. Why do men always think they have to be the best?"

Charles jumped feet first into the pool and sent waves sloshing over the sides. He swam over to Hannah and treaded water beside her. She suddenly laughed and kicked away from the side of the pool. As Dumond bobbed lazily in the bluish water, she put on a one-woman swimming exhibition—two laps freestyle, two laps backstroke, two laps butterfly, then back to freestyle. Before he knew it, she had done fifty laps. It was a short pool, but still.

He was still flutter-kicking in the shallow end when Hannah hoisted her supple body over the side. She patted herself dry and rubbed her hair with a towel. Then she spread the wet towel on her deck chair and lay down, her breasts and flat belly heaving slightly as she breathed. After a few moments, she turned over and undid the strap on her top.

Charles breast-stroked to the deep end and climbed slowly up the steps. He sat in the chair next to Hannah and smiled. "Would you like me to put some suntan oil on your back?" he asked.

"No, thank you. My skin is rather dark, so it doesn't burn easily. Besides, I am not staying long." She closed her eyes and appeared to sleep. Her heavy breathing slowed to a soft, regular rhythm.

Dumond stretched out on his deck chair and watched her. He had an urge to caress her muscular shoulder, but thought better of it.

Suddenly Hannah opened her eyes. "I'll have that drink now," she said.

They agreed to meet in the hotel bar in half an hour. Charles returned to his room, showered, and put on a pair of pleated khaki trousers and a dark green polo shirt. He checked his face in the mirror and decided to shave. Once he'd scraped off his five o'clock shadow, sprinkled on some Gaultier cologne, and combed his thinning, raven-black hair, he thought he didn't look half bad. Women had always found him attractive, with his large black eyes, sensual mouth, and prominent but well-shaped nose.

Charles was first to arrive in the bar. He chose a table near a picture window with a great view of the Mediterranean. The sun was still high in the western sky; seagulls were circling over the water and a handful of bathers were still on the beach. The scene seemed strangely peaceful for a country that had been in a constant state of war for nearly a half century.

Hannah arrived ten minutes later, wearing a low-cut black blouse and white linen pants. Her hair was still damp.

"Sorry I'm late," she said. "I had to make some phone calls. I have to go out on the early flight, 6:55 a.m. I hate getting up so early."

"I have to get up early, too—for me. I have an 8:30 breakfast appointment."

"What do you do?

"I am a journalist."

"A journalist," she raised her luxuriant eyebrows and smiled. "You must meet some very interesting people."

"Yes," he said. "You, for example."

She laughed. "You don't know just how interesting I can be."

A waiter appeared at their table. She ordered a Chablis; he chose a double Chivas on the rocks.

"What publication do you work for?" she asked, as Dumond lit up a cigarette. He held out the pack to her, but she shook her head.

"A weekly newsmagazine called *Actualités*."

"I do not know this magazine. What is its political line?"

"Right-center, pro-government, pro-business. It belongs to one of France's biggest defense contractors, the Larcher Group."

"So that means you basically work for the French military."

Dumond chuckled. "No more than an employee of El Al works for the Israeli military."

"Oh, but I do work for the Israeli military. Like most Israelis, I have served in the army. I am now a captain in the reserves. I have my own Uzi, I can build and defuse bombs, and I am trained to kill with my bare hands. So you'd better watch your step with me, Monsieur."

Charles grinned and sipped his Chivas. "Yes, I'll have to remain on my best behavior."

"And what brings you to Tel Aviv?"

"I am interviewing Amos Oz. That's the 8:30 breakfast appointment I told you about."

"Yes, I saw you reading his new book. A brilliant writer, but hopelessly naive in my view."

"Why is that?"

"He's always going on about peace, and concessions, and accommodation. But you can't have peace with people who want to destroy you. Oz and his friends talk about land-for-peace. What a stupid idea. We give them Gaza and what do they do? They vote for Hamas."

"You can't remain on a war footing forever."

"Then tell the other side to stop killing us. Tell them to put down their arms and stop shooting rockets at us, then maybe we can talk about peace."

Hannah took a small sip of her Chablis, which she had not yet touched. She looked at Charles with flashing eyes.

"How long are you staying in Israel?"

"Not long. Tomorrow, I fly to Amman, then Baghdad. Amman is just a stopover. There are no direct flights between Israel and Iraq."

"And Baghdad, what will you do there?"

"Oh, I'll poke around and see what I can see. My magazine rotates me in there every few weeks. They don't like to keep anyone there permanently because of the security risk."

"Yes," she said, "one wouldn't want to be taken hostage."

Charles started to mention his own hostage experience in Beirut, but thought better of it. Hannah asked a lot of questions. Maybe he shouldn't tell her too much.

"In any case," she went on. "Iraq is not too interesting right now. The insurgency is a problem for the Americans, but Saddam is gone and no one there is threatening Israel. What really worries me is Iran. The Iranians have vowed to destroy us. They are arming Hezbollah against us and they will soon have nuclear weapons. You Europeans think you can negotiate the mullahs out of that. But there is only one way to stop them. When the time comes, either the Americans will do it or we will do it. But it must be done."

"We'll see," said Dumond, putting out his cigarette and draining off the dregs of his whiskey. "Would you care to have dinner?"

"Why not? I have no other plans."

In the subdued lighting of the hotel dining room, Hannah's green eyes and dark honey skin seemed to glow from within. As they continued their conversation over a bottle of red wine, Charles tried to steer away from politics. Hannah told him about her childhood on a kibbutz in northern Israel, her university studies in economics, her brief early marriage to a fellow student, her passion for classical music, and her athletic exploits as a competitive swimmer and black belt in karate.

"But we are talking only about me," she said at last, pushing a strand of hair back from her forehead and tucking it behind her ear. "Tell me something about yourself."

The Frenchman refilled her glass, then his own, and took a gulp. "There's not much to tell, you know. My father was a lawyer in Lille. I grew up and went to the university there."

"What did you study?"

"Journalism, of course."

"And then?"

"Then I did my military service in Germany."

"The Berlin Wall was still standing then, right? It was still the Cold War?"

"Yes, but I spent most of my time shuffling papers in an office and writing articles for the Army newsletter. After that, I went to work for French radio, then for the French national wire service, AFP, and after that, for *Actualités*. That's about it."

"No wife, no children?"

Charles laughed. "If I were married, it would be very naughty of me to be having dinner like this with a beautiful woman, don't you think?"

"So? Most men are naughty. That's my experience."

Charles gazed into her eyes as he finished the last bite of his sea bass. She sipped her wine and looked back at him.

"You can have cream with your coffee, you know," she said in a low voice. "You ate the fish this time."

"That's kosher?"

She nodded. "On the other hand . . ."

"Yes?"

"You can skip the coffee and have me for dessert."

Hannah Avner wasted no time on foreplay. As soon as the door to Dumond's room closed behind them, she pulled off her blouse, wriggled out of her pants and thong, and lay gloriously naked on his bed. Aroused by the sight of her firm breasts and shaved pubis, the journalist stood next to the bed as Hannah unzipped his trousers and took his sex in her hand. She caressed it, gently at first, then pumped it rapidly in her tight fist as if she wanted to finish him off before they had even started. But Charles resisted and shifted his hips closer to her face.

"I don't do that," she said, turning her head away.

"Why?" he asked. "It's not kosher?"

"Certainly not—you're not even circumcised! But I don't do that with Jews either. I just don't like to have a man's penis in my mouth. Expecially one that size."

"It's not bad, eh?" said Charles, with childish glee. He stripped off his clothes and lay down next to Hannah. She wore no perfume and her body still smelled faintly of chlorine from the pool. He kissed her breasts, then slid his head down her flat belly and discovered, to his delight, that she had no objection to oral stimulation—as long as it was applied to her. After several minutes, she began to moan and clutched his shoulders tightly in her strong hands.

Hannah suddenly rolled Charles over on his back and straddled him.

Then she snatched up a foil-wrapped condom from his night table and rolled it onto his sex.

"You're a real take-charge kind of girl," he said.

"You haven't seen anything yet."

Once she had taken him inside her, Hannah heaved her athletic body back and forth with powerful strokes that made her muscular thighs tighten and her breasts sway with the relentless movement. The Frenchman did not last long, but his loud, long groan of pleasure did not slow Hannah's exertions. She continued to slide her pelvis back and forth, up and down, moaning and breathing heavily until Charles was almost in pain. She finally stopped when she felt him soften. She rolled over and checked with her hand to see if the condom was still on. Then she pulled it off and threw it in the wastebasket. "That was quite a discharge," she said. "Mazel Tov."

"Was it good for you?" Charles asked, caressing her cheek as he lay at her side.

"Yes, but I'm not very big on afterglow. Besides I've got to get up and go to the airport in four hours." She stood up and started putting on her clothes.

Charles went into the bathroom, washed himself at the sink, and emerged in a hotel bathrobe.

"Can I have your number before you go?" he asked. "I'd like to see you again."

"It's impossible to reach me on the phone, darling. I'm always traveling."

"How about e-mail?"

"The company reads all my e-mails. Standard security procedure."

"Then what shall we do?"

"Give me your business card. I'll call you the next time I'm in Paris."

He took his wallet out of his pants pocket and handed her a card. She kissed him on the nose and disappeared into the hallway.

CHAPTER

23

C HARLES WENT THROUGH his Saturday morning interview like a zombie, asking obvious questions and losing his train of thought while he scribbled in his notebook. Good thing he was taping it, or he would certainly have missed a lot. He returned to his room at ten o'clock and quickly packed his bags. His head was throbbing.

Fortunately, this cabbie was more interested in driving fast than in talking politics. Charles arrived at Ben Gurion just in time to make his 11:30 flight to Amman. He changed planes in the Jordanian capital and arrived at Baghdad International at three o'clock.

He had been here more times than he cared to count. The airport was basically run by the U.S. military, with uniformed G.I.'s checking the passports alongside Iraqi border police, and Bradley fighting vehicles ringing the perimeter. An American soldier looked suspiciously at the French passport, but he finally handed it to an Iraqi functionary who stamped it and passed it back to Charles.

He was met at the airport by his usual driver and interpreter, a young university student named Rachid, who owned a rust-colored Opel and had a talent for talking his way past checkpoints and driving around charred vehicles. Rachid also packed a Browning 9mm, formerly the standard-issue sidearm of the Iraqi army and now available on the black market for under $100.

The airport highway was once the world's most dangerous stretch of road. Patrols by the Iraqi army had reduced the number of attacks, but there was still no guarantee that one would not be riddled with bullets from a passing vehicle, carbonized by a rocket-propelled grenade fired from the roadside, or blown to bits by a so-called improvised explosive device, the low-tech but lethal land mines that had wreaked havoc with U.S. military convoys.

Dumond chewed his nails during the twenty-minute drive into town. The ride over the cratered road always made him nervous. That was how they'd nabbed him in Beirut years earlier. He had been on the way in from the airport when two cars swerved in from side streets to block his taxi, one in front and one in back. Hooded men had leapt out waving their Kalashnikovs. One of them fired rounds in the air, while others pushed him into the rear vehicle and slipped a blindfold over his eyes. It was the last he had seen of the outside world for six months. He was lucky the first time. But with Islamist lunatics running around hacking people's heads off in front of video cameras, Charles was not eager to repeat the experience in Iraq.

His anxieties surged when they encountered a military checkpoint halfway into town. Surrounded by concrete blast walls, sandbags, and multiple coils of concertina wire, the post was manned jointly by Iraqi and American soldiers.

An Iraqi sergeant looked at Rachid's ID card and addressed him brusquely in Arabic. The driver spoke back, waved his arms in the air, put one hand on his breast and pointed back at Charles with the other hand.

"What's he say?" asked the Frenchman.

"He say I only have student ID, not authorized as a press driver. He want to see your papers."

Charles handed over his passport and French press card. After another brisk exchange in Arabic, a U.S. captain approached the car.

"What's the problem?" he asked the sergeant.

"This man not licensed as press driver, and this man don't have work visa."

The captain studied the papers, then leaned down and looked at Dumond sitting in the backseat.

"I don't understand, Captain," said Dumond in his near-American accent, "I am an accredited French journalist. I come often to Iraq. I have never encountered this problem."

"You gotta understand, sir, the Iraqi soldiers are gettin' kinda hyper 'cause the insurgents have been blowing the shit out of their guys." The captain handed back the papers. "You carrying any weapons?"

Rachid opened the glove compartment and handed over his Browning 9. The Captain checked the clip then calmly fired six shots into a sand barrel behind him to clear the chamber. The close-range detonations set Dumond's ears to ringing.

"Okay, you're good to go," said the captain, handing the empty gun, still smoking, back to Rachid. Two Iraqi soldiers removed a row of metal spikes from the road surface in front of the vehicle and raised the barrier. Rachid drove his Opel slowly through the gate and proceeded on toward the capital.

"Good work, Rachid," said Charles. "I thought we had a big problem there."

"No problem. They just give us shit."

Dumond's arrival at the Hotel Palestine was not much of a relief. U.S. tanks with camouflage netting occupied the parking lot and he had to pass through a U.S.-Iraqi military checkpoint before entering the lobby. Once inside the shabby establishment, he found himself surrounded by gun-toting gorillas from the private security firms that, along with the international press, used the hotel as their base. The presence of foreign media and security people made the eighteen-floor concrete structure a prime target for terrorists. Cynical journalists referred to the Palestine and the neighboring Sheraton, also a foreign press haven, as the "twin towers of Baghdad."

The people at the reception desk remembered Charles from his previous visits and gave him an eighteenth-floor rear room—located high enough to minimize the street noise, and away from the usual rocket trajectory. For that favor, Charles slipped them a $10 bill on top of the $90 room charge.

The air conditioner wasn't working in his room, so he opened a window and set his overnight bag down on the bed. On the night table, next to the telephone, there was a folded blue and white card that read, "Nice

Dreams!" Dumond opened the minibar. The rusting interior was empty. He was tempted to drink from the bathroom tap, but thought better of it. Instead, he splashed some tepid water on his face and returned to the lobby to meet Rachid.

The driver took him to a rendezvous not far from the square where the outsized bronze statue of Saddam Hussein had been toppled by U.S. troops during those heady days when the administration was proclaiming "mission accomplished." Piles of garbage and rubble lined the streets. The facades of the shops and offices were pockmarked by bullet holes and shrapnel from car bombs. Faded election posters were peeling from the walls and blowing in the hot, arid breeze. Grizzled merchants stood in front of their shops, fingering prayer beads. Women in head scarves hurried along the sidewalks, holding their daughters by the hand. The car passed an open-air market where animals were slaughtered and their entrails tossed into an open gutter. The reek of rotting flesh, mixed with the smell of the burning kebabs, almost made Dumond retch.

The Opel came to a stop in front of a grim-looking concrete apartment building. Rachid watched the entrance from the wheel of his car, his finger on the trigger of the reloaded pistol that lay in his lap. Dumond climbed the narrow, dusty stairs to a second-floor flat and softly knocked.

The door opened and a gaunt, bearded man about Dumond's age ushered him inside, then gave him a hug and a kiss on each cheek. He was Jean-François Aziz, son of a French mother and an Iraqi father, who had grown up in Paris and studied political science at Columbia. Aziz spoke Arabic, French, and American English without the slightest accent. As a result, he could swim in many waters without arousing suspicion.

Charles had met him while they were both working as journalists in Beirut. But they had not met the way journalists usually meet, in the bars of local hotels, at press conferences, or on the perimeter of some murderous terrorist strike. No, they had met in the four- by six-foot rat-infested room that they shared as hostages of one of Lebanon's most radical Islamic militias. No other experience in Charles Dumond's life had ever created such a bond. Now that Aziz was working as a freelance journalist in Baghdad, the Frenchman considered him his most reliable source of inside information. He never bothered with the press briefings at the heavily fortified U.S. or French Embassies. Jean-François Aziz was his eyes and ears on what was really going on in Iraq.

"So, *habibi*, you are back in the belly of the beast," said Aziz, with a smile that wrinkled the worry lines on his pale, leathery forehead. "I am making some mint tea. Will you have some?"

Charles smiled and nodded. He pulled a pack of Gauloises out of his shirt pocket and offered one to his host. Aziz took it and gently cupped his hand around the Frenchman's lighter. He exhaled a cloud of smoke. The sounds of voices and passing traffic entered through the open window, along with some tinny Arabic music from a transistor radio. From the top of a nearby minaret, a muezzin was calling the faithful to prayer.

"So many things to tell you, *habibi*, where can I start?"

"Start anywhere," said Dumond. "In a world of chaos, there is no beginning and no end."

Aziz handed his friend a steaming cup of tea. "Yes, you are quite right. And where do you think the chaos is going?"

"Looks to me like the whole region in ready to blow," said the Frenchman. "Hezbollah and Israel at each other's throats, rockets and bombs flying over the border . . ."

Aziz held up his hand. "All that is just part of the old Arab-Israeli death dance. It comes and goes in cycles and follows predictable patterns. Frankly, I am more worried by what is happening here in Iraq."

"The resistance?"

Not just resistance against the Americans, but outright civil war between armed militias struggling for political power. You are starting to see this already—attacks and reprisals between various Shiite and Sunni groups, paramilitary death squads carrying out summary executions, car-bombs killing civilians in the market place, all semblance of civil order breaking down along sectarian lines."

Charles nodded glumly. How could the Americans have made such a foolish miscalculation? They imagined that they could waltz into Iraq under showers of rose petals and establish Western-style democracy—as if mere ballot boxes could create a stable government in a country that has no democratic tradition, an artificial state stitched together from a patchwork of tribes that have hated each other for a thousand years. Saddam was a monster, but nobody in Washington seemed to have realized that his repression was the only thing that kept the lid on this country.

"Why is this happening now, Jean-François? After all, they held successful elections and it looked like they were starting to put together a stable government."

"That's precisely the moment when the power struggles get serious, and everybody pulls out their guns. That was to be expected. But there's another development that could lead to out-and-out war on Iraqi soil. I'm talking about full-scale combat—tanks, artillery, missiles, infantry battles. Thousands of casualties."

"What's that?"

"The Assyrian Christians are trying to secede from the rest of Iraq and form an independent republic."

"This is serious? I thought you told me Ganjibar was a buffoon."

"Ganjibar himself may be a buffoon, but the movement is serious. These people have never considered themselves part of Iraq. Now, with the fall of Saddam, they see their chance to strike out on their own. And keep their oil."

"Are you sure they have any oil?"

"That is what I am hearing. And that's what emboldens them to assert their independence. But the other factions will never accept this—particularly the Kurds, who have been persecuting the Assyrians for centuries, and who have always considered them a servile minority on their own territory."

Dumond blew on the scalding tea and took a tentative sip. "Why would the Assyrians imagine that they could defy the other factions and form a sovereign state?"

"Because they have help, *habibi*. They have built up a formidable army, with artillery, transport, helicopters, and sophisticated arms that no other Iraqi faction can match. Rumor has it that U.S. Special Forces and advisers are secretly embedded in their ranks."

"Maybe they're just trying to maximize their leverage in the new government."

Aziz shook his head. The wrinkles around his eyes were so deep they looked like scars. "They're past that point. Ganjibar's party won five seats in the new parliament. They could have entered the political process by joining a coalition with the Kurds and Shiites. But Ganjibar opted out. He clearly does not want to share power in Iraq. He's striking out on his own."

Dumond fingered the worry beads that he always kept in his pocket when he traveled to an Arab country.

"And so," said Aziz, "the die is cast."

"What do you mean?"

"I am hearing that the Kurds will soon move in to crush this secession movement in its infancy. Other groups are also sharpening their swords."

CHAPTER

24

A S A REPORTER, Sam had always entered the White House through the northwest gate on Pennsylvania Avenue, where he was vetted by armed security guards and made to feel like an intruder. But on this Wednesday evening, dressed in black tie and wielding an invitation embossed with the presidential seal, he was cordially welcomed through the East Appointment gate and ushered into the Yellow Oval room. As a Marine honor guard stood at attention, Sam took his place in the receiving line.

With the First Lady standing dutifully at his side, looking a bit frumpy in her tight pink evening gown, the president was working the crowd like a candidate on the stump. He seemed to be enjoying himself, squeezing hands, slapping people on the back, trading one-liners, calling his guests things like "Billy-boy," "Stretch," and "Thumper."

When Sam arrived in front of the president, Ritter quickly glanced at his name tag and grabbed his hand.

"Hey, Sam, good to see you, fella. I been readin' your stories. How those folks treatin' you in Paris?"

"Fine, Mr. President. No complaints."

"Well that's good to hear. I understand they're not too crazy about us over there. Matter of fact, I'm not real crazy about them either."

Ritter shot him a wink and grabbed for the next hand.

The line moved into the Diplomatic Reception room, where liveried waiters served drinks on large silver trays. The offerings were California champagne, orange juice, and a New York State sparkling water that had replaced Perrier on the White House menu. Sam took an orange juice and noticed that a lot of the other guests did the same. These Evangelicals were not exactly a hard-drinking crowd. As for the president, he had become a confirmed teetotaler after years of hell-raising excess. That was one thing—probably the only thing—that Sam had in common with him.

One man next to Sam did take a glass of champagne. "Don't want to snub the state of California," he said with a sheepish smile.

"The French stuff is better," Sam replied, holding up his orange juice in a mock toast, "but you're not likely to get any in this place."

The man laughed, deepening the heavy creases around his mouth. "You know, we actually make a decent champagne in Israel. The president served it here when our prime minister was visiting."

Sam looked at the man's name tag.

"I'm Lev Karash, the Israeli ambassador."

"Nice to meet you, Mr. Ambassador. Sam Preston of the *Chronicle*."

"Yes, I know. I read your stories out of Paris."

"By the way, I've been meaning to call the Israeli Foreign Office in connection with a story I'm working on. What's your take on Rafat Ganjibar, the Assyrian Christian leader?"

"Ganjibar? He is a great friend of Israel. He contributes a lot of money to Jewish humanitarian causes."

"And what do you make of his movement?"

"We like it. A successful non-Islamic republic in that region, friendly with Israel and the U.S., could be the seedbed for a total transformation of the Middle East. Of course, we have no direct involvement in this struggle."

"And who do you think is arming his militias?"

Before the Israeli could answer, an usher announced that dinner was served and invited the guests to take the Grand Staircase to the State Dining Room. In the crush of moving bodies, Sam was separated from Karash. The ambassador gave him a parting wave and melted into the crowd.

Sam found himself seated between a Baptist preacher and a woman who had written a book on Christian sex practices entitled *For the Love of God.* She had a dyed-blond bouffant hairdo, bright pink lipstick, and a thick coating of makeup that gave her skin a kind of waxy, greasy look. Her eyebrows were painted on and her thick black lashes were fake.

"Some people think God and sex don't go together," she chirped, tucking into her asparagus and artichoke salad. "That's silly. I mean, if we Christians didn't have sex, where would baby Christians come from?"

"Good point," said Sam, gazing at the portraits of past presidents that hung on the walls.

"I mean, just read the book of Genesis," the woman went on. "You'd think all those people ever did was beget and beget and beget. They never stopped! The Bible says Abraham was ninety-nine years old when he begat Isaac, and his wife was ninety. Of course, sometimes it got a little out of hand, so to speak—Onan spilled his seed on the ground, you know, and Lot's daughters got him drunk and slept with him so they could bear his children. But whenever people did really wicked, nasty things, God punished them, like when he 'rained upon Sodom and Gomorrah brimstone and fire from the Lord out of Heaven.'"

"Seems a bit excessive."

"Not at all! That's exactly what sinners deserve. See, there's God's way to have sex and the Devil's way. I've cataloged all this in my book. For example, rear-entry intercourse, anal sex, cunnilingus, and fellatio are the Devil's way."

"And God's way?"

"Caressing above the waist and kissing—no tonguing—followed by the beautiful and traditional frontal congress intended by our Creator as the sublime expression of Christian love. Oh, and you've got to be married, of course. And no condoms."

"Sounds like the Devil's people have all the fun," Sam chuckled.

The woman's eyes glinted under her black lashes. "Until they find themselves in a bottomless lake of brimstone."

Sam turned to the man on his right, who introduced himself as Reverend Conklin, president of the National Christian Council.

"I met somebody who writes for your newsletter," said Sam. "Chris Blassingame."

"Oh, yes. Chris is an important man in our organization. Matter of fact, he's sitting over at the next table next to that Salvation Army guy. See him?"

Sam looked over and saw Blassingame talking animatedly with a man in a dark gray uniform with polished brass buttons. Blassingame caught his eye and waved.

"Chris gets around," said Conklin. "He not only writes for the newsletter, but he travels all over the world to shore up our contacts with like-minded movements."

"Evangelical groups?"

"Not only Evangelicals. We keep in touch with all sorts of folks who can further our cause, including political movements and governments. In fact, we are a powerful political force in our own right. The National Christian Council represents seventy million Christians across the U.S. That's a lot of voters, my friend. I can get the president on the phone whenever I want. And our people meet with him at the White House at least once a month."

"What do you talk about?"

"Everything that interests us—abortion, stem-cell research, Christian education, Intelligent Design, faith-based initiatives, judicial appointments, support for Israel."

"Yes, Chris was telling me about your stand on Israel."

Conklin chewed on a slice of chicken breast and nodded. "We're more Zionist than a lot of Jews," he said. "See, we believe that all the land bordered by the Euphrates, the Nile, and the Mediterranean was covenanted by God to the Israelites. So the Biblical nation of Israel must be restored, and the Second Temple rebuilt, before Christ returns. That's why we are adamant supporters of the Jewish State. I've been on a first-name basis with every Israeli prime minister since Menachem Begin."

After forty-five minutes of eating and chatting, the president rose to speak.

"Ladies and gentlemen, distinguished guests, brothers and sisters," he began in his folksy Western twang, "I want to welcome you all here to this celebration of Christian fellowship. I think you all know that this house is your house, and I am but your humble servant. Well, I'm not always humble—I am the president after all."

Laughter and scattered applause swept through the room.

"Bein' president is a tough job, folks. I mean, it's hard. I get up every morning at the crack of dawn so I can start doing the nation's work—and the Lord's. That means I gotta get to bunk down early. So without further ado, I would like to move on to tonight's musical program. It's a pleasure to introduce a great American artist with a very special message that I want folks to hear all across this great land of ours, and all across the world. It's a message of hope and faith, values and purpose. And I also want to welcome the boys in her band—even if they are French—I mean, nobody's perfect, right?"

More twitters of laughter.

"Ladies and Gentlemen, a warm White House welcome for Princess Tawana and the Les Jambalayas."

At the far end of the room, under a single spotlight, stood Princess Tawana in a low-cut purple evening gown that molded her round contours like a latex glove. Her lips were painted the same shade of purple, and her eyelids were adorned with a glittery lavender eyeshadow. A large seven-pointed star hung from a gold neckchain and dangled in the crevice of her cleavage. Not your standard Sunday-go-to-meeting outfit, Sam thought.

As if to tone down the sultry effect of her costume, Tawana began with a slow, reverential version of "The Old Rugged Cross." She followed it with another quiet hymn, "His Eye Is on the Sparrow," then picked up the tempo with "Will the Circle be Unbroken," which got the audience clapping and tapping their feet.

Three more spirituals followed. Then she announced the final number: "Mr. President, Miz First Lady, ladies and gentlemen. This here is a little tune I wrote that has made a big hit in this country. I can't take much credit for that, because it's the Lord's doing. But I am humbled and honored to be here tonight to sing it for you. And I know that every one of you will understand its message and rejoice."

Without waiting for the applause to die down, she started grinding her hips in time with her tambourine, just as Sam had seen her do in Riga.

The Jambalayas rhythm section picked up the hypnotic beat. Then Tawana stepped to the mike and launched into the now-famous song: *"We gonna win the battle of Arma-ged-don, Arma-ged-don, Arma-ged-don . . ."* The audience all knew the lyrics by heart and some of them started to sing along. More and more voices joined the chorus and people began to clap and wave their hands in the air like a bunch of holy rollers. By the time the Princess reached the last chorus, sweating lustily under the spotlight, almost everyone in the room was on their feet, singing, shouting, and cheering. Sam, who stood but refrained from singing, could clearly hear the president's twangy, off-key voice shouting out the final stanza along with the rest of this bizarre congregation:

Oh, Jesus gonna lead us at Arma-ged-don,
Arma-ged-don, Arma-ged-don,
Jesus gonna lead us at Arma-ged-don,
So you better kneel down and pray . . .

Yes, you better kneel down and pray . . .
Yes, you better kneel down and pray . . .
You better kneel down and pray . . .

At the end of the concert, Tawana was besieged by fans and well-wishers. Normally, Sam would not have joined such a throng, but he was there as her special guest, after all, and it wouldn't do to leave without greeting and thanking her. As he waited his turn, he found himself standing next to a grandly decorated Army general who had been seated at the president's table. One look at the man's name tag and he instantly realized that it was General Richard Runter, head of special operations in Iraq.

"Allow me to introduce myself, General," Sam said, offering his hand. "Sam Preston of the *Chronicle*."

Runter gripped his hand and grinned. "Pleased to meet you, Sam. I know your name. Based in Paris, right?"

"Yes, sir."

"What brings you to Washington? You got tired of eating all that cheese over there?"

Sam chuckled. "I try to avoid that, General. It's bad for my waistline. No, I was invited here by Princess Tawana."

"You did that magazine piece on her, right?"

"That's right."

"Fine piece." The general leaned in closer. "But, frankly, I thought you could have gone into a little more detail about the real Battle of Armageddon."

"I don't really know much about that, sir."

"Well, you better learn. It's all spelled out in the Book of Revelation. Read it—read it as soon as you can."

"What's the rush?"

"Because it's about to happen, Sam. And when it does, you're either with us or against us. Think about it."

"I will, sir," said Sam. "Thank you."

"My pleasure."

Sam made a mental note to check Runter out on the Internet. He'd already been in the news with some controversial statements, but Sam thought this Armageddon stuff was a bit over the top.

When he finally approached the Princess, Sam kissed her on each cheek, French style, while she threw her meaty arms around him and patted him on the back. "Sam, I'm so glad you could come. Isn't this wonderful?"

"You were great. I'm very happy for you."

"Well, the Lord must really be lookin' after us, honey, because this is just the beginning. We off on a big tour tomorrow. And they tell me it's all sold out in advance."

"Well, knock 'em dead, Princess." Sam gave her another peck on the cheek, then stepped over and shook hands with the Jambalayas.

As he followed the crowd toward the exit, Sam felt someone tap him on the shoulder with a rolled-up program. He turned around to see Lisa Taylor sheathed in a long, black, glittery evening gown. She had the elongated grace of a Modigliani painting.

"Lisa," Sam said, and took her hand. "You look wonderful."

"You're not doing too bad yourself, stranger. Even if you have put on a little weight."

"French food," he said with a shrug. "What are you doing here?"

"Dumb luck. They give invitations to the White House press corps on a rotating basis."

"That's great. I mean, it's great to see you. I've been meaning to call you."

"Right!"

"Seriously. Since that last phone call, I thought it was kind of silly not to stay in touch."

"Well, if you really mean that, Sam, why don't you come over to my place for a drink?"

"Should we?"

"Just for a drink, Sam. I know you're married."

They took a cab over to Lisa's apartment located, much to Sam's amusement, in the Watergate, overlooking the Potomac.

"Sorry it's a bit spare," she said as she opened the door. "I spend most of my time at the office, or on the road, so this is just a place to hang my hat."

Lisa was being somewhat disingenuous. The large living room was hardly overfurnished, but the pieces were elegant and expensive. Sam had preferred her old place, a funky studio apartment in Georgetown, near the university, furnished with cheap Ikea couches and folding chairs. He had spent a lot of time there before his transfer to Paris. Lisa had chosen to stay in Washington for the sake of her career; Sam had wanted to break out of the Beltway and explore Europe as a foreign correspondent. Their relationship might have gone further if they had not let their professional priorities get in the way. In the end, Sam thought, they were far too much alike to form a stable couple.

With Sandra, on the other hand, he felt the attraction of polar opposites. He had met her at a Left Bank gallery opening shortly after his arrival in France. He was fascinated by her cat-like eyes, her silky voice, her English accent, and the delicious air of bohemian mystery that surrounded her. They were married three months later, after a brief and torrid courtship. As far as Sam was concerned, Lisa was little more than a sweet memory. But Lisa had never gotten over his sudden passage to another shore.

"I've got some nice Australian Sauterne in the fridge," she said from the kitcken.

"I'll just take a Coke or something."

"Not drinking these days? Boy, that's a switch."

He plopped down on the love seat and picked up a book from the coffee table. It was a collection of aerial photos of Paris. Lisa had Scotch-taped a red arrow over the building that housed the *Chronicle* bureau. "Well, a lot of things have changed in my life, Lisa."

"I know, I know," she said, setting a Diet Coke and a glass on the table in front of him. "Don't remind me."

She held up her Sauterne and clinked glasses with him. "Cheers, Sam, it's good to see you."

"Same here, Lisa."

Lisa sat in an armchair and kicked off her high heels. Even at the end of a long evening, she always looked as freshly groomed as if she had emerged from a Sak's Fifth Avenue box wrapped in silk paper. She smelled faintly of perfume. Sam remembered the scent, and the name: Instant by Guerlain.

"You know, Sam," she said, "I've been thinking about you and this Ganjibar story. I think you might be onto something really big. I keep hearing rumors that his whole movement is being secretly supported by the White House."

"But the U.S. is backing the Iraqi government, we've promoted elections there, we're training their army. How can we support the regime in Baghdad and, at the same time, support a breakaway movement? It makes no sense."

"Look, Baghdad is not in control of anything. The army is a joke, the Sunnis are off the reservation, the Shiites don't want to share power with them, the Kurds run their own show. The president's dream of turning Iraq into a democratic model for the Middle East is a shambles. Maybe he's just crazy enough to think an Assyrian republic could become his new City upon a Hill, or New Jerusalem, or whatever."

Sam drained off the last of his Coke and put his glass back on the table. "He can't just switch horses like that. Public opinion wouldn't support it. Congress wouldn't approve the funds."

"The American public is an idiot! They reelected this jerk. Americans have no memory and no attention span, you know that. As for Congress, he's not asking them for any money yet. But the C.I.A. has a huge slush fund."

"Do you have any proof the U.S. is backing this thing?"

"No, it's just rumor and speculation at this point. But it makes sense. After all, they're getting weapons and ammunition from somewhere. And I happen to know that somebody on the House Foreign Affairs Committee is starting to look into all this."

"Who?"

"I really shouldn't tell you. It was told to me in confidence."

"C'mon, who?"

"Promise you won't tell anybody else?"

"Stop playing kids' games. Yes, I promise."

"Bob Shea."

"That figures. Shea's the last unabashed liberal in the Democratic party."

"He's also a very good friend of mine. Keep that to yourself, too."

Lisa smiled at Sam and folded her legs up under her. "You're so uptight, Sam. Your shoulders are all hunched up. Relax! I'm not going to bite you."

Sam settled back in the love seat and looked at Lisa. Her deep blue eyes, highlighted with just a trace of eyeliner, gazed at him intently. She leaned slowly forward and placed her hand on his.

Sam left it there. "You didn't just invite me over for a drink, did you?"

"No, I didn't."

CHAPTER

25

MARIE CALEDONI HAD BOOKED Sam a room at the Tabard Inn, a quaint but trendy establishment near Dupont Circle that was crammed with antique furniture and modern artwork. The Tabard's bar and restaurant was a popular meeting-place for reporters, politicos, and other power elitists. It was also the place where Princess Tawana and the band were staying.

Sam had been awake since 5 a.m. His eyes always popped open in the wee hours after a transatlantic flight. He usually read or counted sheep until he fell back to sleep. This time, though, thoughts and images of the night before raced through his head.

The dinner had left a strange and troubling memory. Who were these people? How had they taken over the White House, the whole country for that matter? Who was this president, this shallow, mediocre, wisecracking little rooster of a man who put the Bible over the Constitution and led the country on what he called a righteous "crusade" against evil? Thomas Jefferson and Ben Franklin would be rolling in their graves if they could see what this dubiously elected charlatan had done to the separation of church and state, to checks and balances, to Fourth Amendment protections, to the impartial judiciary, to the environment, to America's image in the world. And that general, Runter, with all his end-of-the-world stuff. What the hell was that all about? To think this was the guy in charge of special ops in Iraq. Scary. And Lisa, Lisa. He hadn't wanted that to happen. It was a delicious moment—Lisa was wonderfully skilled in the Devil's ways—but now he felt bad, depressed, guilty. Well, it was done. There was no help for it. But he vowed it would not happen again. He suddenly thought of Sandra and missed the touch of her sleeping body in his bed.

His cell phone rang at 6:30. Sam snatched it up from the night table and read Dumond's number on the screen.

"Hi, Charles."

"Jesus, man, you sound like you just woke up."

"I did. I'm in Washington."

"Sorry, I didn't know."

"What's up?"

"There's a rumor going around that Carnac may announce France's pullout from NATO tomorrow. It's a huge story, man. You better get your ass on a plane right now."

"I'm already booked on an overnight flight. I'll be arriving in Paris at 7 a.m."

"Good. I'll meet you at the Elysée Garden Party. You got your invitation, right?"

"Yeah, but it's at the office. I'll have to swing by there in the morning and pick it up."

"I'll meet you by the bandstand at eleven. Go through the rear entrance, it's quicker."

Sam got up and took a long, hot shower. He let the water beat on his head and trickle down his body, and tried to think of nothing but the embryonic comfort it brought him. Let the clear, warm stream wash away the stain, not of sin, but of stupidity.

At seven o'clock, he walked into the dining room, with its elegant black and white floor tiles and starched tablecloths. At the far end of the room, he saw Chris Blassingame eating breakfast alone.

"Chris," said Sam, pulling up a chair at his table. "What are you doing here?"

"Mornin', Sam. I'm accompanying Tawana and the boys on their tour. I'll be writing about it for the newsletter. Also helping out with the logistics. Our group organized the whole thing, you know."

"No, I didn't know that. I thought it was her French record company."

"Those guys couldn't organize a chicken-fry in a hen house," said Blassingame, slicing off the top of his soft-boiled egg with a neat whack of his butter knife. "The National Christian Council's running the tour. We got her booked into twelve cities—churches, meeting houses, theaters, even a football stadium. Plus radio and TV broadcasts. She's going to be heard by fifty million people on this tour."

"How'd you manage that?"

Blassingame sliced his toast into little slivers and dipped one into his egg, sending its half-cooked yellow spilling over the sides. "I'll tell you a little secret, Sam. When it comes to the entertainment industry, we're more powerful than any network, record company, publishing house, or Hollywood studio. Christian music sells more than jazz and classical put together. Religious books are the hottest sector of the publishing industry, worth more than $3 billion a year."

"Amazing!"

"Well think about it—there's 70 million Evangelicals in America, attending more than 200,000 churches. Christian radio and TV networks control more than 2,000 stations, that reach 100 million people every week. We can turn a record or a book into a bestseller overnight. Look at Tim LaHay's *Left Behind* novels—63 million copies sold and counting. You don't think he did that on his literary merits, do you?"

Sam ordered scrambled eggs and bacon, and took a sip of orange juice. "So that's how you turned 'Armageddon' into such a big hit."

"Why, sure. Don't imagine some obscure little record out of France is going to sell 10 million copies in the U.S. without a big operation like ours pushing it."

"Why that record? What's so special about it?"

"At this crucial time in history, as we head toward the final confrontation between good and evil, we thought it was the perfect anthem and battle cry. When Evangelicals hear that tune, it sends shivers up their spine, Sam, makes 'em want to grab a sword and smite the Devil. It is an incredibly powerful tool for mobilizing the armies of Christ."

"I see," said Sam, munching on an overcooked slice of bacon. "I guess it makes a lot of money, too."

Blassingame grinned, turning his eyes, with their pale blond lashes, into narrow slits. "It makes a whole pack of money. But it's all poured back into the Lord's vineyards. Most of it, anyway. Of course, you have to pay for production, promotion, distribution, artists' royalties, and the like."

"Sure, like any record business."

"Except we don't pay taxes on it, since we're a religious institution."

"Sweet."

Blassingame cut the top off his second egg. "Manufacturing a hit record is the easy part," he said, and sliced up another piece of toast. "What we cannot do, and should not do, is try to manufacture Armageddon itself."

"What do you mean?"

"Well, don't quote me on this, Sam, but some folks are tryin' to jump the gun on the Lord. They think they can bring on the Apocalypse all by themselves. But the Bible tells us we can know 'neither the day nor the hour in which the Son of Man cometh.' We can't force the Lord's hand, we can only be His instruments. That's why some folks in the Evangelical movement don't like what's going on."

"Who's trying to manufacture Armageddon, Chris? What are you talking about?"

"Sam, I can't tell you any more than that right now. I've probably said too much already. If you're as good a reporter as I think you are, you'll figure it out for yourself."

The dining room was starting to fill up with the power breakfast crowd. Sam recognized a senator from Mississippi who was close to the president. He greeted Chris with a big grin, and nodded politely in Sam's direction. At another table, a colleague from the *Washington Post* was talking with a White House speechwriter and taking lots of notes.

Tawana appeared in the dining room and headed toward Sam and Blassingame. She looked strangely ordinary without her jewelry and makeup. She was also the only person in the room wearing a T-shirt and jeans. Tawana didn't care. She always did things her own way. Maybe that's why they called her Princess.

"Hi Chris, hi Sam." She sat down at their table and looked at the menu. "Quite a night, huh?"

"I'll say," said Blassingame. "You were magnificent."

"Where are the Jambalayas?" Sam asked.

"Oh, them," Tawana sighed. "They went out partying. Probably hit every bar in Georgetown, tryin' to get laid. Some of 'em ain't even back yet. I keep tellin' them they oughta listen to the words I'm singin' and behave themselves. But men are men, you know what I'm sayin'?"

"I do," said Sam. "I do indeed."

Tawana picked up a piece of cold toast from Sam's plate and popped it into her mouth. "Speakin' of men, they had some crazy-ass people in that place last night."

"In Georgetown?" said Blassingame.

"Naw, I ain't talkin' about no Georgetown. I'm talkin' about right there in the White House. Like that general. What's his name?"

"Runter."

"That's it. General Runter. You know what that man told me? He said Armageddon was at hand, I mean the real battle of Armageddon. Said it was just about to happen, and he wanted me at his side singin' when it did. He tried to give me an open ticket to Baghdad. 'When the time come,' he say, 'I'll call you, and you fly right over there and meet me.' Man, I've heard some crazy pickup lines in my time, but that takes the cake."

"But you told me yourself you believe Armageddon is about to happen, Tawana," said Sam. "You told me that right there in your dressing room in Riga."

"Yeah, that's right, but I ain't flyin' to no Baghdad on no open ticket to sing for it, honey. When the Lord want to call me, he'll just rapture me right up to Heaven. I sure ain't goin' there in no airplane."

Sam laughed and looked over at Blassingame. The Evangelist was not smiling. He peered straight into Sam's eyes and said, "You see what I'm talking about?"

CHAPTER

26

INSPECTOR ELEFTHERIOS THRAKIS STEPPED over the yellow police tape and entered the open door of room 29. It was a dingy single with shower on the second floor of the Hotel Olympos in central Athens. Cheap furniture, dirty curtains, no view to speak of. Its main appeal was the price: $38 a night. But the man on the bed wouldn't have to pay for it anymore. He had been dead for at least eight hours, according to the medical examiner, George Kropias, who had gotten there just before the inspector.

A police photographer was shooting the scene from all angles, throwing a garish light on the nude body with his flash. It wasn't a pretty sight. The victim was a male in his late thirties, graying hair, muscular build. He had a woman's stocking over his head, tied tight at the neck. He still wore a condom.

The inspector leaned over and looked closely at the victim's blackened face. "Strangulation?"

"No," replied the medical examiner. "Crushed windpipe. Looks like one clean blow to the neck. The stocking was probably part of some kinky sex thing."

"Lovely," said Thrakis. He turned to one of the younger detectives, who was taking measurements and writing them down in a notepad. "What do we know about this guy?"

"Name is Nikola Lefkosias. He's been living here for a little over a week. Flew in from Paris July 6, on Air France flight 2332."

149

"Profession?"

"No regular job. Maybe dealing drugs. He hung out at the Club Macaramba over in Plaka. It's a techno place—loud music, lots of hashish, coke, and Ecstasy going around. Seems he was into all that. Drugs and women. The night clerk at the hotel says he often came back with some girl he'd picked up in the club."

"Who saw him last?"

"The night clerk, sir."

"Get him up here. I want to talk to him."

"He's off duty now, Inspector. Left at noon. But he told me earlier that Lefkosias came in around two with a tall, well-built woman, about twenty-five years old. Very good looking, he said."

"What time did she leave?"

"He didn't see her leave, Inspector. He says he might have been dozing off. Or she might have gone out the ground-floor ladies room window."

Thrakis stepped closer to the bed and removed a strand of blond hair from the stocking. He handed it to the medical examiner.

"I've already taken some samples from there, Inspector," said Kropias, waving a little plastic pouch in the air.

Thrakis looked at the tanned, hairy, muscular body. "Are we sure he came in with a woman? There's a lot of transvestites in those clubs."

The detective smiled. "From the clerk's description, sir, I'm pretty sure it was a woman."

"A pretty strong woman, don't you think, to kill a man with one blow? I don't know a lot of hookers who can do that."

"The clerk said she didn't look like a prostitute. She was very classy. Well dressed. Spoke French."

The inspector rubbed the thick black stubble on his chin. "What about the motive?"

"Seems to be theft, sir. The chambermaid said he had a briefcase. It's missing, along with his wallet."

"Briefcase. Do we know what was in it?"

"Afraid not, sir."

Kropias slipped on a pair of white latex gloves, leaned over the bed, and removed the condom. He held it up to the light. "No DNA on this, I'm afraid. It's unused."

The inspector shook his head in disgust. "She could have at least waited for the poor bastard to shoot his load."

The other men laughed. But Thrakis did not. Death did not amuse him. It was not always tragic—Greeks had a pretty high threshold for tragedy—but it was always ugly. And stupid. The most frustrating thing about his job, he thought, was that he could track down killers, but he could never undo their deeds.

CHAPTER

27

GEORGES CARNAC STOOD RAMROD straight on the reviewing stand and saluted the column of light armored vehicles that clattered down the Champs Elysées in the direction of the Place de la Concorde. Behind them, wearing tall, black-plumed hats and gray parade uniforms, marched the students of the Ecole Polytechnique, France's elite military academy. Then came a mounted regiment of the Garde Républicaine, their polished silver parade helmets gleaming in the late morning sun. Three Mirage-2000 fighters roared over the famous thoroughfare at low altitude, trailing red, white, and blue jetstreams behind them. Standing ten-deep along both sides of the avenue, onlookers applauded and waved French flags.

Carnac was born to stand tall under tricolor bunting and salute. He had fought as a young officer in the Algerian War, and briefly contemplated a military career before going into politics. He even approached politics in a military way—charge ahead, take-no-prisoners, into the breach. He had held many ministerial portfolios and won many elections during his long career. Trouble was, Carnac never seemed to have any idea what to do once he had won office. Unlike his controversial leftist predecessor, who had nationalized and denationalized major companies, sent French troops to fight in Africa and the Middle East, and dotted the Parisian landscape with architectural monuments to his own pharaonic glory, Carnac's main claim to fame was that he had called—and lost—early parliamentary elections that left him on the sidelines for

152

most of his first term. So he played the role that he was best at: the ceremonial president.

July 14th, Bastille Day, is a grand occasion for French pomp and circumstance, but it is not a good day to try to move around the 8th arrondissement of Paris. Sam could not get off at his usual RER stop at the Etoile because it was closed for the duration of the military parade. Instead, he had to get off at Auber-Opéra and walk a half-mile to his office.

When he opened the door, he found Woodridge and Kemp, dressed in almost identical cream-colored summer suits, sitting in the conference room with their feet up on the table and watching the parade on TV.

Woodridge gave Sam a quizzical look. "What are you doing here, Preston? I didn't expect you back until tomorrow."

"My business back home didn't take as long as I thought, so I came back early. Didn't want to miss the Elysée garden party."

"Yes. Umm, Bradley, would you excuse us a moment?"

"Sure, Clive. No problem." Kemp got up and left the room, closing the door behind him.

Woodridge pursed his lips and looked silently at Sam.

"What's up, Clive?"

"Sam, I didn't know you had any family in Washington."

"I don't. Why?"

"Because you asked to take a couple of days off to attend to 'urgent family business' back in the States."

"That's right."

"So, I was just wondering if you could enlighten me as to the reason for your presence at a White House dinner night before last, and at the Tabard Inn yesterday morning."

"Look, Clive, I got invited to the dinner by Princess Tawana. I thought it would be a chance to show the flag, do some reporting, networking. It's all company business, right?"

"Not if you don't declare it as company business and get it approved by your superior—in this case, me. Why didn't you tell me you were going to Washington?"

"I knew you wouldn't approve it."

"Quite right. We've got twenty correspondents in the Washington bureau. Why in God's name would I send you there on my tight budget?"

"That's why I didn't ask."

"And who paid for the trip? You don't expect me to believe you went there on your own nickel?"

Sam shook his head. "Tawana's press agent gave me a ticket. I didn't think it was that big a deal to be honest."

"Sam, you know as well as I do that we can't take freebies. It's unethical. The Frogs may do that sort of thing, but we're Anglo-Saxons. We must be above suspicion, like Caesar's wife. Don't you agree, Sam?"

"I know it was dumb."

Woodridge leaned back, cocked his thumbs behind his suspender straps and jutted out his lower lip. "I tell you what I'm going to do, Sam. I won't tell New York—this time. But I want you to reimburse the agency that gave you the ticket."

"But why, Clive? What difference does it make now?"

"Why? Because there's a right way to do things and a wrong way. You chose the wrong way."

Sam shook his head in disgust. "You know what pisses me off most of all, Clive? You and I have been friends and colleagues for ten years. We've been down in the trenches together, and we've had some good laughs together. Now you find yourself a little higher than me on the corporate totem pole and you start talking to me like some British sahib to his house boy. Fuck you, Clive."

Woodridge clicked his tongue. "Sam, Sam. You know, I genuinely like you, and I admire your work. But sometimes, you're your own worst enemy. Shape up, old boy. I'm really in your corner, but you've got to help me out."

There was a knock on the door. "Clive," Kemp shouted. "We better head out. We'll be late for the garden party."

"Be right out, Bradley." Woodridge stood up and shook his trousers to straighten the creases. "Oh, by the way," he said, giving Sam a little tap on the shoulder, "I wasn't expecting you back today, so I've given your garden party invitation to an old school chum who's over here on holiday. Didn't think you'd mind."

"You did what?"

The door closed behind Woodridge, leaving Sam sitting alone in the conference room while the military music droned in through the open windows and images of marching soldiers and tanks flickered across the TV screen.

He sat there seething for a few minutes, then pulled out his cell phone and dialed the number of Carnac's spokeswomen, Corinne Malonna.

He could hear the brassy marching music behind her when she answered.

"Corinne, this is Sam Preston at the *Chronicle*."

"Hello, Sam. Sorry, I don't hear you very well. I am here with the president and the music is quite loud. How can I help you?"

"I've misplaced my invitation to the garden party. Any way you can get me in?"

"Of course. I'll call the guardhouse at the front gate and leave your name."

"Thanks so much, Corinne. You are wonderful!"

"It's no trouble, Sam. I must go now. See you later."

Sam arrived at the main entrance of the Elysée Palace at eleven o'clock and took his place in the long line of people who were waiting, invitation in hand, to enter the presidential residence. It was a mixed bunch: military officers in ceremonial uniforms, ministers and ambassadors in dark suits and designer ties, journalists like Sam in shabbier suits, and, as a result of Carnac's demagogic youth outreach, hordes of rowdy kids from the working class, immigrant suburbs in white track suits with hoods, or baggy jeans with the crotch at knee level. Funny that Carnac's leftist predecessor had never seen fit to invite the huddled masses onto this hallowed republican ground. It took a vote-hungry conservative to do that. The irony is that most of these kids didn't vote; they burned cars.

It was nearly half past eleven when the gendarmes finally waved Sam through the front gate. He crunched across the gravel courtyard, marched up six red-carpeted steps, and entered the tall glass door that led into the marble entrance foyer. Carnac spent a lot of time in this very spot gripping and grinning for the cameras alongside visiting foreign dignitaries. That was a big part of the ceremonial presidency, probably the part he enjoyed most. It didn't matter whether the visitor was an African dictator, an Arab sheikh, a German chancellor, or Jack Ritter. They all got the same handshaking, backslapping welcome.

Sam knew his way around the Elysée after his years of attending press conferences, briefings, treaty signings, New Year's greetings to the press and, of course, July 14th garden parties. The Salon Napoléon III was crammed with guests, milling about, sipping champagne, or bellying up to the buffet tables to fill and refill their plates with pâté and salmon canapés. There were even more people in the adjoining Salle des Fêtes, with its gilded ceiling and twelve glass chandeliers.

Sam exited the salon through a row of side doors and stepped out into the sun-dappled rear garden. It was a splendid day, if a little on the warm side, and the grassy, tree-lined park was filled with people. Some were standing around chatting, others were sitting cross-legged on the lawn, still others were listening to the Garde Républicaine orchestra. Mostly, though, they were eating and drinking—especially the journalists, who looked on the opportunity to pig out at the Elysée as one of their more enjoyable perks.

Along both sides of the garden, elaborately decorated food stands offered up the wares of France's different regions: wines from Burgundy, cured hams from Savoy, oysters from Normandy, scallops from Brittany, bouillabaisse from Marseilles, spicy boudin sausage from Guadeloupe, goat-meat ragout from Corsica, choucroute from Alsace, ice cream and pastry from Nice. And, from every part of France, it seemed, there was cheese—Camembert, Roquefort, Pont l'Evêque, Brie, Reblochon, Epoisse, Bleu d'Auvergne, Chèvre des Pyrénées, Munster, Neufchâtel, Tomme de Montagne, Vacherin. . . . It was the infinite variety of cheese, Sam thought, that best reflected the richness and complexity of French society. As De Gaulle famously put it, "How can you govern a country that has 365 cheeses?"

When Sam finally reached the bandstand in the middle of the park it was well past 11:30. Dumond pointed at his watch. "What kept you?"

"You don't want to know. Why didn't you tell me you were going to the Middle East?"

"The trip came up all of a sudden. I hardly had time to pack my underwear. Good thing I brought my rubbers, though."

"You scored?"

"Big time! I'll tell you all about it later. Right now, we've got to work on our game plan. I am told that Carnac may announce his NATO pullout today. This is a big deal, Sam. It's a major break between Paris and Washington over security and military issues. And it's the perfect peg for our arms sale story. We've got to be ready to go with it."

"It's too soon, Charles. We don't know the whole story. With just a little more time, we can flesh it all out from the stuff in that envelope I sent you."

"What envelope?"

"Didn't you get my phone message? I said I was sending you an important envelope."

"Oh that. It never showed up."

"What do you mean it never showed up?"

"I never got it. Maybe you didn't put enough stamps on it."

The Garde Républicaine band struck up the Marseillaise and everyone turned their eyes toward the palace. Standing at attention on the rear steps of the Elysée were Georges Carnac and the key members of his cabinet. Everyone in the garden was singing the sanguinary words of the French national anthem—except the foreigners and the *banlieue* kids, who didn't know them.

"He's going to mingle with the guests now," said Charles, shoving Sam in the direction of the presidential entourage. "Now's our chance to talk to him."

Carnac, though a tall man, was barely visible in the middle of the knot of well-wishers, political supporters, and autograph seekers that circled around him as he waded into the crowd. He was loving it—smiling, laughing, shaking hands, kissing cheeks, chatting amiably with constituents and reporters. At times like this, it was hard to believe that his approval rating was under thirty percent in the national opinion polls, even lower than Jack Ritter's.

Sam had trouble moving in close enough to hear the president's words. But Dumond, taking advantage of his smaller size and sharp elbows, soon found himself face-to-face with Carnac.

"Mr. President," he shouted over the buzz and babble of the crowd, "is there anything to the rumors that you will pull France out of NATO?"

The president, known to be a bit hard of hearing, leaned close to Dumond and cupped his hand behind his right ear. "What was that?"

Dumond repeated the question, louder this time.

Carnac straightened up. "I prefer not to comment on that for the moment. But we can all ask ourselves what is the purpose of a Cold War alliance in a post-Cold War world?"

The president moved on, gripping, smiling, signing, chatting. Dumond emerged from the knot and grabbed Sam's forearm.

"Did you hear what he said?"

"No," said Sam. "I couldn't hear fuck-all."

"He's gonna do it."

"That's what he said?"

"That's what he meant. He's going to announce it in his TV interview. I'm certain."

At 1 p.m., following a time-honored ritual, the president retired to his office and gave a televised interview to two well-known French journalists. It was a live interview, but hardly a spontaneous one. The questions were submitted and vetted in advance by Carnac's in-house media guru (who happened to be his own son). The answers were prepared by his staff, polished and rehearsed—though no amount of media coaching could ever turn Georges Carnac into a smooth performer on camera.

The interviewers, typical products of the TV star system, never followed up with tough or embarrassing questions that might limit their access in the future. But no one ever took them to task for not providing aggressive, penetrating, and factual coverage of the news. In France, even more than in the U.S., television news was pure entertainment. It didn't matter if a popular anchorman was caught taking bribes or fabricating interviews, as long as his show led the ratings. In America, an anchor who did that wouldn't last ten minutes.

True to form, the two journalists began with a couple of softball questions. Then came the big moment. "Monsieur le Président," said Philippe Poirier of Télé-Première, "We've been hearing rumors about a big change in French security policy. What can you tell us about this?"

Carnac cleared his throat with a rasping, guttural sound. "Ahh, yes, Philippe Poirier, there are always rumors on every subject—*n'est-ce pas?* And a president should not comment on every rumor. But this is a matter of vital interest to the French people and, naturally, as president of the republic, I owe you a frank answer."

The president turned his gaze away from his interlocutor and looked right into the camera, his tired brown eyes moving ever so slightly as he read from a teleprompter.

"As you know, French defense and security policy has been, since the time of President De Gaulle, the cornerstone of our national sovereignty and independence. During the first four postwar decades, France linked its security and defense apparatus with that of the NATO alliance. But with two important particularities. First, in the early 1960s, our republic developed an independent nuclear deterrent, *la force de frappe*, which remains exclusively in French hands. Second, in 1966, President De Gaulle withdrew France from NATO's integrated command. That meant France would remain in the alliance, but would not put its men and matériel under any centralized NATO command structure."

"And you are planning to change that?"

"Do not interrupt me, Monsieur Poirier."

"I beg your pardon, Monsieur le Président."

"Today, I believe that a Cold War alliance that was established, under American hegemony, to counter Soviet power has no reason to exist after the collapse of the Communist bloc in Europe. Current American attempts to project NATO operations beyond the European sector—to Iraq, the Gulf, the Middle East, for example—have no other purpose than to protect America's oil supplies. Therefore, my fellow citizens, I have decided, effective August 1, to sever France's remaining ties with the North Atlantic Treaty Organization. In its place, I propose to consolidate ongoing efforts to create an independent European defense pillar, in which France, naturally, would play a leading role."

In the Salle des Fêtes, where a pack of French and foreign journalists were huddled around a large-screen TV set, an initial moment of stunned silence was followed by the din of a hundred voices all talking at once. Some reporters ran out of the room with cell phones clapped to their ears. Others typed furiously on their laptop computers. Others, with tape recorders or notepads in their hands, strained to hear the rest of the interview. It was one of those electric, adrenaline-pumping moments in the news business when it seems that the world is about to shift on its axis.

When Sam returned to the office, he found Woodridge and Kemp glued to the conference room television. He could see from the sag of Woodridge's lower lip that he'd had more than a few glasses of champagne at the Elysée. Sam pulled up a chair.

On the screen, the CNN anchor was interviewing Mike Gold, a former Defense Department official and now a policy analyst at one of Washington's leading right-wing think tanks. Dubbed the "Black Knight" for his advocacy of doomsday scenarios during the Cold War, Gold was now one of the main theoreticians of the neoconservative clan that practically dictated White House foreign policy these days.

With his silver hair, pudgy face, and dulcet-toned voice, he could almost have passed for a preacher. But Gold cared nothing about religion. Like his friend and fellow neocon Bill Cordman, his only concern was maintaining and expanding American power. And he had always regarded France as an obstacle, minor but annoying, in America's path to world dominance.

"Richard," he said, speaking slowly in a mellifluous baritone, "this announcement by President Carnac doesn't surprise me at all. The French have never been interested in their own defense. Ever since 1870, they have done nothing but capitulate and wait for us to come bail them out of trouble. For most of the postwar era, France had one foot in NATO and one foot out—just enough to be protected from the Russians, but not enough to pull their weight in the alliance. So their formal departure will have virtually no impact on NATO's organizational cohesion or combat readiness."

"But that's not entirely fair, is it Mike?" the anchor interrupted. "Just a few years ago, Carnac offered to rejoin NATO's military command and restore France to full membership."

"That offer was totally bogus, Richard. Do you know what Carnac demanded in exchange? That the entire southern sector of NATO—controlling half its assets plus the U.S. Sixth Fleet—be put under a French commander. That preposterous condition was obviously a nonstarter."

"Mike, you seem to be implying that the French are cowards—'surrender monkeys,' as their critics love to put it. But let's look at the facts. The French were leading players in the U.N. peacekeeping force in Bosnia, their fighter pilots flew alongside ours during the NATO action in Kosovo, they fought in the U.S.-led coalition during the first Gulf War, and they are currently taking part in the peacekeeping force in Afghanistan. That's a lot of military action for 'surrender monkeys,' isn't it?"

"Richard, I don't want to debate this thing point by point. If you look at the overall record, going back to the end of the Revolutionary War period, you will see that the French have never been loyal allies of the United States. They proved that with their opposition to our antiterrorist action in Iraq, and they've just proved it again today."

"Thank you, Michael Gold, senior fellow at the Legacy Foundation. We'll be back with more reactions after these messages."

"Ha!" Woodridge chortled. "What do you expect Mike Gold to say? He's practically built a whole career on French-bashing—even though he owns a vacation home in the south of France. An old friend of mine from the *Financial Times* has a place in the same village, and he tells me Gold buys a lot of wine and cheese at the local market."

"The hypocrite," Bradley snickered. "At least he could have said something nice about French cuisine."

Woodridge muted the sound and leaned back in his chair. "Right. Big story for us, lads. Have to approach it as a team. Here's how I see it. I'll do the overview, handle the interview contents, immediate reaction.

Bradley, you look at the potential consequences—whether this might weaken NATO, possibility of other countries pulling out and joining France in a rival defense alliance, what this means for Franco-American relations, all that sort of thing."

"You got it, Clive."

"And me?" said Sam.

"Well, Sam, since you managed to get in there after all, I think you could do a nice color piece on the garden party. Set the scene, the people, the food, the music, the ambience. You know, a featury kind of thing. You're awfully good at that. Right, lads! Off we go. Copy by 8 p.m."

CHAPTER

28

THE MACARAMBA BAR IN ATHENS'S trendy Plaka district was a typical techno club, centered around a raised platform on which d.j.'s mixed and scratched at their turntables from 8 p.m. to 4 a.m. Late at night, when the place was jammed, strobe lights, smoke machines, pulsating electronic music, and recreational drugs combined to produce an orgiastic cocktail of sensations. But on this Saturday afternoon, shortly after 6 p.m., the place was dead.

The man who took a seat at the long bar and gazed intently around the room was not the kind of customer you usually found in the Macaramba. With his beaky nose, Neanderthal brows, and brush-cut salt-and-pepper hair, he bore no resemblance to the curly-locked young Adonises who came every night to get high on Ecstasy and cruise for women. And yet, Eleftherios Thrakis was looking for a woman.

The youthful, long-haired bartender paid no attention to him. He was busy stacking the cooler with bottles of Corona, Desperado, and Smirnoff Ice.

When the barman finally turned around, two objects on the bar attracted his attention. One was the badge that identified the brush-cut customer as a cop. The other was a photo of Nikola Lefkosias.

"Inspector Thrakis, chief of homicide," he said in a voice made gruff by years of smoking filterless Greek cigarettes. "Have you ever seen this man?"

The bartender picked up the grainy mugshot, photocopied from Lefkosias's passport, and studied it in the dim light. "Yes, I have seen him. He was in here every night for the past week or so. He'd drink Red Bull and vodka at the bar, dance with the girls, disappear for a while, then come back and drink some more. But I don't know his name. Look, if he was dealing drugs, I don't know anything about it, okay? We get two hundred people in here every night. I can't control what every individual customer does in this place."

"I am not interested in drugs."

The bartender put his elbows on the bar and rested his chin on the palms of his hands. "He was a good-looking guy, very muscular, macho, you know? The kind the chicks go for. Went home with a different girl every night. Is he in some kind of trouble?"

"Not anymore. He's dead."

The bartender let out a low whistle.

"Did you happen to notice the woman he left with last night?"

"Did I notice? Every man in here noticed her. She was a drop-dead knockout—great dancer, sexy as hell. All the guys were hitting on her. But your guy won the lottery."

"I'd say he lost," said Thrakis dryly. "Do you know anything about her? Was she in here before? Do you know where she lives? Where she works? Anything at all?"

The bartender shook his head. "Sorry. I never saw her before last night. If she had ever been in here another time, believe me, I would have remembered."

"Did you notice her hair color, eye color?"

"Blond hair, shoulder length. The eyes, well, they were light, maybe blue or green."

A man who had been sitting alone in a booth doing paperwork came over and took a seat at the bar. "I'm Dionysos Mikouris," he said, and shook the inspector's hand. He was thick-necked, broad-shouldered, somewhat taller than Thrakis. "I own this joint. Try to keep the trouble-makers out, but you know how it is with these kids. They get all hopped up on booze and Ecstasy and the next thing you know, they're snorting and fucking in the shithouse."

"I'm from homicide," Thrakis grunted. "Snorting and fucking are not my department."

"Good," said Mikouris. Without his asking, the bartender placed a tall glass of ouzo and shaved ice on the bar in front of him. He took a sip. "That broad you're looking for. A friend of mine, kind of a business partner actually, was in here last night. We were all talking about her, how hot she was, you know, and he swore he'd seen her on his flight in from Paris yesterday."

"Did he mention the airline?"

"Air France. He said she sat right across the aisle from him."

"Would he remember the seat number?"

"I can ask."

Mikouris picked up the photo of Nikola. "And this guy—this *malaka*. He was trying to peddle some crap he had in an envelope. Some kind of documents he brought from Paris. My security guys overheard him talking about arms sales or something. I don't think he found any takers—unless maybe the broad snatched them."

Thrakis smiled slightly under his bushy mustache. "You would make a good detective."

"Me? That's a laugh. I'm the kind of guy cops are always hassling."

The bartender looked again at the photo. "You know something?" he said, scratching the bridge of his nose with a dirty fingernail. "The kids are always snapping pictures of each other on their cell phones. Like the guys take shots of hot chicks and vice versa, then they e-mail them to their friends. It's kind of a game—they're like, look what I scored tonight, you know? If you want, I can ask around later and see if any of them got a picture of the girl."

"That would be helpful," said Thrakis, placing his business card on the bar. "If you have any luck, perhaps you can e-mail it to me."

Mikouris sucked the ice at the bottom of his glass and tapped the detective lightly on the forearm. "Hey, do me a favor, Inspector. Tell your colleagues in the drugs and alcohol division to lay off the Macaramba. They've been giving us a lot of shit, you know."

Thrakis scooped up the badge and photo and put them in his wallet. "I'll see what I can do."

"Thanks." Mikouris squeezed the detective's outstretched hand. "You know, now that I think of it, my friend told me something else about that broad. Something kind of weird."

"Weird?"

"Yeah. He said he went in the toilet right after her and there was piss all over the seat."

"Charming."

"But look—a broad sits down to pee, right? So how does she piss on the toilet seat?"

CHAPTER

29

M IGUEL CARVALLO PACED up and down the portside deck
of the *Empress* and gazed out at the sea. As he looked at the azure
water, dancing with a million reflections of the bright noonday sun, he
saw a small craft approach from the direction of the mainland. In the
distance, he took it for a fishing boat. The Brazilian removed his sunglasses and studied the progress of the vessel.

"Sergei," he shouted to the white-clad figure standing near the bow.
"Tell the skipper I'm coming up there. There's a boat approaching from
the port side."

"Right away, Mr. Carvallo."

By the time Carvallo had made his way forward and climbed up to
the pilot's cabin, the craft was less than one hundred yards away. The
half dozen or so men on board sat in deck chairs with deep-sea rods in
their hands.

"Looks like a holiday fishing expedition, sir," said the skipper, a lanky
Dutchman who sported the kind of long, broad sideburns that were in
fashion in the 1970s.

"Give them the usual warning," said Carvallo.

The skipper flipped some switches and picked up a radio microphone.

"This is the *Empress*, out of Malta. Request to identify yourself."

Scratchy static emerged from the radio speaker, followed by a male
voice. "Copy that, *Empress*. We are the *Malizia*, out of Monaco, on a deep-
sea fishing expedition under hire by a party of six U.K. citizens. Over."

"Now hear this, *Malizia*: the *Empress* is a military craft working under cover for the Italian Coast Guard on an antismuggling mission. You are in Italian waters. Your presence in this sector is considered hostile. I must order you to withdraw immediately to a distance of five nautical miles. Repeat: withdraw immediately to a distance of five nautical miles. Over."

"Copy that, *Empress*. Would like to comply, but we're having engine trouble. Will leave the sector as soon as we complete repairs. Over."

The skipper cut the mike and looked at Carvallo. The Brazilian scratched his groin and spat into a waste can. "Tell the son of a bitch if he's not out of here in fifteen minutes we'll blow his ass out of the water."

"Now hear this, *Malizia*: You have fifteen minutes to clear the sector. Beyond that limit, we will consider you hostile and take defensive measures. Over."

"Copy that, *Empress*. We're working as fast as we can. Will keep you informed. Over."

Carvallo picked up a pair of binoculars and scrutinized the cruiser bobbing on the waves off the port bow. "I don't like the look of these guys. They're on a deep-sea fishing cruise and nobody's sunburned? Look at those motherfuckers—they're white as sheets."

The skipper raised his own binoculars to his eyes.

"These clowns are working for somebody," Carvallo barked. "Get rid of 'em."

"You want us to fire on them immediately, sir? We've given them fifteen minutes. And they've probably radioed our coordinates to their people ashore. If they are working for a foreign service, it's not a good idea to sink them."

Carvallo continued looking through his binoculars. "How much time do they have left?"

"Seven minutes, sir."

"Warn the fuckers again."

The skipper turned the mike back on. "Hear this, *Malizia*: You have seven minutes to clear the sector. Repeat: seven minutes. Over."

"Read that, *Empress*. We've identified the problem and are proceeding with repairs. Will advise upon completion. Over."

Carvallo sat down and lit a cigarillo. "They're stalling for time. The bastards are up to something."

"Sir, all I see over there is fishing equipment and deck chairs. They might actually be a commercial cruise operation."

"Well they're going to be an ex-commercial operation if their asses are not out of here in five minutes."

Carvallo took a Corona beer from the minifridge under the control panel and popped the cap off with the opener on his keychain. He took a gulp and relit his cigarillo. Pacing slowly back and forth in the cabin like a caged tiger, the Brazilian kept his eyes riveted on the *Malizia*. He puffed nervously on his cigarello until it nearly burned his fingers, then crushed it out and sat down. He tapped his foot on the floor and checked his watch again. "Two minutes. Get ready."

"*Empress*," said the voice in the radiophone speakers. "We've completed our repairs. Starting engines now. Will be clear of the sector in two or three minutes. Over."

"Copy that, *Malizia*. Thank you for your compliance."

"No problem, *Empress*. Have a nice day!"

The *Malizia* slowly turned and headed back in the direction of the mainland. As the craft withdrew into the distance, the skipper studied her again with his binoculars. On its port-side deck, visible to the *Empress* only after the turn, he saw a wet suit, aqualung tanks, and a pair of flippers.

"Sir, did you notice that diving equipment on the deck of the *Malizia*?"

Carvallo picked up his binoculars. "Oh shit!"

The detonation set off Carvallo's arsenal and sent a blinding white fireball high into the air. The detritus of the *Empress* covered a radius of more than one hundred yards, and multiple, delayed explosions of the various and sundry ordnance continued for several minutes. The largest pieces of the hull sank immediately in the deep Mediterranean waters. The other bits floated listlessly on the waves. After ten minutes, the *Malizia* circled back and returned to the smoke-enshrouded zone for a final inspection. When the cruiser encountered the first pieces of debris, its skipper fished a wooden board out of the water. It still had a label stapled to it.

"Looks like Tel Aviv was wrong about the cargo, boys," he laughed. "This says, 'canned tomatoes.'"

The commando leader laughed, too. He was not at liberty to tell the other crew members that Miguel Carvallo had taken his equal opportunity policy one step too far when he started shipping Pakistani centrifuge parts to Iran in his tomato crates.

CHAPTER

30

THE PESH MERGA ENTERED the Christian town of Tareq
shortly after 3 a.m. on Tuesday, July 18. The five hundred battle-
hardened Kurdish soldiers, armed with Kalashnikovs, mortars, and hand
grenades arrived in a convoy of Toyotas and armored personnel carriers
"liberated" three years earlier from Saddam Hussein's defeated army.
The first units that rumbled into town met scattered resistance from the
small Assyrian militia contingent that patrolled the streets at night to
guard against possible terrorist attacks on the local church. But this was
no lone bomber with an explosive belt strapped around him. It was a
full-fledged military assault, and the rag-tag Christian militia was no
match for it.

The Kurds mowed down the town's defenders with ruthless efficiency,
leaving their bodies where they fell. Then they went through the streets
banging on doors, smashing windows with rifle butts, and herding the
terrified residents into the square in front of the Byzantine church. The
men and boys were shoved into APC's that quickly drove off into the
night, leaving the women shrieking in anguish and the children crying
and clinging to their skirts.

The Pesh Merga commander stood on the church steps and surveyed
the scene. He knew the men would not return, but now he had to deal
with the others. He raised a megaphone to his lips and shouted out his
orders to the wailing, shivering assemblage. "You are on Kurdish soil,"
he barked. "We are liberating this village, and others in the region, so

that Kurdish people can live here. Your men will be well taken care of in a transit camp until we can arrange their transfer to another part of Iraq. Meanwhile, as proof of our magnanimity, I will give you fifteen minutes to collect your belongings and vacate the town."

One voice rose above the din of crying women and children. "Where shall we go?" It was a teenage girl with large brown eyes and tear-stained cheeks. She was still dressed in her nightgown.

"You, my pretty, you can stay here," said one of the officers with a snicker that set the other soldiers to laughing.

The commander struck him on the nose with a hard backhand blow, drawing blood and bringing the laughter to an abrupt halt.

He spoke again into the megaphone. "You can walk to Mosul in two days. But I advise you not to remain on Kurdish territory, or we might not be so charitable next time."

Under the watchful eye of the Kurdish soldiers, some of whom had already started removing silver, jewelry, and other valuables from the dwellings, the women and children returned to their homes to collect what they could. The Pesh Merga had commandeered all the cars and trucks on the streets, but they allowed the evacuees to load their belongings onto donkey carts. There were not enough carts to hold it all, and many women had to wrap their pitiful goods in sheets or blankets and sling them over their shoulders.

The crying and moaning continued unabated as the soldiers herded them onto the road and watched the lumbering column slowly disappear into the starry night. By 5 a.m., all the townspeople were gone and the soldiers were bivouacked in their former homes.

At 5:30, Rick Runter was awakened by his aide-de-camp as he slept in his quarters at Camp Steel Dragon, inside Baghdad's heavily fortified Green Zone.

"There's a call for you, sir."

The general put on his glasses, glanced at his alarm clock, then took the receiver. "Runter."

"Sorry to wake you, General. Davidson here."

"What's up, Colonel? I assume it's pretty damn important."

"Yes, sir, I'd say so. We just got word that a Pesh Merga unit has attacked the town of Tareq. The men were all carted off in APC's—no word yet about their fate—and the women and children were ordered to evacuate on foot. The Pesh troops are dug in there now."

"What the hell do they think they're doing?" Runter growled. "The Pesh are supposed to be working with us on rebuilding the Iraqi army. Why would they attack a town?"

"It's an Assyrian Christian town, sir. According to reports we have received from the evacuees, the assailants said it was Kurdish territory and they were liberating it."

Runter took a deep breath and rubbed his thumb along the gilded edges of his bedside Bible. "Colonel, I want those Pesh bastards whacked to kingdom come. I don't want a man left alive. We have to teach them a lesson. But we can't do this ourselves. The Assyrians have to do it."

"I'm not sure they have the capability to do it alone, sir."

"I didn't say anything about doing it alone. We have a whole Special Forces battalion embedded in Ganjibar's army, wearing their uniforms. Have the Green Berets move in there with the Assyrians. And don't hold back the firepower. I want an awesome show of force."

"Yes, sir."

At 10 a.m., as the Pesh Merga troops relaxed in front of confiscated TV sets, hung out their laundry, and munched on food pilfered from the homes of the banished Christians, six unmarked Blackhawk attack helicopters buzzed in low over the desert. They were still a mile away when they unleashed a barrage of Hellfire missiles that blew off the roofs and toppled the walls of a row of ancient mud-brick houses near the center of town. The choppers circled overhead and fired another round of missiles as their .50-cal machine guns raked the streets where panicked Kurdish fighters were firing back at them with their AK-47s.

Meanwhile, a column of Bradley fighting vehicles, also unmarked, clattered up the same road the Pesh Merga had taken the night before and entered the town with their 120-mm cannons firing at anything that moved. One thousand Green Berets and militiamen, all in Assyrian uniforms with green and brown battle paint on their faces, arrived next in a fast-moving convoy of APC's and armored Humvees, leaping out with their assault rifles spitting fire and lead in every direction. More Hellfire missiles crashed into the buildings where the Pesh Merga had retreated and dug in. Thick clouds of smoke rose over the town. The streets were strewn with dust, rubble, and bodies—those of the Christian militiamen killed the night before and the Kurds who were still oozing blood onto the road. The noise was deafening.

Lying on their bellies, two U.S. weapons sergeants loaded and fired shells from their 84-mm M-3 antitank recoilless rifles. Each impact blew a hole the size of a refrigerator into the side of a building. The besieged Kurds riposted with RPGs and automatic weapons, but they were hopelessly outgunned. When the gunfire began to subside inside the buildings, the Green Berets led their Assyrian comrades on a house-to-house cleanup, kicking down doors and hurling grenades into what, until the night before, had been the humble living rooms of a thousand Christian families. Fragments of furniture, paintings, family photos, and religious statues lay in smoking heaps, along with chunks of brick, mortar, and body parts.

The last pocket of resistance finally collapsed, and two dozen Kurds emerged from their smoking refuge with a white bedsheet on the end of a rifle and their hands on their heads.

The Special Forces colonel in charge of the operation raised his assault rifle and took aim. "The general said to whack 'em all. Let's fuckin' do it."

He fired into the hapless band. Other Green Berets and Assyrians did the same. Moments later, the remaining Pesh Merga lay in a tangle of bleeding flesh. The Kurdish commander, the man who had waved the white flag, writhed in pain and gasped for air. "You American bastards!" he groaned. "This is not your fight."

The colonel finished him off with a rifle burst between the eyes. Then he stepped into a collapsed dwelling and snatched up a crucifix that had fallen among the rubble. He threw it on top of the mound of bodies. "May God have mercy on their souls."

CHAPTER

31

ON THIS WARM JULY EVENING, Sam and Sandra dined on the open terrace of the Brasserie du Théâtre and admired the illuminated Chateau de Saint Germain just across the road. The buff-colored renaissance palace was touted in all the guidebooks as the birthplace of Louis XIV, but the locals paid little attention to it. The chateau was just part of the décor of Saint Germain, often considered a suburb of Paris, but in reality an ancient town with its own traditions and history. Part of that history included its role as the final home of England's exiled King James II, who spent his last years in the chateau as the guest of his fellow Catholic Louis XIV. When the émigré king died in 1702, he was entombed in the Eglise de Saint Germain, right next door to the Brasserie.

Sandra thought of poor King James as she nibbled on an olive and gazed over at the colonnaded church. "Isn't it strange," she said suddenly, "that one of our English kings is buried right here in Saint-Germain?"

Sam shrugged. "Americans are not real big on English kings."

"Still, think about it. One day he was one of the most powerful men in the world. The next day, he was a lonely exile, stripped of his crown, vilified for his supposed crimes and follies."

"And what were they?"

"Mainly trying to cram his religion down the throats of his people."

"Reminds me of Jack Ritter."

Sandra laughed and took a sip of her white wine. "You're certainly not going to compare your cretinous president to a king?"

"Why not?" he smiled, and sprinkled Tabasco sauce on his steak tartare. "They both came to power through family connections, got promoted beyond their abilities, and put their personal religious beliefs over their political responsibilities to their people."

"I'm not so sure about that last point," said Sandra. "Don't you think most Americans share Ritter's religious fanaticism?"

Sam munched on a handful of *pommes frites*. "No," he said. "Most Americans are religious, but they're not all fanatics. The people I met at that dinner in Washington can't possibly be representative of the country at large. There was a woman made up like a tart who was literally drooling over Christian sex practices, a general telling me the end of the world is at hand, and the president himself assuring everybody he was doing God's work right there in the White House."

Sam looked up at the twilight sky and watched a flock of swallows make its last swooping circle before nesting under the roofs and gables of the old buildings around the square.

"Did you see anybody you knew there?" Sandra asked.

"Sure, Princess Tawana and her band."

"I mean any journalists. Old colleagues, people you know in Washington."

Sam took a sip of Perrier. "Oh, you know, I recognized a few faces at the dinner and at the Tabard Inn. But no one I really know, if that's what you mean."

They rented a movie on the way home from dinner—a French comedy guaranteed to take anyone's mind off the problems of real life—and were just settling down to watch it when Sam decided to check the headlines on CNN.

"This just in," said the news anchor. "According to U.S. military sources, units of the Assyrian Liberation Army this morning repelled an attempt by Kurdish Pesh Merga forces to take over the Christian town of Tareq, sixty kilometers west of Mosul. The Kurdish troops had invaded the town during the night, removing some five hundred men and boys in transport vehicles, and forcing the evacuation of the remaining townspeople, mostly women and children. At ten o'clock this morning, local time, A.L.A. forces entered the town and dislodged the Kurds after a brief firefight. Casualties were said to be heavy on the Kurdish side, but we have no precise figures."

The accompanying video footage, provided and heavily edited by the U.S. Army, only showed Assyrian troops firing automatic rifles, running through the streets, and entering smoking buildings. There were no shots of bodies, aircraft, or heavy weaponry. And nothing to suggest a direct U.S. role in the fighting. CNN ran the same images over and over in a loop.

"I want to stress," the anchor continued, "that our only information on this comes from the Pentagon. We have no independent witness of the fighting. But CNN's Roger Ellison was able to interview some of the refugees on the road from Tareq to Mosul. Roger?"

The scene shifted to western Iraq, where the CNN correspondent, holding a microphone and wearing a flak jacket over his denim shirt, stood at the side of a desert track. "Richard, this desolate stretch of road was the only way out of hell for the roughly one thousand women and children who were expelled last night from the town of Tareq. According to the witnesses we have talked to, the Kurdish forces entered the town at about 3 a.m., neutralized the local security forces, and carted off the men and boys to an uncertain fate. The women and children were then forced to walk down this road in the direction of Mosul. It was here that a U.S. army patrol intercepted the refugees and transported them to a Red Cross shelter in Mosul. We were not allowed to film any interviews with the refugees, but the ones I spoke to described chilling scenes: bodies of Assyrian security forces lying in the streets, looting and pillaging of their homes by the Kurds, and, of course, the seizure of their men, and their own forced evacuation. Richard?"

"Roger, do you have any eyewitness accounts of the retaking of the town by the Assyrian Liberation Army?"

"No reports of the actual fighting, but some refugee sources telling us of helicopter squadrons flying overhead in the direction of Tareq, followed by loud, repeated explosions."

"Helicopters and loud explosions. Now wouldn't that suggest that the U.S. was aware of, or perhaps even condoned, the counterattack? The U.S. controls all the airspace over Iraq, right?"

"That is correct. Nothing can fly over Iraq without U.S. knowledge and permission. But I stress that these eyewitness reports are unconfirmed, and U.S. officials denying that any type of aircraft was involved in this incident. Richard?"

"One final question before we break, Roger. Do we have any idea why the Kurds would attack this particular town?"

"Richard, refugees telling us the assailants wanted to remove the Christian inhabitants and restore Kurdish control. It sounds like a classic case of ethnic cleansing, with this twist: the town is part of the Assyrian Christian enclave that is demanding increased autonomy and may even push for outright independence. That is something the Kurds, not to mention the Shiites and Sunnis, would strongly oppose. Some analysts saying this may just be the opening battle of a broader civil war. They note, for example, that four Christian churches in Baghdad and Kirkuk were targeted by car bombs yesterday, leaving at least six dead and twenty-five wounded. So there may be a pattern developing here. Richard?"

"Roger Ellison with that live report from Iraq. We'll be back with more after this."

Sandra hit the mute button. "Right! There goes our quiet evening," she huffed.

"Why do you say that? I don't cover Iraq."

"No? It seems to me you manage to cover everything. Gospel singers, White House dinners, secret arms sales, terrorist attacks."

"Come on, Sandra, you can't blame the news cycle on me. That's my job—shit happens and I write about it. But there is no reason for some skirmish in Iraq to ruin our evening."

"Oh no? How long will it be before that bloody phone rings? I give it two minutes."

"Don't be silly, darling."

The telephone rang in the hallway.

"Oh fuck!" Sam grumbled. He got up and snatched the receiver.

"Hello!" He could hear the irritation in his own voice.

"Howdy Sam, sorry to bother you so late. This is Hal Carpenter from Rafat Ganjibar's office. Remember me?"

"Of course. What is it?"

"Well, I know it's mighty inconvenient so late at night and all, but Rafat really wants to talk to you. It's real important, Sam. You saw what happened over there in Iraq?"

"Yes, I just saw it on CNN."

"It's pretty bad. Rafat's madder'n a wet hornet. He wants to talk to you about it."

"Hal, that happened two thousand miles from here. I don't cover Iraq. I cover France."

"Rafat's in France, Sam. You're the only reporter he trusts. You remember what I told you about dancin' with the one that brung you? Rafat has something mighty important to say, and he wants to say it to you."

Sam sighed audibly. "Okay, okay, put him on."

"He won't talk on the phone. He wants to see you in person."

"Tonight?"

"Right now. He's sent me over to get you in his car. In fact I'm right outside your gate."

"How do you know where I live?"

"Oh, that's easy! Your address is on the Internet. The driver just punched it into his GPS system and here we are. We're waitin' for you with the engine runnin'."

"Oh, shit," Sam muttered. "Alright, I'll be out in five minutes."

He put on a jacket and went back into the TV room. Sandra had already put the disc in the DVD player and was watching the movie alone. "Don't say anything, Sam. Duty calls. Don't explain. Don't apologize. Just go."

He knew better than to try to kiss her goodbye at a moment like this. "Sorry, Sandra," he said. "I'll be back before the movie's over."

"Just be careful, Sam. I hate it when you go off in the night like this. If you knew how much I worry about you."

Sam opened the iron gate and locked it behind him. Ganjibar's black Audi was idling in the driveway. He opened the back door and got inside.

"Evenin', Sam," said Hal with a toothy grin. "Glad you could make it."

"I'm not sure how glad I am. Let's go."

"Look, Sam. Lemme explain the situation. It's pretty hairy."

"I saw the TV reports."

"Naw, I'm not talkin' about what happened over there. I'm talkin' about Rafat. He's in a whole mess of trouble. The Frogs are buzzin' all around him like flies on horseshit."

Sam cocked his head in the direction of the driver.

"Oh, don't worry about Dominique," said Hal. "Sucker don't speak a word of English. Ain't that right, peckerhead?"

The driver took no notice.

"See?"

"Okay, go on." Sam folded his arms and leaned back into the creamy leather upholstery.

"Well, first off, some folks from the Labor Ministry come out to his headquarters and started asking questions about who all worked there, and why their salaries weren't declared, and why he didn't pay Social Security, and yada, yada, yada."

"He doesn't declare their salaries? Why?"

"Aw, you know. That's the way they do it in Lebanon. Everything's cash under the table, barter, you scratch my ass and I'll scratch yours. It's just a different culture. They all think like camel traders over there."

"That won't wash in France. This is the most rules-oriented, bureaucratic country in the world."

"That's what we've been tryin' to tell him. Tikhani's been tearin' his hair out tryin' to make him do everything legal and regular like. But Rafat won't listen to anybody. He always thinks he knows better."

"Okay, so he'll pay some fines and do it right next time. What's the big deal?"

"Hold your horses. That ain't all. Then they did the same thing at this Lebanese restaurant he owns out in Neuilly. Seems everybody workin' out there from the cook and the waiters to the lady who cleans the damn toilets was off the books. And he wasn't payin' the VAT on the money he was takin' in."

"Not good."

"Wait a minute! Then the inspectors from the Finance Ministry got in on the act and went over all his accounting records, such as they are. They say he wasn't payin' corporate taxes or personal income taxes. They claim he owes 'em a couple of million euro, plus fines, and he may even face criminal charges for tax evasion."

"Sounds like he's really in the shit."

"You ain't heard the worst of it, Sam," Carpenter sighed. "Two days ago, the cops called him in for questioning about the church bombing. Get this—they suspect he ordered the bombing himself. Can you imagine that?"

"Why would he do that?"

"They say he was tryin' to draw attention to his movement or somethin' like that. Anyway—this is the bad part—they put him under formal investigation for complicity in a terrorist activity. If they convict him, he could get locked up for ten years or more. They took his passport and told him not to leave the country. And the damn judge can throw him in preventive detention any time he wants."

"You think he really did it?"

"Blow up his own damn church? Are you on drugs or somethin'?"

"They must have some kind of proof."

"Oh, they dragged some raghead kid out of a prison cell, told 'em Rafat had paid him to plant the bomb under the altar. Plea-bargain stuff—tell a lie about somebody and they cut your time. You know how that works."

"Lie or not, he's got a witness against him. I suggest he get a good criminal lawyer."

"Tikhani's workin' on it," said Carpenter. "But listen, Sam, that's all just the backdrop so to speak. All this shit that just happened over there in Iraq is really serious. Rafat says it's the beginning of a civil war, with every crazy son of a bitch in the whole damn country trying to crush his movement. He says he's gonna fight back hard. But he really needs the support of the American people now. That's where you come in."

"What does he expect me to do?"

"I'll let him explain it. We're almost there."

The Audi crossed the St. Cloud bridge, turned right along the river-front drive, and came to a stop in front of Ganjibar's headquarters.

Hal took out his cell phone. "Rafat? We're out in front."

Two minutes later, the heavy iron and glass door opened. A tall, broad-shouldered man in a black raincoat emerged and surveyed the street. Then he turned and waved to the man behind him. Rafat Ganjibar waddled toward the car. His gargantuan frame looked even more bloated than the last time Sam had seen him, doubtless due to the pastries he indulged in whenever he was under stress.

The bodyguard opened the rear door of the car and checked inside. He made a brusque sign to Hal. "*Yalla!*"

Hal quickly shook hands with Sam. "That's my cue to leave."

"Wait a minute," said Sam. "Aren't we going inside?"

"No. Rafat thinks the offices are bugged. The car's the only secure place to talk."

"*Fissa! Fissa!*" The bodyguard raised his voice.

"Okay, okay, Musa, I'm leavin'. Don't have a cow!"

Rafat squeezed his corpulence into the back seat next to Sam. He smiled with his wet, protuberant lips and offered a limp handshake.

"Hello, Sam. It is nice to see you again. I am grateful to you for coming."

The bodyguard got in the front passenger seat and slammed the door.

The driver turned around. "*On va où, Monsieur le Président?*"

"*N'importe, Dominique.* Drive anywhere you want."

The car made a U-turn and headed back toward the St. Cloud bridge and the Bois de Boulogne.

"You are well? Your family?" said Ganjibar.

"Yes, Rafat, we're fine, thanks. But I don't have much time."

"I understand, my friend. I will get right to the point. There is big political plot against me and Christian movement. They want to kill me and destroy my people. You see, first French, they try to make us trouble. Administrative nonsense, tax, salary, all these kind of thing, you know?"

Sam nodded. "Hal filled me in."

"Do not listen to this idiot. I will tell you. The French, they try to say I bomb my own church. How I bomb my own church? Church is house of God! But they say, you know, they got this Algerian boy —drug dealer, car thief, bad, bad person—and he say I pay him to bomb church. Now is big investigation starting. You see, they try to destroy me because they not for freedom and democracy and Christian religion."

"Who's they?"

"All of them! French, Kurds, Sunni, Shiite. They all hate us. They all work together, you see? You see what they do to our village? And same day, they bomb our churches in Baghdad and Kirkuk. Is starting big civil war against us. We must fight back. You see?"

"What will you do?"

"Sam, you are my friend. I like you very much. And I need your help. I need you to tell whole story to American people. Then they force Ritter to recognize our government, and help us fight our enemies. They are your enemies, too, you know?"

"But you don't have a government. You have an independence movement. It's not the same thing."

"That is what I want to tell you, Sam. I want you to be first to know, because I trust you, you understand? Sam, in one week, I am going to declare unilateral independence of Assyrian Republic. Formal declaration, big press conference, everything. Then the French, they can't do nothing to me because I am foreign head of state, have diplomatic immunity. And American government they have to recognize us. And they have to help defend our territory. Otherwise, the whole thing go up in smoke. All hope for democracy in Middle East, for Christian religion, for independent oil supplies—everything go up in smoke."

"But why would the U.S. recognize a secession against a sovereign state that they support?"

"Because, Sam, they already backing us. Secret support. But big, big. They do everything for us—construction, infrastructure, arms, oil development. They even put U.S. troops in my army. They wear my uniforms and they fight for us. President Ritter, he don't want the world to know about this. But now we make him stand behind us. Is like, when you deflower virgin, you know, she gonna have your baby. You got to marry her."

"I'm not sure you can pull off a shotgun wedding with the U.S. government, Rafat."

"You will see. You will see. I have proof of what I say. Photos, videos, documents, blueprints, bank statements, everything. When this comes out, Sam, American government have to choose. They are for us—a pro-Western, Christian democracy—or they are for Baathists and Islamists and terrorists in Baghdad. They must choose. They must choose."

The car turned off the main axis that cuts through the Bois de Boulogne and followed a narrow, meandering road through the thickly wooded forest. Every fifty yards or so, the headlights caught the garish, scanty costume of a prostitute.

Ganjibar gazed out the window for a moment. Then he licked his moist lips and turned back toward the journalist.

"But Sam, you must not write this immediately. I make this announcement in one week. No one must know about declaration before this. Already, I receive death threats. If my enemies, they know my plan, then they try to kill me to prevent it."

"Rafat, if I can't write any of this, what good is it to tell me about it?"

"Because I want you to know true situation. If anything happen to me, Sam, I want you to tell the whole story to the world."

"You don't seem to understand how the American press works. If I have important information, it's my responsibility to verify the facts and publish them. I can't just tell a story the way you want, when you want, to produce the effects you want. It doesn't work that way."

"But, Sam, that is true story."

"How can I verify it? Who are your contacts in Washington? Who are the military officers working with your army? Who is in charge of construction projects, oil development? Where is the money coming from?"

"Sam, I give you all that. I told you I have proof—documents, photos, everything. I put this in sealed envelope for you. I leave it in safe with Maître Tikhani. He is like a brother to me. If anything happen to me, Sam, he give you these documents."

"And if nothing happens to you?"

"Then maybe I show you anyway. Depends on how Washington react to my declaration of independence."

The driver dropped Ganjibar and the bodyguard off at his apartment on the Avenue Foch, just a few blocks west of the Arc de Triomphe, then headed back to Le Vésinet with Sam. Fifty miles overhead, a National Security Agency satellite was sending data from Ganjibar's onboard GPS system to a parabolic dish in Langley, Virginia. Thanks to certain enhancements, notably the microphones that had been surreptitiously inserted into the Audi's hi-fi speakers, the device transmitted more than mere geographic coordinates into the skies.

CHAPTER

32

ON THE MORNING of Wednesday, July 19, the mood was tense in the small conference room off the Oval Office, where Jack Ritter gathered with the key members of his security team: Vice President Cordman, C.I.A. Director Trenton McBride, Secretary of Defense Ronald Chandler, National Security Advisor Nick Adams, Attorney General Tony Firelli, and the president's top political adviser, Chuck Granger.

Ritter's jaw was clenched, and his thin-lipped gash of a mouth radiated anger and determination. "Gentlemen, let's cut right to the chase here. Our project has been put in imminent peril by the attack on Tareq. We'd all hoped to see a gradual, peaceful separation by our Assyrian friends, with adequate time to establish our presence there and complete the infrastructure we need to support democracy and assure our security needs. Now it looks like we're facing the possibility of all-out civil war in that sector. What are our options? Ron?"

The square-jawed secretary of defense—mockingly dubbed "the Stallion" by the Washington press corps—adjusted his rimless glasses and glanced down at his yellow legal pad. "Mr. President, I'll start with what I call the industrial strength option: we could rapidly embed twenty thousand troops with the Assyrians and upgrade the armament with Apaches, Bradleys, heavy artillery, cruise missile batteries, night-fighting optical equipment, pilotless Predator attack drones, and F-18 air cover. The problem with all that is that it will leave tracks. Our involvement will become obvious to everyone."

"So? That's got to happen sooner or later, right?"

"Later is much better, Mr. President. As you said, we need time to complete the infrastructure and dig in. If we are seen directly supporting a breakaway movement against a sovereign state—a state we ourselves have been trying to create, I might add—it will become a worldwide crisis. The international community won't stand for it."

Ritter snickered. "Tough titties! They didn't stand for it when we went into Iraq in the first place. What's the U.N. gonna do, nuke us?"

"Mr. President," said Chandler, "I wouldn't joke about that. The French have already warned that they would use nuclear weapons against any state that posed a terrorist threat to their vital interests."

"Ganjibar's no terrorist. He's just fighting for democracy and freedom for the persecuted Christians."

"Let me remind you, Mr. President, that one man's freedom fighter is another man's terrorist. If the French construed his actions as a threat to their vital interests, by withholding oil supplies, for example, it might fall under their definition of an actionable nuclear situation. And we don't just have French nukes to worry about—there's also the Chinese, the Indians, the Pakistanis, the North Koreans, and, if we don't stop them in time, the Iranians."

"Hmm," said Ritter, frowning and stroking his chin. "So where does that leave us?"

"I think we have three steps to take. First, we reinforce the Assyrians' defense capability, but discreetly, so they can resist attacks by the Kurds and the other militias for as long as possible. We don't have to worry about the Iraqi national army moving against them at this point. They're under our control and, frankly, they're not much of a fighting force."

"That's not what we've been telling everybody."

"Just for the benefit of the folks in this room, Mr. President, take my word for it—they're piss-poor."

The meeting erupted in laughter. Ritter guffawed louder than any of them. Despite his best efforts to appear serious and engaged on occasions like this, the fraternity boy in him was never far under the surface.

"The other problem with the Iraqi national force, of course," Chandler continued, "is that they're all at each other's throats. The Shiites,

Sunnis, and Kurds are all jockeying for position within the army, and we have reports of Shiite death squads operating out of their Defense and Interior Ministries running around the country murdering Sunnis and Kurds. In short, the Iraqi armed forces are a disaster."

"How about the other two steps?"

"Well, I think it is absolutely essential that we redouble our efforts on the military infrastructure and oil field development. The airport is nearly finished, but the construction of the underground complex still has a long way to go. We have to do it by tunneling, rather than open-air excavation, to evade detection by surveillance satellites. It's a huge project. We need crews working day and night. But that's going to cost a lot of money. Tens of billions. It's just not in the Pentagon budget."

"Trent?" The President looked at the C.I.A. director. "Can your slush fund handle it?"

McBride shook his head. "No way, Mr. President. With Iraq, Afghanistan, Pakistan, Iran, North Korea, and Al-Qaeda to worry about, we're stretched way too thin as it is."

"Chuckie-boy, could we get Congress to approve emergency funding?"

Granger, an unimposing man with a bald, egg-shaped head, soft, round cheeks, and granny glasses, leaned forward and looked at Ritter with a sardonic smile. It was Granger's tactical brilliance and political ruthlessness that had taken a man of modest abilities and meager experience and made him, first governor of New Mexico, then president of the United States. Theirs was an old friendship and a successful partnership. Granger was never afraid to tell Ritter what he thought; the president, for his part, usually did what Granger told him to do.

"Jack," said Granger. "I have to level with you. The polls show that a large majority of Americans want us out of Iraq, they think you lied about why we went in there, and they don't think America has reaped any benefits that are worth the sacrifice. Apart from the Christian right—and even they are divided on this—there is no constituency that would support major new funding for this operation. As for Congress, considering our anticipated losses in the midterm elections, and the deficits due to our tax cuts—heading toward $400 billion this year—there isn't a snowball's chance in hell that they would come up with more money. Sorry to be so blunt, but that's how it is."

"I don't understand, Chuck. If deficits are a political problem for us, why did we cut taxes?"

"So you could get elected," Granger snorted.

"Mr. President," Cordman interrupted, "I think maybe it's time to draw on your discretionary fund. We've dipped in rather sparingly until now. Maybe we should open the spigots. But funding's not technically a security issue, so I suggest we discuss that separately."

"Right." Ritter nodded at his avuncular vice president. "Now, let's see, where were we?"

The defense secretary held up his pencil. "I was just coming to the third step on the military option."

"Okay, Ron, go on."

"Mr. President, it is the strong recommendation of General Runter that we deploy tactical nuclear weapons in the subterranean complex. That is a grave decision, and it is yours to take. But Runter argues, and I agree, that given the potential nuclear threat I just described, and particularly from Iran, we will need such a deterrent to defend the enclave and our broader interests in the Middle East."

"Hold on there," said C.I.A. chief McBride, tugging at the goatee that served to hide his receding chin. "I'm not sure it's a good idea to introduce a nuclear pawn on the Middle East chessboard. Besides, a deterrent is only useful if people know about it."

Chandler wheeled around and glared at McBride. The two men, former classmates at Georgetown, had been crossing swords in Republican administrations going back to the Nixon era. Chandler could not disguise his contempt for a man who, in his view, lacked the backbone needed to defend America's interests in a perilous world. McBride, for his part, considered Chandler to be an incompetent hothead; he took a malicious delight at seeing a succession of retired generals publicly call for Chandler's resignation because the secretary of defense, in their expert opinion, had screwed up the Iraq operation by trying to do it "on the cheap."

"They'll know about it when we want them to know about it," Chandler snapped. "And as for what you call the Middle East chessboard, the nuclear pawns are already there—in Israel and Pakistan today, maybe in Iran tomorrow. And they would have been in Iraq now if we had listened to you and called off the invasion."

"With all due respect, Ron, you know that's bullshit."

"Oh yeah? That assessment was based on your own intelligence reports."

"As doctored and distorted by certain people in this room. I warned you guys that you wouldn't find any WMD's in Iraq."

"Now, boys," said Ritter with a hatchet-slash smile. "Let's let the past bury the past and move on. That's what the American people want us to do."

"Exactly," said Cordman, eyeing McBride with an off-center smirk.

"Bill," said Ritter, "what's your feeling on this nucular deployment thing?"

"I agree with Ron," replied the vice president. "It won't hurt to put them in there protectively. Nobody else has to know about it for now."

"Nick?"

"I'm with the director on this one, Mr. President," said the national security adviser, with a nod in McBride's direction. "I'd be very leery about injecting a nuclear capability into this volatile theater."

Ritter looked around the table as if he were counting heads. Then his close-set gray eyes seemed to blur and stare off into the distance. There was a long, awkward silence.

"Gentlemen," he said at last. "This is a weighty decision. I'm going to need some time to think and pray over it. You all know I believe I'm here at the bidding of a higher power, and I want to be sure I'm doing His will on this."

"With all due respect, Mr. President, I suggest you pray fast," said the secretary of defense. "We need to clarify our position before events spin out of control."

"Right." Ritter stood up, stretched, and looked at his watch. "No wonder I was gettin' hungry. It's almost lunchtime."

As the other men rose and headed out of the conference room, Cordman grabbed the president's arm. "Mr. President," he said in a low voice, "there's one other important matter we have to deal with. I've asked Tony and Trent to stay behind and discuss it with you."

"Can't it wait till after lunch?"

"No, Jack, it's urgent."

Ritter sighed and slumped back down into his chair. "Alright, Bill, what's up?"

"Mr. President, we have a situation in Paris. As you know, we've repeatedly sent word to Ganjibar to stay cool and keep a low profile. That's apparently not his style."

Ritter loosened his tie. "Bill, you've already told me that. What's so urgent?"

Cordman cocked his head in the direction of the C.I.A. director.

"Mr. President," said McBride, "Ganjibar's communications have been under N.S.A. surveillance for some time. Last night, he met secretly with Sam Preston of the *New York Chronicle* and told him he was about to declare unilateral independence and force the U.S. to publicly recognize and support his state."

"How could he force us?"

"Use your head," Cordman said. "He can blackmail us, threaten to reveal details about our involvement there, our military presence, our funding, the secret oil development. If that kind of thing comes out too soon, it will screw up the whole damn project."

The president nodded. "Preston. I met him at the Evangelical dinner the other night. Seemed like a nice fella."

"Jack," the vice president cut in impatiently, "nobody's nice in the liberal media. The point is that Preston now has secret information about Ganjibar's plan. He hasn't published anything yet, but he could do so at any moment. Or he could talk to other journalists about it."

"I hate reporters."

"The real problem, here, Jack, is Ganjibar. If he goes through with this thing, shit's gonna hit the fan. He's a loose cannon, he's corrupt, he's perfidious, and he may even be an out-and-out criminal. The French think he himself was behind the church bombing and they are probably right."

"Why would he do that?" asked Ritter.

"Draw attention to his movement, win sympathy, attract donations. He's out of control, Jack. When the time really does come to unveil this little state as a model Mideast democracy, Ganjibar is the last one we'd want as its leader."

"Okay, Bill, you made your point. So what do we do about him?"

"My recommendation, Mr. President," said Cordman, "is to terminate with extreme prejudice."

"Excuse me?"

"Eliminate him, Jack. Remove him from this vale of tears."

"Are you saying we should assassinate him?"

"If I may," the attorney general interjected, clearing his throat, "I wouldn't phrase it quite that way, Mr. President. And I wouldn't say 'we.' The legal situation is this: Executive Order 12333 forbids agents of the U.S. government to 'engage in, or conspire to engage in, assassination.' But it doesn't say we can't outsource the job."

Tony Firelli was a past master of legal and ethical pirouettes. He was the one who had provided the theoretical justification for the brutalizing of prisoners by the U.S. military, wholesale eavesdropping on American citizens, denying of trial rights and habeas corpus to terror suspects, and the shameful practice of "rendition"—handing prisoners over to accommodating governments who were even less squeamish about torture than the current U.S. administration. All this in the name of the vast and vague war powers claimed by the president in the wake of the infamous terrorist attack on New York.

"So it's illegal if we do it, but legal if we get somebody else to do it, is that what you're saying, Tony?"

"Precisely, Mr. President," said Firelli. "In a war situation, like the present one, executive power must be supreme and unhindered. You may do whatever you deem necessary in the name of national security."

"In other words, Jack," said Cordman, "it's legal if we say it's legal."

The president drummed his fingers on the conference table. "Maybe it is legal. But I'm not too sure about this. I mean, Ganjibar is a God-fearing Christian and all."

"Mr. President," said Firelli. "Let me remind you that you allowed more than one hundred souls to be executed when you were governor of New Mexico. Most of them were Christians. One was even a Bible-thumping, born-again convert, and you let her die. You even made fun of her on television."

"That's different. They all had fair trials."

Firelli raised his thick black eyebrows. "*All* of them?"

Ritter shrugged. "Well, almost all of them. I think there might have been one or two mistakes in there—but, hey, we're all human."

Cordman let out a loud sigh. "Jack, we're wasting time. Every minute we spend talking about it is a minute closer to the time when Ganjibar opens his mouth and fucks up the whole operation. He's planning to declare independence less than a week from now. We gotta take him out."

The president frowned. "You got a backup for him?"

"Yes," said McBride. "A former seminary student from Mosul, George Shaheen. Got an MBA at Harvard, worked on Wall Street, and has an excellent relationship with us. He's smart, he's discreet, he's reliable. And he's got a good group of people around him over in London—not a bunch of loonies and sycophants like Ganjibar. He's perfect for the job."

"And he's a good Christian? Don't forget, this is a Christian republic we're talking about."

"He's a big supporter of the Assyrian church, a generous donor, a lay reader, and almost became a priest himself."

"And he's a family man? Not into little boys or anything like that?"

"Married with two children, Mr. President."

Ritter nodded. "Okay. Let's do it. Who you gonna outsource it to, the Israelis?"

"Not this time," said Cordman. "They are too close to Ganjibar. They wouldn't go along with it."

"Actually, Mr. President," said McBride, "it's better you not know the details of the plan."

"He's right," said Firelli. "Deniability is crucial in a situation like this."

"Done!" Ritter stood up and rubbed his belly. "But what are you gonna do about the reporter?"

"Preston?" said Cordman. "I say we scare the bejesus out of him."

CHAPTER

33

T HE OAK LOGS BURNED brightly in the Oval Office fireplace. The crackling fire gave off little heat, thanks to the trans-
parent thermal screen in front of it. It was a sweltering July day in
Washington and the air-conditioning was turned up to the maximum.
But there was nothing Jack Ritter loved better than a cheery blaze, so
the fireplace functioned year round and the hell with the White House
electric bill.

Ritter settled into his favorite armchair, facing his guest. There was
no one else in the room. General Runter had specifically requested a
private meeting about urgent military matters.

"Well, Rick, how are things going over there in I-raq?"

"I have to level with you, Mr. President. Iraq's a mess. There's been
some semblance of a government following the elections, but the
army's a joke, the resistance is still very active—they're averaging
seventy-five attacks a day—and the country's teetering on the edge of
out-and-out civil war. There's no way we can pull our troops out any-
time soon."

"What's the good news?"

Runter's eyes lit up, and he leaned toward the president with his elbows on his knees. "The good news, Mr. President, is the Armageddon
Project."

Ritter nodded and gave the general a tight smile. "Where do things
stand, Rick?"

"Construction of the underground facilities is about two-thirds finished. The civilian airport, which actually doubles as a state-of-the-art military airbase, is virtually completed. The weaponry and ordnance continue to arrive in covered truck convoys. We're hiding it all underground, of course. Our troops are secretly embedded in, and in control of, the Assyrian Liberation Army. And the oil-field development is proceeding apace."

"Excellent."

"But there's one thing missing, Mr. President. And only you can provide it: tactical nuclear warheads."

Ritter jutted out his jaw. "We've been discussing that with the security team. I'm still ponderin' it over. To be honest with you, I'm not yet convinced."

"Then allow me to convince you, Mr. President. There is a tactical reason, a strategic reason, and what I like to call a transcendent reason to do this."

"Okay, Rick, lay it out for me."

Runter stood up. "I hope you don't mind if I walk around a little while I talk, Mr. President? That's the way I like to do it when I talk to my staff officers—and when I teach Sunday School, I might add."

"Be my guest," said Ritter, with an impish grin. "But don't walk too fast, or my eyes'll get sore followin' you around the room."

"Mr. President, the tactical reason is simple: a nuclear-armed Assyrian Republic, which in reality will be an American colony and military base, will serve as a deterrent to other nuclear powers in the Middle East."

"Okay, Rick, I got that."

"The strategic reason is also simple. The Assyrian Republic can be a staging ground for preventive strikes against the Iranian nuclear facilities. This is the aspect that most interests our Israeli allies. In fact, they consider themselves virtually at war with the mullahs ever since their Hezbollah surrogates started kidnapping Israeli soldiers and lobbing rockets over the border."

"You know something?" said Ritter. "Somebody oughta get on the phone with Hezbollah and tell 'em to stop doing that shit."

Runter ignored the remark. "So we've been working together with the Israelis on targeting Iran. Our assessment is that at least 400 targets would have to be hit, starting with the underground centrifuge plant in Natanz. Now, if this were done with conventional airborne weapons, it would require something in the neighborhood of a thousand strike sorties. The Israelis would like to do it, but don't have the air power, or the reach, to do the job on their own."

"Couldn't we do it without them?"

"We could, Mr. President, but we might lose a lot of planes to Iranian antiaircraft batteries. We would also have to carpet bomb to make sure we knocked out underground facilities, which would cause a lot of civilian casualties and drive all the Muslim countries batshit. Finally, our targeting would be less precise and our firepower less effective than if we made surgical strikes with cruise missiles and tactical nukes. Natanz is buried under seventy-five feet of earth and rock. We'd really need a B61-11 to take it out."

"Rick, you're starting to lose me here. What's a B61-11?"

"That's a tactical nuclear bunker-buster."

Runter stopped pacing back and forth and stood right in front of Ritter's armchair, causing the president to look up to him like a churchgoer gazing at the pulpit from a front-row pew.

"Forget all that military stuff, Mr. President. The real reason—the transcendent, prophetic, and apocalyptic reason to do this—is all spelled out in the Book of Revelation: 'These shall make war with the Lamb, and the Lamb shall overcome them: for he is Lord of lords, and King of kings: and they that are with him are called, and chosen, and faithful.' That's us, Mr. President. That's the United States of America. We are called and chosen to fight alongside the Lamb in the terrible, final battle of good against evil: the Battle of Armageddon."

"I am quite familiar with Revelation, General. But why do we need nucular weapons to fight it? When the time comes, won't Jesus come back with a whole band of angels in white linen and smite the evildoers with a 'sharp sword' and a 'rod of iron'?"

"With all due respect, Mr. President, that was written two thousand years ago. Take it from me as a military man, when Jesus comes back, he's gonna need a hell of a lot more than swords and iron rods. The forces of the Antichrist have modern arms. We've got to give the Lamb the very best high-tech, precision-guided, lethal-force weaponry—and a bomb-proof underground command center—if we want to win this battle. And that, Mr. President, is what the Armageddon Project is really about."

"Cordman and Chandler say it's about establishing Middle East democracy and developing independent oil supplies."

"That's precisely why I wanted to see you alone, Mr. President. Cordman and Chandler—all their cockamamie neocon theories were drawn up by a bunch of egghead Jews and secular humanists. But you and I are God-fearing, born-again Christians, Mr. President. I'm telling you, with every ounce of faith and conviction that is in my soul, that we are entering the End Times right now. It is your privilege, and sacred duty, to preside over the preparation of a nuclear-armed forward base for the battle of Armageddon. That is why the Lord put you in the White House at this point in time. Think of it, Mr. President. My God, what a glorious destiny!"

Ritter gazed at the blazing logs in the fireplace. They danced, and glowed, and spewed golden flames into the air like a burning bush. The president closed his eyes tight, bowed his head, and clasped his hands over his breast. After a long moment of silence, he looked up at the general with a beatific smile. "Rick," he said. "Let's go for it!"

CHAPTER

34

THE ELEGANTLY LANDSCAPED Buttes Chaumont park, with its lakes and cascades and rocky outcroppings, is the proud centerpiece of Paris's 19th arrondissement. The area was once a model of peaceful cohabitation among the Jews, Poles, Armenians, Greeks, Germans, Spaniards, and Italians who started moving here in the late 1800s to work in the local industries. After World War II, they were joined by Africans and Arabs from the former French colonies.

In recent years, the teeming neighborhood had broken down into competing, sometimes warring, communities. And nothing was more alarming than the rise of Islamic fundamentalism in this once-tolerant melting pot. One by one, long-bearded Salafists had taken over local cafés, restaurants, butcher shops, and groceries, and turned the 19th into a hotbed of Muslim radicalism.

Its focal point was the Al Taweed mosque, situated a few blocks south of the Buttes Chaumont, tucked among high-rise, low-rent apartment blocks bristling with satellite dishes to bring in Al-Jazeera and other Arabic stations. Al Taweed didn't look much like a mosque. It had no minaret, no pointed arches, no tiled courtyards, no gilded calligraphy on the walls. It was just a squat, three-story gray concrete building that was once a furniture warehouse. Its prayer room was a windowless, bunker-like chamber whose only adornment was the thick, overlapping layers of oriental carpets on the floor.

In a corner of this room, Walid Karouche knelt on a rug, surrounded by six young neighborhood youths. The others were dressed like typical Parisian teenagers—jeans, oversized sneakers, baggy sweatshirts. But Walid, also known as *le guide*, wore a white robe and red kaffieh headdress. His traditional vestments and unkempt black beard made him seem older than his twenty-four years. So did his mastery of the Koran and of Salafist philosophy, which he had learned in his pious family and dispensed with charismatic fervor to his young disciples.

The imam and other officials of the mosque claimed that Walid had no formal role there. But he would come every morning to pray and gather in a corner with his young disciples, who would listen, mesmerized, to his soft voice and hard words.

"Look at you, my brothers," he would say. "The French say you are citizens of their country, but they consider you as scum and treat you as vermin. Your fathers came here to work, yet they have no work. And you will have no work. You can study all you want in their schools, my brothers, no one will give you a decent job. Do you know why? Because you are Arabs. You were born here, but this is not your home. It will never be your home."

Some of the young men nodded their heads and mumbled.

"But you have a far better home than this blasphemous French republic, my brothers. You have Islam. You are Muslims. That is your true identity. That is who you are. And to be true Muslims, you must follow the faith and obey the law with all your heart and mind."

"How can we know the law? We cannot read the true Koran. We can hardly speak Arabic."

"I will teach you the Koran, and I will teach you Arabic. And when you are ready, I will send you to a school in Damascus, the Abu Nahir school, where you will perfect your knowledge among fervent and pious believers."

Even in the cold neon light of this windowless room, Walid seemed in the eyes of the youths around him to glow with some inner fire. His black eyes burned with fervor, but his voice had the sweetness of milk and honey. The harshness of the scornful world outside, their problems and failures at school, the lure of alcohol and drugs and petty delinquency, all this was shut out by the doors of the mosque. And this beautiful man, this shepherd, this righteous guide, he could show them the way to a far better life and a higher calling than anything they could hope for as citizens of a secular French republic that despised them.

"But it is not enough to learn the Koran, my young brothers. You must learn to defend it against the enemies of Islam. And do you know who are the enemies of Islam?"

"The Jews," said one boy.

"The Christians," said another.

"The Israelis . . . the French . . . the Americans."

"All of them, young brothers. All of them and more. Including those among us who were born into Islam but do not keep its laws. They are all our enemies. And we must show them no pity."

The young men mumbled their agreement.

"And that is why, my young lions, you will be taught the use of arms along with the Koran. At Abu Nahir, our brothers will turn you into fierce warriors. And then the bravest and purest among you will be chosen to cross into Iraq and do jihad against the infidels and the kafirs who have dared to invade a Muslim country and defile the holy land of Islam."

"The Americans!"

"Yes, my dear friends, the Americans. They not only desecrate our land, they incarnate all that is odious and blasphemous in the modern secular world—capitalism, globalization, sexual promiscuity, racism, subjugation of the poor and downtrodden, support of the Zionists against our Arab brothers. Who among you is ready to take up your sword against the American infidels and drive them from the land of Islam?"

Every young man kneeling on the rug alongside Walid eagerly raised his hand.

"May God's blessing be upon you all, my noble brothers. You shall be God's soldiers. And those who fall in battle will be glorious martyrs. They shall go instantly to Paradise, to bathe in rivers of honey and lie with sweet celestial virgins in eternal bliss."

One youth, the youngest and smallest of the lot, rose up on his knees and moved closer to the guide.

"Master," he said. "Why must we cross into Iraq to fight the infidels? Can we not fight them here as well?"

"When the time comes, Samir, we shall fight them here, *inch'Allah*, just as our brothers in Amsterdam struck down the blasphemous film-maker Van Gogh. For now, our most urgent need is to defend our brothers in Iraq."

The imam, a short, middle-aged man with dry, pale skin and a well-trimmed graying beard, entered the prayer room and glanced disapprovingly at the small gathering in the corner. The imam's message was that of a merciful and compassionate God, a God of tolerance, peace, and brotherhood among men. From what he occasionally overheard, he was not so sure the young man in white robes was preaching the same Islam that he espoused and strove to teach his flock. But Walid Karouche was the scion of a prominent Salafist family. The imam could not afford to alienate them by banning this self-appointed guru or other Salafist radicals. In spite of his own moderation, he feared that the extremists were hijacking his mosque.

Other worshipers were filing in to take part in the formal Friday prayer session. Walid and his group joined them and soon the whole congregation, all men, were kneeling and pressing their foreheads on the ground as the imam intoned verses of the Koran.

When the prayers ended, Walid's group dispersed. But the guide put his hand gently on Samir's shoulder.

"Did you mean what you said about fighting the infidels right here in France?" he whispered.

"Yes, master Walid."

"Are you prepared for martyrdom, young brother? Do you understand what that means?"

"Yes, Walid. I am ready."

"And that is what you truly want?"

"More than anything."

Walid kissed the youth on both cheeks. "Then I have a mission for you."

CHAPTER

35

GEORGES CARNAC'S LIMOUSINE pulled up at The Break-ers at 10 a.m. The vulgar extravagance of this seaside mansion, with its incongruous arches and columns, its pretentious balconies and outsized chimneys, seemed to the French president the perfect emblem of American materialism and excess. He knew from his briefing book that this flamboyant fortress, coyly referred to as a "cottage," had been built by one of the most ruthless of America's Gilded-Age robber bar-ons, Cornelius Vanderbilt II. It was here that Jack Ritter resided during the G8 summit. How fitting, thought Carnac.

French troops under Rochambeau had bivouacked in Newport just before marching to join the Americans in their decisive victory at York-town. But it seemed to Carnac that the two countries were now sepa-rated by a gulf as wide as the Atlantic Ocean that stretched out beyond these immaculately manicured lawns.

On this Saturday, July 22, Ritter received him in the library, surrounded by beautifully bound old books that no one had ever read. The American president had proposed a tête-à-tête meeting, without aides, interpret-ers, or notetakers, so that the two men could speak openly and frankly. He also knew that Carnac's English was not perfect, which would give Ritter a tactical advantage. Vice President Cordman and Chuck Granger had thoroughly briefed him on what to say. But they were never sure that he would remember, or follow, their game plan. Ritter liked to wing it in private meetings like this. And that's when he sometimes got into trouble.

Ritter stood and greeted the Frenchman with a firm handshake. "Welcome to Newport, Mr. President," he said, "the proudest showplace of American capitalism. Men like Vanderbilt, Bell, and Wetmore all prospered on the free market and built these beautiful mansions as a monument to the American way of life."

Ritter took a seat on a Chesterfield couch and waved his guest to a matching leather armchair. Carnac looked around the high-ceilinged room, with its thousands of books, crystal chandeliers, and white marble fireplace.

Despite the formal politeness, there was no warmth or cordiality between the two men. Deep down, in fact, they had always detested one another. Carnac had contempt for the American's ignorance and provincialism; Ritter scorned the Frenchman's pretentiousness and the weakness of the once-grand country he represented. Carnac's recent decision to pull France out of NATO had further poisoned the personal chemistry. It was clear from the outset of this tense encounter that they were not there to exchange pleasantries

"Very impressive villas, Mr. President," said Carnac. "But we in Europe have a different way of life—older, gentler, less dazzling, perhaps. Yet we remain attached to it, and we will defend it. We are also attached to principles like human rights, sovereignty, multilateralism, and respect for international law."

"Oh, we respect international law, too. In fact, we wrote most of it ourselves."

A sardonic smile crossed the Frenchman's lips. "Then perhaps you have forgotten Article 4 of the U.N. Charter."

"Article what?"

"Article 4—the one that outlaws 'the threat or use of force against the territorial integrity or political independence of any state.'"

The vertical crease between Ritter's small, close-set eyes deepened. "Look, Georges," he said, "I thought we'd agreed to disagree on Iraq, if that's what you're referring to. Saddam was a threat to world peace, so we liberated his country. End of story."

"I'm not talking about your ill-advised invasion, Mr. President. I am talking about the Assyrian revolt that you are arming, funding, and encouraging in defiance of international law."

"Now wait a minute," said Ritter, raising his voice. "Americans naturally have sympathy for a valiant little Christian community fighting for its survival, but my government has no involvement in that struggle. None whatsoever."

"Then perhaps you can explain where all the Assyrian arms are coming from, and who is paying for them."

"Private donations for missionary work. You can scoop up a lot of money in a collection plate every Sunday."

"Twenty-five billion?"

Ritter's eyebrows shot skyward. "Twenty-five billion? What the hell are you talking about, Georges?"

"Let us stop beating the bush, Mr. President. France has intelligence services. We know all about your secret fund in Switzerland. And we know exactly who was your point man. Roland Peccaldi was one of my closest personal friends before he betrayed me—and before he allowed your agents to buy him off. It was actually rather clever of you to use a Frenchman to cover your tracks and provide deniability."

"I don't know what you're talking about."

Carnac leaned forward and looked at Ritter with a carnivorous smile. "I would never want to call you a liar, Jack. I prefer to think you have merely forgotten some details. Allow me to refresh your memory."

"I'm all ears."

"Roland Peccaldi is the one who set up the secret Swiss bank fund for you, first to arm the Assyrians, and to set up a puppet republic with its own international airport, army, banking system, and multinational businesses. But most of all, you and your friends are planning to exploit the large oil field that has recently been discovered on the Assyrian territory, the one that Bullington is developing under a no-bid contract. All of this, naturally, is in violation of international banking rules, the U.N. charter, and the NATO charter—not to mention several U.S. laws."

Ritter frowned but said nothing. He stood up and walked slowly around the room, looking at the rows and rows of bookshelves. He stopped and pulled out a leather-bound volume. Then he turned around and held the book up so Carnac could read the gilded letters on its cover: Holy Bible.

"Let's just say I obey a higher law," said Ritter, tapping the book's cover with his index finger. "Are you a Christian, Mr. President?"

"I am a Roman Catholic."

"That's close enough. Do you read the Bible?"

Carnac smirked at the suggestion. "In France, Mr. President, we never mix religion and politics. We fought for a century to separate church and state. That is a foundation stone of our republic."

Ritter walked toward the Frenchman, still waving the book in his hand. "Well, we fought hard for our freedom, too, but we didn't chop off any heads or banish God from the hearts of our leaders. Read the Book of Revelation, Georges, and you will see that we are entering the End Times. We're on the brink of Armageddon, the final battle between good and evil. You're either with us or against us. You got to choose sides. Which will it be?"

"With all due respect, Mr. President," said Carnac, looking up at Ritter with an air of disbelief, "I think you are quite mad."

Ritter stepped closer to the Frenchman, until he was practically hovering over him. "Hell is mighty hot, and eternity is a long time, Georges. Better think it over. I'll tell you something else you need to think over. You mentioned secret bank accounts a while back. Yours is holding about $50 million that came from your buddy Saddam Hussein back when you folks were cozyin' up to him, selling him nucular power plants and all kinds of weaponry. We know the whole story, chapter and verse."

"Those were legitimate commissions," Carnac protested, "destined for the Gaullist party campaign fund."

Ritter grinned and gave his Bible a loud thump. "Then why did they wind up in your private account in Luxembourg? I can tell you the account number if you don't believe me. Imagine what the French press would do with that. You wouldn't just be out of a job. You'd be in jail. Is that what you really want, Georges?"

"Are you trying to blackmail me?"

"No more than you are. But I'll make a deal with you—you keep quiet about the Assyrians, and I'll keep quiet about your bank account."

Carnac stood up. At six foot two, he towered over the American. "Mr. President," he said in a voice choked with anger, "I think this conversation is over."

"Have it your way, Georges. But think about it, my friend. Think about it."

CHAPTER
36

I T WAS SATURDAY MORNING and Sam felt good. He and
Sandra had slept late and lingered deliciously together in bed for the
first time in weeks. Now, drained and satiated, he was relaxing on a chaise
longue under a parasol, sipping a diet Coke and reading a Tom Fried-
man column in the *Herald Tribune*. Sandra was working in her studio
with the door open. He could hear the tink-tink-tink of her hammer
and chisel on stone. They needed more quiet time together, Sam thought.
But he knew this morning's balmy lull was just the eye of the frightful
storm that was breaking over his life.

Alfie was on the lawn beside him, gnawing on a plastic chew-toy in the
shape of a Big Mac. Sam reached down and kneaded the floppy skin over
the dog's neck. The mongrel closed its eyes and purred like a kitten.

The phone rang in the kitchen.

"I'll get it, Sandra," he said, folding his paper and slipping his feet
into his sandals.

He skipped up the back steps and grabbed the receiver.

It was a recorded announcement. "Hello. You have an important
e-mail message. Please check your e-mail now. Hello. You have an important e-mail message. Please check your e-mail now. Hello . . ."

Sam slammed down the receiver. He returned to his chaise longue
and unfolded the paper.

"Who was it, Sam?" Sandra asked, shading her forehead with the flat
of her hand.

"Some phone solicitation. They told me to read my e-mail. I hung up."

"Why don't you read it? Maybe you won something."

The phone rang again.

"If that's the same message I'm gonna rip out the phone."

Sam didn't bother with the sandals this time.

"Hello!" he barked.

"Allo there, Sam. How ya goin', mate?"

"Oh, hi Nigel. Sorry, I wasn't expecting you."

"Yeh, you did sound a bit snappy there. Everything okay? Sis okay?"

"We're all fine, Nigel. Are you headed this way again?"

"No. In actual fact, we're off to Switzerland. I've got to take two more weeks' holiday before the end of the month or I'll lose 'em. You know how that is."

"I don't, actually, Nigel. Well, look, enjoy Switzerland. I'll call Sandra."

"Right-o, mate. Good talking to you."

Sam stuck his head out of the kitchen door and flashed a phone sign at Sandra with his thumb and little finger. He outlined a pot-belly with the palm of his right hand and assumed a stooping, slope-headed Neanderthal posture.

"Is that Nigel?" said Sandra, heading toward the back steps. "I wonder what that's about. He never calls unless he needs me to do something."

She wiped her hands on a paper towel and took the receiver.

"Hello, Nigel . . . Uh-huh . . . Right . . . Oh, dear . . . Well, couldn't you put it off for a week or so? . . . No? . . . Right . . . Well, I'll have to talk it over with Sam first. I'll call you back."

Sam gave her an inquiring look as she hung up the phone.

"Now don't explode. You're always ready to blow up at Nigel, but I want you to promise to stay calm."

"I promise."

"You really promise?"

"I promise. What is it?"

"Well, Mummy's not feeling well and Nigel wants me to come look after her while he goes off on holiday."

"What? That weasely, selfish, gas-guzzling, semiliterate cretin wants you to come all the way from France so he can go roving off yet again in his stupid camping-car? I don't believe this!"

"Sam, you promised you wouldn't blow up. You promised. I know he's annoying, but he's the only brother I've got. What do you say?"

"No! Absolutely not! I wanted to spend a quiet weekend with you. I'm not going to give it up so Mr. Comic-book brain can go sit by a lake somewhere and play with his water toys. No! No way! No!"

Sandra took a deep breath. "I don't know what to do. Mummy's apparently not feeling well at all. She's having trouble with her asthma."

He threw his hands up in the air. "Look, you deal with it. I've told you what I think."

He opened the fridge and drank a long gulp of diet Coke from the plastic bottle. As he headed upstairs, he could hear Sandra dialing Nigel's number.

In the guest room, which doubled as his home office, Sam turned on his iMac desktop and drummed his fingers while he waited for it to boot up. He slid the mouse over to the Safari button and called up his e-mail.

There was one, just in, from Charles Dumond: "Still no sign of you-know-what. Did you have right address? Call when you get a chance. Must tell you about hot times in Tel Aviv and other important matters."

Sam shook his head. What the hell happened to that envelope? Of course it was the right address.

The second e-mail came from a sender named "A. Friend" and bore the subject heading "URGENT MESSAGE!" That would be the phone solicitation thing. Somehow it got past his Spamguard.

He called up the message, but what he saw on his screen was not spam: "Sam Preston, drop all Iraq-related matters immediately. Publish nothing, say nothing, do nothing. We are watching you closely. See attachments."

There were four jpeg images attached to the message. Sam downloaded them and sat up with a start when the images took shape on his screen.

The first picture showed Sandra working in the garden with Alfie at her side. It looked like it was taken that morning.

The second showed their Peugeot, parked out on the street in front of the house with the license number clearly visible.

The third one showed Sam, buck naked, shaving in his upstairs bathroom. It also appeared to have been shot that morning with a telephoto lens.

The final image was a detailed map showing the way to Sam's house.

A new message popped up: URGENT PART II. It contained the same pictures, apparently doctored on Photoshop, splattered with realistic-looking blood.

Sam switched off the computer and wiped his sweaty palms on his shirttail. He went to the window and peered out from behind the thin white curtains. The four-story apartment building across the street, with balconies on every floor, would provide a perfect vantage point for taking those photos. Or for firing rifle shots into the house and garden.

Sam closed the metal shutters in the guest room and bathroom. Then he scurried down the stairs and found Sandra sitting at the kitchen table in tears.

"I can't deal with this, Sam. I can't deal with it. Now Nigel is proposing to drop Mummy here in his bloody camping-car and then go off to Switzerland. He's furious. I don't know what to do."

He put his hand gently on her shoulder. "Sandra, why don't you just cut through all the aggravation and go to Dover?"

"But you said no. You were so adamant."

"I've thought it over, and I've changed my mind. It's better to keep peace in the family."

Sandra took his hand in hers. "But what about our weekend?"

"When is Nigel leaving?"

"Monday morning."

"Let's drive up to Normandy today and spend the night at that bed-and-breakfast in Veules-les-Roses. We can have a nice little moment together by the sea, and I can drive you up to the ferry port in Calais tomorrow afternoon. You'll be in Dover for dinner."

She wiped her face and blew her nose with a paper napkin. "I'd like that. That would be lovely. Oh, but what about Alfie? Should we take him to the kennel?"

"Nah, takes too long. I'll be back here tomorrow evening. Let's just leave him a lot of food and water. We can ask Nicole Danton to come over and let him out in the garden during the day."

"Oh that's such an imposition."

"Nonsense. That's what neighbors are for. She's always coming to us for favors. How many times has she asked you to pick up her kids at school?"

"Well, maybe it's not such a big thing to ask."

"Of course it isn't. I'll take her the key while you pack the bags. I want to be out of here in fifteen minutes."

"What's the big rush, dear?"

Sam held her against him and smiled. "I want to make love to you by the sea."

CHAPTER

37

TUCKED INTO A NOTCH between the towering cliff walls along the English Channel, Veules-les-Roses is a Norman village full of climbing rose bushes, narrow stone fishermen's houses, grand nineteenth-century villas, and thatched-roof cottages along the river Veules—a one-kilometer-long, crystal-clear stream dotted with mill wheels and stocked with trout. A seaside village this charming would normally be crawling with vacationers and tourists in mid-July, but the rough pebble beach and chalky-white water—due to the constant erosion of the cliffs —kept the crowds down to a tolerable level.

Sam and Sandra sat on the terrace of the Café Tropical, watching the sun set over the Channel. This was their favorite weekend getaway, located less than two hours' drive from their home.

Sandra dipped her finger into the thick, creamy cap of her Belgian draft beer and licked off the foam. "Why can't we do this with French beer?" she asked.

"Because French beer sucks," Sam said.

Sandra reached out and held Sam's hand. "You're so tense, dear. What's the matter?"

Sam shook his head. "It's nothing. Just work stuff."

"Why don't you tell me about it? It'll help get it out of your system."

"No, I don't want to talk about it."

"Is it something secret?"

"Yes. I mean, I'm not trying to keep secrets from you, but I'm working on things that are secret, if you see what I mean."

"Not really. It seems like you're always investigating murky things, dangerous things, like that church bombing, and that fat Iraqi chap, what's his name?"

"Ganjibar."

"Right. Ganjibar. I was so worried when they drove you off in his car the other night, Sam. I wish you wouldn't do things like that. What if they'd killed you, or taken you hostage?"

"This is France, Sandra, not Iraq."

Sandra sipped her beer and gazed at the horizon.

"But someone could kill you, right? They shot that man right on the Place St. Michel the other night. You knew him. You could have been sitting there with him. Don't you ever think about that?"

"No," he lied. "If I did, I couldn't do my job."

"Then why don't you do some other job? You're not married to the bloody *New York Chronicle*."

"Because this is what I was born to do. It's what I like to do. I do it well. And maybe it can do some good."

"But is it worth all the stress and aggravation? You're always telling me the *Chronicle* doesn't appreciate you, they shortchange you on raises, they pass you over for promotions."

"The story I'm working on now can change all that. It's the story of a lifetime, Sandra. This will be the number-one headline in every newspaper in the world. It will make history."

"My God, is that what you want? Make history? Are you really that ambitious?"

"No, Sandra, I'm not ambitious. You want to know what ambition is? Let me tell you about Bradley Kemp. I watched his act back in New York. In editorial meetings, he would always hedge his words until he saw which way the managing editor was leaning, then swing right in behind him. At receptions, you could be talking to him and his eyes would be shifting this way and that, then he would cut you off in midsentence and dash off as soon as someone more important entered the room."

"How gauche."

"Wait, you haven't heard the best part. Once, when I was still in New York, he offered me a bit of friendly advice. 'If you want to get ahead here, Sam,' he told me, 'you have to get the attention of the senior people.' He says, 'Take me, for example. I only use the men's room by the executive offices. That way I'm always running into the bosses. They ask how I'm getting along, what I'm working on. All that's good for my career.' I mean, can you imagine that? Talking about his career while he's holding his dick? Now that's what I call ambition."

"What a smarmy little man."

"So I don't have Bradley Kemp's kind of ambition—that's probably why he's leapfrogged over me. But I'll tell you what I do have: I take a certain pride in playing the game well and being respected for it. I played varsity basketball when I was in college. I was not a big star. I was a team player, and the team hung together. But when hotdogs like Bradley Kemp start scoring points for their own glory, the team loses its soul, and playmakers like me have no one to pass the ball to anymore."

"So what do you do then?"

"You jump as high as you can, and go for a slam dunk."

The fiery red ball was almost touching the horizon now. In the after-glow of the long midsummer evening, Sam and Sandra strolled hand in hand along the beach. The tide was coming in, the heavy, churning Channel surf that crashed into the rocks and exploded into white spray and rattled the stones on the beach. In just a few minutes, the waves would be pounding the base of the chalk cliffs, wearing them down bit by bit, as they had been doing for thousands of years.

Seagulls were wheeling overhead, diving for their unsuspecting prey just under the surface, rising again with small fish wriggling in their beaks. Sam watched it all and marveled at the power, the beauty, and the brutality of nature. Sandra watched, too, silent, almost awestruck. The dying glimmer of daylight threw a golden blush on her cheek. Sam drew her to him, kissed her, and held her tightly in his arms to protect her from the rising wind.

Sunday went quickly, too quickly. Rising late, they had coffee and croissants at the seaside café. A walk along the willow-shaded banks of the river Veules; a visit to the port, where fishermen and their wives hawked the morning's catch behind their wooden stands; a quick lunch of *moules frites* at their favorite seafood restaurant, and it was time to leave for Calais.

They didn't talk much during the two-hour drive. They had said the important things last night. Now it all had to settle. But Sam felt the closeness of his wife and, from time to time, put his hand on her knee. She would let it stay for a moment, then return it to the steering wheel. She was right. For better or worse, he was the driver and he had to stay in control.

CHAPTER

38

IT WAS 5:30 WHEN the ferry pulled away from the dock and chugged slowly toward the open sea. He could see Sandra on the rear deck, clutching her bag in one hand and waving to him with the other. He waved back and watched her silhouette grow smaller and smaller until it finally disappeared altogether.

The drive back to Le Vésinet took longer than usual. He avoided the motorway and took back roads. Save on tolls and see more of the countryside, he told himself. But, in truth, he was in no hurry to return to the dark, empty house. At least he would have Alfie to comfort him.

When he drove up to the front gate, Sam was surprised to see all the metal shutters open; he had closed them before leaving. Then, as he crossed the garden, he saw that the kitchen door was ajar.

Sam climbed slowly up the back stairs and pushed the door. The kitchen was a shambles—broken plates and glasses everywhere, the refrigerator wide open and the contents thrown all over the floor, Alfie's dish overturned and his food pellets scattered everywhere. In the living room, all the books and CDs had been pulled off the shelves, the couch cushions pulled apart, the lamps knocked over. Same thing upstairs: the master bedroom was turned upside-down, clothes pulled out of the closets, dresser drawers dumped on the bed; the guest room was less disheveled, but Sam's old iMac computer had been dismantled and the hard drive removed. Thank God he'd thought to take his laptop with him to Normandy. That's where he kept his vital data.

Then he noticed the red stain on the edge of the rug, just in front of the bathroom door. He opened it and saw Alfie sprawled motionless on his back, his soft underbelly exposed, his tongue hanging out, and his dull open eyes staring at the ceiling. He was surrounded by a puddle of blood that was still oozing from the deep razor slash across his thorax.

"Alfie! Oh God!" Sam cried, and put a towel to his face to keep from vomiting.

Then he heard a noise downstairs. Someone had pushed the door open. His heart was racing. He snatched up a heavy brass lamp in his sweat-slick hands and headed slowly down the stairs. He heard another door slam.

"Sam?" called a woman's voice. "Sam, is that you up there? Are you okay?"

"Nicole," he replied. "Somebody's torn the whole place apart."

"I can see that," she said. "All these break-ins in the neighborhood. Honestly, where are the police? I mean, it makes you wonder why you pay your taxes. I was telling Jacques that just the other day."

Sam stared at Nicole with his mouth half-open as he struggled to catch his breath. "Nicole," he said at last, "didn't you notice anything unusual going on here? Didn't you hear anything? I mean, you live right next door."

"Oh, I heard something that sounded like plates breaking, but I thought maybe you and Sandra were back and were having a fight. You know, a little lovers' quarrel? I didn't want to intrude on that. I know you Americans are different, but, you see, we French are very discreet."

"Somebody's tearing my house apart and you're discreet?"

"Well, perhaps I should have taken a closer look, but, you know, tend your own garden as Voltaire said."

Sam hustled Nicole toward the door. "C'mon, we gotta get out of here."

"Don't you want me to call the police?"

"No," he snapped as he followed her through the door and hastily locked it behind him. "Don't bother. I'll take care of it."

Sam drove his car to the RER train station and pulled into the empty parking lot. He listened to the rapid pulse in his temples and pondered his next move. Until this terrible night, his investigation had seemed to him like an intriguing game. Now he was afraid. If he went back to the house, they might kill him. He thought of going to Dover to tell Sandra what had happened, to comfort and be comforted by her, and to warn her of the dark forces that were lurking out there somewhere, wishing him and his wife no good. But it was too late to get back to Calais for the last ferry. And he could not wait until morning to tell Sandra. She would be expecting his call tonight.

He took out his cell phone and dialed Sandra's number.

"Sam, is that you?" he heard her say. He had always found her breathy contralto voice very sensual on the phone. Now it had an anxious edge.

"Hi Sandra. How was the trip?"

"Oh, the usual. Rough crossing. Bar full of drunken Arsenal fans who threw up all over the floor. But I'm none the worse for wear. Nigel picked me up and brought me to Mummy's. He was right to want someone to stay here with her, Sam. She's not doing terribly well. I expect I'll be here till Nigel and Glennys get back."

"Sandra, it might be best to stay there even longer. We're not safe in Le Vésinet."

"What do you mean?"

"I found the house ransacked when I got back. Someone had gone through the whole place and trashed everything."

"Oh my God, Sam! Did they steal anything?"

"Not that I could see. Only my hard drive."

"Who could have done such a thing?"

"I don't know. But it's related to my Iraq story, the arms sales, Ganjibar, all that. I got threatening messages about it in my e-mail on Saturday. That's why I was in such a hurry to leave for Normandy."

"Sam, why didn't you say so? You're always doing this—not telling me things to protect me. When I find them out later, it's ten times worse. Don't you know you can share your problems with me? That I can maybe even help you solve them?"

"Not this one, Sandra. I feel like I'm being sucked up into a tornado and you can't come where it's taking me. The best thing you can do is stay put for now, keep cool, and take care of your mother. I'll come over there as soon as I can."

"Where are you going to stay?"

"With Charles."

"What about Alfie?"

"Sandra, Alfie is dead."

The sob on the other end of the line was the most heart-rending sound Sam had ever heard.

Charles Dumond was dozing in front of a TV movie, some French costume drama starring Gérard Depardieu. He was startled by a late-night knock.

"Who is it?" he demanded.

"It's me, Sam."

Dumond opened the door to find his friend standing on the landing with an overnight bag in his hand and a computer case over his shoulder.

"Are you planning to move in or something?" he asked.

"Yes," Sam said, and pushed past the Frenchman. "Quick, lock the door. You gotta put me up here for a couple of days."

"Calm down, Sammy. You're shaking. Do you want a cognac or something?"

"No! Listen to me, Charles, this is serious. They're after me. They've sent threatening e-mails. They just ransacked my house and killed my dog."

Dumond tightened the knot on his terrycloth bathrobe and sat back down in his armchair. "Who's they?"

"I don't know. It could be anybody. It could be the C.I.A., it could be the D.S.T., it could be Peccaldi."

Charles raised an eyebrow. "Peccaldi? I don't think so."

"Why not?"

"Don't you follow the news? Peccaldi's dead."

"Dead?"

"Sam, you are supposed to be a reporter. This has been all over the radio and TV all weekend."

"How did he die?"

"They say he slipped in the shower yesterday morning and hit his head. Massive cerebral hemorrhage. Bingo."

Sam sat down on the couch. "You believe that? About the shower, I mean."

"Of course not. He was done. Just like Francis de Granville—remember the guy who supposedly committed suicide in his office at the Elysée a few years back? Two bullets in his right temple—not one, but two—and he was left-handed. C'mon!"

"So who killed Peccaldi?"

"Who didn't have a reason to kill the old bird? He betrayed everybody—his clients, his party, his henchmen, his president. Everybody except De Gaulle."

Sam glanced at the flickering TV screen. Depardieu was staggering around in a musketeer costume and waving a sword in the air.

"Who do you think?"

Dumond shrugged.

"And who's after me?"

"I don't know that either. I told you this could be dangerous business."

Dumond agreed to accompany Sam out to Le Vésinet the next day. Sam didn't really want to go back there so soon. The cleanup could wait, but not Alfie. Sam could not just leave the poor beast up in the bathroom in this summer heat. It might be dangerous to go back, but with Dumond at his side, Sam felt reassured.

Sam did a double take when he opened the garden gate. The metal shutters were all closed. He took out his key and opened the kitchen door. Everything was exactly the way he and Sandra had left it on Saturday. Even Alfie's dish was sitting in the corner, full of food pellets.

Sam went from room to room with the Frenchman in tow. In the living room, the shelves were tidy, not a book or CD out of order. The couch cushions were in place, the lamps upright with working bulbs. No sign of debris or broken glass on the floor. Upstairs, all was in order in the bedroom, the clothes hanging neatly in the closets, the drawers closed, the bed made. In the guest room, nothing seemed amiss; the iMac was intact and sitting in its normal place.

Sam drew a deep breath and opened the bathroom door. Alfie was gone, the tile floor was spotless, fresh towels hung in their place on the racks.

The two men looked at each other.

"I don't get it," Sam muttered.

"Sammy," said the Frenchman, "are you sure you're okay? You've been under a lot of stress these days, you know. Maybe you hallucinated this thing."

"Charles, I did not hallucinate. I saw it with my own eyes."

Dumond patted his friend on the shoulder. "I know you think you saw it, Sam, but look around you."

Sam kneeled down and pointed to the red stain on the rug at the entrance to the bathroom. "What about this, Charles?"

CHAPTER

39

O N MONDAY, JULY 24, Rafat Ganjibar's chauffeur sat at the wheel of the Audi and waited for his boss to emerge from his building on the Quai Alphonse Le Gallo. He gunned the idling engine and cranked up the air-conditioning. The temperature outside was over ninety-five degrees, and the chauffeur knew that Ganjibar would berate him mercilessly if the car was not precooled.

It was nearly noon when he saw Musa the bodyguard advance cautiously toward the car. Musa peered slowly up and down the street, then beckoned to Ganjibar and opened the rear door.

The sound of a motor caught the chauffeur's attention. He glanced in his rearview mirror and saw a youth approaching from behind on a red Honda scooter. He noticed that the rider was wearing a thick coat despite the sweltering heat. "Watch out," he shouted to the bodyguard. "Watch this guy!"

Musa rudely shoved Ganjibar down onto the rear floor of the car. He whipped out his .45 automatic and fired three shots at the cyclist. Two seconds later, the whole neighborhood was shaken by the powerful blast from the youth's explosive belt.

The Audi was ripped open like a tin can and blown into the side of the building, where it caught fire, then exploded when the flames ignited the fuel tank. Other nearby cars were also in flames; their alarms shrieked in an ear-splitting cacophony. That noise was soon amplified by human screams, as passersby, once over the initial shock, reacted to the scene of horror in front of them. A young woman lay bleeding on the sidewalk. Her skirt had been blown to tatters. Two men knelt at her side; one tried to stanch the deep wound on her thigh with his handkerchief, the other frantically called the emergency services on his cell phone.

Body parts from the Audi's occupants were all over the sidewalk, mingled with pieces of the bomber. The boy's head, perfectly intact, had been blown off by the blast and rolled to a stop ten feet from the car.

Judge Bertrand Bouvard sucked his pipe and studied the smoldering tableau. The flaming vehicles had been extinguished and emergency workers joined police in the macabre task of assembling and sorting the body parts and putting them into separate plastic bags.

The Paris police prefect, Jacques-Marie Trigani, stood at Bouvard's side and contemplated the gruesome scene. "What do you make of it, Monsieur le Juge?" he asked.

"I'm not sure," he answered grimly. "I only know it is not what it seems."

The barrel-chested investigating magistrate, head of the Justice Ministry's antiterrorist section, had observed every kind of crime scene in his long and illustrious career of chasing bomb-throwers, hijackers, and political assassins across Europe and beyond. It was he who had collared the famous Red Brigade terrorist Carlo *"il Carnivore"* Benedetti in South Africa. He had also uncovered a plot to blow up the U.S. embassy in Paris, traced a jetliner bombing to the Syrian secret services, and nabbed the members of an Iranian death squad who had dared to come to Paris and cut up an opponent of the Tehran regime with knives from his own kitchen. As a result of his success in putting terrorists of every stripe behind bars, Bouvard was himself a terror target. His bodyguards had narrowly saved him from an assassination attempt several years earlier. Since then, he had started carrying a .357 magnum in a shoulder holster.

"And what do you think, Monsieur le Préfet?"

"Offhand, I'd say it is the same bunch that bombed Ganjibar's church."

"And do you know who they are?"

"We're hard at work on the case, Monsieur le Juge."

"So am I. And I do not know who they are."

Bouvard tapped the bowl of his pipe on the sole of his shoe and put it in his pocket. He could hardly disguise the contempt he felt for elite-school civil servants like Trigani who knew nothing about law enforcement and thought only of their next promotion or ministerial portfolio. For his part, Bouvard had turned down promotions in order to keep his fingers on the bloody, beating heart of crime fighting.

Trigani straightened up and tightened the knot on his tie as a camera crew from Télé-Première approached the two men. He made a brief, uninformative statement and promised a thorough investigation. Bouvard waved the microphone away. "I never comment on an investigation in progress," he said curtly.

Trigani excused himself and settled into the back of his limousine with a female aide. They were late for a luncheon at the prime minister's residence and sped off toward the St. Cloud bridge.

Bouvard stepped over the yellow tape and paced around the carcass of the Audi. He observed the gaping hole at the building's entrance, where the glass doors had been pulverized to powder. There were spatters of blood on the ground floor window frames and pockmarked facade of the building. Bark and branches had been blown off the scorched trees on both sides of the street. Powerful blast, he thought. Extremely powerful blast.

"Inspector," he said to one of the dozen police officers still working on the crime site, "you see that fragment of skin and hair over the window there? Have one of your men collect it in a sample bag, please. It will help with identification."

There was no mystery about the occupants of the Audi. Ganjibar's car, driver, and bodyguard were well known to French authorities, who'd long had them under surveillance. As for the bomber, his ID papers and photos of his intact head enabled investigators to identify him within hours of the blast.

At 3 p.m., just as he was returning from lunch at his usual *plat du jour* bistro near the Palais de Justice, Judge Bouvard received a phone call from Chief Inspector Gérard Morin of the *police judiciaire*.

"Monsieur le Juge, we have identified the perpetrator in the Ganjibar killing."

"That was fast work, Morin."

"His name is Samir Fahrani, sixteen years old, high-school dropout, unemployed. Lived with his family in a low-rent housing block on Avenue Jean-Jaurès. Police record shows some petty delinquency. But the family says he straightened out when he started going to prayers at Al Taweed in the 19th arrondissment."

"Al Taweed," Bouvard repeated, and struck a match to light his pipe. "I know about Al Taweed. They've been recruiting young jihadists there for months. The imam claims he knows nothing about it."

"Sir, this boy didn't have much contact with the imam, according to his family. They say he took informal Koranic and Arabic lessons there under a kind of self-styled guru.

"His name?"

"Walid Karouche."

"I've had my eye on Karouche. Have him brought in for questioning."

CHAPTER

40

AFTER RETURNING FROM LE VÉSINET that Monday morning, Sam called in sick. Until he knew who had raided his house and what it meant, he had decided to stay at Dumond's place and lie low. When he got back to the Frenchman's apartment, he fixed himself a ham sandwich and turned on CNN.

At half past noon, the hyperventilating anchor read a breaking news dispatch. "According to wire service reports just in, Rafat Ganjibar, the leader-in-exile of Iraq's Assyrian Christian minority, was assassinated today by a suicide bomber in front of his office in the Paris suburb of Boulogne. This footage was shot just minutes ago by Reuters —as you can see it contains some rather explicit images of the carnage that some viewers may consider shocking. We have just established an audio hookup with CNN's Jim Enderman at the scene. Jim, what can you tell us?"

"Richard, as you can probably see on the video footage, the black Audi SUV carrying Ganjibar, his bodyguard, and driver has been reduced to a charred hulk of twisted steel. All three occupants killed instantly. Police officials here saying the car was blown up by a suicide bomber who approached the left side of the parked vehicle on a motor scooter and detonated the belt after being fired upon by Ganjibar's bodyguard. Officials describing the device as extremely powerful, pointing out that this is the first time we have seen a Middle East-style suicide bombing on French soil—a worrisome development in their eyes."

"Jim, we're looking at graphic images that remind us all too well of scenes from Baghdad. Do officials there see any link between this bombing and the Kurdish attack on the Assyrian Christian enclave in Iraq last week?"

"At first glance, Richard, it would appear to be related to the situation in Iraq. It is possibly a retaliation for the Assyrian Liberation Army's overwhelming counterattack against the Kurds in the village of Tareq last Wednesday. On the other hand, French government sources telling us Ganjibar was involved in some controversial business activities here and may have been the victim of a Mafia-style rubout, though that would seem inconsistent with a suicide bombing. We have no official word yet on the identity of the bomber, but witnesses describe him as a dark-skinned young man between fifteen and eighteen, wearing a heavy coat, riding a red Honda motor scooter. Richard?"

"Jim, the AP has just reported that a group called 'the Avenging Scimitar of Allah the Omnipotent' has claimed responsibility. A statement posted on an Islamist Web site praises, and I quote, the 'glorious young jihadi who struck in Paris this morning. There are more like him who are racing toward martyrdom and eager to fight the enemies of God, the Jews, the Crusaders and their stooges.'"

"Richard, if that is authentic, that would appear to be the same people who last month bombed St. Jean de Patmos, the Assyrian church here in Paris, with which Ganjibar was affiliated. But officials working on that case saying they still do not know who is behind that group."

"Stay with us, Jim, we'll be back after a short break."

Sam picked up the remote and flipped through the other news channels. They were all reporting the same thing, with the same images. Nobody, in the news business at least, seemed to know much more than the contents of the initial wire reports. But Sam knew more. A lot more. There was no doubt in his mind that the hit was related to Ganjibar's impending declaration of independence.

A beep on Sam's cell phone alerted him to an incoming text message. He checked the screen: "Meet at pyramid 1:15. Urgent. RT."

He couldn't place the initials at first, but after a quick flip through his address book, he figured it out. Robert Tikhani, Ganjibar's lawyer.

Sam knew Tikhani was holding something for him. And they both knew that it was now red hot, virtually radioactive.

Sam took the Metro four stops down to the Louvre-Palais Royal station. He sprinted across the colonnaded Rue de Rivoli, and entered the vast open courtyard of the Louvre. There was a huge crowd of camera-snapping tourists hovering around the top of the so-called inverted pyramid—convinced, after reading *The Da Vinci Code*, that the Holy Grail, whatever that was, was buried underneath it. An even larger group was lined up at the museum's main entrance under the big I. M. Pei pyramid. Good call, Tikhani, Sam thought. If anyone wanted to melt anonymously into a crowd, this was the place to do it.

Sam surveyed the open plaza, but could not spot Tikhani anywhere. Then his eyes fell on the dyed orange hair of Professor Daniel Rappola, the one he'd met on his first visit to Ganjibar's office. Rappola was sitting at the edge of one of the triangular fountains. He saw Sam and gave him a discreet nod.

The professor was surrounded by Japanese shutter-snappers, German backpackers, and whitebread American college kids, many of whom were splashing their bare legs in the water. Sam took off his shoes, rolled up his trousers, and plopped down next to Rappola with his legs in the water.

"You have heard?" Rappola said softly, facing in the opposite direction from Sam and seeming to be talking to himself.

"Yes," Sam whispered as he looked at his legs swirling around in the water.

"Tikhani could not come. The police are searching his office. He sent me here to give you something."

"You brought the file here?"

"Of course not. It's in a safe deposit box in the USB headquarters in Zurich, 59 Bahnhofstrasse. The number is written on a discarded Metro ticket under my shoe. The bank is expecting you. Ask for Mr. Zellman. Bring your passport."

"Then what?"

"*A vous de jouer*. That's up to you."

Sam looked up at the apex of the pyramid. The polluted Parisian air had coated the glass panels with dust, and rainwater had turned it into a sinuous pattern of grimy rivulets. Probably not what Pei had in mind for this proud architectural jewel.

Rappola stood up and calmly walked away. Sam continued to contemplate the pyramid for a moment, then swung his legs over the side of the fountain, rolled down his trousers, and put his shoes back on. When he had finished tying the laces, he picked up the used Metro ticket and slipped it into his pocket.

CHAPTER

41

NAPOLEON ONCE CALLED the *juge d'instruction* "the most powerful man in France." And Bertrand Bouvard was, without a doubt, the most powerful of all the country's 550 investigating magistrates. He was widely feared and hated in international criminal circles, of course, but even government officials had reason to worry about what his relentless digging might uncover. The hundreds of dossiers that lined his cramped second-floor office in the Palais de Justice probably contained enough information to bring down a half-dozen ministers, and maybe even the president himself. But Bouvard was not interested in political transgressions. His job was hunting terrorists. And he was very good at it.

On this Monday afternoon, he sat staring at a pile of notes and documents, trying to make sense of what seemed like a kaleidoscopic puzzle. Like most investigating judges, he was assigned to work on dozens of cases simultaneously. Often the different trails crossed, as links and common elements emerged. And sometimes, several apparently divergent investigations suddenly morphed into one.

The sudden death of Roland Peccaldi intrigued and frustrated Bouvard. Unless he was assigned the case by the *procureur*, or state prosecutor, the judge had no jurisdiction to investigate Peccaldi's death. Moreover, such an investigation was now impossible since the state medical examiner, probably acting on direct orders of the interior minister, had immediately ruled the old man's death an accident. Case closed. But Bouvard was not so sure.

Though he was forbidden to delve directly into the Peccaldi affair, there were other ways to hook into it. Bouvard had been officially assigned to probe the murder of Peccaldi's henchman, Michel Lanzatti. His preliminary investigations pointed to a professional hit by operatives in Peccaldi's milieu. That was one hook.

Bouvard also wondered if that morning's murder of Rafat Ganjibar might also be tied somehow to Peccaldi. Perhaps not, but the timing of their deaths, just two days apart, did not seem entirely coincidental.

In any case, Ganjibar's murder did not appear to be a simple act of religious fanaticism. Bouvard's brief initial interrogation of Walid Karouche an hour earlier had already revealed an interesting anomaly: how could a twenty-four-year-old jihadi, held by the Americans in a high-security military prison in Iraq, calmly walk out of there and make his way back across the Syrian border without some kind of collusion? And what was the meaning of the expensive Breitling watch he wore on his right wrist? Karouche was now cooling his heels in preventive detention, and Bouvard aimed to subject him to a grueling round of interrogation over the next four days—the maximum time for holding suspects without charge. And there would be charges, no doubt.

Then there was this Nikola Lefkosias character. Two-bit hustler, drug dealer, and information peddler, not a likely player in any terrorist network. But Bouvard knew from information he'd garnered from the D.S.T. and other agencies that Lefkosias was closely linked to Lanzatti, and therefore to Peccaldi. He also knew that the Greek had suddenly fled the country on an Air France flight to Athens on July 6, just one day after Lanzatti's murder. Bouvard lost his trail at that point. But there were ways of finding it.

The judge relit his pipe, put his feet up on his desk, and leaned back to contemplate the one piece of artwork that adorned the drab walls of his office: a framed reproduction of a cubist painting by Georges Braque. The judge was forever finding in its angles and intersecting lines the most interesting patterns that he had never noticed before.

He picked up his phone and dialed the antiterrorist section of the *police judiciaire.*

"Morin," he said. "Bouvard here. Have you heard anything from Interpol about this Lefkosias character?"

"They called me back just a moment ago, Monsieur le Juge. I am typing up my notes."

"What do they have?"

"Quite a lot. Turns out Lefkosias was murdered in a cheap Athens hotel one week ago. The local homicide guys have a tentative suspect—a French-speaking woman who hooked up with him in a techno club the night of the murder. She apparently killed him with a clean karate chop to the throat. They've sent us a grainy cell phone snapshot of her dancing with Lefkosias in the club that night."

Bouvard sucked on his pipe. "Have they identified the suspect?"

"Not yet, but they know she flew in that morning from Paris on Air France 1232. The Greeks have her seat number, 36C. They are requesting access to the Air France passenger list."

"Out of the question. Air France is our national airline. Europe or no Europe, I won't have a bunch of Greeks bigfooting on our turf. Tell them we will check the list and get back to them if we find anything."

"A wise move under the circumstances, Monsieur le Juge."

"What circumstances, Morin?"

"A French-speaking woman flies into Athens on Air France, zeroes in on Lefkosias, administers a professional hit and disappears into the night. Could be our own services, don't you think?"

"I don't think, Morin. I verify."

"*Naturellement.* But there is one other pertinent detail you should know about this female suspect."

"Which is?"

"She's apparently a man."

CHAPTER

42

"S AMMY BOY, I HAVE a lady friend coming over for dinner to-night. You remember the one I told you about from Tel Aviv?"

"The El Al stewardess?"

Dumond nodded and made a juvenile masturbatory gesture with his right fist. "You are going to bust your jeans when you see her, man. Just remember, I saw her first."

"If you're so worried about male competition, why don't you two go off and have a romantic dinner somewhere else?"

"It was her idea to come over. I told her you were staying here, and she said she wanted to meet you."

"Jesus! You didn't tell her about the story we're working on?"

"Do you think I'm nuts? Oh, by the way, your little package finally arrived. The cretins in the mailroom had misplaced it."

"Oof! I was getting worried."

Dumond handed over the worn manila envelope. Sam put it in his shoulder bag, alongside his laptop. "Thanks. I'll read it on the train tomorrow. Did you make a photocopy?"

"I didn't have time. We'll go over it together when you get back from Zurich. Then we publish the fucker."

Charles answered a knock at the door. One of the most stunning women Sam had ever seen walked in clutching an airline crew bag in one hand and a bottle of champagne in the other. She smiled and kissed Charles on both cheeks.

"Sam, meet Hannah Avner. Hannah, this is Sam."

The tall, broad-shouldered young woman stepped forward and kissed Sam's cheeks as well. "Hello, Sam. I am happy to meet you. Charles has told me so much about you."

Sam glanced at Dumond. "Don't worry," the Frenchman giggled, "I didn't tell her about the morals charge in Vegas."

The American shook his head and looked at Hannah.

"I know," she said with an alluring smile. "He's always joking. Like a little boy."

Dumond opened the champagne and poured three glasses. "Normally, Sam here doesn't drink. But I thought he just might have a little champagne in your honor."

Sam hesitated, then touched his glass to Hannah's and Dumond's. "To the three of us," he said, and took a sip. The fine bubbles tickled his tongue and he felt a delicious warmth in the back of his throat. It was good stuff. But he put the glass back on the table and resolved to leave it there.

"Charles tells me you used to play basketball," said Hannah, settling in next to Sam on the couch.

"I played some college ball at Yale."

"And were you good?"

"Good enough to make the varsity squad. Not a big star, though, just a team player."

"Yes, I like that better. Teamwork. All stick together and help each other, like on my kibbutz."

Hannah wore no perfume, but Sam could smell the faint, sweet odor of her shampoo, along with a trace of chlorine. She ran a hand through her damp hair and shook her head. "I didn't have time to dry my hair after I went swimming," she said. "I must swim every day, you know, to keep fit."

"Yes, you do seem very fit."

Charles called to them from the kitchenette. "Knock it off, you two."

Hannah laughed and waved an index finger at him. "You Frenchmen are always so jealous. You think every time a man and woman look at each other, they are thinking of sex. It's not true."

"In America," said Sam, "men and women don't look at each other at all. They pass on the sidewalk and look the other way."

"Because they are afraid of their sexuality," said Hannah. "In Israel, men and women enjoy looking at one another. If I find a man attractive, I look at him, and I want him to look at me. It is a little game. Usually it goes nowhere. But it is nice, don't you think, Sam?"

"Maybe I got out of the habit since I got married."

"Oh, I don't think so," she said, looking into his eyes as he looked back. "Those kinds of habits, one never forgets."

Charles laid three plates on his kitchenette table. "Dinner is served," he said. "I've made spaghetti carbonara. It's got ham and fresh cream, Hannah, so I'm afraid it's not kosher."

"Oh I don't care. It is only in Israeli restaurants or on the plane that I must keep kosher. I am totally secular—in every sense of the word."

They ate and talked and laughed far into the night. Charles and Hannah—mostly Charles—consumed a bottle and a half of lightly chilled Brouilly on top of the champagne. Sam drank Perrier.

It was after midnight when Charles and Hannah retired to the bedroom. Sam set his cell phone alarm for 6:30, stripped down to his jockey shorts, and bunked down on the couch. After a few minutes, he heard the heavy breathing and groaning of the lovemaking couple in the next room.

Once his friends had quieted down, Sam dozed off. But his sleep was fitful. He thought of the envelope in his bag, and the trip he had to take in the morning. He thought of Rafat Ganjibar and Roland Peccaldi and Michel Lanzatti, and of his wrecked house and poor Alfie. He thought of his sweet Sandra, across the Channel, nursing her mother and, probably, missing him. And, he had to admit it, he thought of the lovely Hannah Avner and the smell of her shampoo.

At 3:30, the bedroom door opened. Sam had been only half asleep. He saw Hannah emerge and go into the bathroom. Then she flushed the toilet and drew a glass of water from the kitchenette tap. Instead of returning to the bedroom, she walked softly toward the couch.

"Sam," she whispered, "are you awake?"

"Yes." Her athletic form was silhouetted by the dim light that filtered in from the street. He could see that she was wearing Charles's terrycloth bathrobe, loosely tied and quite revealing. She had a damp, womanly smell, faint but intoxicating.

"Charles said you are going to Zurich tomorrow. I must go there too, to meet up with a crew from Tel Aviv. Do you want to fly there together?"

Sam cleared his throat. His mouth felt dry. "I'm taking the train," he whispered.

"I can take the train, too. I don't have to be there until the afternoon."

Sam thought for a moment, then shook his head. "I don't think so, Hannah. I have a lot of stuff to read. I need to be alone so I can hunker down over it."

She smiled and patted his bare shoulder. "Okay, I understand. But maybe we can meet there. Give me your cell phone number."

Sam sat up and took his wallet out of his shoulder bag. He slipped out a business card and handed it to her. "It's on here," he said. "Good night, Hannah."

"Good night, Sam. I hope to see you tomorrow."

CHAPTER

43

SAM'S TRAIN PULLED INTO the Main Zurich station shortly after 2 p.m. on Tuesday. He had traveled light—just a shoulder bag containing his laptop, a couple of magazines, and, of course, the envelope he'd gotten from Nikola.

He had studied the documents carefully during the four-hour train ride. Some of the details were still murky, and some of the arms invoices were coded or contained only part numbers. It would take a specialist to sort that all out. But he understood enough to know that Roland Peccaldi was at the center of a massive arms operation, funded out of a numbered account at the Banco Bersalino in Lugano.

Sam still had no idea where the funds came from. The bank statements listed only account numbers of the parties that had wired the money into Lugano. But there was a huge amount of cash in the account, several billion dollars. The documents also showed transfers between Peccaldi's account and four other accounts at the Banco Bersalino.

Peccaldi's documents did not contain statements for the other accounts, so it was impossible to know how much money was in them or where it came from. Sam guessed that the old Gaullist had access to only one account, and that the rest of them were controlled by other people, perhaps for different purposes. No point calling the Banco Bersalino for a clarification: Swiss banking secrecy, even after it was shaken by the Nazi gold scandal, remained a formidable barrier to any outsider seeking information about numbered accounts.

As for the arms shipments, some of them came through Miguel Carvallo, but there were many other merchants involved in Peccaldi's overall network. There were dealers in Seoul, Taipei, Tel Aviv, Cape Town, Rio de Janeiro, Miami, New Orleans, the Bahamas, the Cayman Islands. All with obscure names and discreet addresses. The recipients were no less varied: procurement offices in Turkey, Egypt, Jordan, Kuwait. The one that most intrigued Sam, and the one that received the lion's share of the shipments, was a certain A.L.A. Logistic and Support Center, located in Istanbul. The journalist strongly suspected that this was Ganjibar's Assyrian Liberation Army. If so, then Peccaldi's operation would seem to be at least one conduit for the billions of dollars in American military aid that Ganjibar himself had told him about. And that is what Sam hoped Ganjibar's documents would confirm.

Sam walked down Zurich's famed Bahnhofstrasse, a busy thoroughfare shaded with double rows of lime trees, and home to more banks per square foot than any other street in the world. He strolled along the sidewalk, trying to pass for a casual window shopper, stopping from time to time to look at the displays in the luxury boutiques that offered everything from designer suits and fine shoes to cameras and, of course, Swiss watches.

Four blocks down from the train station, he stood before the main branch of the United Swiss Bank. Its monumental columns were topped by the sculpted heads of a peasant patriot, a mother, the Roman god Mercury, and William Tell, the mythic Swiss hero who shot an apple off his son's head with a bow and arrow. Sam pushed through the heavy revolving door and found himself in an immense foyer of reddish brown Tessin marble. He gazed up at the twenty- by thirty-foot skylight and the ornate moldings that surrounded it.

A uniformed security guard, attracted by this curious visitor, approached Sam and addressed him in German. The journalist tried answering in French, then switched to English when it became apparent that the guard could not, or would not, speak one of his country's three official languages.

"May I see your passport sir?" The guard demanded.

Sam pulled the document out of his wallet and handed it over.

"And what is your business in the bank?"

"I'd like to see Mr. Zellman."

"Do you have an appointment?"

"No. But he knows I am coming."

"Please wait here."

The guard returned shortly with a young woman in a smart-looking business suit.

"Hello, Mr. Preston. Herr Zellman has been expecting you. Unfortunately, he is busy at the moment. I am his assistant, Heidi Krüger."

"I don't actually need to talk to him. I'd simply like to access a safe-deposit box. I have the number here."

"I can help you with that, sir. Follow me, please."

The woman led Sam down an elevator into the deep, fortified bowels of the building. After taking his passport information, she unlocked a heavy metal grille door and entered a room whose walls were surrounded with gleaming brass deposit boxes. She unlocked the one bearing the number Sam had given her and placed it on a large marble-topped table in the center of the room.

"I will leave you now," she said. "Please press the buzzer by the door when you are finished."

"Thank you."

Once the door had closed behind her, Sam opened the lid and removed an inch-thick envelope that bore his name in Ganjibar's own handwriting. He put it into his shoulder bag, closed the lid on the deposit box and buzzed Heidi Krüger.

When Sam emerged from the air-conditioned bank into the July heat outside, he noticed that his shirt was soaked with sweat and his hair was damp. He clutched the bag under his elbow and cut through a narrow side street, past the twin-towered Cathedral Münster, down to the banks of the river Limmat. He was tempted to sit at an outdoor café and have a cold drink, but decided to find a less exposed place. Perhaps he was just being paranoid, but he had the distinct impression that he was being watched.

From previous visits to Zurich, he remembered a café on the east bank of the river, Le Sélect, where one could sit and read newspapers all day for the price of a coffee. He could see it from where he was, on the other side of the Limmat, some two hundred yards further down. He had almost three hours before his train back to Paris. It would be the perfect place to wait.

He entered the Sélect and spotted a table in the rear corner. The café offered a selection of newpapers mounted on long wooden batons. He took one down from the rack, although he knew from past experience that they were all in German, a language that he did not read.

After ordering a coffee from the woman behind the counter, Sam spread the newspaper out on his table and pretended to read. Then he discreetly pulled Ganjibar's envelope out of his bag and laid it next to him on the corner bench.

He slipped out some papers. There were photos of Bradley fighting vehicles, Cobra helicopters, and armored personnel carriers surrounded by smiling Assyrian troops in their cinnamon berets. Other photos showed senior U.S. military officials, including General Rick Runter himself. He was wearing neatly pressed camouflage fatigues and grinning at the camera with his arm over the shoulder of an Assyrian officer. Defense Secretary Ron Chandler appeared in several pictures, apparently reviewing troops or briefing Ganjibar's men. In one captioned photo, he was shown shaking hands with General Jamil al-Waradi, supreme commander of the Assyrian Liberation Army, in Waradi's office.

Another shot showed Ganjibar grinning with Ritter and Cordman in front of the Oval Office fireplace. There were bank statements that documented regular, and substantial, payments into the personal accounts of Ganjibar and other senior officials of the Assyrian Liberation Movement, presumably from a C.I.A. slush fund.

Other items showed the extent of the infrastructure that had already been put in place on the Assyrian territory: photos of the sprawling airport complex, the cavernous underground facilities, the oil rigs, and what looked like the beginnings of a pipeline construction project.

There were also some bizarre letters from the National Christian Council and other American Evangelical groups, referring to the End Times and the "final battle." One letter, handwritten by Reverend Conklin himself, informed Ganjibar that a group of Evangelical leaders had just met with Ritter at the White House and received "assurances of financial, logistical, and military support sufficient to ensure the triumph of your glorious and divine mission."

Among the more technical documents, there were bills of lading for shipments of hand grenades, mortar shells, assault rifles, missiles, and numerous other items, all addressed to the A.L.A. Logistic and Support Center in Istanbul. Bingo, Sam thought. That mysterious Istanbul address was indeed a procurement arm of Ganjibar's army.

After twenty minutes, Sam had seen enough to know that the self-styled Assyrian Republic had received large quantities of munitions through Peccaldi's network, among other sources, and that the Ritter administration was solidly behind the operation. It would take days to sort it all out, he thought, but the two files together contained a thorough and devastating record of U.S. support for an illegitimate government, an illegal army, and a corrupt political leader—not to mention circumvention of Congress, deceit of the American people, and betrayal of the Iraqi parties that had bought into the U.S.-backed democratic process.

Sam felt a wave of anger and contempt welling up inside him. He wasn't sure what he could do with this information—there were powerful forces lurking out there that would stop at nothing to prevent its publication. But he knew that, one way or another, he had to get the story out. It was his duty, not only as a journalist, but as a decent American citizen who was outraged at the hijacking of his country, its values, its image, and its place in the world, by a band of cynical profiteers and self-righteous religious zealots.

"*Haben Sie ihre Zeitung fertig gelesen, mein Herr?*"

Sam looked up to see a portly old Züricher smiling at him and pointing to his newspaper with a stubby finger. He did not quite understand the words, but caught their gist. "*Ja, ja, fertig,*" he said, and handed over the paper.

"*Danke schön.*"

"*Bitte schön.*"

Sam started to panic. He suddenly realized that he was holding a sheaf of papers that could bring down the Ritter presidency, perhaps even change the course of history, and there he was sitting in a Zurich café pretending to speak German and making a conspicuous fool of himself. He felt hot, sweaty, light-headed. He put the envelope back in his shoulder bag, left some coins on the table, and walked out.

His cell phone rang as he walked along the quay. It could only be Dumond—just before leaving Paris, he had bought a new phone with a prepaid card so that his location could not be tracked. He had given the new number to no one but Charles.

"Hello, Sam. This is Hannah."

"Hannah."

"Yes. You know that number on your business card did not work, so Charles gave me your new number. Are you in Zurich?"

"Yes."

"Where are you now?"

"Near the Café Sélect, on the Limmat Quai."

"Oh, that is not very far from my hotel. I am at the Dorfer Waldhaus on Kurhausstrasse. It turns out I don't have to fly out until tomorrow morning. I've just had a nice swim. Perhaps you can join me here for a drink?"

"I don't have much time, Hannah. I have to catch a train back to Paris."

"What time is your train?"

"Six o'clock."

"It is only four now. You have plenty of time. Besides, I have something you need."

"What's that?"

"Can't you guess?"

"No."

"Aren't you missing something?"

Sam dug his hands into his pockets. Used Metro tickets, some loose change, a wadded up Kleenex.

"Oh, shit! I forgot my key."

"You win the prize!" she laughed. "We found it on the coffee table after you left this morning. Charles asked me to give it to you. He had to leave for London, so he won't be there to let you in tonight."

"God! How could I be so stupid? It must have fallen out of my pocket when I laid my pants over the chair last night."

"Now you see why men should always keep their pants on," she said playfully. "But, listen, it is no problem. You just take a taxi to the Dorfer Waldhaus. We have a drink, a little chit-chat, I give you the key, and you have plenty of time to catch your train."

"Okay, I'll be there in five minutes."

CHAPTER

44

THE DORFER WALDHAUS TURNED out to be quite a fancy place nestled up in the hills over Lake Zurich, with an outdoor swimming pool, clay tennis courts, and even its own nine-hole golf course. Sam called Hannah's room from the reception desk.

"Hello, Sam. I am just stepping in the shower after my swim. Come up to my room, 514. The door is unlocked."

Sam took the elevator up and found Hannah's room at the far end of the corridor. He opened the door and stepped inside. The furniture was modern, elegant, expensive. A sliding glass door led out onto a private balcony with spectacular view of the lake and the snow-capped Alpine peaks in the distance. Rather grand digs for an employee of a money-losing airline, he thought. Perhaps El Al got rooms here on a barter agreement.

"I'll just be a minute," said Hannah over the noise of the shower. "I've ordered some champagne. Pour yourself a glass."

Sam stepped over to a marble-top table, where a bottle of Moët & Chandon sat chilling in a silver ice bucket.

From that vantage point, through the half-open bathroom door, he could see Hannah's tan body only slightly blurred by the translucent shower glass. She was shampooing her hair, with her arms raised and her breasts bouncing with the rapid scrubbing movements. Even through the glass he could see the dark, round circles of her nipples, and felt an involuntary stirring in his groin.

"It's too bad you weren't here earlier," she said. "You could have joined me in the sauna. It was lovely."

Sam was tempted to have some champagne. After all, he had taken a little sip at Dumond's the night before and that didn't hurt. He remembered the titillating sting on the tip of his tongue, the pleasant warmth in the back of his throat. Perhaps it would calm his nerves. Then he glanced once more at Hannah's exquisite form and decided that one source of intoxication was enough.

"I don't drink alcohol, Hannah," he called to her. "I'm going to take a soft drink from the minibar."

"Help yourself. I'm coming right out as soon as I rinse my hair."

Sam grabbed a bottled Diet Coke, but the opener was missing from the end of the chain. He looked on top of the fridge, then inside it, with no luck. He opened a dresser drawer. There was no bottle opener, but the other contents were startling: alongside the usual Gideon Bible, there was a Glock 9mm pistol, a security badge issued by the Israeli Defense Ministry, four passports with Hannah's picture but different names and nationalities, and a thick stack of new $100 bills—maybe $20,000 in all. The enchanting young lady in the shower stall was clearly no ordinary airline stewardess. Sam felt his heart pounding in his chest.

He picked up his bag, moved toward the door, and gently turned the handle, careful to make no noise that could be heard over the shower. He ran to the end of the hallway and entered the stairwell. He knew he could not exit the hotel via the ground floor. If Hannah had been laying a honey-trap for him, she would surely have colleagues watching the lobby. He scrambled all the way down to the underground parking garage.

Just as he emerged from the stairs, he spotted a well-dressed middle-aged woman sliding in behind the wheel of her Mercedes.

"Excuse me, madam," he said, limping toward the car. "I've just twisted my ankle rather badly. Can you give me a ride up to the street level so I can take a taxi?"

She shot Sam a disdainful look. "Take the elevator," she snapped, then closed and locked her doors. The Mercedes backed abruptly out of its parking space and sped away.

"Fuck you, lady," Sam muttered to himself.

"Excuse me."

He turned to see a young woman at the wheel of a white Miata convertible.

"I can give you a lift if you like. I was just leaving. Hop in."

"Oh, thank you," said Sam. He settled into the bucket seat and closed the door. "Would you mind putting up the top?"

"Don't want anybody to see you with me? I understand." She looked over at him and winked. Sam found her quite attractive, with her long black hair and slinky top, even if she was wearing perhaps a tad too much makeup.

She closed the roof and started the engine. The Miata emerged from the garage at a rapid clip, followed a winding road for a hundred yards or so, then turned onto Ramisstrasse and headed toward the lakefront.

"Where are you taking me?"

"You wanted a taxi, right? Just trust me."

The powerful sports car sped across a four-lane bridge and headed toward Burkiplatz Square at the end of Bahnhofstrasse. On the far side of the traffic circle, the Miata screeched to a halt behind a lone taxi.

"You're in luck," said the woman with a cheery smile. "I could have taken you to the train station, but you would have had to wait in line."

"Thank you," said Sam. "You're very kind."

"Don't mention it. Take care of your ankle."

Sam opened the rear door of the taxi and slid into the back seat.

"Where to, buddy?" said the driver.

"Out of town. Anywhere." Sam struggled to catch his breath. "How did you know I spoke English?"

"The way you're dressed. Your haircut. You could only be American. I used to live in New York. Drove a cab in Brooklyn."

The man's accent was pure Flatbush Avenue, without the slightest trace of foreign inflection.

"You're American?" Sam asked.

"No, I'm German. My parents moved to America just before the war. I was born in Brooklyn, have an American passport. But I moved back here in the seventies, married a Swiss girl. Bought a little house just outside of Zurich. It's nice here."

The taxi turned onto the Mythen Quai, and proceeded south along the Seestrasse on the western shore of the lake.

"Running from someone?" said the driver, catching Sam's worried eyes in the mirror.

Sam nodded. "My girlfriend's husband."

The driver smiled. "I thought it might be something like that. It's always the women that get us in trouble, you know what I mean?"

Sam did not reply. He looked out the window at the passing chalets, with their wooden balconies and painted shutters and window boxes full of geraniums. Such a peaceful little country, he thought. And it had managed to stay that way, through two world wars, by not choosing sides.

"If you like, I can take you somewhere he can't find you," said the driver. "I got an empty apartment in a village twenty kilometers from here. For 150 francs, you can stay there tonight. Fact, you can stay there long as you want. I can give it to you for five hundred a week."

Sam considered the offer. It could be a trap. But on the other hand, he had to hide somewhere quickly. He assumed Hannah's confederates would be watching the train station, the airport, perhaps the main hotels. His escape routes were severely limited. He couldn't just stand on the roadside and hitchhike back to France. He decided to take the chance.

"Okay" he said. "But I don't have any Swiss money."

"There's an ATM up the road. You can get cash there."

"Take me there."

Five minutes later, the taxi pulled to the side of the road and stopped.

"The ATM is just in front of that pharmacy. There is also a dispenser of condoms if you like."

"No condoms, thanks," said Sam. "I don't think I'll be needing them for a while."

The driver laughed. "Yeah, I guess it's better to leave it in your pants. I'll wait for you here."

Sam drew five hundred francs from the machine with his Visa card and stuffed the receipt in his pants pocket.

The car continued along the same road for twenty minutes or so, then took a right turn at a small intersection and headed up a winding hillside road. From the increasingly higher altitude, Sam could see the vast expanse of the lake and the forested hills on the far shore.

"Where is this village?" Sam asked. "Seems like a long way."

"Just up the road. You'll have lots of peace and quiet up there."

The taxi came around a final turn and entered a flat stretch of road. One hundred yards further, alongside a fast-moving stream, they came upon a few chalets and farmhouses. The car pulled off the road and stopped.

"The apartment is in that first chalet on the left, on the ground floor," said the driver. "Belongs to my wife's family. We rent it out during the ski season, but it's hardly used in the summer."

The driver got out and opened Sam's door. He was not a tall man, but beefy and thick-necked like a wrestler. He led the American to the chalet and opened the door with his key.

"It's just a simple place, as you can see, but I think you'll find it comfortable. There's a fridge, toilet, shower, hotplate. The couch pulls out into a double bed. It's already made up with fresh sheets."

Sam looked around the spare but clean room "Fine. This will do. What is the name of this village?"

"Ort, just a little hamlet. The closest real town is Horgen, the place where we turned at the bottom of the hill. When you're ready to return to Zurich, or wherever you're going, give me a call. Here's my card. The key's on the hook there."

"Thank you. You've been very helpful. Good night."

"That will be two hundred francs, in advance."

"You said 150."

"That's for the room. There's also a fifty-franc deposit for water and electricity. I'll check the meter when you leave."

"Whatever." Sam peeled off two 100-franc notes and handed them to the man.

"Then there's the fifty francs for the taxi fare."

Sam pressed another note into the man's hand.

"Thanks, buddy. Oh, one other thing."

"Yes?"

The man handed Sam a crumpled piece of paper.

"This fell out of your pocket by the car. You should hold onto it, or destroy it. You can be traced with an ATM receipt, you know. You wouldn't want your girlfriend's husband to track you down."

Sam looked at the printed paper, which contained his credit card number, date and place, and withdrawal amount.

"Thanks," he said, and tore the receipt into small pieces. He watched the taxi drive off, then closed the door. He looked at the name on the business card: Klaus Rosen.

Sam lay down on the couch and dozed for a few minutes. He was awakened by his cell phone. Dumond's name flashed on his screen—his was the only number Sam had entered into the new phone's memory.

"Where the hell have you been, man?"

"I'm still you-know-where." Sam could hear the hollow fatigue in his own voice. "I'll be back tomorrow."

"Don't come back to France whatever you do."

"Why?"

"They're looking for you."

"Who?"

"Everybody—the *police judiciaire*, the C.I.A., the D.S.T. You are a suspect in the Ganjibar killing. There's an Interpol warrant out for your arrest."

"How do you know?"

"Sam, I've told you before, I have good contacts with the French services. I can't explain it on the phone. I'm just warning you not to come back here."

"This is ridiculous. I'm an accredited correspondent. There's nothing to link me to the Ganjibar murder."

"Wake up and smell the coffee, man! People in power can link anybody to anything they want—you should know that. Wherever you are —and don't say it on the phone—you should sit tight and wait for this to blow over."

"I can't do that."

"Why?"

"Because I have to get this story out. It's too important."

"Sam, I am warning you to lie low. Don't try to be a hero. And watch out for Hannah, she's a Mossad agent. The first time I had dinner with her in Tel Aviv, her colleagues snuck into my hotel room and copied my hard drive. That's how they knew we were onto the arms sales."

"Now you tell me."

"I just found it out myself. Do you think I would be shagging her if I knew that? She's a killer, Sam, a hired gun."

"Then why did you give her my key?"

"What key? What are you talking about?"

"You didn't give her the key before you went to London?"

"I never went to London, Sam."

In Sam's racing, feverish mind, Hannah's game plan suddenly seemed clear. She must have pinched the key out of his pocket while he slept. Her people obviously knew about Ganjibar's file. They must have been watching Rappola when he met Sam at the Louvre. Either that or Rappola was working with them. But the safe deposit box was in Sam's name, so they needed him to retrieve the file. Hannah's role was to lure him into her bed and kill him, or drug him, and snatch the envelope. Sam thought with a pang of her exquisite body in the shower, those perfect brown-tipped breasts. Jesus, that was close!

"Do me a favor, Charles," Sam said. "Call Sandra and tell her I'm okay, tell her I love her. Her cell phone is 0600859384. If I call, they're likely to trace it. They've probably got her number under surveillance."

"Okay. But you better remove the battery from your own phone. Otherwise they can trace you even if you're not on line."

"I didn't know that."

"And Sam . . ."

"What?"

"Don't blame me for all this. Remember, you said you were in."

CHAPTER

45

SAM POPPED THE BATTERY out of his phone, then drank a glass of water from the kitchenette tap. He felt a numbing fatigue coming on, but he knew he could not sit tight. Klaus Rosen—or Hannah or God knows who else—was liable to come back and kill him. Maybe Mossad or the C.I.A. had traced the call he'd just received. He could not stay there with those explosive files in his bag.

It was just after six when he squeezed out of a back window. He jogged across a wet, grassy field until he came to a large barn. He stopped there for a moment to catch his breath and make sure he was not being followed. The coast seemed clear. He continued along a narrow footpath that ran parallel to the gurgling stream. There was still plenty of daylight, so he decided to avoid the main road until he was well out of town. He clutched the shoulder bag tightly against his side and marched along at a rapid clip.

After he had followed the stream for about a mile, moving ever higher up the hillside, Sam joined the road and came upon an isolated restaurant. The place looked open, but the parking lot was empty. He checked his watch. It was 6:30, way too early for most Europeans to think about dinner. Sam didn't dare go inside: he could not chance being noticed in case Rosen or anyone else came looking for him. Instead, he decided to wait in the shadows behind the building, where a row of fir trees provided cover.

Sam had not been out of the chalet more than ten minutes when Klaus Rosen's taxi came to a halt in front of the building. A metallic gray SUV with tinted windows pulled up and parked just behind it. Four men climbed out of the second vehicle as Rosen approached the door and knocked sharply. There was no answer.

The others looked silently at Rosen. The taxi driver pulled a key ring from his pocket and opened the door. The four men rushed inside with automatic pistols drawn, each one holding his weapon out in front of him with a double-handed combat grip. They fanned out to the four corners of the apartment, kicked open the door to the WC and the shower. The place was empty.

"Where is he, Klaus?" asked the commando leader.

"I don't understand, Micah," said the taxi driver. "I left him here a half-hour ago."

"Who handled the surveillance?"

"We had a video camera on the front door," said one of the other men, "and infrared sensors tracking the movement inside. Our monitors indicated no exit from the safe house."

"Who wired the place?"

"We had a technical team in here overnight just before the American arrived in Zurich."

"Was the system verified?"

"Everything seemed to work fine, but they didn't have time for thorough testing. It was a rush job, you know."

"Great!" fumed Micah. "All that fucking technology just waiting to go on the fritz. Meanwhile, the guy calmly waltzes out the back window. Look, the screen is still open."

Micah turned toward Rosen. "And you—why didn't you stay here and stake out the place with your own eyeballs?"

"For that matter," said another commando member, "why didn't you just break his neck and snatch the bag once you got him here?"

"I'm not a professional operative, Lev. I'm a taxi driver and a part-time informant, okay? My assignment was to get him to the safe house, period. If you wanted to put the moves on him, you should have had one of your own agents on the case."

"We were overextended," sighed Micah. "Our people were staking out the hotel, the Bahnhof, the airport. You were only part of the third-string backup."

"Look, Micah, I did what I had to do. I got the guy in here and I notified your people."

"Rosen's right," said Lev. "It's not his fault. I don't understand why our surveillance team didn't just grab the guy's bag when they saw him leave the bank. It was too complicated to lure him to the hotel."

Micah shook his head. "It was too dangerous to try that on a public street in broad daylight. If the snatcher had been caught by the cops, the whole operation would have been compromised—plus the bag would have wound up in the hands of the Swiss. Hannah said it was safer, more discreet, to honey-trap him."

"Bullshit!" said Lev. "I think she just wanted to fuck the guy."

"You're wrong," said Micah. "Hannah's frigid. She gets absolutely no pleasure from sex. Whenever she screws someone, it's like punching a clock at the factory gate."

"What a waste!"

"I wouldn't be jealous if I were you, my friend," said Micah. "Half the guys she fucks wind up dead."

"Why she didn't just pop him in the hotel room?"

"Fire a Glock 9mm in a five-star Swiss hotel? The police would have been all over her in two seconds. Besides, her team had the lobby staked."

"So how did he slip out?"

"I don't know—maybe the parking garage."

"Why wasn't that watched, too? Who made this meshuggenah plan?"

Micah shrugged. "Hannah was the squad leader. They'll surely be asking her about that in Tel Aviv. Headquarters just called her back for debriefing. I think she's in deep shit."

"Come on, we're wasting time," said Lev. "We have to find this bastard now and take him out. He can't have gotten far on foot."

"Right," said Micah. "Let's comb the whole area."

At 7:40, a Vauxhall squareback drove into the restaurant parking lot pulling a vintage aluminum caravan with GB plates. A man and woman in their mid-sixties got out of the car and headed into the restaurant. Other cars began to arrive, but Sam kept his hopes pinned on the Brits. Every car that drove past the restaurant or entered the parking lot sent a heart-pumping shot of adrenaline coursing through his veins. The wait seemed endless.

At 8:10, a white Mercedes taxi pulled up in front of the restaurant, followed by a gray SUV. Sam was horrified to see Klaus Rosen get out of the taxi and go inside. He could hear the blood whooshing through his temples as he crouched down low behind the trees and prayed that Rosen and his friends would not search the grounds. Two minutes later, Rosen exited the establishment and shook his head in the direction of the SUV. He got back into his taxi, started the engine, and drove off rapidly, followed by the other vehicle. Sam clutched his bag and listened to his own rapid breathing.

It was nearly dark when the couple emerged at nine o'clock. They walked slowly toward their car. The woman was chatting with that inimitable English earnestness about how cool the night air got up in the hills.

"T'is, actually," replied her husband.

Sam stepped forward and smiled amiably. "Excuse me, sir," he said. "Are you headed back to England by any chance?"

The man looked at his wife, then back at this tall Yank who seemed to come out of nowhere. "Why do you ask?"

"Well, you see, I've been hiking across Switzerland on holiday, but I just now got word on my cell phone that my mother-in-law has taken ill back in London. I've got to dash back there. I was hoping I could perhaps get a ride with you. I'll pay for the petrol."

The man was about to speak when his wife cut in. "Your mother-in-law is English? What's she got, the poor dear?"

"She gets these terrible asthma attacks, ma'am," said Sam. "On top of her emphysema. It gets so bad that they have to hospitalize her and put her under an oxygen tent. My wife—she's English, too, of course—my wife says they're not sure she'll pull through this time because the old girl also has a chest infection, maybe even pneumonia. Sounds pretty bad. That's why I have to get back as soon as possible."

"Well, we *are* headed home," said the woman. "Dear, don't you think we could take this nice gentleman back to England with us?"

The man studied Sam silently. "You say you've been trekking across Switzerland in those shoes? With no gear?"

"I left my gear with some friends," said Sam. "I thought it would be easier to hitchhike with just the clothes on my back."

"Rubbish!" said the man. "Come on, Norma, hop in the car. This chap's a con man or a car thief."

"Oh, dear," said the woman.

As soon as he heard the doors slam and the engine start, Sam made his move. He stepped up on the rear ladder of the caravan and grabbed hold of an unused bicycle rack with both hands. The driver exited the parking lot and headed west along the climbing, winding road. As Sam had hoped, the frequent turns prevented the car from building up any great speed, so he was able to hold on without too much difficulty.

Some twenty minutes later, Sam jumped down from his precarious perch when the car stopped briefly at a crossroads near the entrance to a village. A road sign identified the place as Rosseau. It was 9:30 now, and night had fallen. He could see the lights of a hotel-restaurant on the right side of the road, just one hundred yards further down.

CHAPTER

46

S AM TOOK A TABLE at the Kleine Gasthof and ordered a bowl of oxtail soup. He reckoned he was now some twenty kilometers west of Rosen's chalet. It was ten o'clock now; most of the other diners had finished their meals and left.

When the young blonde waitress returned with his soup, Sam noticed that she was looking at him rather strangely. He must be a sight, he thought. He was all dusty, his hair was a mess, his shirt, even in the cool of the evening, was damp with sweat.

"Are you all right, sir?" she said in English.

"I'm fine. Why?"

"It's just that you are very pale. You are sweating and shaking. Perhaps you have a fever? Would you like an aspirin?"

"No thanks," Sam said, and drew a deep breath. "I just need to sleep."

"We have rooms here if you like."

"How much?" Sam asked, trying to calculate how much Swiss money he had left.

"It's eighty francs, breakfast included."

"Okay."

"Very good, sir. Room two on the second floor. The key is on the door."

"Thank you."

Sam quickly ate his soup, along with two rolls and butter, and ordered a cup of decaf coffee. When he had finished, he picked up his shoulder bag and headed for the stairs. "If you don't mind," he said, handing the woman four 20-franc notes, "I'll pay in advance. I'd rather not sign the book. I don't want anyone to know I'm here."

"Not a problem, sir." She put the bills in the cash register and smiled sweetly at the American. "We Swiss are famous for our discretion—and neutrality. Enjoy your sleep."

The room was modest—just a simple pine bed and table, a couple of wooden chairs—but it was neat as only Swiss hotel rooms can be. There was a sink with a mirror, but the toilet and shower were outside on the landing. The single window looked out on the main road. Sam drew the curtains and bolted the door.

He went to the sink, threw some cold water on his face, and checked himself out in the mirror. He looked a mess: white as a sheet, dark circles under his eyes, his chin covered with stubble. He wanted to brush his teeth, but he had not planned to stay in Zurich overnight and did not bring his kit—or deodorant, which was starting to be a problem.

Sam stretched out on the bed, stared at the freshly painted ceiling, and quickly dozed off. His sleep was troubled by the noise of passing cars, by strange creaking sounds on the stairway, and by his own feverish dreams. He was running down a country road, alongside a stream, across a field, and finally into a thick forest. He was fleeing from something, but did not know what. He was gripped with fear, but the faster he tried to run, the more some mysterious force seemed to hold him back like tangled vines clutching his thighs. He suddenly came upon a clearing. There was a church in the middle, with a tall, sharp-pointed steeple, and bells tolling jubilantly, as if to herald a wedding. He pushed the heavy double doors and proceeded down the center aisle. On the left side, the congregants were all waving Bibles and singing a cacophony of different hymns. On the right side, Muslim men in turbans and white linen robes were ululating and striking themselves in the face with Korans until they bled. In the front of the church, Princess Tawana was leading the rapturous singing of those on the left side; Osama bin Laden, his graying beard reaching all the way to the ground, was cracking a whip and directing the self-mortification of those on the right. Sam suddenly realized that he himself was completely nude. As he walked down the center aisle, the congregants on both sides bowed down to him, then continued their frenzied devotions. When Sam approached the sanctuary, he saw a bed at the foot of the altar. It had fine silk sheets of purple and scarlet. Behind the altar, dressed like a bishop in red robes with a blue stole and gleaming white miter, stood the smiling president of the United States, Jack Ritter. Rafat Ganjibar was at his side, also in priestly garb. Ganjibar was licking his pouty lips and sprinkling holy water on the bed, where a nude woman lay on her back with her legs spread wide and her sex, totally devoid of pubic hair, gaping like an open wound. She wore a pearl necklace, golden rings and bracelets, and clutched a gold cup in her left hand. A purple veil covered her face. The singing and ululating got louder and louder as Sam mounted the steps to the sanctuary. Ritter and Ganjibar smiled at him and held up their arms in blessing as he climbed upon the bed and prepared to deflower the one who, he now understood, was destined to be his bride. Just as Sam prepared to couple with the throbbing red gash, Ritter leaned down and lifted the woman's veil. Leering hideously at him, with painted scarlet lips, long black eyelashes, and a thick layer of white, unctuous makeup on her face, was Hannah Avner.

CHAPTER

47

JACK RITTER'S 150-ACRE RANCH in Loco Lobo, New Mexico, was a perfect reflection of the man: simple, virile, earthy. It boasted one hundred head of cattle, whitewashed stables, a fifty-foot well with a windmill pump, and a log-bordered sandbox for pitching horseshoes—a favorite presidential sport. There was also a swimming pool, tennis court, and indoor gym—his wife had insisted on those amenities—but Ritter preferred to spend his time like a real cowboy, riding his horse Trigger, mending fences, and clearing brush. His adopted Western ways contrasted sharply with the Boston Brahmin style of Quentin Ritter, but the old man had long since stopped looking for any similarities between himself and his son.

Since Jack Ritter's election, the ranch served as a Western White House, the place to which he frequently repaired when he wanted to get away from all those "Washington insiders" and recharge his batteries in God's own country. Thanks to modern communications, and a small army of staffers who followed him everywhere, he was able to work here as easily as he did in the Oval Office.

On this Wednesday morning, dressed in snakeskin boots, faded jeans, and a plaid shirt with mother-of-pearl snaps, he sat on a cowhide-covered couch in front of a crackling fire. As he did in the White House, Ritter always kept a fire going here in his den, confined behind a thermal screen so that it didn't compete too much with the air-conditioning system that ran day and night in the summer months. The fireplace, with its rough-hewn wooden mantelpiece topped by a mounted pair of steer horns, was in fact the vital nucleus of the presidential ranch. It was here that Jack Ritter received his visitors and transacted most of his business.

When he arrived for the 10 a.m. intelligence briefing, accompanied by the vice president, Trenton McBride took a seat near the fireplace and immediately regretted it. In spite of the thermal screen, he could feel heat coming from the crackling logs. And he didn't like feeling heat.

It did not help matters that McBride wore a business suit. Cordman, who had his own ranch in Montana, was dressed like the president in jeans, boots, and a plaid shirt. But even Ritter had to admit that this former corporate executive, with his bulging midriff and comb-over white hair, looked somewhat ridiculous in a cowboy costume.

"Trent," said the president, "Bill here tells me there's some problems on the Armageddon Project."

McBride stroked his goatee and tried, as far as possible, to lean away from the fireplace. "Mr. President, I'll start with the Ganjibar issue. I wanted to shield you from the details, but now there's a little snag so you need to know what's happening."

"What's up?"

"As you know, Ganjibar, his driver, and bodyguard were killed by a suicide bomber on Monday."

"I know that. Some Mohammedan kid. I assume he's got no connection to us?"

"Not directly. But the person who assigned this, uh, task to him, and provided the explosive belt, does, in fact, have a relationship with us."

"We have relations with suicide-bomb folks?"

"Sir, we have relations with lots of people that neither you nor I would want to sit next to at dinner. That's the nature of intelligence work."

Ritter shook his head disapprovingly. "Okay, go on."

"Let me explain the background, Mr. President. The guy who arranged this thing, the guru, so to speak, is a twenty-four-year-old French national of Algerian origin named Walid Karouche. He grew up in a very pious Salafist family."

"What the hell is that?"

"The Salafists, sir, are the most radical fundamentalists among the Muslims. They are the purest of the pure. They take literally every word in the Koran, abhor the modern world, and shun all those, including moderate Muslims, who do not share their views. They want to live as people lived when the Prophet walked the earth."

"How can people be so backward?" said Ritter. "Don't these folks know the world has moved on since the olden days? This is the age of globalization, satellite TV, the Internet."

"Oh, they know all about satellite TV and the Internet, sir. Those are among their most powerful tools."

"In other words, they curse the very tools they're usin' against us."

"That is correct, Mr. President. In this case, as I say, Walid Karouche was steeped in Salafism from an early age. His brother-in-law was a Salafist imam who was actually expelled from France for his radical preaching. Walid was following in his footsteps. He attended an Islamic school in Damascus, Abu Nahir, where he perfected his skills in Arabic, Koranic studies—and guerrilla warfare."

"In a religious school?"

"Not actually in the school, sir, but under the tutelage of militant Islamic radicals who have infiltrated it and recruit jihadists among its students."

"I get it. Kinda like an R.O.T.C. for the bad guys."

"Something like that, Mr. President. Anyway, Walid Karouche was one of the most brilliant and talented of the young jihadis and was eventually selected to lead a handful of new recruits over the Syrian border into Iraq. From there, they were taken under the wing of Iraqi insurgent leaders. But Karouche was captured by our forces early last year, shortly after entering Iraq, and was imprisoned at Abu Ghraib."

"Abu Ghraib, huh?" said Ritter. "Was he one of the folks who were, uh, mishandled by the grunts over there?"

"No, Mr. President. Karouche was immediately recognized as a potential asset because of his prestige and influence with the Salafists back in France. He was separated from the other prisoners and given a special treatment by our elite trainers. They subjected him to an intensive process of indoctrination, alternate application of pain and rewards, and some unorthodox methods including hypnosis, psychotropic drugs, and, especially, the attentions of some lovely young ladies. In the end, his twenty-four-year-old hormones overcame his religious convictions, and he was turned."

"Turned?"

"He joined our side, Mr. President. He became a valuable sleeper—and was very well paid for it, I might add. We exfiltrated him back through Syria to Paris. There, he started to recruit for the Iraqi resistance, but he kept us informed of exactly who he was sending into Iraq, when and where. We have been able to track them thanks to microchips bound in the pocket Korans that Karouche gave them as going-away presents. And they, in turn, have led us to resistance elements that we have been able to neutralize. One of Karouche's recruits, in fact, unwittingly led us to the entourage of the Al-Qaeda terrorist, Abu Musab Al-Zarqawi. He was one of several sources that enabled us to pinpoint Zarqawi in Baqouba."

"And we nailed his ass with a 500-pound bomb," said Ritter with a broad grin. "Maybe this Karouche guy will lead us to bin Laden next time. That boy sounds like one hell of an asset."

Cordman glared at McBride with his half-sneer. "Go on, Trent. Now tell the president the rest of the story."

McBride clutched the armrests of his chair and slid it a couple of inches away from the fireplace. "Well, Mr. President, you know the old story about the best-laid plans going awry. We decided to use Karouche to recruit a kid for the Ganjibar job."

"I warned you against that, Trent. He was too valuable an asset."

"In hindsight, Bill," McBride growled, "I'd have to say you were right. You're always brilliant in hindsight. This looked like a good plan, and all the senior people at Langley signed off on it."

"Okay, okay, boys, let's move on," said Ritter. "So what's the problem, Trent?"

"The problem, Jack," Cordman jumped in, "is that thanks to a very bad decision on the director's part, we have lost one of our most valuable moles in Western Europe."

Ritter's gaze turned from Cordman to McBride.

"Mr. President," said McBride, "I'll get right to the point. One of France's top investigative magistrates, Judge Bouvard, has traced the link between the bomber and Karouche. He brought Karouche in for questioning. With help from the French D.S.T. and D.G.S.E., he established that Karouche had not escaped from Abu Ghraib, as his cover story had it, but had in fact been released by us and remained in contact with the agency. In short, he has identified Karouche as one of our assets. Our station chief at the Paris embassy, Jason Winthrop, has been declared persona non grata and the French foreign minister has called our ambassador in for an explanation. So we have a big diplomatic crisis on our hands."

"Well that's just great, Trent. Nice work! Carnac's been raggin' me ever since we went into Iraq. Now you hand him a hot poker to ram up my ass."

Ritter closed his eyes and pinched the bridge of his nose. He took a deep breath and let it out slowly. "So what do you propose we do about this little flap?"

"We'll do what we always do in such cases, Mr. President," said McBride. "We'll deny any knowledge of Karouche and his activities. In espionage, as in adultery, the cardinal rule is: admit nothing."

Ritter shook his head and toyed with his wedding ring. "Well at least we got Ganjibar out of the way, so we can move ahead with the project."

"Wait, Jack, there's more," said Cordman. "Tell the president about your little friend in London, Trent."

McBride ran a hand through his graying sandy hair. "It's about the new guy, George Shaheen. He was approved by the Assyrian ruling council the day after Ganjibar was killed."

"Good."

"Bad, Jack," said Cordman. "He's fucking us over."

"Now I wouldn't put it quite that way, Bill," said McBride. "Let's just say he wants to be his own man."

"He's fucking us, Trent," Cordman fumed, and turned to the president. "Jack, this ungrateful son of a bitch is telling our people he wants us to pull out of the Assyrian territory—arms, personnel, equipment.

He wants to negotiate an agreement with the other Iraqi parties that would make the region semiautonomous and guarantee its religious freedom within a federal arrangement. In other words, no independent republic, no U.S. bases, and no American control of the oil reserves."

"How the hell does he think he's gonna pump the oil without our technology and equipment?" Ritter demanded.

"The French could do it, the Dutch, the Brits," said McBride. "He wants to open the whole thing to competitive bidding."

"That's outrageous!" Cordman snapped. "We've already given the contract to Bullington. They've made a huge investment there. We can't go back on our word."

"Pipe down, Bill," said Ritter. "What about the oil revenues?"

"Instead of fighting a civil war over it," McBride explained, "he's talking about negotiating a revenue-sharing agreement with the other Iraqi regions in exchange for their recognizing Assyria's administrative autonomy. He calls it an 'oil for peace' initiative."

"That's the most preposterous thing I've ever heard of," Cordman shouted.

"Bill, will you calm down?" said the president. "You're gonna have another damn heart attack."

"I'm sorry, Jack," said Cordman, gulping down a glass of water, "but oil is something I take very seriously. Our whole energy future depends on it. This is too important to leave in the hands of some camel jockey over there in London."

"Let me get this straight, Trent," said Ritter. "He wants all our men, our equipment, and our oil rigs out, right?"

"That's correct, Mr. President."

"What about the nucular weapons?"

"He doesn't know about the nukes."

"Did Ganjibar know about 'em?"

"Of course not," Cordman interrupted. "We kept our deployment plans top secret. But Ganjibar knew a hell of a lot about the rest of the project. If his file leaks out in the press, there'll be hell to pay."

"What file?"

Cordman again sneered in McBride's direction.

The director coughed, blew his nose loudly into a handkerchief, then stuffed it back in his pocket. "Mr. President, we knew from our electronic surveillance that Ganjibar intended to leave a file for the journalist Sam Preston documenting the details of the project. He said he was going to keep it in his lawyer's office safe. But when our team went in there, the safe was empty."

"And where's Preston now?"

"Mr. President, I'm sorry to say, we, uh, lost him."

"You lost him?"

"He moved out of his house after we rattled his chain. He was staying with Dumond, his French reporter friend. But now he's left there. We had been tracking him through his cell phone, but he has apparently changed phones."

"I don't believe this, Trent. You're tellin' me you have no idea where he is? We give you $50 billion a year and you can't even track some weasely hack from the *New York Chronicle*? No wonder you can't catch bin Laden."

"Actually, we know Preston went to Zurich yesterday. He might still be in Switzerland. Mossad is looking for him there."

"What's Mossad want him for?"

"Mr. President, if Preston indeed has his hands on that file and publishes its contents, the political fallout would be at least as devastating to the Israeli government as it would to ours."

"I don't get it."

"Think about it, Mr. President. The Israelis are heavily implicated, along with us, in a secret operation to arm, train, and finance a breakaway Christian movement that has been battling several Islamic factions on the territory of a Muslim country."

"So what's wrong with fighting the Islamists? That's what the war on terror is all about. It's normal for the Israelis to help us fight terrorists. That's why we gave them a green light to go into Lebanon and hit Hezbollah."

"The timing is terrible for them, Mr. President," McBride continued. "They're currently involved in top-secret talks with Hamas to obtain recognition of Israel in exchange for a Palestinian state. This could be the last best chance for peace."

"Hold it, hold it! I thought Hamas was the folks who swore to destroy Israel."

McBride took a deep breath. "It's a Nixon-in-China thing, sir. The thinking is that only the real radicals have the street creds to make peace with Israel. But if the details of the Armageddon Project leak at this point, that's the end of the secret talks. Then they could be in for another fifty years of turmoil and bloodshed. No one in Israel wants that. The Israelis have voted for a moderate government that could guarantee peace and security. Are you following me, Mr. President?"

"Pretty much," said Ritter. "But what's the bottom line here?"

"The bottom line is that the Israeli national interest would be gravely threatened by any Armageddon revelations. And that's why they're after Preston."

"They tryin' to kill him?"

"They may be."

"Should we let 'em do it?"

"There's not much we could do to stop them at this point, Jack," said Cordman. "They're still pissed at us for terminating Ganjibar. Our leverage with them on this issue isn't great. Oh, and by the way, the French are looking for Preston, too. They think he was somehow involved in the Ganjibar hit, that he was one of our agents."

"Was he?"

"Of course not!"

"Well, you know what I think?" said Ritter, absently stroking his chin. "With the Frogs and the Israelis on our ass over this Ganjibar business, we oughta lie low and let Mossad handle this guy. It might solve a problem for all of us if they took him out."

Cordman nodded.

"Bad idea, Mr. President," said McBride. "If we knowingly allow foreign intelligence services—even allied ones—to kill American journalists, where does it stop? What's to prevent them from taking out our military attachés and field agents? We have to draw the line."

"Let the Israelis deal with this, Trent," said Ritter. "After all, we're not our brother's keepers. If that story gets out, we're all in deep shit."

"Even if the Israelis do take care of Preston," said Cordman, with a murderous glance at the director, "that would still leave another problem."

"What's that?" said McBride.

"You, Trent. Don't you think you've done enough damage for one tour of duty?"

"I serve at the pleasure of the president, Bill," McBride snapped. "And if you knew how much information I have on your sweetheart financial deals with Bullington, not to mention your role in compromising my field agents, you would shut your goddamn trap."

"I'm not afraid of you, McBride," Cordman shot back. "You're all fluff and bluff. It's time we got someone with a little backbone to run the agency." Cordman turned to Ritter. "Well, Jack, what's your pleasure?"

The president shifted his eyes back and forth between Cordman and McBride. "I hate to tell you, Trent, but I think Bill's right. We need a change."

McBride scooped his papers off the varnished pine coffee table and abruptly stood up. "You'll have my letter in the morning, Mr. President. As for you, Bill, I'm afraid you're going to regret this."

CHAPTER
48

SAM TOSSED AND TURNED half the night. He didn't fall into a deep sleep until nearly 6 a.m. When he awoke it was nearly noon on Wednesday. The room was stifling and he was soaked with sweat. He also had a throbbing headache and, perhaps, the beginning of a fever. He revived somewhat after a cold shower, and proceeded to wash his shirt in the sink. He pressed it in a towel and put it on wet. In this heat, it would dry quickly.

He went downstairs and ordered a black coffee from the young woman behind the counter.

"How did you sleep?" she asked.

"Not great. I have a headache. Would you have an aspirin?"

"Sure. Tablet or effervescent?"

"Tablet."

She handed him a foil-wrapped packet, then watched him tear it open and swallow the contents, followed by a sip of hot coffee.

"If you want to shave," she said, "there's a pharmacy in the village. You can buy some disposable razors and shaving cream."

He touched his cheek with the back of his hand. His face felt like sandpaper.

"Good idea."

"And your shirt, perhaps you'll want to touch it up with an iron? I can lend you one."

"Thank you." Sam appreciated the young woman's helpfulness, but he was beginning to wonder if she was showing lapses in the legendary Swiss discretion. After all, it was his business if he wanted to look like a slob. But that, of course rubbed up against the Swiss obsession with neatness. Complicated people, these Swiss.

When he returned from the pharmacy, Sam asked if he could use the phone. He needed to make an urgent call but did not dare use his cell phone.

"Of course, sir. Right at the bottom of the stairway. But you'll need a phone card. I can sell you one if you like. The minimum is ten francs."

"Thanks. Can you put it on my bill?"

"No problem."

Sam stepped into the stairwell, pushed his card into the slot, and dialed a number that he had written in his wallet. After four or five rings, a sleepy male voice answered.

"Allo."

"Nigel, it's Sam."

"Sam. How ya goin', mate? I was just tryin' to get a little kip after lunch."

"Sorry to wake you, Nigel, but this is urgent. Are you in Switzerland?"

"Yeh. I'm at a place called Arth, on the Zuger lake. I just got here this morning. Glennys is back in England."

"You went on holiday alone?"

"Yeh. See, just as we were about to leave on Monday morning, Sophie's husband called us and said she'd gone into labor a month early. They were just about to wheel her into the operating room for a cesarean—some kind of complications, you know. Glennys said we had to be there—first grandchild and all that—but I said no blinkin' way."

"Your daughter was having a cesarean and you left anyway?"

"Bloody hell, man, I'll lose my last two weeks of holiday if I don't use it up by the end of the month. I don't mind being on my own, actually. There's other campers here—nice blokes. Only trouble is, without Glennys, there's nobody to cook and clean up."

"Nigel, listen to me. This is a matter of life and death, do you understand?"

"That's what Glennys said. I told her, 'Rubbish, everything will turn out fine.' And in actual fact, it did. They just called me this morning. Sophie's fine, kid's fine, strappin' little tyke with operatic lungs. I could even hear him screamin' in the phone. So I told Glennys, I said, 'You see, Glenn, all that fuss for nothin', you coulda come here and caught up to Sophie at the end of next week.' But you know how women are, eh, mate?"

"Nigel, shut up and listen to me. Somebody is looking for me. They're trying to kill me."

"What are you on about? You been readin' too many spy novels or something?"

"Nigel, I am dead serious. I need help and you are the only one I can turn to."

"Well that's real flatterin', you know what I mean, Sam? You don't call us all year, you don't come visit, you don't even send us a bloody Christmas card, and now I'm the only one you can turn to?"

"Listen. I am hiding in a little town thirty kilometers northwest of Zurich. I am going to be tracked down and killed like an animal if you don't pick me up in your camping-car and get me out of here. I have to get to England immediately."

"What? Did I hear you correctly? You want me to cut short my holiday and give you a ride to England? You must be joking, Sam."

"Nigel, I don't have time to argue with you. If you don't do it, not only will you make your sister a widow, but you will prevent the publication of a story that could change the whole world."

"Sounds pretty intriguin', Sam, but what's in it for me?"

"I'll pay for your petrol."

"What else?"

"Whatever you want. Jesus, I don't believe this."

"Tell you what, mate. I'm actually kinda bored here on my own, to tell you the truth. So I'll take you back to England on one condition."

"What's that?"

"There's a huge Wine & Beer World hypermarket in Calais. I'll fill my camping-car with Newcastle Brown Ale and you pay the tab. Deal?"

"Yes, Nigel, anything you want, for Christ sake."

"Right. Where are you?"

"A roadside hotel called the Kleine Gasthof in a village called Rosseau just off the A4. Look it up on a map."

"Don't need a map. I can just punch it into my GPS. But it's gonna take me a while to pack up all my gear. I couldn't make it before, say, three o'clock."

"Just get here as quick as you can."

"You could say thanks, Sam."

"Thank you, Nigel. God bless you. Now get your butt over here."

When Sam hung up, he saw that the woman at the counter was watching him. "Don't forget the iron, sir," she said.

It was nearly 3:30 when Nigel's white whale of a camping-car pulled up in front of the gasthaus. It was piled high with surfboards, rolled-up sails, dune buggies, and dirt bikes. Watching from his first floor window, Sam saw his brother-in-law get out, scratch his bollocks, and head for the door.

Sam scrambled down the stairs, freshly shaven, wearing a neatly pressed shirt, and clutching the precious shoulder bag under his arm.

"Nigel. Let's go."

"Hold your horses, Sammy. I'm just gonna have a cup of java before I get back behind the wheel. We'll be driving half the night—and you know how much I hate that."

While Nigel sat by the window and calmly stirred his coffee, Sam went up to the counter to pay his bill.

"Let's see, sir, the room was paid in advance. You owe me ten francs for the phone card, one franc for the aspirin . . ."

"And put my coffee on his tab, miss," said Nigel, as he dumped a packet of sugar into the steaming cup.

"So, that's fifteen francs altogether."

Sam handed her some coins and nervously pulled at the straps of his bag while he waited for Nigel to finish slurping down his coffee.

"There's one other thing, sir."

"Yes?"

"I forgot to tell you. After you went up to your room last night, a taxi driver from Zurich was in here looking for a tall American with a shoulder bag like yours."

"Did he say why?"

"He said the person he was looking for had left his apartment key in his cab. He wanted to return it."

"Did you tell him I was here?"

"Of course not. You asked me not to. He also asked at another hotel down the road."

"What did he look like?"

"Average height, heavyset, and, well, he looked Jewish to me."

"Thank you."

Sam grabbed Nigel by the shoulder and yanked him up from the table. "C'mon, Nige, we gotta move."

"Bloody hell, man! I haven't finished my coffee."

"Yes you have."

Shortly after leaving the hotel, Nigel turned right onto the A4 motorway and headed north.

"Got everything you need on board," he told Sam, waving grandly around the cabin. "Fridge, hi-fi, DVD player with surround sound, hotplate, microwave, shower, bog. Bloke could spend his whole life in here and never want for anything."

"Uh, Nigel," said Sam, who was strapped into a pivoting seat-pod to the driver's left, "we can't go through France. We'll have to cut through Germany and Belgium, and take the ferry at Ostend."

"You're joking, mate. It's twice as long that way."

"I can't go to France. The police are looking for me in France. In fact there's an all-points Interpol warrant for my arrest, so I can't get caught going across any borders."

"What did you bloody do, Sam, kill someone?"

"No, but I am suspected of it by the French. Whatever you do, don't drive into France. If you do, you can get arrested as an accomplice."

"Oh great! That's just lovely! What about Wine & Beer World in Calais? You promised, Sam. That's the only reason I agreed to pick your sorry carcass up in Rosseau."

"Relax. I'm sure there's a duty free shop on the Ostend ferry."

Nigel shook his head in disgust. "There's no more duty free. They packed that in years ago."

"But they still have shops on the boats. It's cheaper than in the U.K."

"I know those ferries. They don't carry Newcastle Brown."

"Then buy a different ale, for Christ sake."

"They're not the same. It's not fair. It's not fair, Sam. You're not playing straight with me."

They drove on in silence for more than an hour. The muscles in Nigel's clenched jaw were twitching and his lower lip was jutting out. He was not just angry at Sam; he was angry at himself for getting trapped in his brother-in-law's road movie hallucinations. He should have just said no, no fucking way. But he let himself get sweet talked, bent over backward out of the goodness of his heart, reached out to a friend in need, and look at the thanks he got. Not even a case of Newcastle Brown. Change the world, eh? The world could go bugger itself for all he cared.

They were still thirty kilometers from the German border when Sam suddenly remembered that he had not been to his office, or even called in, for the past two days. Damn, he thought, Woodridge is going to be livid. No, not Woodridge, he was off in the South of France working on his tan and guzzling the local wine. Bradley Kemp was running the show in his absence. He could handle Bradley. Bradley was a preening, strutting peacock, but deep down, he was a wimp.

"Nigel, can I use your cell phone?" Sam asked.

Nigel didn't answer.

"Nige, I asked if I could use your cell phone. I have to call my office."

"Use your own. I'm not going to pay for your phone calls on top of everything else."

"I can't use mine. It's liable to be traced. Don't worry, I'll pay you for the call."

Nigel drove on in silence for a moment, then mumbled, "It's on the dashboard."

"Thanks."

Sam picked up the phone. It was the latest model Nokia with built-in still and video cameras, an integrated game system, a TV interface, and wireless Internet access. You could also make calls with it. Sam dialed the office number.

Bradley picked it up on the first ring.

"*New York Chronicle*. Kemp speaking."

"Bradley, this is Sam."

"Sam, where the devil are you? It's like you dropped off the face of the earth. Clive's off on vacation, you've been AWOL since Monday, and I'm here alone fighting alligators. Look what's happened here—your friend Ganjibar is assassinated, Roland Peccaldi dies, Carnac's pulling out of NATO. I've got no help here. I'm going nuts."

"Look, Bradley, I can't explain it all on the phone. I'm in a life-or-death situation. I'm in trouble."

"You bet you're in trouble, Sam. In fact, you're fired."

"What the fuck are you talking about, Bradley?"

"Haven't you heard? There's a big cost-cutting drive back in New York. Heads are rolling all over the place. Considering your erratic behavior recently, terminating you was a no-brainer. Clive barely dodged a bullet himself. They're transferring him to Detroit as soon as he gets back from vacation."

"Who's the new bureau chief?"

"I'm in charge here, Sam. And I'm telling you to get your buns in here and clear out your desk. I have two new guys coming in and I need the office space."

"Bradley, you don't understand. I am sitting on a very big story here. I've got to get it into print fast."

"Not in the *New York Chronicle*. You're history here, Sam."

"Okay, Bradley, okay. I understand. But there's just one more very important thing I have to tell you."

"What's that?"

"You are a contemptible, conniving, self-promoting, ass-licking, shit-eating little prick."

"Sam, have you started drinking again?"

"Go fuck yourself, Bradley. It'll be the biggest thrill you've had all year."

Sam turned off the phone and put it back on the dashboard.

Nigel glanced at him out of the corner of his eye. "You seem to have a very weird relationship with your colleagues."

Sam folded his arms and gazed at the highway that stretched out in front of them. "He's not my colleague."

As they approached the Swiss-German border on the A4 near Hoher-Randen, Nigel told Sam to lie down on a couch in the rear compartment and cover himself with a blanket. "They usually wave us right through Continental borders these days," he said, "but you never know. I have a better hiding place for you when we take the boat."

The German border police watched passively as the camper drove slowly through then picked up speed on the other side.

"See what I told you?" said Nigel. "I don't know what they pay them for. How are we supposed to keep terrorists from coming over and killing us in our beds if these blokes won't even check passports at the border?"

"Aren't you glad they didn't?"

"Yeh, this time. But I'm talking about the principle of the thing, mate. It's like they got their priorities all wrong."

Nigel put a Willie Nelson album on the CD player and Sam promptly fell asleep to the singer's nasal drone. He must have been exhausted, because he slept a long time. Nigel shook him awake at a service station parking lot.

"Rise and shine, mate. Better take a mighty piss, 'cause you're going to be immobilized for quite a while."

Sam was surprised to see it was nighttime. "Where are we?"

"Just outside Ostend. You slept right across the Belgian border. They just waved us through again."

Sam went into the shop and got a coffee from one of the automatic vending machines. In France, the machine-brewed coffee was drinkable but this Belgian stuff was wretched. Sam drank two sips and threw the cup in the trash barrel. He went to the toilet, urinated prodigiously, then splashed some water on his face. Nigel was waiting for him at the cash register.

"Be my guest," he said, handing him the bill for a full tank of diesel fuel—ninety euros. He also put a copy of *Motor World* magazine on the counter. "Get me that too, would you?"

Sam picked up a couple of ham sandwiches as well, which brought the bill to 110 euros. He paid in cash.

The two men strode side by side across the brightly lit parking lot and chewed on their sandwiches. It was late at night now and most of the spaces were empty. Among the few cars that came and went, Sam watched a green Volkswagen Golf with Swiss plates circle the lot, then pull into a slot just opposite the caravan.

Sam pulled Nigel's sleeve. "That green car. I think it followed us from Switzerland."

"Don't be daft, there's a million Swiss cars goin' all over Europe. Nobody's following you. Look, there's two blokes got out. They're not paying the slightest attention to us. They're just going in to take a dump or something."

Nigel started the engine and backed out of his space. The men had still not returned to the green car when the camper drove off in the direction of Ostend.

"See what I mean?" said Nigel. "Those guys are still in there shakin' their willies. Don't get paranoid, Sam. You'll make me nervous."

The camping-car drove into the ferry port parking area just as the last boat, the 11:30 overnight, was sounding its foghorn to signal an imminent departure. Nigel sped toward the ticket window, but the barrier went down and the massive, three-deck ship eased away from the slip and chugged slowly out into the harbor.

"Damn!" said Sam.

"It's your fault, mate," said Nigel. "You took so long over a coffee and a piss back there that you made us miss the bleedin' boat."

"What'll we do?"

"Sleep in the camper and catch the first ferry out tomorrow."

"Where are you going to park?"

"Right here, at the ferry port."

"Not a good idea, Nigel. It's too exposed. And you might get arrested."

"Bollocks, I do it all the time. That's the beauty of owning a camping-car. You can do what you bloody well please. Anyway, I'm the captain of this little ship, and I say we're staying right here."

Nigel gripped two handles under the rear couch and pulled it out into a bunk bed. From a storage box underneath it, he removed a red-and-white plaid sleeping bag and handed it to Sam.

"There you go, mate. Pleasant dreams."

Sam stripped down to his shorts and curled up in the bag. He was asleep in minutes.

CHAPTER
49

ISRAEL'S NEWLY ELECTED PRIME MINISTER, Itzhak Berg, was known as a centrist. But like his more hardline predecessor, like all previous Israeli leaders, in fact, he put his top priority on ensuring the security of his fellow citizens. He knew he had to be especially vigilant on that score since the militant Hamas movement, sworn to destroy the Israeli state, had recently taken power in the Palestinian territories.

Belying early hopes that political power would make the group behave responsibly, Hamas's armed wing soon broke a 16-month cease-fire with a spate of suicide bombings, short-range rocket attacks, and the kidnapping of an Israeli soldier. Upping the ante, Hezbollah, the Lebanese Shiite militia, kidnapped two Israeli soldiers and killed eight in a bold cross-border raid.

Berg responded with air strikes on the Beirut airport and other Lebanese targets believed to house Hezbollah militants and arms. When Hezbollah replied with a murderous barrage of rocket attacks on Haifa, Berg ordered an infantry incursion into Lebanon that sparked international protests and, some feared, would herald a new Israeli occupation. That was not Berg's goal, but he had no intention of allowing Hezbollah to remain on his northern border and continue raining rockets on his people. Armed and financed by Iran, with matériel and logistical support from Syria, Hezbollah represented the fanatical rejection front that was determined to push Israel into the sea.

The sudden flare-up of hostilities, and Hezbollah's unexpected tenacity on the battlefield, convinced Berg of two things: Israel's supposedly "invincible" army could not hope to defeat its opponents by military force alone, therefore he must find an urgent solution to the Israeli-Palestinian conflict that had been raging for more than half a century. "It's now or never," Berg told his closest aides. And so, despite his public refusal to negotiate with Hamas, he seized the occasion to enter into top-secret talks with them. Perhaps a former hawk like Berg and the most militant of the Palestinian factions could accomplish what all others before them had failed to achieve: peaceful coexistence.

What Berg envisioned was no less than a definitive land-for-peace deal that would trade Palestinian statehood for a formal end to hostilities. Once there was an agreement with the Palestinians, Berg reasoned, most of the other Arab states would finally make peace with Israel. And the bitterness that fueled anti-Israeli sentiments on the so-called Arab street would disappear like the foul waters of a dried-up swamp. That was his hope.

But Berg's bold plan was complicated by a covert operation launched under his predecessor. The Prime Minister did not know much about it, but what little he had heard was not at all to his liking. Shortly after the secret talks began, Berg summoned General David Posner to his office for a private briefing.

"What is this Armageddon Project all about, General?"

Posner, chief of staff of the Israeli army, and hierarchical head of the state security services, got up from the cabinet table and walked over to a stand containing maps of the region. He flipped to a map of northwestern Iraq. With a wooden pointer, he indicated an area that was circled in red.

"Prime Minister," he said in clipped, military tones, "this enclave is inhabited mostly by Assyrian Christians. Their main political organization, the Assyrian Liberation Movement, has been demanding autonomy and was preparing to secede from Iraq and declare itself an independent republic."

"You say *was* preparing?"

"Yes, sir. As you know, their leader, Rafat Ganjibar, was assassinated two days ago. His designated successor, George Shaheen, seems to favor administrative autonomy within an Iraqi federation."

"Do we know who killed Ganjibar?"

"Responsibility was claimed by a group calling itself 'the Avenging Scimitar of Allah the Omnipotent.' To the best of our knowledge, though, no such group exists."

"Where did that name come from?"

"It first cropped up in connection with the bombing of an Assyrian church in Paris in June. The French suspect, we think correctly, that Ganjibar himself was behind the blast and that he made up the group's name as a smoke screen. The people who killed Ganjibar then borrowed the same name in order to cover their own tracks. Rather clever of them, in fact."

"Who actually killed him?"

"We think the C.I.A. farmed this out to a French-based terrorist network."

"Why would the Americans do such a thing? Ganjibar was their ally."

"He was also our ally, sir. But Washington lost confidence in him. He was about to declare independence, which the Americans felt was premature and would compromise their project."

"*Their* project?"

"Yes, sir. The Americans have been secretly arming and financing the Assyrians, embedding their own soldiers in the ranks of the Assyrian militia, carrying out extensive infrastructure and oil development in the territory."

"I see. Building an American colony in the Middle East. Apart from the oil, what is their interest in doing this?"

"Threefold, sir. The Ritter administration sees it as a future model of pro-Western democracy in the Middle East, as a major U.S. military base in the region, and as a possible launch pad for preemptive strikes against Iranian nuclear facilities."

"What is our involvement in this project?"

"We have been working closely with the Americans on the military aspects of it—particularly by supplying arms via various international networks, training Assyrian commandos, and sharing targeting data for a possible strike on Iran. If we agree with the Americans on one thing, it is that Iran must never be allowed to become a nuclear power. We estimate they are only three to five years away from building atomic weapons—and they are already testing multiple warhead missiles with enough range to hit us."

Berg frowned. "We do not need the Americans to deal with Iran. If and when we decide to take out the Iranian nuclear sites, we can do it ourselves, just as we did with Iraq's Osirik reactor in 1981."

"It's a much more difficult task, sir. The facilities are deep underground, scattered, some located in heavily populated civilian areas. The Americans have satellite data and technical capabilities that we lack."

"For example?"

"Stealth bombers and laser-guided cruise missiles with tactical nuclear warheads."

"Nuclear weapons? Are they mad?"

"These are high-precision bunker busters with a relatively low radioactive yield. We are not talking about Hiroshima here."

"And I'm not talking about nukes, period. We may have our own deterrent, but I would never use it in a preemptive tactical strike. That's unconscionable. General, I want us to sever our involvement with this project immediately."

"There are political issues to consider, sir. Our pulling out would profoundly displease the Americans."

"That wouldn't be the first time," Berg snorted. "I am prime minister of Israel, not a vassal of the United States."

"I'm not just talking about the administration, sir. I am talking about the religious right, the Evangelicals. Along with the American Jewish community, the Evangelicals have been our strongest allies and advocates in the U.S. They are Christian Zionists, absolutely committed to the consolidation and security of the Israeli state."

"Yes, I know about those people. They are committed to us as long as it advances their wild dreams of some apocalyptic endgame. Their political support has been useful to us, General, but at the end of the day, they are neither our friends nor our brothers. They see us only as stepping stones toward the universal triumph of

Christianity, they do not embrace us as Jews. We are merely actors in their phantasms."

"Sir, I am not a religious man, nor are you, I gather. But the Evangelicals are very wedded to this project. They actually see it as a staging ground for the final battle of Armageddon. I have heard General Runter talk of this in the most explicit terms."

"They're mad."

"Perhaps, but they are quite powerful and, for now, they are supporting us. I would think twice before I alienated them."

"General, I am adamant in my decision. I want us to sever all ties with this so-called Armageddon Project."

"Very good, sir. But that will not erase our past involvement, nor the negative repercussions on the peace talks should the extent of it be revealed."

"And how would it be revealed?"

"There is an American reporter on the loose in Europe with a file that could bring down the Ritter administration—and thoroughly compromise our own interests and security—should he manage to publish it."

"Who does he work for?"

"The *New York Chronicle*."

"We have good contacts with the *Chronicle*. Perhaps we can prevail upon them to suppress the story on security grounds."

The general shook his head. "No good, sir. He would only publish it somewhere else, or pass it on to a colleague. He already knows too much. He must be stopped."

"How?"

"By whatever means it takes. We have a team tracking him now. They almost neutralized him in Zurich last night."

"Neutralized him? General, let me tell you something. I am well aware of my predecessor's policy on nonmilitary killings, but I will not stand for it. We may track down and eliminate terrorists who kill Jews. But we do not kill journalists, do you understand?"

"And if the story gets out?"

"We must do all we can to prevent that—short of murder."

Micah Lebedev sat behind the wheel of the SUV, sipping coffee from a paper cup and munching on a bread roll. He was parked in front of a bakery in the Swiss village of Knonau, some eight kilometers north of the Zuger Lake. He and his comrades had been combing the area for more than twelve hours, checking every café, restaurant, and hotel they could find within a radius of twenty kilometers around the safe house.

The only lead they had come up with was a strange report by a service station manager outside of a village called Rosseau: he said he saw a tall man with a shoulder bag clinging to the rear of an old aluminum caravan with U.K. plates. The sight was so peculiar, said this witness, that he had watched the vehicle continue on down the road and he could swear he saw the man jump off a hundred yards further on. But the team's inquiries in and around Rosseau produced no further leads. Micah had ordered a squad out of Bern to see if they could pick up the trail of the British caravan, but he had no great hopes of that.

When Micah's cell phone rang, he was hoping that Rosen or one of the others had come up with something. Instead he heard the tense voice of Mossad's Bern station chief on the other end of the line.

"New orders from the highest level, Micah. Do not terminate. Repeat: do not terminate. Intercept the package by all means, but without prejudice. Understood?"

"Yes, of course. But it is a pity. We were so close."

Micah flipped the phone off and put it back in his pocket. He wiped the crumbs from his chin with a balled-up paper napkin and started to throw it out the window. Then he suddenly remembered he was in Switzerland and put the wadded paper in his pocket instead.

"Bern says to stand down," he muttered to the others. "Grab the package, but no wet stuff."

"How the fuck can we grab the package if we don't know where the guy is?" said Lev, exhausted and cranky after the long, fruitless pursuit. "And why did you tell Bern we were so close?"

Micah wheeled around and glared at Lev. "Did you actually expect me to tell the station chief we've lost him?"

"I'm not ready to give up, Micah."

CHAPTER
50

EARLY THURSDAY MORNING, Sam was awakened by the bright sun that shone directly into his eyes as he lay on the rear bunk. Nigel, who preferred the niche above the driver's seat, was well protected from the dazzling light and continued to snore loudly while Sam opened and closed cabinet doors in search of some instant coffee. Finally roused by the noise, Nigel began to stir, indulged in a flatulent detonation followed by a loud yawn.

"Right," he said. "Time for a bit o' breakfast, then we're off."

He slid down from the bunk, scratched the sweaty crack of his bare buttocks, then peed in the toilet with the door open. Seemingly unaware of his own flop-bellied, hangdog nudity, he slid two frozen scrambled-egg-and-sausage breakfasts into the microwave and pushed the start button. In the four minutes it took to thaw and heat the food, he had slipped back into his previous day's garb—a dirty T-shirt and a pair of lime-green nylon track pants.

They ate at a fold-down breakfast table that practically crushed Sam's knees. "Kinda tight quarters in here," said Nigel, generously displaying a mouthful of half-chewed egg, "but everything works, you know what I mean?"

Sam nodded and swallowed his dry, tasteless food.

"And speakin' of tight quarters, mate, you're going to have to squeeze into that storage box I've built in the back, under that rear couch. The Brits do things right and check everybody's passport. You've got to hide until we get to the other side, otherwise you're likely to get arrested at the border and we'll both be in trouble."

"You want me to hide in that box?"

"Don't worry, I'll empty it out first. There's an airspace under the lid, and I'll get you a Coke bottle to piss in. It's only a four-hour crossing. Plenty of time to catch up on your sleep."

Nigel opened the door and jumped down on the tarmac. "I'll just go get the ticket, then we'll tuck you in and off we go."

Sam opened the top of the storage box and inspected its contents—extra pillows, blankets, rubber boots, a tool box, and two sixpacks of Newcastle Brown. He removed everything but the blankets and pillows, then carefully placed his shoulder bag in a corner of the box. It would be a tight squeeze, he thought. He'd have to bend his knees to fit inside.

"Bloody hell!" Nigel raged when he returned to the camper. "They tell me they discontinued service to Dover in 2002. We'll have to go to fucking Ramsgate and drive twenty miles to Maxton. I swear to God, Sam, it's just one thing after another with you. I'm really gettin' fed up with all this."

Nigel sat on a bar stool and opened his copy of *Motor World* magazine, a heavily illustrated gazette for fans of auto and motorcycle racing. He looked at the draft beer taps and was tempted to order a pint of dark ale, but he had a drive ahead of him and decided to be responsible. He ordered a half pint.

Like most bars on board the channel ferries, this one contained a motley assortment of snoring backpackers, French and Belgian tourists headed over to gawk at Big Ben and the Queen's Horse Guards, and noisy British families returning from their holiday homes and rentals on the Continent. And then there were the folks like Nigel, the camping-car crowd, that normally prefer to keep to themselves in their own rolling cocoons but, for the time of the crossing, are forced to mingle with the ordinary lot of tourists.

Nigel checked his watch and decided it was time to make his move on the onboard shop. It was one level down. The elevator was out of order so he had to walk—as much as he hated getting any exercise when it didn't involve his recreational exertions. The shop was a big one, but nothing like the hyper-depot in Calais. Bloody Sam! He'd promised.

Nigel wandered up and down the aisles looking at the cartons of cigarettes, boxes of Dutch and Cuban cigars, shelf after shelf of cognac, pastis, armagnac, Swiss chocolate. That looked good. He picked up four large Tobler bars with crushed almonds. Glennys would like that. Maybe it would mollify her after he dashed off and left her holding the baby so to speak. Crikey, nobody could really blame him for that. A man's gotta do what a man's gotta do.

When he arrived at the beer and ale section, he looked desperately for his favorite Newcastle Brown. None to be found anywhere. There was Watney's Amber, St. Peter's Cream Stout, Chelsea Brown, O'Sullivan's, Guinness. The closest thing he could find was Kilkenny ale. Irish stuff. Bloody Irish, always causing trouble. But their beer wasn't so bad. He piled six cases onto a dolly and wheeled them to a cash register.

"That's 260 pounds sterling, sir."

Nigel paid with a credit card and made sure to keep the receipt. This one's on Sam, he thought, and chuckled to himself.

"I'm afraid you'll have to carry them down by hand, sir, the elevator's out of order."

"Oh bloody hell," he groused. "Reckon I'll have to make a few trips, then."

He picked up two cases, leaning backward under the strain. "I'll be back for the rest of the lot in a minute," he groaned.

"Take your time, sir."

Nigel trod down the stairs, huffing and puffing and cursing Sam for not being there to help him. He couldn't take his boxes all the way to the camper; no one was allowed on the car deck during the crossing. He left them at the bottom of the stairs and went back for the rest. Twenty minutes later, beet red and gasping for breath, he stacked up the last two cases then returned to the bar for what he considered was a well-deserved half-pint.

Down in the bowels of the *Roi des Belges*, meanwhile, Sam was getting nauseous from the lingering automobile fumes, the heat of his confined space, and the relentless pitch and roll of the ferry. The combination of physical discomfort and anxiety was almost unbearable. He could not wait to emerge from this hellish sarcophagus and breathe the fresh, free air of England.

CHAPTER
51

NIGEL WAS AWAKENED by a voice on the ship's PA system announcing their imminent arrival in Ramsgate. He stretched, let out a loud, beery belch, and headed for the stairs.

People were already jamming the stairwell, waiting to join their vehicles. Nigel wormed his way through the throngs of tourists, whiny kids, and backpackers, until he found himself at the very bottom. Some bloke was sitting on top of his stack of boxes—actually had the cheek to put his grotty bum on Nigel's ale. But it was a young guy, about six foot tall and fourteen stone with tattooed biceps the size of a York ham. Nigel did a quiet burn, but said nothing.

When the boat finally docked, people rushed to their cars, leaving Nigel to trundle his stash over to the camping-car as best he could. He was furious when he finally got to the camper and stacked the boxes outside the passenger-side door. It was all Sam's fault, he fumed. He'd make him bloody pay for it.

Sam was relieved when he heard the footsteps and voices of people coming to rejoin their cars. But no Nigel. Christ, where was Nigel? Finally, he heard him open the door, wheezing and cursing under his breath, and start shoving things around inside the van.

"Hurry up," Sam shouted. "I'm dying in here."

"Hold your bloody horses, Sammy. We gotta get through customs and passport control first."

The gargantuan vehicle rolled slowly up the ramp and took its place in line. For what seemed to Sam like an eternity, it inched forward toward the customs barrier, two hundred yards from the dock. He was afraid exhaust fumes might be leaking into his compartment, so tried to breathe as little as possible lest he be asphyxiated by carbon monoxide.

The customs officer glanced at Nigel's passport. "Welcome home, sir. What have you got in the vehicle?"

"Just my camping gear and personal effects."

"I see. Been on holiday have you?"

"Yeh."

"And what countries did you visit, sir?"

"Switzerland. I mean I also drove through France, Germany, and Belgium. But mainly Switzerland."

The officer scrutinized the passport, flipped through the pages, then bent down to Nigel's level and looked him in the eye.

"Right. Did you bring anything back from abroad? Any merchandise, goods, equipment, food, plants, Swiss watches?"

"Nah, nothing like that. Just some stuff I bought on the boat."

"What did you purchase onboard, sir?"

"Oh nothing much, just some chocolate bars, and, uh, a few cans of ale. You know, the usual."

"Is that the ale in those boxes I see behind you?"

Nigel turned around and eyed the boxes. "Yeh, that's it. Kilkenny. Not as good as Newcastle, mind you, but that's the best they had."

"Quite."

The officer paced slowly toward the rear of the camping-car, and studied the motley assortment of bikes, wheels, boards, and sails that were attached to the roof. He put his face up against the back window and eyed the contents of the vehicle. He walked behind the camper, kneeled, and scrutinized the rear panel. Then he returned to the driver's-side window.

"Sir, there's a little problem back there."

"What's that?"

"You've lost a bolt. Your rear license plate looks like it's about to fall off. You'll want to get that looked at."

"Oh, right. I'll see to that right away. Thank you, officer."

"And there's a bit of a customs violation, I'm afraid."

"Customs violation?"

"Yes, sir. I've counted six cases of ale in your vehicle. Limit's two. I'm afraid I'll have to collect thirty pounds duty, and a thirty pound fine for the violation."

"What? Sixty bloody quid just to bring some ale into my own country? That's outrageous."

"You have a right to contest the levy, sir, but I'd have to impound the vehicle until your case is reviewed by the customs magistrate."

"Bloody hell!" grumbled Nigel. He pulled out his wallet, peeled off three twenties, and forked them over.

"Right you are sir. Thank you very much, and here is your receipt, lovely. Drive safely, and enjoy the ale. Not at the same time, of course."

"Very funny," Nigel growled and drove through the raised red and white barrier. He wound through the tangled streets of Ramsgate for ten minutes until he found the entrance to the A256 and took it south in the direction of Dover.

Sam had not understood all the words exchanged between Nigel and the customs officer, but he gathered that there had been some altercation and feared that his brother-in-law's short-fuse temper would get them both thrown in jail. He was relieved when he felt the vehicle drive away from the customs post, but now he wondered why Nigel did not stop and liberate him from his stifling box. He banged loudly on the lid.

"Nigel," he shouted. "Stop the van and let me out. I'm about to suffocate in here!"

"Not yet, Sammy," Nigel shouted back. "Gotta put some distance between us and the port so no one will know we slipped you through. Cops might have followed us, you know. Can't be too careful, mate."

Sam banged harder on the lid. "Nigel, you idiot! Let me out of here!"

"Stop whinging, will you?"

Finally, some five miles out of Ramsgate, Nigel pulled over. Sam heard him fiddle with the padlock. Then the lid was raised and he saw Nigel's jowly red face hovering over him.

"How ya goin' Sam. That wasn't too bad, was it? Hope you didn't shit yourself in there."

Sam gripped the edges of the wooden compartment and hoisted himself up. His back and knees were aching and his freshly washed shirt was once again dusty, sweaty, and wrinkled. He stretched and rubbed the back of his neck.

"Tell you what you need, mate. A half pint of ale. That'll calm your nerves."

Sam let out a deep breath. "No, thanks, Nigel. You know I don't drink alcohol anymore."

"One little ale wouldn't hurt you. Do you some good, in actual fact. C'mon, I'll have one with you."

In his frayed and frazzled state, Sam was tempted. Maybe there'd be no harm done if he stopped after one.

Nigel ripped the lid off the top box and took out two cans of Kilkenny. He popped one open, took a gulp, and handed the other to Sam.

"Don't you have any in the fridge?" Sam asked.

"You're joking, mate. You gotta drink your ale at room temperature."

The thought of drinking warm beer suddenly made Sam ill. He was still too much of an American for that. "On second thought, Nigel, I'll have a Coke—if you have a cold one."

"Oh, yeh, that I keep in the fridge. Blimey, just the idea of a warm Coke makes me want to puke."

When Nigel pulled the camper into his garage, he and Sam got out and started undoing the gear on the roof. It took them a half hour to get it all down and stored away. Then they hauled the cases of ale out of the vehicle and stacked them in the corner of the garage. "Reckon that'll hold me for awhile," he said. "Too bad it's not Newcastle."

"Drop it," said Sam. "Some other time, we'll go to Calais and I'll buy you all the Newcastle Brown you want."

"It's the least you could do, mate."

"Thanks, Nigel. You may not realize it, but you've probably saved my life. I appreciate it."

"Aah, don't mention it. C'mon inside. Glennys is probably over at Sophie's, otherwise I'd get her to fix us some food. I'm starved."

"Nigel, listen. I'm a hunted man. I think the best thing for me to do is stay in your camping-car for a while."

"You're not going to pick up Sis at Mum's?"

Sam shook his head. "It's too dangerous, Nigel. I'm pretty sure they've got her under surveillance."

"Who?"

"The C.I.A., Mossad. The Frogs."

"Sam."

"Yeah?"

"You realize you're mad, don't you?"

"Nigel, I can't explain it to you right now. I'm just telling you that I am in danger, your sister is in danger, and if anyone knows I am staying here, you and Glennys are in danger. I have to lie low for a few days. Let me stay in the camper."

"Suit yourself, mate. There's still some frozen dinners in the fridge. You've got the bog, bottled water, electricity, everything you need."

"Thanks. And it's best not to tell Glennys I'm here. The fewer people know about it the better."

"Alright, Sam. You're daft, but alright."

When the automatic garage door closed, Sam sat alone in the dark and tried to collect his thoughts. The silence was a welcome change after the noise of the road and Nigel's incessant chatter. He rubbed his face and considered his next move.

Though Sandra was in Dover, only two miles away, direct contact with her was out of the question. He switched the light on, opened his bag, and pulled out a notebook. Then he took the cap off a felt-tipped pen and began to write:

Dearest Sandra,

I have asked Nigel to hand-deliver this note to let you know I'm okay. I can't see you or talk to you on the phone right now. I can't even fully explain the reasons why. Let's just say the story I have been working on has upset certain parties. I have a plan to put everything right. Just sit tight and wait to hear from me. If you like, you can send a letter back via Nigel. But whatever you do, don't use your cell phone, and don't tell anyone you have been in touch with me or even know where I am. You are probably being watched at your mother's house. Stay calm and don't worry. Everything is going to be fine. Trust me. And if you hear any bad things about me, don't believe them.

I love you,
Sam

P.S. Destroy this letter once you've read it.

Sam folded down the table, pulled his computer from the shoulder bag, and plugged its adapter into the AC outlet behind the driver's seat. He booted up his G4 PowerBook and called up a blank Word document. He took out the two envelopes, opened them, and spread their contents on the table. Then he began to type:

The Armageddon Project
Summary and overview of the key documents pertaining
to secret U.S. involvement in an illegal political and
military operation in Iraq
By Sam Preston

Out of habit, he had begun his text in a journalistic way, but it was not really a news story. It was a roadmap intended to guide the reader through the dozens of documents contained in the envelopes, to explain their significance, and to suggest a possible response to the dire and dangerous situation. In writing up his report, Sam relied not only on the documents, but also on his own interviews, analysis, and observations. In short, it was a comprehensive account of the Ritter administration's boldest, maddest undertaking. If he ever had a great piece of writing in him, he thought, let it be this urgent denunciation of high-level wrongdoing. He knew this was the story of his life.

Sam had been writing nonstop for four hours when he finally decided to take a break. He looked in the fridge and found a frozen meatball and spaghetti dinner. He and Sandra didn't have a microwave at home, but the instructions on the package looked simple enough. He popped the plastic-wrapped packet in the oven and pushed the start button. Several minutes later, he pulled the steaming pasta out and plopped it onto a paper plate.

While he ate his overcooked spaghetti, he turned on the small TV set that was mounted on the opposite wall. He flicked the remote looking for CNN, but could only get local channels. Most were silly daytime dramas, soap operas, game shows, and sitcom reruns. Finally, he landed on the BBC World Service. He was flabbergasted to see his own face on the screen behind the anchor desk.

"French authorities," said the anchorman, "are looking for American journalist Sam Preston, formerly of the *New York Chronicle*, in connection with the assassination in Paris last Monday of Iraqi Christian leader Rafat Ganjibar. Preston, a respected Paris-based correspondent, was severed by the newspaper this week for reasons apparently unrelated to the Ganjibar case. Preston was last seen in Zurich, Switzerland, and is now believed to be in hiding somewhere in Europe. He is the object of an Interpol arrest warrant and British authorities have joined their European colleagues in the search for the murder suspect. Earlier today, the BBC's Trevor Chillingsworth spoke with Bradley Kemp, Paris bureau chief of the *Chronicle*."

Kemp's smug, cherubic face appeared on the screen.

"I want to stress that Sam Preston no longer has any connection with the *New York Chronicle*," said Kemp. "He was terminated as part of a broad reduction in force, and not for any connection he may or may not have had to the assassination of Mr. Ganjibar. I can say, however, that he had close ties to Ganjibar and his entourage. I have turned his office files over to the French authorities and the *Chronicle* is cooperating fully with the investigation."

Bradley Kemp, you shit. True to form right to the end. Was there a living, breathing human being that he would not stab in the back to move up one step more on the ladder of his boundless ambition?

Sam flipped through other channels. More daytime garbage, commercials, rock videos. Then he hit ITV news, which was also running a piece on him. They showed the same ghastly mugshot from his French press card.

"Who is the mysterious murder suspect Sam Preston?" said the anchor. "To find out, ITV's Gloria Farley caught up earlier today with his friend, American Gospel singer Tawana Pickens. Here is her report."

The scene switched to a shot of the windswept journalist standing next to Tawana by a stone parapet overlooking the sea. "I am here at Dover Castle, where Princess Tawana Pickens, the U.S. Gospel superstar, has just finished a rehearsal for tonight's outdoor concert. Tawana, Sam Preston has interviewed you, traveled with your band, and written about you. What is he really like?"

"Well, I tell you one thing, Gloria, he sure ain't no killer. I known a lot of bad dudes where I grew up, and I can tell you for sure, Sam Preston don't have that kind of evil in him. He's a true gentleman, and a great journalist. If he's in trouble today, I think it's because Satan is tryin' to mess with him 'cause he's too good a person. Satan don't like good folks."

God bless you, Princess Tawana, faithful friend, stalwart singer, buxom black beauty. You don't know it yet, but you may just be the guardian angel who is going to save me, and perhaps the rest of the world, from the real agents of mischief right here on earth.

The garage door opened and Nigel knocked on the side of the camper. "I've just been over to me mum's house," he said. "Didn't tell Sis I was hiding you in the camper, but I had a hell of a time explaining why I came right back from Switzerland. Nobody can believe I cut short my holiday. Can't believe it myself in actual fact."

Sam handed Nigel the letter he had written to his wife. "If you don't mind, Nigel, could you take this to Sandra?"

"I just got back from there, mate. I'm not gonna turn right around and drive to Dover again."

"Nigel, it's urgent. The TV news is presenting me as an assassin. Sandra's sure to see it and worry herself sick. You've got to put this letter into her hands. Oh, and I need a pack of big manila envelopes."

"Oh yes, sir. Right away, sir. Will there be anything else, sir?"

"As a matter of fact, Nigel, I'd like you to take me to Dover Castle tonight."

"What, just like that? A little sightseeing to while the time away, is it?"

"Not sightseeing, Nigel. I have to meet someone there, someone who can help get me out of this mess."

"Sam, Winston Churchill doesn't live there anymore."

CHAPTER

52

T HE CAMPING-CAR ENTERED the parking lot at half past seven on Thursday evening. Sam told Nigel to park as close as he could to the castle, with its sprawling battlements and towering twelfth-century keep. It was in the maze of tunnels carved into the cliffs under Dover Castle that Churchill and Vice Admiral Ramsay had coordinated Britain's defenses in World War II and directed the heroic evacuation of 388,000 British soldiers from Dunkirk. Now, Sam hoped, the historic fortress would play a role in his own extraction from danger—and perhaps in the salvation of another embattled democracy.

No sooner had Nigel parked the camper than the opening guitar riff from the Beatles' "Ticket to Ride" rang out from his dashboard.

"What's that?" asked Sam.

"My cell phone," Nigel replied with a smug smile. "I just downloaded it for two quid. Nice, eh?"

He picked up the phone. "Allo, allo! . . . Yeh . . . He's fine, luv. Got 'im right by my side."

Sam shook his head and wagged his finger furiously in Nigel's face.

"Sorry, Sis," said Nigel with a malevolent chuckle, "can't tell you where we are. Top secret and all that, you know . . . Right, will do. Ta!"

Nigel put his phone back on the dashboard and looked over at Sam with a patronizing grin. "Your wife sends love, Sammy. But I'll tell you something, mate, you really are ridiculous with all this secret agent stuff."

The London-based Mossad unit had been monitoring Sandra's cell phone 24/7. Now, thanks to Nigel's indiscretion, they knew exactly where to find Sam Preston. The geographic coordinates of Nigel's Nokia—51°07'49"N, 1°19'14"E—pointed precisely to the parking lot of Dover Castle. Within five minutes, a midnight blue BMW exited the underground garage of the Israeli Embassy on Palace Green, and headed east on Kensington High Street in the direction of Westminster Bridge. Under normal conditions, the eighty-mile drive would take just under two hours. But traffic was heavy on this Thursday evening.

At precisely eight o'clock, one hour before the scheduled concert, a van drove up and parked twenty yards from the camper. On its side was painted the smiling face of a black woman and the words: "Princess Tawana and the Jambalayas—European Tour—Save Your Soul with New Orleans Gospel."

"Nigel, drive the camper right next to that van, quick."

"You're jokin'. We've already got a good spot and the car park's starting to fill up."

"For fuck's sake, Nigel, just do it."

Sam could see the side door of the van slide open. Tawana stepped out, followed by the other band members, and, finally, a skinny white man with a bad toupee.

"Hit it, Nigel, we're gonna miss them."

With a great sigh, Nigel started the engine, backed out of his spot, and headed toward the van. The musicians were pulling their instruments out of the rear luggage compartment. The camper's headlights caught Tawana in their beam. Sam opened the door and jumped out.

"Tawana," he called.

She turned and looked in his direction.

"Sam! What are you doing here, boy? Don't you know they lookin' for you?"

She gave him a big hug when he approached. "You need to get your little white butt out of sight."

"I had to see you, Tawana. It's urgent. When are you going back to the U.S.?"

"No time soon, baby. We just startin' a European tour."

"I need somebody to take an envelope to Washington."

"Well you in luck. Chris Blassingame is going back there tomorrow. I know you didn't do nothin' bad, Sam. That's what I told those folks."

"I saw it, Tawana. Thank you."

"Listen, baby, we got to go get dressed and set up. But I'm gonna send Chris back out here to see you. You in that white camper?"

Sam nodded.

Tawana cackled loudly. "Man, that's a big mother, ain't it?"

She gave him a kiss on the cheek and went off to join the others.

The blue BMW hit a snarl going through Elephant and Castle. A semi had broken down just before the junction with the Old Kent Road and traffic was backed up for a quarter mile eastbound. The Mossad driver suddenly swerved right, into the opposite lane, and slalomed his way through a column of oncoming cars, triggering a discordant chorus of automobile horns.

As he cut back into the eastbound lane, the driver clipped a motorcyclist who was speeding down the median to avoid the traffic jam. The heavy bike was knocked sideways into the path of a slow-moving westbound car. The rider bounced off the hood, rolled over twice on the ground, then sprawled motionless in the middle of the road. By that time, the BMW had passed the immobilized lorry and turned into the Old Kent Road.

Sam got back in the camper.

"Aren't we goin' in with your friends?" Nigel asked.

Sam shook his head. "Too dangerous. I can't afford to be spotted."

"What? We're not even gonna hear the music?"

"Go buy yourself a ticket, Nigel. I'll pay you back for it when I get some pounds."

"Thanks, Sam." Nigel opened the driver's side door and jumped out. "I'll leave you the key, in case you have to move her. You're not in a proper parking spot, you know."

He trotted off in the direction of the Cannon's Gateway entrance, leaving Sam alone in the camper. It was starting to get dark now. The nighttime illumination threw a golden light on the battlements. Before long, he heard an announcer speaking from the outdoor stage just behind the massive stone walls. "Ladies and gentlemen, the Dover Jazz Festival is proud to present a little lady who has just finished a smash tour in the United States and is here tonight to sing for your enjoyment and sanctification. Let's give a warm welcome to Princess Tawana and the Jambalayas!"

Over the applause, Sam could hear the first notes of an up-tempo spiritual, "Down By the Riverside." Tawana's powerful voice, amplified by the sound system, was bouncing off the old walls that, in ages past, had heard the shouts and clatter of battling soldiers, and heraldic trumpets hailing jousters on horseback.

Back at the accident scene, meanwhile, a team of paramedics was loading the immobile form of the motorcyclist onto a stretcher as the police and emergency vehicles swept the scene with red and blue lights. The accident victim had two broken arms, a crushed hip, and a concussion, but the spine was intact and his blood pressure was steady. The paramedics thought his survival chances looked good if they could get him to the emergency room within an hour. But his condition was serious, with a strong possibility of internal bleeding.

From eyewitness accounts, policemen at the scene learned that the car that struck the bike was a midnight blue BMW M6 coupe whose license number began with PG, and that the vehicle had turned onto the Old Kent Road headed east. The Metropolitan Police headquarters in London immediately sent out an all-points bulletin in search of the hit-and-run car.

The BMW merged onto the M20 motorway near Swanley and headed southeast. Dover Castle was now sixty miles away. The driver floored the accelerator and the sleek, powerful coupe hurtled toward its destination at a speed of 125 mph.

At 9:30, as it passed under a highway bridge near Gillingham, the car was snapped by a radar camera. The image of the vehicle and its license plate was immediately transmitted to London, where monitors had been on the lookout for a BMW with PG plates. A new bulletin went out, locating the blue car on the M20 headed east.

Sam saw Blassingame emerge from the Cannon's Gateway and head toward the camper. He cracked the door open and signaled to him.

"Hello, Sam," said Chris, holding out his hand. "I hope I'm not shaking hands with an assassin."

"If you believed that, Chris, I don't think you'd have come out here."

"Of course I don't believe it."

Blassingame climbed into the camper and took a seat on the rear couch, next to Sam.

"Thanks for coming, Chris. I'm in big trouble and I hope you can help me out."

"I'll do my best, Sam, but I got big troubles to deal with, too. That's why I have to rush back to Washington tomorrow."

"What's up?"

"Everything's going to hell in a handbasket over there. First of all, Reverend Conklin got caught in a hotbed motel with his secretary."

"The guy I sat next to at the White House dinner?"

"That's him. Turns out Conklin and her had something goin' on for quite a while. Then some smart-ass reporter from the *National Enquirer* took a picture of 'em coming out of a Motel 6 in Falls Church, Virginia. The reverend's resigned and all, big press conference, broke down in tears in front of the cameras just like old Jimmy Swaggart did when they caught him with his pants down. It's been all over the papers. Didn't you see it?"

"No. I've been out of touch the past couple of days."

"Well, that's just the tip of the iceberg. Even before the Conklin scandal, the Evangelicals were bitterly divided over whether or not to support Ritter on Iraq. A lot of 'em were antiwar to begin with—in fact, most Christian groups were urging the president not to invade Iraq in the first place. They swung behind him after the invasion, but now this Armageddon thing has put 'em in a quandary. Ganjibar's folks have been hittin' us up for funding and the White House was urging us to pony up big time.

We've already shoveled millions into the operation—including most of the profits from Tawana's hit record, if you want to know the truth."

"Didn't anyone wonder what was being done with the money?"

"That's what I'm fixin' to tell you. A lot of us are starting to think that General Runter and them are going too far. They're not just preparing for the final battle, they're trying to start it themselves, even talking about preemptive nuclear strikes to trigger the Apocalypse. But you see, Sam, like I told you before, mortal man can't decide when Armageddon's going to happen—we can't hold a gun to God's head and make Him jump. God's gonna choose the moment when He's good and ready. It's like it's written in Revelation: 'Thou shalt not know what hour I will come upon thee.'"

"So the Evangelicals are turning against this project?"

"Some of 'em are, but others are still gung-ho. It's tearin' us apart. And this new guy they got over in London, this George Shaheen fella, he's trying to keep us at arms length. See, he's real close to his church hierarchy, and you know those Eastern Orthodox folks, they don't live their religion the way we do."

"But Ganjibar was Orthodox too."

"Fact is, Ganjibar didn't give a hoot about religion. He just used the Evangelicals to advance his own cause, which was basically to turn his territory into a big filling station, free-trade zone, and duty-free hypermarket for his own benefit. We didn't realize that at first, but when it finally dawned on us, a lot of us thought we'd been had by some carnival shill. And Ritter was his main tout."

"What about your friend Carpenter? Didn't he believe in Ganjibar?"

"Oh Hal, Hal's a nice fella, but he's not playin' with a full deck if you know what I mean. We used to call him snapper-head back in school."

"I thought he was a doctor."

"That's a good one," Blassingame guffawed. "If Hal Carpenter has an M.D. degree, he found it in a Cracker Jack box. Look, Ganjibar just used Hal because he was a nephew of Johnny Allgood—you know, the big televangelist? Anyhow, Hal's back in Alabama now. After Ganjibar was killed, the French expelled him as an undesirable alien. Sounds about right. He always was a bit of a space cadet."

"Seems like you folks have a big mess on your hands."

"I reckon," Blassingame sighed. "Now I got to go back there and do what I can to fix things up, at least from a public relations perspective. That's my real specialty."

Blassingame gazed out the window at the castle's battlements. "Those old stones," he mused. "Looks kind of like the old city of Jerusalem. You know, maybe we ought to spend more time looking backward to our roots rather than forward to trying to make the End Times happen. I honestly think we went off the rails somewhere, you know Sam? We need to think more about the real message of Jesus—peace, tolerance, justice, love, the sermon on the mount—and less about trying to leverage our political power. Jesus said we should leave all that to Caesar. 'My kingdom is not of this world,' he said."

"Chris, let me tell you something," Sam said. "I'm not particularly religious. In fact I haven't been to church much since I was a kid. I believe the sermon on the mount, the Ten Commandments, those are good rules for us right here on earth. But some powerful people have been playing by other rules, and that's why things have gone off the rails, as you put it. I think I know a way to start putting things right. I can't explain it all, but you can help me do this if you trust me."

"I do trust you, Sam. I think you're a good guy."

"Then take this and guard it with your life." Sam handed him the envelope containing all his files and his overview text, which he had burned onto a CD-rom. "When you go back to Washington, deliver it to Lisa Taylor at the *Chronicle* news bureau on Connecticut Avenue. Tell her it's from me and it's urgent. But don't say anything about it on the phone. Just go up there and hand it to her. Will you do that, Chris?"

Blassingame took the envelope. "I will, Sam. Now I'd better get back in there and see what's happening. Take care of yourself."

"You, too, Chris, and Godspeed."

As soon as Blassingame stepped out of the vehicle, Sam locked the door and placed his shoulder bag in the rear storage locker. Then he sat down and waited.

CHAPTER

53

BACK AT THE ISRAELI EMBASSY in London, radio techni-
cians were carefully monitoring the police emergency frequency.
From the information that they relayed to the BMW, the commandos
knew they were being pursued as potential manslaughter suspects. But
the team was now so close to its prey that the squad leader
decided not to abort the mission unless the Brits were really closing
in. The embassy kept him informed of the latest police bulletins through
his earpiece.

The BMW exited the motorway at 10:05 and headed into Dover via
the Archcliffe Road. The onboard GPS directed the Israeli driver street
by street through the unfamiliar town—Constable's Road, West Norman
Road, Harold's Road, and, finally, to the visitor's parking lot at Dover
Castle. They had Nigel's license plate number, of course, but that was
hardly necessary. His camper was hard to miss.

Sam sat on the rear couch, listening to the music echoing from within
the castle walls. Suddenly he heard a knock on the door. Would that be
Nigel? Blassingame?

"Who is it?"

"Fire brigade, sir. I'm afraid you'll have to move your camper. You're
in an emergency vehicle access zone."

"Oh, sorry," said Sam. He settled into the driver's seat and started
the ignition. In the external rear-view mirror, he saw a man dressed in
black standing by the door.

Sam had never driven a lumbering craft like this before, but the automatic shift looked pretty straightforward. He backed the camper out and slowly cruised some fifty yards until he found an empty space at the end of a row of parked cars. Lucky to find that end spot, he thought. He could never have fit Nigel's boxcar into a normal slot.

Sam yanked on the parking brake. There was another knock on the door. He saw the same man in the mirror.

"Yes?"

"Fire brigade again, sir. Thanks for your cooperation. I'll just need you to sign this for me."

"Sign what?"

"Routine thing, sir. The security police already wrote your vehicle up. They've called in a tow truck to remove it."

"What?"

"But I've just filled out a form saying you vacated the illegal spot. They'll leave you alone if you just countersign it. Save you a lot of bother and a hundred quid fine."

Sam felt his throat tighten as he looked around the cabin for something to block the door with. "It's not my vehicle. I'm not signing anything."

"Suit yourself, mate."

Sam heard the clank of a heavy object against the door, then the groan of bending metal as the man outside pried the lock with a crowbar. Seconds later, he yanked the door open, burst into the cabin and pointed a Beretta 9mm pistol at Sam's head. "Don't make a fucking sound," he snarled, and pinned the American up against the door to the WC.

Two other men entered the vehicle. They rifled through the camper, ripping open cabinets, tearing up cushions, looking under the seats, pulling down wall panels.

"Where is your shoulder bag?" demanded the man who was pinning Sam down. Sam could feel his hot, fetid breath on his cheek.

Sam did not reply at first. The gunman doubled him over with a stiff kick in the groin, causing him to writhe on the floor in exquisite pain.

"Where's the fucking bag?" his assailant growled once more, and struck Sam on the bridge of his nose with the barrel of his gun. Sam's glasses fell on the floor and shattered.

"In the storage locker under the rear couch," Sam gasped.

One of the other men pulled out the locker. Inside, along with some blankets and pillows, he recognized the black and gray shoulder bag from the surveillance photos provided by the Swiss team. He snatched it up and began to unzip the flap.

"Code red!" the gunman suddenly shouted, pressing on his earpiece with his index finger. "Cut and run! Cut and run!"

As the two other men scrambled through the door, the commando leader pointed his Beretta at Sam's forehead. "Don't make a peep, Preston, or I'll come back here and blow your fucking head off." Then he was out the door.

Sam lay shaking on the floor, still feeling the deep, dull pain in his lower abdomen. He heard the whine of a powerful automobile engine, followed by squealing tires.

He slowly rose to his knees, crawled to the couch, and hoisted himself up. The bag was gone, his computer was gone, but the documents were safe—for now. He knew it would not take long, though, for the commando to realize that the bag they had seized contained only magazines, scrawled notes, and his PowerBook. They would be back for the files. He thought they might kill him to shut him up—or more likely torture him to make him reveal the whereabouts of the documents.

For a brief moment, Sam considered driving away in Nigel's camper, but the outlandish vehicle was too conspicuous. If he left on foot, he would be easy to track down. He was trying hard to think clearly but his head was throbbing and his mind had drifted into a dreamlike state. He heard the opening measures of "Armageddon" reverberating off the ancient stones and feared that he might be facing his own End Times on this warm July night.

Suddenly he saw a lone policeman standing at the entrance to the Cannon's Gateway at the far end of the parking lot. He slipped out of the camper and, crouching low, made his way along the row of parked cars.

"Excuse me, officer," he said.

The startled constable looked at the tall, disheveled man with the Yank accent and a bleeding cut on his nose.

"Good God, man. Have you been mugged or something?"

"I want to turn myself in."

"Turn yourself in? What for?"

"My name is Sam Preston. There is an Interpol warrant out for my arrest. I'm wanted for murder."

The sergeant's freckled face turned pale for an instant, then quickly regained its reddish hue. "Just stay right where you are, sir," he said, and snatched a walkie-talkie from his belt.

"Captain, this is Douglas at the castle. I've got a chap named Preston here wants to turn himself in." The constable cupped his hand over the mouthpiece. "You the one wanted by the French?"

Sam nodded.

"Yes, Captain, that's him. You'll need to send a car over here to take him into custody. No, he doesn't appear dangerous."

Sam was booked at the local police station on Ladywell Road, then transferred to the Kent County Constabulary in Maidstone, some forty miles from Dover. Before locking him up, the police allowed him to make one phone call.

"Sandra, it's Sam."

"Sam, oh my God! I was so worried. I thought they'd killed or kidnapped you."

"I'm fine. I'm okay."

"Nigel called and said his camper had been trashed and you were missing."

"I'm all right. I'm safe now."

"Where are you?"

"In British police custody."

"Sam, what's happening? You're all over the TV news. They say you killed Ganjibar. The French are looking for you, Interpol's looking for you . . ."

"I'm in good hands, now, Sandra. I'll be okay. This is all a misunderstanding. We'll settle it quickly. I'll be home soon."

"When can I see you?"

"I'll let you know, Sandra. The police are saying my time's up on this call. I'll call you back when I can. Don't worry. Everything's okay. I love you."

"I love you, too, Sam."

The contents of Sam's computer bag elicited a great deal of interest from the Mossad analysts in London. It was clear from the various notes, downloads, and files contained on his G4 hard drive that the American possessed much of the story of the Armageddon Project. But it was equally clear, particularly from the comprehensive overview he had prepared, that he was not fully aware of the Israeli role in all this.

To be sure, the presence of Israeli weapons and civilian arms dealers in the overall scheme was noted. But the direct government role in arming, financing, and training the Assyrians was not. Nor was the fact that Israeli and American military officials were sharing targeting information for possible Iraq-based strikes on Iran. No, the onus of Preston's exposé was squarely on the Ritter administration, Ganjibar's people, and the American Evangelicals. Perhaps Israel could live with this after all. They had little choice now, in any case. Preston was in British custody and his file was floating out in the ether somewhere.

CHAPTER
54

O N RETURNING FROM LUNCH on Friday afternoon, Reg Hillenbrand took a special elevator to the bottom level of the U.S. Embassy in London and punched his ID code on an electronic lock. The station chief's office was windowless and not particularly spacious for an official of his rank, but it had the advantage of being discreet and bugproof. After reading over several computer files and e-mail messages, Hillenbrand closed and locked his office door, then picked up an encrypted phone. He dialed the hotline number, a special satellite linkup that connected him with Trent McBride's office in Langley, Virginia.

The two men had old school ties that went back to their Georgetown days. Unlike their classmate Ron Chandler, Ritter's power-drunk defense secretary, McBride and Hillenbrand had shared a youthful idealism that followed them through their decades of government service. It was hard not to become cynical and opportunistic in the intelligence field; both men had in fact been involved in their share of louche operations. But they had managed to cling to some sense of what their mission was really about—protecting the American republic against the myriad forces that were working to undermine and destroy it. And they knew that those forces did not all wear enemy uniforms.

"Trent, it's Reg," he said when he heard the director's tired voice on the other end. "How's it going?"

"I'm packing boxes and preparing to brief my successor—if the Senate ever confirms him."

"They'll confirm him alright, even if he is an incompetent crony of Bill Cordman's."

"That's why we have to see this thing through while I'm still in charge, Reg. What's the status?"

"Preston's in British police custody."

"How'd the Brits nab him? They haven't been particularly helpful on this thing."

"It's complicated. Let me run you through the past twenty-four hours. You know about the Mossad agent who was bird-dogging Preston and his French buddy?"

"The stewardess."

"Right. The one we code-named Mata Hari. She almost nailed Preston in her hotel room in Zurich, but he got out through the parking garage."

"Slipped away from Mossad? How the hell did he manage that?"

"He had help. One of our female agents scooped him up in a sports car and delivered him to a taxi driver who also works for us. Actually, the guy is a double-dipper. Mossad hires him on Swiss jobs, but they don't know he's really one of our agents."

"What's his name?"

"Klaus Rosen."

"What did he do with Preston?"

"Took him to a Mossad safe house up in the hills outside Zurich. But he made sure the Israelis didn't catch the guy. He screwed up their electronic surveillance equipment and stalled until Preston escaped and made a run for it."

"Why didn't our people pick Preston up at that point?"

"Rosen lost him. He couldn't communicate with us because he was with the Mossad team. His basic mission was to make sure they didn't kill Preston or get ahold of his file."

"How did Preston turn up in England?"

"We're still not sure how he got across the Channel. But we picked up his trail last night when we intercepted some Mossad communications out of their London Embassy. They had apparently zeroed in on

Preston in the parking lot of Dover Castle. By the time we learned that, they had a team on the way to Dover."

"And we couldn't beat them there?"

"Not without a helicopter—which we didn't have, thanks to Ritter's budget cuts. By the time we got there, they had already roughed Preston up and snatched his computer."

"Did they get the file?"

"Not sure. The British police were closing in on them, so they cut and ran. That's when Preston turned himself in to the Brits for his own protection. Now the French are trying to extradite him in connection with the Ganjibar murder, which, as you well know, he had nothing to do with."

"Where is the file?"

"No idea, Trent."

"Dammit! I just hope he got it into safe hands. The story's got to come out, Reg. Something has to stop Ritter and Cordman before they push this country off a cliff—or set off a nuclear holocaust in the name of Armageddon."

"This isn't a personal vendetta, is it Trent? You're not just paying them back because they sacked you?"

"Reg, I'll be honest with you. I don't like either one of them, no more than I like Ron Chandler. The president is an ignorant zealot, and Cordman is an evil and corrupt warmonger. Am I settling a personal score with them? You bet. But it's much bigger than that, Reg. I could swallow my pride and forgive a personal slap in the face. But I can't tolerate what they are doing to our country, and to the rest of the world for that matter."

CHAPTER

55

A S SOON AS HE LEARNED of Sam's arrest, Bertrand Bouvard requested, and London authorities promptly approved, a rogatory commission that empowered him to question the journalist on British soil. On Saturday, July 29, the judge arrived at the towering glass-and-steel headquarters of New Scotland Yard with his secretary and Chief Inspector Morin of the *police judiciaire* in tow.

The Metropolitan Police provided Bouvard with a corner office on the tenth floor, overlooking the bustling traffic on Victoria Street. It was bigger and sunnier than his cramped quarters at the Palais de Justice, but to Bouvard's taste it lacked charm. No sooner had he hung up his blazer behind the door than he lowered the blinds to approximate the dimmer light of his own office back in Paris. In the dazzling glare of day, he thought, one missed all the subtleties and nuances.

Bouvard sat behind a desk and adjusted the lamp so that its beam faced away from him. It would not shine directly into the eyes of the suspect, but it would make it more difficult for him to scrutinize the face of his interrogator. Morin drew up a chair next to, and slightly behind, the judge. He gave a nervous little smile to the Scotland Yard detective who had been assigned to attend the session.

The Brit nodded but did not return the smile. Like most of his colleagues at Scotland Yard, Lieutenant David McKewan regarded these rogatory commissions as an intrusion on his turf—especially when these Frog investigators showed up with all their fastidious airs and tried to give lessons to their British counterparts. Sometimes he thought that the English Channel was not wide enough.

Bouvard pulled a pipe from his pocket and struck a match.

"Sorry, Judge," said McKewan. "It's against the rules to smoke anywhere in the building."

With his match suspended in mid-air, Bouvard stared at the detective over the tip of the flame. He slowly shook it out and placed the pipe on the desktop. A few crumbs of tobacco fell out. McKewan got up and wiped them off with his handkerchief, then shook it over the trash can. The judge eyed him silently as he returned to his chair.

"Let us proceed," he said finally. "Bring the suspect in."

Since his transfer from the Kent County Constabulary on July 28, Sam had been held in a basement cell at the headquarters of the Metropolitan Police. It was small and spare, but the bunk had a firm mattress and was actually more comfortable than the pull-down contraption in Nigel's camping-car. Here in the confines of New Scotland Yard, protected from his pursuers, he slept better than he had for a long time. He'd also had the benefit of some fresh clothes, a shave and a shower.

Sam had just finished his lunch of sausage, beans, and chips when two constables, a man and a woman, opened the door to his cell and took him upstairs via a secure elevator. He was afraid they might handcuff him, but apart from gripping each arm, the officers treated him respectfully.

When they reached room 1010, McKewan opened the door and ushered them inside. He motioned Sam to a chair directly in front of Bouvard's desk. The constables left the room and stood guard in the corridor outside.

"Monsieur Preston," said Bouvard in French. "This is not the first time we meet, I believe?"

"No, Monsieur le Juge. I interviewed you for a profile I did in the *Chronicle* a couple of years ago."

"Yes," said Bouvard with a slight smile. "I'm afraid that was a waste of time. You see, I almost never talk to the press, and when I do, I never discuss my work. All you gleaned from our little talk, as I remember, is the fact that I smoke a pipe and have a Braque reproduction on my wall."

"Just a minute," McKewan interrupted. "You'll have to do this in English, Judge. I am assigned to observe this interrogation to guarantee that the prisoner's rights are respected under British law, and I don't understand a word you're saying."

Bouvard looked at the detective and frowned. "This cannot be," he said in his halting English. "This is French judicial procedure. Besides, my *greffière*, she does not understand English."

"Your what?"

"My *greffière*, my secretary, she transcribe the deposition." He nodded in the direction of the demure young woman who was sitting on a couch with a steno pad on her knees.

"Sorry, sir. I'm afraid you'll have to do it in English."

Bouvard stood up slowly and walked to the door. He pulled a small black address book from his inside coat pocket.

"Morin," he said to his colleague. "Here is the direct number of Sir John McAllister. Please call him on your cell phone and inform him of this problem."

"Oui, Monsieur le Juge." Morin took the address book and left the room.

The judge picked up his pipe and stuck it, unlit, into his mouth. The room was quiet except for the sound of his dry sucking and the distant rumble of traffic on the street below. McKewan folded his arms across his chest and stared silently at the Frenchman.

At fifty-two, with his prominent ears and long jug-shaped face, Bouvard was easy to write off as an unimaginative French civil servant plodding his way toward a cushy retirement. But his eyes, black and shiny as wet ink, reflected a keen intelligence. He was a man of few words, and what he did say never reflected the full extent of this thinking. Those who did not understand his cryptic manner often underestimated him. McKewan had just made that mistake.

Five minutes later, Morin returned with an attractive young woman at his side.

"*Bonjour, Monsieur le Juge*," she said in impeccable French. "I am Detective Lauren Peterson. I will take over the observer duties here."

McKewan gave her a quizzical look.

"The director says you can stand down, Dave," said Peterson. "He'd like to see you in his office."

Bouvard turned his attention back to Sam.

"Why did you turn yourself in?"

"For protection."

"From whom?"

"I was being pursued by Mossad, the C.I.A., probably the D.G.S.E."

"Why would they be pursuing you?"

"I possessed information that certain parties sought to suppress."

"About what?"

"Illegal U.S. activities in Iraq."

"Iraq does not concern me, Monsieur Preston. I am investigating an assassination committed on French soil."

"What makes you think I was involved?"

"I will ask the questions," said Bouvard. He glanced furtively at Detective Peterson, then picked up his pipe. He struck a match and drew a volley of deep puffs until the tobacco glowed in the bowl and a cloud of acrid gray smoke rose over his head. Peterson observed him disapprovingly, but said nothing.

The judge stood up and began to pace back and forth behind the desk. "You were curious some years ago about my method, Monsieur Preston. It is quite simple really. I use my intuition to solve puzzles. Sometimes, when the pieces seem to make no sense, you line them up differently and a whole new picture appears before your eyes. Pieces that seemed totally irrelevant at first suddenly provide essential clues."

Bouvard stopped pacing. He placed his hands on the back of his chair and leaned slightly forward, pipe clenched between his teeth, his gleaming black eyes fixed on Sam. "I think you may be such a piece, Monsieur Preston."

Sam looked up at the judge, but the glare from the desk lamp blurred his view. He could feel damp circles forming under his arms.

"In fact, I find this piece in more than one place. It appears all over this intriguing tableau—it is the common element that seems to tie everything together."

"I don't follow you."

"How is it that a simple American journalist is in contact, within a very short period, with all the protagonists in this drama? How is it, for example, that he lunches regularly with the C.I.A. station chief in Paris, a certain Jason Winthrop? That he interviews Roland Peccaldi twelve days before his sudden, I would say, curious death? That he meets with Michel Lanzatti and Nikola Lefkosias shortly before they are both murdered? That he was one of the last people, outside the immediate circle, to meet with Rafat Ganjibar before he was assassinated—assassinated, I might add, in the very car that you rode in on the night of July 18?"

"Ganjibar was killed by an Islamic suicide bomber. You certainly don't think I arranged that?"

"Not you, but you might have provided essential reconnaissance information to the people who did—the kind of car he drove, the hours he kept, his security arrangements, his political intentions."

"You say 'might have,' but you have no proof."

"I am working on that, Monsieur Preston. But I have no doubts about the basic facts of this case: your friend Jason Winthrop ordered the attack on instructions from Washington. It was arranged by a C.I.A. mole posing as an Islamic radical."

"Then why don't you ask Winthrop if I was involved? He'll tell you I had nothing to do with it."

"Alas, Winthrop has diplomatic immunity. I cannot interrogate him. All we can do under international law is declare him persona non grata and expel him from France, which we have already done."

"Then ask your Islamic radical. I've had no contact with anyone like that. I don't even know who you are talking about."

"Of course you had no contact with him. In a compartmentalized operation, it would have been unthinkable."

"This is all circumstantial," said Sam, raising his voice. "What concrete evidence do you have that I was involved?"

"We have testimony by a certain Hal Carpenter to the effect that he picked you up in Ganjibar's car on the night of July 18, and that you later drove off with Ganjibar, his chauffeur, and his bodyguard for a long discussion in the Bois de Boulogne."

"That's true, but what does it prove?"

"And we have your fingerprints from the inside of the car."

"Any passenger in that car would have left prints. This is ridiculous."

"Not so ridiculous, Monsieur Preston. Why are you so agitated if you have nothing to hide?"

"And what motive could I possibly have to help kill Rafat Ganjibar?"

"Orders from above, Monsieur Preston, orders from above. Like many of your journalistic colleagues, you might well be an honorable correspondent of the C.I.A. But unlike your friend Winthrop, you have no diplomatic immunity."

"You are making a big mistake," Sam sighed. "I'll admit there are some curious coincidences, and I realize it would be politically expedient for your government to convict an American in this affair. But you should know, as a man of the law, that you have no evidence, no corroborating witnesses, and no case. None of this will stand up in court."

"We shall see about that in due course, Monsieur Preston. By the time we get you extradited to France, I believe I will have assembled all the hard evidence I need to convict you."

CHAPTER

56

ON MONDAY, JULY 31, the receptionist at the *Chronicle*'s Washington bureau called Lisa Taylor and told her she had a visitor. When Lisa arrived in the waiting area, she saw a scrawny-looking man in a straw-colored toupee and a red-and-white seersucker suit. He looked like the kind of crank who occasionally shows up at the offices of news organizations to complain about some article or warn the press about a Communist plot to poison the water supply.

This man did neither. He was polite and well spoken, even if he did have a reedy voice and a hillbilly accent. He apologized for coming without an appointment and taking up her time. Then he handed her a thick envelope.

"This is from Sam Preston," said Blassingame. "He says it's urgent."

Lisa turned white. "Have you seen Sam? How is he? Where is he?"

"He's fine, ma'am, but I can't tell you where he is. In his current situation, you understand, he has to be discreet."

Lisa examined the envelope. Sam had handwritten her name on it. Her heart was racing. "Thank you, Mister . . . ?"

"Name's not important, ma'am. I thank you for your time." Blassingame gave her a little smile and a nod, then turned and headed for the exit.

When Lisa got back to her office, she closed and locked the door. Then she opened the envelope. Inside it, there was another sealed envelope, and a folded one-page letter:

Dear Lisa,

I know you'll be surprised to hear from me, dear friend, but I also know I can rely on you to help me in my hour of need. Do NOT read the contents of the inside envelope, or your life will be in danger as mine is now. I beg you to get this immediately into the hands of your friend Bob Shea. Tell him to read the CD-rom and study the documents carefully, and then to take whatever action he may find appropriate. I have been prevented from publishing this information, but the world needs to know about it. I hope you are well. I'll be back in touch when I can.

Love,
Sam

Lisa read the letter over several times, then picked up her phone and dialed a direct line on Capitol Hill.

"Bob? It's Lisa. Can I see you?"

CHAPTER

57

WHEN HISTORIANS LOOK BACK on it all, perhaps they will see in the stark gray pages of the *Congressional Record* for Monday, August 14, the decisive turning point in America's recovery from a long season of moral and political decadence:

> *THE SPEAKER.* Persuant to the rule, the gentleman from Massachusetts will control 10 minutes. The chair recognizes the gentleman from Massachusetts.
>
> *MR. SHEA.* Mr. Speaker, I rise today to address this house on a grave and urgent matter. The contents of the envelope I am holding, as verified and supplemented by my congressional research staff, contains dramatic, documented proof of high crimes and misdemeanors committed by the president and vice president of the United States.
>
> I will of course share them fully with you, fellow members of Congress, and I expect that they will be thoroughly examined by this body. For I am confident that you will conclude, as I have, that the acts to which I refer warrant nothing less than the impeachment of the president and vice president. I speak of acts far graver than the sexual indiscretion that, some years ago, prompted this body to seek the removal of a president.
>
> Mr. Speaker, the 10 minutes you have allotted me are insufficient to spell out the details that have prompted my allega-

tions. I will simply enumerate the charges that I would hope, and expect, this body to adopt in the form of formal articles of impeachment once the Judiciary Committee has fully examined the evidence.

Article 1: The president and vice president have circumvented the budgetary oversight powers of Congress by secretly funding an armed movement in rebellion against a legitimate foreign government.

Article 2: They have usurped the war powers of Congress by carrying out a foreign military expedition in ways, and for reasons, that were not properly presented to, or approved by Congress.

Article 3: They have violated Executive Order 12333, of December 4, 1981, which forbids officials of the U.S. government to conspire to carry out assassinations.

Article 4: They have solicited and extorted monies from foreign governments and individuals with the purpose of funding illegal operations.

Article 5: They have violated the First Amendment guarantees of freedom of the press by seeking to suppress information deemed embarrassing to the administration.

Article 6: They have violated the Fourth Amendment protections against unreasonable searches and seizures, by ordering electronic and other forms of surveillance on U.S. citizens without seeking judicial approval or respecting due process of law, as required by the Constitution and the Foreign Intelligence Surveillance Act.

Article 7: They have condoned torture, cruel and unusual punishment, and unlawful imprisonment in violation of the terms of the Geneva Convention on the Treatment of Prisoners of War, to which the United States has been a signatory since 1949.

Article 8: They have violated the Constitutional principle of habeas corpus by denying the right of so-called 'unlawful enemy combatants' to have legal representation, to see the evidence against them, or to challenge their detention. In so doing, they have stripped the judiciary branch of its powers of judicial review.

Article 9: They have abused executive power in contravention of the checks and balances prescribed by the Constitution.

Article 10: In their privileged dealings with the Evangelical Christian community, including large-scale, illegal campaign financing, and in numerous other ways, they have flouted the consitutional separation of church and state.

Mr. Speaker, in the limited time you have allowed, it will not be possible for me to address the administration's ineptitude and criminal negligence in its handling of a catastrophic natural disaster; its fiscal recklessness in running up a $400 billion deficit by cutting taxes and sharply increasingly defense spending; its ideologically motivated attempt, now happily abandoned, to privatize and ultimately destroy a Social Security system that has served since the New Deal to protect our country's weakest and neediest citizens from poverty, suffering, and degradation; or its short-sighted focus on oil, and spurning of renewable energy research, which will leave us forever at the mercy of the very oil sheikhs and Middle East despotisms that are in fact financing our most ruthless and fanatical enemies.

All that, Mr. Speaker, belongs to a broader national debate that should be undertaken in the interests of the citizens of this country. As for the ten articles of impeachment proposed above, they clearly merit, in my opinion, the removal of the president and vice president from the high offices that they now occupy.

Therefore, Mr. Speaker, I move that this house immediately adopt an impeachment inquiry resolution and send this matter to the Judiciary Committee for further examination and such action as the committee may see fit to undertake

THE SPEAKER. The question is on the motion offered by the gentleman from Massachusetts.

The question was taken.

THE SPEAKER. In the opinion of the chair, the majority of those present have voted in the affirmative.

CHAPTER

58

S AM DID NOT STAY LONG in British custody. With the help
of a court-appointed barrister, he was able to resist a formal French
extradition request on the grounds that the case against him was based
solely on circumstantial evidence. Though he railed about the obstruc-
tionist "rosbifs" in London, Judge Bouvard was secretly relieved, for he
himself had begun to have doubts about Sam's guilt. More to the point,
after discovering that a transvestite French agent had killed Nikola
Lefkosias in Athens, the judge had received strict orders from the Elysée
to lay off the Ganjibar case.

Meanwhile, back-channel U.S.-British diplomatic contacts initiated
by Congressman Bob Shea succeeded in winning Sam's release so that
he could testify in the House Judiciary Committee's impeachment inquiry. By the time the red tape was completed, though, he had only
twenty-four hours to get to Washington for his first appearance before
the committee on the afternoon of Monday, August 21.

There was no time to go to Dover and see Sandra. Their reunion was
limited to a single night at the Heathrow Holiday Inn. Over dinner,
Sam started to fill her in on all that had happened since their last weekend together in Normandy. But there was too much to say, and it was
not a time for talking. Instead, they retired to their room. After that
long period of danger, anxiety, and uncertainty, they bonded physically, hungrily, almost violently, then fell asleep in one another's arms.

There would be plenty of time to talk once he got back from Washington.

With an 8:41 flight to catch, Sam awoke early, showered, and packed his bag. He awakened Sandra with a kiss on the forehead. She opened her eyes wide and clutched him tightly to her breast. There were tears on her cheeks.

"Oh, Sam, I can't bear to let you leave again so soon. I'm afraid something dreadful is going to happen."

He lay down on the bed and caressed her arm. "Nothing is going to happen, Sandra. The file is out of my hands now. No one is after me. I'll just go testify and then our lives will go on as before."

"I don't believe that. You're still in the middle of this. It's so big. All the cameras will be on you. All that pressure, all that scrutiny. All those powerful people who consider you the enemy. They'll try to tear you down, Sam. They'll destroy you. They'll destroy us."

"Sandra, I've told you there's nothing more to fear. Maybe I'll have some uncomfortable moments in the spotlight. But I have no choice. I've got to do this. The world has to know what I know."

"But they've got the file now. Why do they need you?"

"Because documents aren't enough. The public doesn't understand paper trails. They need witnesses. They need drama. They need live testimony under the TV lights. People have to see all this unfold in their living rooms. This isn't some courtroom hearing about an insurance claim. It's the indictment of a president in the full glare of public opinion. These people cannot be allowed to hijack our country and trample on everything we stand for in the world. I have to do this."

Sandra wiped her cheek with a corner of the bedsheet. "You know, Sam. I used to think you just went through life, day by day, doing your job, interviewing people, writing stories, thinking of nothing beyond the next paycheck or promotion."

"I guess I did."

"I even had a secret scorn for you sometimes, because I thought you didn't believe in anything, or even care about anything really important. Then when you started working on this political, arms sale, Middle

East stuff, I was excited because I saw a spark in you, then a flame. And now . . ."

"What?"

"And now I'm afraid the flame is going to burn us up. And I almost wish for the old you, going blithely through the motions, reading your newspaper on the lawn chair all weekend and thinking about dinner."

"It's too late for that, Sandra."

The hearing room was jammed with spectators, reporters, and TV cameras when Sam arrived at 4 p.m. and made his way to the witness table. The hubbub began to subside as he laid a notepad next to the microphone under a stroboscopic volley of electronic flashes. The Judiciary Committee chairman, Representative J. Cooper Helmsley of South Carolina, tapped his gavel and officially opened the hearing.

"Mr. Preston," said Helmsley in a gravelly voice, "I'm going to start this thing by swearing you in as a witness before this committee. Raise your right hand."

Sam raised his hand.

"Do you promise to tell the truth, the whole truth, and nothing but the truth, so help you God?"

"I do."

"Thank you. Now will you now state your full name and occupation?"

"Samuel Wilkes Preston, journalist."

"And who is your employer, Mr. Preston?"

"At the present time, Congressman, I'd have to say I'm self-employed."

A ripple of laughter crossed the room. Helmsey tapped his gavel. "Mr. Preston, I want to return to the circumstances of your, uh, current employment status and other related matters that reflect on your credibility as a witness. But first, I must give the floor to Congressman Shea of Massachussetts, who has requested your appearance here as a witness today. Congressman?"

"Thank you, Mr. Chairman," said Shea, whose prematurely gray hair gave him a distinguished air that contrasted nicely with his lean, boyish face. He looked good under the TV lights and he knew it. Sam gazed up at his smiling countenance, his clear eyes and perfect teeth, and thought of Lisa.

"Mr. Preston, thank you so much for coming here today to testify in this very important inquiry. I know you have been through some trying moments in recent days, and I very much regret the circumstances under which you have been wrongfully accused and detained in London. Before I proceed with my questions, I want you, and this committee, to know the French Embassy has just informed me that all charges against you have been dropped. In other words, you are appearing here today as a free man, unblemished by any suspicion of wrongdoing, and able to fulfill your duty as a patriotic citizen, as indeed you have done throughout your distinguished career as a journalist."

"Thank you, Congressman."

"Mr. Preston, you were the source of many of the documents that formed the original basis for this inquiry. They have, of course, been supplemented by other documents, including extensive research done by my staff on the Foreign Affairs Committee. But since the material you provided is so central to this case, I wonder if you could explain to this committee how these documents came into your possession."

"Congressman, they came from two sources. The first batch, if you will, was given to me in Paris by a man named Nikola Lefkosias. Lefkosias and a certain Michel Lanzatti had approached me earlier with a view to selling the documents."

"Did you pay for these documents?"

"No sir, they were given to me."

"Where did they come from?"

"My understanding is that Lanzatti had obtained them from the office of the late Senator Roland Peccaldi of France, with whom he had a close working relationship."

"And what was the nature of those documents?"

"They traced numerous arms sales and deliveries, payments, bank transfers, and deposits, most of them overseen by Senator Peccaldi."

"I will remind the gentlemen of this committee that they have all been given copies of those documents, which we will discuss in detail at a later time. What about the other set, Mr. Preston?"

"The other set was made available to me by the lawyer of Rafat Ganjibar."

"Rafat Ganjibar, the assassinated leader of the Assyrian Liberation Movement, is that correct?"

"Yes, sir."

"And what was the nature of those documents?"

"They essentially concerned secret arms shipments to the Assyrian Liberation Army in Iraq, many of them arranged by Peccaldi with funding that was apparently provided by agents of the U.S. government. There were also numerous documents—letters, photos, affidavits—that demonstrated strong support for the Assyrian Liberation Movement by members of the Ritter administration and by certain influential leaders of the American Evangelical community. Other documents refer to extensive oil drilling activities in the region controlled by the A.L.A."

"And what company or companies were doing the drilling, Mr. Preston?"

"Only one company appears in the documents I saw, sir: the Bullington Group."

"Again, gentlemen, these documents have been shown to you and will be subject to, I am sure, considerable discussion at a later date. Mr. Preston, why did Mr. Ganjibar make those documents available to you?"

"He was afraid that he might be an assassination target and wanted to make sure that the full story of his relationship with the Ritter administration would be revealed in that event."

"He told you that personally?"

"Yes, sir."

"And when did you meet with him?"

"On two occasions, Congressman. The first meeting was at his office in Boulogne on June 19. He told me about his plans to push for an independent Assyrian republic, and showed me architectural plans for his future capital city."

"Did he discuss any military matters?"

"He showed me a video about the A.L.A., which included shots of uniformed troops and a lot of military hardware."

"Did he indicate to you how all this was funded?"

"He was vague on that point, sir, only saying that he received large donations from Assyrian Christians and from the American Evangelical community."

"What about support from the U.S. government?"

"I would say he intimated that he had backing from the Ritter administration, but did not say so explicity on that occasion."

"What about the second time you met him? Was he more explicit about links to the administration?"

"Absolutely. This was on July 18, right after the Pesh Merga attack on the Assyrian village of Tareq in Iraq. Ganjibar summoned me to Boulogne and we talked for a long time in his car. He was very agitated and told me he was going to formally declare the independence of the Assyrian Republic within a week. He would do so, he said, to force the Ritter administration to reveal the nature of its ties to his movement, the full extent of its backing."

"What did that backing consist of?"

"According to Ganjibar, it was extensive—financial, military, economic. He said U.S. troops were secretly embedded in his army, that Bullington was drilling oil wells there under U.S. military supervision, that large quantities of arms were being shipped into that zone through a network organized by the U.S."

"Did he ever mention nuclear weapons?"

"No sir."

"Now, Mr. Preston, you said Ganjibar was afraid of being assassinated."

"He said he had received death threats."

"From whom?"

"He didn't specify that, Congressman, but he had a lot of enemies—the Shiites, the Kurds, the Sunnis, the various Islamist militias."

"Would that list of enemies include the Ritter administration at this point?"

"That would be pure conjecture on my part, Congressman. But one could see how Ganjibar might be viewed as a liability, and that his threat to reveal his ties with the U.S. might be considered as a dangerous and hostile act by the administration. Again, that's merely my conjecture."

"Gentlemen, we will return to this vitally important question later in these hearings, as my staff has uncovered facts that go far beyond the realm of conjecture."

A rumble of murmurs and mutterings filled the committee room and a burst of electronic flashes lit up Shea's handsome face from every angle. Photographers jabbed one another with their elbows as they jockeyed for position. Sam, too, was bathed in TV lights and peppered with flashes. Helmsley tapped his gavel and called for order.

"Mr. Preston," said Shea, "you have been a most helpful witness. Do you have anything to add to your testimony?"

"No, sir."

"Thank you."

The murmurings continued, as Sam poured himself a glass of water from the pitcher in front of him and took a drink. Helmsley tapped the gavel again.

"Ladies and gentlemen," he said, "it's getting late, so I am going to adjourn this hearing until nine o'clock tomorrow morning. At that time, I want to continue with the questioning of Mr. Preston by myself and other committee members."

As he stood up and gathered his papers, Sam was surrounded by photographers and reporters shoving microphones in his face. He waved off their questions. "Guys, I have told the committee everything I have to say on this."

"Why were you fired from the *Chronicle*?" shouted a reporter from Fox News.

"That's got nothing to do with these hearings."

"Why did Ganjibar talk to you and no one else?" asked another reporter. "Did you have some special deal with him? Were you on his payroll?"

Sam buttoned his jacket and pushed toward the exit. "So long, guys, I'll see you tomorrow."

Just as he reached the door, he saw Lisa Taylor smiling at him.

"Sam, you were wonderful," she whispered in his ear as he leaned forward to give her a peck on the cheek. That fleeting moment was captured by a dozen cameras, and relayed live to millions of TV screens around the world.

In her mother's living room back in Dover, Sandra watched and wondered who this elegant-looking young woman might be. Probably just a friend or colleague. But she was troubled by the apparent intimacy of the gesture, the whispering in her husband's ear, that manicured hand on his shoulder. She wasn't sure exactly what she feared. But he was so far away.

When the hearing resumed on Tuesday, August 22, Helmsley himself opened the questioning. At sixty-nine years old, he was regarded as an elder statesman among the Republican leadership, a former restaurant owner from Charleston who had opposed integration in the 1960s, fulminated against Vietnam War protesters, denounced the teaching of evolution in public schools, equated gun control with totalitarianism, and considered the United Nations a one-world conspiracy against American democracy, free-market capitalism, and Christian values. In short, he stood at the opposite edge of the moral and political universe from the journalist who was seated at the table in front of him.

"Mr. Preston, I'm going to start with a simple question and I want a simple answer. Are you an alcoholic?"

"Excuse me?"

"You heard me, Mr. Preston. Are you an alcoholic?"

"I don't have to answer that question, sir. It is irrelevant to this hearing."

"Mr. Preston, I am the chairman here, not you. I decide what is relevant. Are you pleading the Fifth Amendment on this question? In other words, are you saying that the answer would tend to incriminate you?"

"Of course not. I simply refuse to answer a question that has no bearing on the subjects under discussion here."

"Mr. Preston, you have sworn to tell the truth and the whole truth. If you don't plead the Fifth, and you still refuse to answer, I hope you realize that I can hold you in contempt of Congress."

"I still won't answer that question, sir."

"Well, in fact, you don't need to. Because I know the answer. According to my information, you are a member of Alcoholics Anonymous. You attend regular A.A. meetings at St. Marguerite church in Le Vésinet, France—that's about the only time, I might add, that anybody ever sees you in a church."

Laughter erupted in the committee room, causing Helmsley himself to smile even as he lightly rapped his gavel.

"Mr. Preston, do you deny that you attend these meetings?"

"I don't have to deny anything."

"Well now, Mr. Preston, I have never attended an A.A. meeting myself—and I think that's to my credit—but I have done a little research, and I happen to know that whenever anyone gets up to speak at such a gathering, they preface their remarks with the statement, 'My name is so-and-so and I am an alcoholic.' Is that correct?"

"You have your information on that, Congressman, you don't need me to support it."

"Then I presume that, from time to time, you have stood up there in St. Marguerite church and declared, 'My name is Sam and I am an alcoholic.'"

"Presume what you like, Congressman. I am not going to speak to that."

Bob Shea, sitting to Helmsley's left, leaned toward his microphone. "Mr. Speaker," he said in his flat-voweled Boston accent, "I object to this line of questioning. Mr. Preston is here as a witness. He is not a defendant in a criminal trial."

"Congressman, this isn't a Sunday school picnic we're holding here. It's an inquiry into the possible impeachment of the president of the United States. Mr. Preston has made some grave charges against the president. I think this committee, and the American people, have a right to know about the character and credibility of this witness."

"On the contrary, Mr. Chairman," Shea retorted, "I think the American people are going to see that you are a bully who prefers to take cheap shots at a witness rather than examine the substance of his testimony."

Murmurs rumbled once again through the room and cameras flashed the faces of Shea and Helmsley as they stared murderously at one another.

"Congressman," said Helmsley with his exaggerated Southern gentleman manners, "I would respectfully ask that you keep your partisan opinions to yourself while I continue questioning the witness. But since you want me to talk substance, I am only too happy to oblige. Now, Mr. Preston, I have obtained some interesting information concerning your activities at the *New York Chronicle*. That is your former employer, correct?"

"Yes."

Helmsley slipped on a pair of rimless reading glasses and studied some papers on his desk. "Among the documents that this committee has subpoenaed from the *Chronicle*, I have some expense reports here that you turned in to their Paris bureau. I'd like you to explain some items to me."

Sam took a sip of water, then folded his hands on the table.

"For example, on July 10, you claimed reimbursement in the amount of $295 for a pair of Gucci sunglasses purchased over the Internet with your credit card. Did you buy these glasses for yourself?"

"No sir. The report explicitly states that it was a gift for a source."

"A bribe, you mean?"

"No sir. It is perfectly legitimate, from time to time, to make gifts to sources and contacts who help us gather news."

"According to my information, Mr. Preston, the *Chronicle*'s Code of Ethics limits such gifts to fifty dollars in value. Beyond that amount, I would consider any such gift a bribe, and a violation of your company's rules. Am I right?"

"That's your opinion, sir. I considered it a legitimate news-gathering expense."

"Well, it's true that $295 is not a very large sum. It is much smaller, for example, than the 925 euro—over a thousand dollars—that you spent on a first-class plane ticket to Athens, purchased on your corporate Amex card. Was that for a professional trip or a little weekend by the sea?"

"Again, it was news gathering. And the ticket was not for myself."

Helmsley raised his bristly white eyebrows and smiled wryly. "Another gift for a source?"

"Not a gift. It was to enable the source of certain vital information to escape from a threatening situation."

"Mr. Preston, let's not beat around the bush here. That ticket was for Nikola Lefkosias, right?"

"Yes, sir."

"And you have already testified that Mr. Lefkosias was the source of your first set of documents, is that correct?"

"Yes."

"And you have told this committee, under oath, that you did not pay for those documents. I assume you remember making that statement yesterday?"

"Yes."

"Mr. Preston, that is a very serious admission. It would appear from your own testimony that you in fact paid for those documents with a thousand dollar plane ticket. In which case, you have committed perjury before this committee."

Sam shook his head. "No, sir, I did not. It was not a direct payment. Mr. Lekfosias got no personal benefit from it except to extricate himself from a life-threatening situation. I would add that he was murdered in Athens a week later, which I think is a pretty strong indication that his life was in danger."

The buzz and drone from the audience again filled the chamber.

"Well, Mr. Preston, I'll leave it to our committee lawyers to examine the perjury question. But I would like you to tell me whether you actually published any information you obtained from Mr. Lefkosias. In other words, did your company derive any benefit whatsoever from the money you, in fact, misappropriated on its behalf?"

"I never had the opportunity to publish it, sir, because the *Chronicle* fired me before I could do so."

"Fired you, according to my information, for negligence, repeated unexplained absences, insubordination."

"Congressman, I was let go along with a dozen other staffers as part of a general reduction in force. I was not fired for cause."

"Well, that's what I'd call putting the best face on an embarrassing situation. I think this committee, and the American people, will understand from the facts I have laid before them that you were a dishonest and untrustworthy employee."

"Congressman, I reject and resent that characterization."

"I am merely stating obvious facts about your moral lapses, Mr. Preston, lapses that go far beyond your professional activities. You are a married man, are you not?"

"Yes."

"How long have you been married?"

"Four years."

"Were you married in a church?"

"No sir, in a civil ceremony in Paris."

"Well, now, I understand that the French do things that way—keeping God out of the most sacred bond that exists between a man and a woman. But I assume you still exchanged vows?"

"It was the standard French act of marriage, sworn before the mayor."

"Did that, uh, French act include a vow of fidelity?"

"I believe so."

"You believe so? Well, then, would you mind explaining to the committee the nature of your relationship with a certain Miss Lisa Taylor?"

Sam's face turned red and the room erupted once more.

"Order," Helmsley shouted. "I call this chamber to order. Answer the question, Mr. Preston."

"Lisa Taylor," said Sam with a slight quiver in his voice, "Lisa Taylor is a former colleague at the *Chronicle*. I worked with her in the Washington bureau before my transfer to Paris. I went out with her at that time."

"According to my information, Mr. Preston, you have been out with her, or maybe I should say in with her, far more recently than that. Can you explain, for example, what you were doing in her apartment at the Watergate between 11 p.m. and 1 a.m. on the night of July 12? I have security camera images here that document that fact."

Sam glared at Helmsley and took a sip of water. Then he rose slowly to his feet and began to speak in a loud, angry voice.

"Mr. Helmsley," he said, "I have had enough of your insulting and outrageous insinuations about my character and my personal life. I have no apologies to make about my character. I have strong values, which may not be your values, sir, but I believe in them and I live by them. As for my personal life, that is no business of yours—no more than the personal lives of my former colleague and my wife, both of whom you have deeply wounded here today."

The noise level around him rose steadily, but Sam continued. "And since you are so intent on talking about personal morals, Congressman, let's talk about yours. Three divorces, five draft deferments that kept you out of Vietnam, a conviction for assault on two civil rights workers who committed the crime of ordering a meal in your restaurant, and, from what I read in the papers, a possible federal investigation into your relations with a certain lobbyist who is now serving a jail term for handing out millions of dollars in illegal campaign contributions to Republican members of Congress."

Helmsley pounded furiously on his gavel. "Sit down, Mr. Preston. You are out of order."

"No, sir, you are out of order. You and your whole band of self-righteous, narrow-minded, mean-spirited hypocrites. You want to hand out lessons to the rest of us, hold us to your pin-headed rules with your pious incantations while you violate the Constitution, line your pockets, invade sovereign countries on spurious pretexts, and make a mockery of this great nation in the eyes of the entire world."

As TV cameras zoomed in on Sam's face under a battery of electronic flashes, Helmsley continued to pound his gavel like a roofer hammering down a rebellious shingle.

Sam pointed his finger at the chairman and leaned down close to the microphone. "You, Mr. Helmsley, your party, and your president have almost succeeded in destroying everything that was great and admirable about America, just as you have sought to destroy me here today. I hope the American people will realize what you are doing, and oppose it, before it is too late. As for me, Congressman, I am a free man, with a clear conscience, and I am going to walk out of this chamber right now. If you want to hold me in contempt, that's fine with me, because the contempt I feel for you and your ilk at this moment, sir, is beyond measure."

Back in Dover, Sandra sobbed uncontrollably as she watched Sam's image flicker across her TV screen. She had never felt him so strong, or loved him more deeply, than she did at that moment—even though she was hurt and humiliated by Helmsley's odious words. She prayed they were not true. But if they were, she hoped Sam would tell her, explain it all, make it right. Otherwise, her pain would be too deep to bear.

Sam's phone call came an hour later, just as Sandra was preparing for bed.

"Did you see it?" he asked.

"Sam, who is this Lisa Taylor? What is that all about?"

"She's an old girlfriend, who is still a friend, and who was instrumental in getting all this out into the open. She's a good person."

"But did you sleep with her?"

"She was my girlfriend before I met you, Sandra."

"Since then?"

Sam hesitated. He could hear Sandra's rapid breathing on the other end of the line. "Yes I did. In one weak moment last month. It was like taking a drink when I know it will destroy me. But I know I'll never take a drink again. Because I don't want us to be destroyed. Do you understand what I'm saying?"

He heard her sobbing. "Why?"

"I was weak, Sandra. I'm very sorry. I'm afraid I'll never be perfect, but I can promise to try. Can you forgive me?"

"It hurts, Sam. God, it hurts. It will take time."

"We have time. I'm coming home tomorrow. I love you, Sandra."

CHAPTER

59

S IX MONTHS LATER

Jack Ritter had taken this walk many times, but never had the occasion been more dramatic. As he headed down the red-carpeted corridor, his arms dangling stiffly at his sides with his thumbs turned in as usual, he saw the reporters with their flashing cameras and TV lights as an enemy army lying in wait. When he finally reached the podium in the East Room, joined on one side by his wife and two sons, and on the other by his parents, Quentin and Susan Ritter, he stood silently for a moment and waited for the reporters to take their seats. Then he stepped up to the microphone, put on his glasses, and read from a prepared text.

"My fellow Americans, I stand before you today as a man who is bloodied but unbroken. The charges that have been leveled against me have been motivated from the start by partisan politics and by a shameful attempt on the part of my opponents to win, by slander and deceit, the prize that escaped them in the ballot box.

"The charges are baseless, wrongfully argued, legally flawed, morally reprehensible. I will maintain to my dying day that I have done nothing wrong in my exercise of this nation's highest office, have committed no crime, have violated no law.

"In these times of exceptional danger facing our nation, my administration has had to adopt exceptional means of protecting our citizens from perils that our forefathers could never have imagined. In that context, my fellow Americans, I have done no more, and no less, than my duty. Those who level these charges against me today are allies of the very forces of evil that threaten our democratic nation. But I say to you today, in the words of the Book of Proverbs, that 'The righteous shall never be removed: and the wicked shall not inhabit the earth.'

"My fellow citizens, apart from Jesus Christ and the Holy Bible, nothing is dearer to me than the grand old flag of the United States of America. It stands for all the good, decent, hardworking, church-going folks that make this nation great and prosperous. It is for their sake, to spare the American people the agony and divisions of an impeachment trial, and to spare my family the anguish and pain of this disgraceful witch hunt, that I come before you today to announce my resignation as president of the United States.

"I wish my successor well, and I pray that God's blessing and grace will be bestowed upon the American people and the Republic for which they stand."

Ignoring the bedlam of shouted questions from the press pack, Ritter stepped back from the podium. His family gathered around him and, with tears, hugs, and audible sobs, shared his pain.

Back in Le Vésinet, Sam and Sandra sat enthralled as they watched this extraordinary drama unfold on CNN. Sam found himself feeling strangely sorry for Ritter, just as he had more than a quarter-century earlier, when Richard Nixon stood at the door of his presidential helicopter and, with a clenched but quivering jaw, waved good-bye to the White House for the last time. Sam had never thought of his denunciation of Ritter's misdoings in personal terms. Now he saw the fragile, human side of this disgraced and defeated president. Jack Ritter was not a bad person. He was just a weak and limited man, promoted far beyond his true abilities, and prey to keener minds with darker ambitions.

On the TV screen, CNN senior correspondent Fox Krieger, his silver beard impeccably clipped as always, stood before the backdrop of the White House with a microphone in his hand. "Well, there you have it, Richard," he said, "Jack Ritter announcing his resignation as president of the United States. A dramatic, tragic moment in the history of this nation."

From Atlanta, the anchor asked the veteran newsman for his thoughts on the meaning of it all.

"Richard, this announcement not really coming as a surprise at this point. The House had been expected to vote the articles of impeachment this afternoon and refer the matter to the Senate for a trial presided over by the chief justice. Unofficial head count in the Senate showing the upper house leaning toward conviction. That process would have lasted for several grueling, incapacitating weeks. So the president cutting his losses and, as he put it, sparing the country an agonizing and divisive spectacle whose outcome would seem, at this point, to be inevitable. I should add, Richard, that the latest public opinion polls were running more than 70 percent in favor of the impeachment of President Jack Ritter."

"Fox, this announcement widely expected, as you say, but where does it leave us? Where do we go from here?"

"Well Richard, this is a very unusual situation, but there is a clear precedent for it in the Nixon resignation back in 1974. At that time, you may remember, Nixon's vice president, Spiro Agnew, resigned in the face of corruption charges. President Nixon, as mandated by the Constitution, named Gerald Ford to replace Agnew. Thus when Nixon himself later resigned to avoid impeachment over the Watergate affair, the unelected Gerald Ford became president."

"Fox, that all seems rather complicated. Can you spell out for us exactly how it applies to the present situation?"

"It's going to follow pretty much the same scenario, Richard. As we all know, former vice president Cordman resigned two months ago in the face of multiple allegations of influence peddling, insider trading, and perjury. At that time, President Ritter named Senator Frank Connelly of Nevada to replace Cordman, and the Senate approved that choice. So Connelly will now become president. We will see his swearing-in ceremony live from the Capitol rotunda in just a few minutes."

"Fox, before we cut away to that historic event, tell us what kind of president you expect Frank Connelly to be. Does he represent a clean break from the Ritter administration, continuity, or something in between?"

"Richard, I'd say something in between. He's a senior figure in the Republican party, so there's some continuity there. On the other hand, Connelly, a Vietnam war hero, has been a vocal opponent of the way the Iraq war and occupation have been carried out, and he's opposed to the more ideological, faith-based, low-tax, high-deficit policies of his predecessor. In short he's a more traditional, fiscally conservative Republican. He's also shown an ability to reach out to the Democrats on key issues, so we may expect him to make a bipartisan appeal for national unity and healing."

"Fox, one last thing—any idea who Connelly might choose as his own vice president?"

"Richard, his staff telling us they have several names on the short list. But the name we're hearing most often is that of Senator Chip Nagor of Indiana, also a Vietnam vet, harsh critic of the Iraq invasion, fiscal conservative, and in many ways a man cut from the same cloth as Connelly. Richard?"

"Thank you, Fox Krieger there at the White House. And now we're going to move to the Capitol Rotunda for the swearing-in of Frank Connelly as the next president of the United States."

The image cut to Capitol Hill, where CNN congressional correspondent Max Feldman stood some ten yards away from a dais and a lectern that had already been emblazoned with the presidential seal. A large delegation of congressional leaders from both houses and both parties was visible behind him.

"Richard, in just a few moments, Frank Connelly and Chief Justice James Emerson will step up on the podium behind me for the oath of office. The podium set up on the very spot where the bodies of presidents from Abraham Lincoln to John Kennedy and Ronald Reagan have lain in state. The choice of venue here very symbolic. Aides to the future president telling us that he chose to take the oath here in the Capitol Rotunda as a sign of unity, of bipartisan cooperation, and of deference to the role of Congress under the Constitution. No formal speech planned, but we are told that the new president will address a brief message to the nation. Richard?"

"Max, I see the president-designate and the chief justice approaching the dais just behind you, so let's go directly to the oath of office."

Connelly raised his right hand and placed his left hand on the Bible. He was normally a man with a sunny manner and a ready grin, but at this moment his demeanor was as solemn as his dark gray suit.

The chief justice raised his own right hand and administered the oath.

"You, Frank B. Connelly, do solemnly swear."

"I, Frank B. Connelly, do solemnly swear."

"That you will faithfully execute the office of president of the United States."

"That I will faithfully execute the office of president of the United States."

"And will, to the best of your ability . . ."

"And will, to the best of my ability . . ."

"Preserve, protect, and defend the Constitution of the United States of America."

"Preserve, protect, and defend the Constitution of the United States of America."

"So help you God."

"So help me God."

The last words were followed by spirited applause from the invited dignitaries, greatly amplified by the acoustics of the rotunda. The Marine band struck up "Hail to the Chief" as Connelly shook hands with the chief justice, an ultraconservative appointee of his predecessor, and with the congressional leaders who, until recently, had been his colleagues on Capitol Hill. Among them was Bob Shea of Massachusetts, whose national popularity had skyrocketed during the impeachment hearings and who was now considered the front-runner for the Democratic presidential nomination. As Connelly and Shea shook hands, their eyes locked briefly on one another.

Then the new president returned to the podium and waited for the chamber to fall silent.

"My fellow Americans," he said in a firm, resolute voice, "this is no time for celebration. It is a very sad moment in our nation's history. I am honored to stand before you as president today, but I would have given anything to have our proud nation avoid the circumstances that put me here. I am not here to criticize my predecessor—let history be his judge. Nor will I deliver any ringing inaugural address. What our country needs now is action, not rhetoric. I simply want to inform you of the immediate steps I intend to take as president.

"First, I am nominating Senator Charles Nagor of Indiana for the office of vice president, subject to Senate approval.

"Second, this afternoon, I will sign an executive order pulling all U.S. military personnel and equipment out of the so-called Assyrian Autonomous Region immediately, and making any future deployments there, and throughout the territory of Iraq, subject to the request and authorization of duly elected regional and national officials there.

"Third, I will propose modifications in the Patriot Act and the Foreign Intelligence Surveillance Act to ensure that the rights, privacy, and freedom of expression of our fellow citizens are respected according to the strict letter of the Constitution and the application of due process of law.

"Apart from those initial concrete steps, I want to pledge to you, my fellow citizens, that I will strive to restore the constitutional balance prescribed by our forefathers; that the executive branch, under my authority, will pursue its mission in partnership with Congress, with all due respect for the rights and prerogatives of the people's representatives and of the judiciary branch.

"I will have more to say to you in the coming days and weeks, my fellow citizens. But at this solemn and painful time, I simply want to ask for your cooperation, your understanding, your prayers. Let us all reach out to one another, for the love of our country and the principles on which it was founded, and together put this long, dark night behind us."

Sandra's eyes were glistening as she took her husband's hand in hers. "Well, Sam, you said you wanted to change the history of the world. Are you satisfied?"

"Not really."

"What more did you want?"

"I wanted to be president."

"Oh, you mad fool." She pushed him over on the couch and gave him a long, hard kiss. Sam groped for the remote and turned off the TV.

CHAPTER
60

I T WAS 5 A.M. IN BAGHDAD and all seemed quiet in the Green Zone. This sprawling, heavily fortified quarter on the banks of the Tigris River formerly housed Saddam's presidential palace and the villas of his top government officials. Saddam and his henchmen were long gone. In their place, behind twelve-foot concrete blast walls topped with concertina wire and circled by M1 Abrams tanks and Bradley fighting vehicles, was the administrative nerve center of the U.S.-occupying force and the fledgling Iraqi government that operated under its tutelage. And in the middle of the complex stood Camp Steel Dragon, home of the U.S. 82nd Field Artillery, the 89th Military Police Brigade, and the special operations senior staff.

Captain Andy Felker stirred his coffee and surveyed the bank of video monitors on the wall in front of him. He scanned the screens one by one: the base entrance, the administrative housing blocks, the senior staff headquarters and briefing rooms, the arms depots, the PX, the soldiers' barracks. Suddenly something attracted his attention in the officers' mess. There was a strange movement, a blurry figure wandering among the tables, crouching, advancing, crouching again.

Felker pushed some buttons in front of him and called up video images of the mess and galley from all angles. He turned a dial and zoomed in tight on the mysterious figure.

"Eddie!" He nudged the elbow of Captain Edward Hollinger, who had been dozing at his side. "Eddie, we've got penetration in the officers' mess. Check this out."

Hollinger sat up and squinted at the screens. He saw a man in boxer shorts and a sleeveless undershirt clutching an automatic rifle in one hand, opening and closing the doors of refrigerators and lockers with the other.

"Holy shit, Andy. That's General Runter."

"It sure is. What the fuck is he doing in the officers' mess at 5 a.m.?"

"By the looks of that M-16, I don't think he's looking for a midnight snack. Hit the sound."

Felker punched another button and suddenly the general's voice emerged from a pair of wall-mounted speakers.

"Where is the filthy bitch? I know she's in here somewhere. Come out you fornicating slut! I'm gonna blow your ass away for Jesus!"

Runter moved erratically among the tables, knocking over chairs, turning around in circles with his finger on the trigger of his M-16.

Felker flipped a switch and activated his own microphone. "Uh, General?"

Runter started at the noise and fired several rounds into the air. "Who's that?"

"General, this is Captain Felker up in base security. How are you doing this morning, sir?"

"Felker! We've gotta kill the whore of Babylon. She's hiding in here."

"Sir, what makes you think anyone is hiding in the officers' mess? The area is monitored by security 24/7."

"Jesus told me she was in there. He just came to me in a dream, Captain. He said, 'Rick, I need you to kill the whore of Babylon, and then I'll come.'"

"Uh, Jesus told you he was coming? To the Green Zone, sir?"

"Hell no, you dumb bastard. He's coming to Armageddon to fight the final battle. I want every man on this base mobilized, dressed in white linen robes. He's gonna need us at his side. But first I gotta kill the whore of Babylon."

Felker switched off his mike and turned to Hollinger. "Call the 89th MPs and tell them we have a situation in the officers' mess. Runter's gone berserk. He's armed and dangerous. I'll try to keep him talking."

He turned the microphone back on. Runter was turning over tables, shelves, and serving carts, sending shattered plates and silverware clattering across the linoleum floor.

"Sir," said Felker. "We're trying to help you out here. Do you have a description of the individual you're looking for?"

"Of course I have a description, Felker. It's written right there in Revelation 17: 'And the woman was arrayed in purple and scarlet color and precious stones and pearls, having a golden cup in her hand full of abominations and filthiness of her fornication. And upon her forehead was a name written, MYSTERY, BABYLON THE GREAT, THE MOTHER OF HARLOTS AND ABOMINATIONS OF THE EARTH.'"

Felker stared at the monitor and blinked rapidly, a nervous tic that he developed at times of stress. "Sir, I've checked the security logs up here, and there's no report of anyone by that description entering the base."

"Felker, you idiot. The Whore of Babylon doesn't need to come through a military checkpoint. She's like Satan, she can be material and immaterial, she can fly like a bat, crawl on her belly like a snake, wriggle through keyholes like a centipede. That's why I gotta find her, and I gotta kill her." Runter opened the door of a cold-storage locker and fired a few rounds into a frozen side of beef.

Hollinger put his phone down and signaled to Felker to turn off the microphone.

"The MPs have called in some Special Forces guys and they have the mess surrounded," he said, "but it's locked and barricaded from the inside. They've also searched his quarters. You're not gonna believe this."

"What?"

"He's plastered his room with pictures of black women with their butts in the air and their crotches spread open. The MPs said he downloaded them from a Web site called 'blackbooty.com.' And he's scrawled 'Kill the Whore of Babylon' all over the walls with magic marker."

"Jesus! He's lost it."

"Totally."

"What should we do?"

"The MPs said we should keep him talking."

"Why don't they just break the door down and grab him?"

"They're afraid he'll use his weapon against them, or himself. They want us to play for time, wear him down."

Felker took a deep breath and looked at his watch. Five-thirty. His palms felt sweaty as he flipped the microphone back on.

"Uh, General. Felker here. Sir, it's getting toward breakfast time. Don't you want Cook to come in there and whip you up some scrambled eggs and bacon? Why don't you unlock the door and let him in?"

"Felker, any sonofabitch tries to come in here, I'll blow his fucking head off. I'm not kidding. Jesus told me to kill the Whore of Babylon and I'm not coming out until I've wasted the bitch."

"We can send in some reinforcements to help you, sir, if you'll just open the door."

"Felker, are you out of your mind? As soon as I open that door, the Whore will fly out of here like a bat out of hell and we'll never catch her. No, Felker, I gotta do her by myself. Gotta do it for Jesus. Gotta do it for Jesus. Do it for Jesus. It's a written order."

"Sir, did you say you were acting on a written order?"

"That's right, Felker. It is written in the 138th psalm: 'O daughter of Babylon, who are to be destroyed; happy shall he be, that rewardeth thee as thou hast served us. Happy shall he be, that taketh and dasheth thy little ones against the stones.'"

There was a knock on the door. Felker turned off the mike.

"Captain," said a soft voice on the other side. "This is Reverend Truehart. I want to talk to the general."

Felker checked the video monitor next to the door and recognized the base's respected Protestant chaplain. He buzzed the door open and gave Truehart, who held a major's rank, a salute.

"Morning, Captain. Bad business, eh?" There was something reassuring about the chaplain's smile. Felker didn't go to chapel much, but he'd always liked Daryl Truehart's gentle, low-key manner. It was like a calm island amidst a raging sea of testosterone and adrenaline.

"Let me talk to him, Captain. I think he may listen to me."

Felker switched on the mike and gave his seat to the chaplain.

"General, this is Daryl Truehart. Can you hear me, General?"

"I hear you. What a glorious day, Reverend!"

"Every day the Lord gives us is glorious, General."

"Yes, Reverend, but this is the morning of the Last Day. The end is near, the prophecy will soon be fulfilled. All we've worked and prayed for will soon come to pass. Rejoice, Reverend. Rejoice."

"I rejoice each morning when I wake up, General, and each night when I go to sleep. I rejoice that the Lord has made us in his likeness, to be His servants on earth and follow His law. And General, I rejoice in the message of the Gospel and the Ten Commandments—that we should love our neighbor as ourselves, that we should be merciful and compassionate, that we should not kill, or lie, or steal, or covet, that we should judge not lest we be judged."

"Yes, Reverend. But we must also smite the enemies of the Lamb, 'for he is Lord of lords, and King of kings: and they that are with him are called, and chosen, and faithful.'"

Truehart wiped his forehead with a handkerchief. He took a sip from the paper coffee cup that Felker had set before him.

"General, there is a chain of command in the universe, just as there is a chain of command here on earth. Soldiers like you and me don't make the law of the land, we merely defend it. Am I right?"

"That is correct, sir. We are under civilian leadership."

"And we Christians don't make God's law, we must follow it."

"Right again, Reverend. We are but His humble servants."

"Yes we are, right down to the very last day. But, General, it is not ours to know or choose that day."

"Reverend, the day is at hand. Jesus just told me that in a dream."

"General, there are times when a dream is simply a dream. I am a man of God, but I don't presume to talk to the Lord. I can only divine His will through my own heart and mind. And I'll tell you what I think He wants you to do now, General."

"What's that, Reverend?"

"Put down the gun, General. Put down the gun and open the door."

"I, I can't do that, Reverend. I'm on a mission. A mission for Jesus."

"Rick," said Truehart, his voice hardly louder than a whisper, "put down the gun and open the door. I want to come in there and pray with you, Rick. I think it's time for us to pray."

Runter made no answer. He pulled out a chair and sat down slowly. He laid his M-16 on the table in front of him, but kept his finger on the trigger.

"Rick, I'm going to recite the 23rd Psalm with you. When we get to the end I want you to open the door and let me come in and pray by your side."

Runter put his head in his hands and stared at his rifle. He was getting tired. It was such a long night.

"The Lord is my shepherd; I shall not want," Truehart began, and Runter joined in.

"He maketh me to lie down in green pastures: he leadeth me beside the still waters."

In a darkened hallway downstairs, a small group of MPs and elite Green Beret troops huddled around the main door to the officers' mess.

"He restoreth my soul: he leadeth me in the paths of righteousness for his name's sake."

Two demolition specialists quietly attached a fifty-gram wad of Semtex plastique explosive to the door.

"Yea, though I walk through the valley of the shadow of death, I will fear no evil: for thy rod and thy staff they comfort me."

The Green Berets stepped back from the door and readied their M-16s. The MPs removed the safeties on their sidearms.

"Thou preparest a table before me in the presence of mine enemies: thou anointest my head with oil: my cup runneth over."

A Green Beret major held up his hand and counted off the seconds on his fingers, five, four . . .

"Surely goodness and mercy shall follow me all the days of my life: and I will dwell in the house of the Lord forever."

The blast blew the lock off the door. Eight soldiers burst in, dropped to a battle crouch, trained their weapons on Runter.

At the same instant, a second charge detonated. Six more soldiers rushed through the rear door and hit the deck.

Runter cradled his M-16 in his arms but made no move. He slowly drew his legs up and crouched into a fetal position, his hands still gripping the weapon. His eyes were wet with tears.

Through the main door, still obsured by smoke, Daryl Truehart walked slowly toward the general.

Runter did not move. The chaplain put his hand on his shoulder. "Rick, give me the gun," he said softly. "Armageddon can wait."

EPILOGUE

CONNELLY DID A CREDIBLE JOB during his first six months in the White House. He had gotten nearly one third of the U.S. troops out of Iraq—some 40,000 men and women who returned to their families and their lives after a long season in hell. There were many physically and psychologically wounded among them, but they were more fortunate than the 3,000 who came home in steel boxes. Within two years, the president promised, most of the remaining U.S. forces would be out. The U.S. would continue to provide aid for reconstruction, but the democratically elected authorities of Iraq, for better or worse, would be fully responsible for administering and defending their own country. On the domestic front, Connelly had raised taxes and restored some of his predecessor's deep budget cuts in education, health, and renewable energy research. But it would take at least another generation to chip away the deficits left behind by the Ritter administration.

As for Ritter himself, he had returned to New Mexico and assumed the titular presidency of an oil company owned by a syndicate of investors put together by his father. It was actually a sinecure, which paid him a million dollars a year to put on a suit and show up at a few board meetings. Quentin Ritter wasn't about to let his son actually have a hand in running things. So the former president of the United States spent most of his time down on the ranch, riding horses, clearing brush, and playing horseshoes.

Bill Cordman was the one who really landed on his feet. He had nothing to fear from prosecutors now, since Ritter's last official act as president was to issue him a blanket pardon. He was back on his ranch in Montana—for some reason conservatives all had to have ranches somewhere—and was hard at work on his memoirs. His literary agent had put them up for auction and got a high bid of $5 million for the disgraced ex–vice president to write five hundred pages of turgid, self-justifying prose under the title *In My Own Good Conscience*, a book that many would buy but few would read. (No one had thought to solicit Ritter's memoirs, since the idea of his actually writing a book lacked credibility in the eyes of the publishing community.)

From his ivory tower perch as the newly installed president of Georgetown University, Trenton McBride had watched the downfall of Ritter and Cordman with undisguised glee. He was less pleased by the ex-veep's publishing coup, especially since his own memoirs had so far found no takers.

In France, Georges Carnac was history—though not a very distinguished chapter of it. His last year in office had been tarnished by allegations of political scandal and mysterious leaks about secret bank accounts. Carnac's hyperactive, ravenously ambitious successor had proposed some bold domestic reforms—like privatizing the postal service and national railroad, drastically slashing the ranks of French civil servants, reining in pensions and other entitlements—but he had backed down on most of it in the face of crippling national strikes. He made some cosmetic attempts to improve Franco-American relations, but made it clear that France would not return to NATO, and, frankly, did not get along well with the new American president. In private, Connelly told his staffers to keep "that yapping French attack poodle" away from him.

At the *New York Chronicle*, too, there had been many changes. The cost-cutting and head-rolling had continued. Many of the overseas bureaus had been closed; international coverage was handed over to the wire services and a handful of roving reporters. The business-side executives, who had relegated the once-powerful editors to the role of hired help, decided that American readers and advertisers didn't care enough about foreign news to warrant a big investment in covering it.

There were those who thrived in the new environment, however. Bradley Kemp had been called back to New York and made deputy editor, pending his inevitable anointment as editor in chief once he succeeded in pushing his boss aside. No one expected that to take very long. Clive Woodridge had quit the newspaper rather than move to Detroit. He was now doing public relations for a posh golf and tennis club in Surrey, where he spent most of his time happily downing gin and tonics in the bar.

Charles Dumond was still working for *Actualités*. He had his own foreign affairs column now, and spent a lot of time on the road. Sam tried to have lunch with him every few weeks. For a long time, he had been angry over what he considered Dumond's manipulation of him for the benefit of the D.G.S.E. But the Frenchman had explained, and Sam finally came to accept, that his relationship with the French intelligence service had been limited to occasional information sharing; that he had never pursued his collaboration with Sam at the behest of the agency or reported Sam's activities to them. In order to save a friendship he valued, Sam concluded that French journalists simply had a different code of ethics and agreed to turn the page.

Sam's own life was simpler now. He'd had his brief moment of glory—appeared on the cover of *Time* magazine the week he testified. But when he made the rounds of the newspaper offices back in New York and Washington, he couldn't find a job. Not only did the *Chronicle* refuse to hire him back—hardly surprising under the circumstances—but the *New York Times*, the *Washington Post*, and a half dozen other dailies and newsweeklies also turned him down.

An old friend at the *Chronicle*, the former deputy editor who'd been eased out to make room for Kemp, explained it to him one day over a lunch of corned beef and cabbage at P.J. Clarke's on East 53rd.

"Sam," he said, "you're a great journalist, some would even say a national hero. But it all comes down to this: in this day and age, when the media are controlled by corporate interests, when the advertisers rule the roost and the business-side boys call the shots, nobody wants to hire a whistle-blower. All these interests are so interlocked that an investigative reporter like you is just too dangerous to keep around.

They're all scared to death of what you might uncover in their own backyard. Sorry, pal, but that's how it is."

But Sam got a break. Shortly after his return to France, a New York publisher had approached him about writing a book based on his Armageddon investigation. They had originally suggested that he do a fictionalized version. Sam told them he was a reporter, not a novelist, and could only write the true story. The publisher had agreed and now he was hard at work on the project, living frugally on the advance, but happy to be plying his trade once more.

Sandra was starting to have some success with her painting and sculpture; she'd had some gallery shows in Paris, sold a few pieces, and there was talk of doing something in New York. She was freer to travel now, in any case, since her mother had moved to a nursing home. That left Nigel freer, too. The Mossad commando had trashed the interior of his camper, but he used the insurance settlement to buy an even bigger vehicle. Thus he and Glennys could continue traipsing across Europe and taking vacation pictures of each other.

On this beautiful July morning, Sam and Sandra walked hand-in-hand to the open air market in Le Vésinet. Trailing behind them on a leash, a rambunctious boxer puppy named Megiddo sniffed the sidewalk and stopped to pee on a lamppost. Piled high on the vendors' wooden stands, the eggplants, tomatoes, squash, plums, and apricots were vibrant in the summer sun. Sandra picked up a cantaloupe melon and sniffed it.

"I'm going to buy some hamburger buns at the bakery," said Sam.

"Hamburger buns?"

"Yeah, and get us some gound beef at the butchers, will you? I'm going to throw some burgers on the barbecue. Charles and his new girlfriend are coming to lunch. I want to feed them some real American food."

"Why don't you just order pizza?" she laughed. "Knowing you, you're liable to burn the meat. I mean, you always do, Sam."

"Nonsense," said Sam, yanking Megiddo back from a much larger dog's rear end. "I'm an excellent barbecue chef."

Sandra took her place in line at the vegetable stand. "I'll make a big salad. At least there'll be something to eat if you carbonize the beef."

"I'll meet you back here," Sam said, and headed off in the direction of the bakery.

The baker didn't actually have hamburger buns, so Sam chose some Viennese rolls that were vaguely the right shape. They were a bit too fancy to wrap around a grease-dripping slab of ground meat, but they would do. Once he slathered on the ketchup and chopped onions, nobody would know the difference.

Sam entered Le Méditerranée and spotted his neighbor Jacques Danton standing at the bar nursing a beer. Danton did not notice him at first. His head was buried in the newspaper that lay open on the counter.

"Hi, Jacques," said Sam, as he sat on a stool next to the scientist. "What's happening?"

Danton looked up. Through his thick glasses, his eyes had a wild, manic expression that seemed at odds with the beatific, open-mouthed grin on his face. "Have you seen this?" he said, rapping his finger on the front page of the *Figaro*.

Sam picked up the paper and read the headline: "CHINESE CLAIM SUSTAINABLE FUSION REACTION." Underneath it, there was a subhead that read, "Successful experiment heralds inexhaustible energy supply." There were related articles on potential commercial applications, the physics of fusion, and the sharp plunge of oil stocks on Wall Street.

"Jesus," said Sam, "this is a revolution!"

"More than a revolution, it's a paradigm shift," said Danton with a triumphant tone. "Remember when I told you hydrocarbons were doomed? You didn't want to believe me. But I was right, Sam. Internal combustion engines are history. We can stop worrying about carbon emissions and global warming. And, best of all, we can tell the whole Middle East to go stuff it."

"Not so fast," said Sam, turning to the jump page. "This is just one experiment—remember the 'cold fusion' fiasco in the eighties—the famous Fleischman and Pons hoax?"

Danton smiled and shook his head. "That was lights and mirrors stuff. This is for real. Read the article—the Chinese have unveiled a sustainable prototype reactor that can produce 1000 megawatts. They're promising commercial service within five years. Their secret research program was decades ahead of everybody else. Meanwhile, you Americans stinted on fusion research and bet everything on oil. Now you can buy your energy from the Chinese—actually the Chinese and the French, since we're going to help them build the commercial reactors."

Sam skimmed through the various articles, then handed the paper back to Danton. "Yeah, it's a paradigm shift, alright."

Danton nodded triumphantly. "We should drink to it. Want a beer?"

"No thanks. I gotta meet Sandra at the market. But, hey, I'm grilling a bunch of hamburgers for lunch. Got a couple of friends coming over. Why don't you guys join us?"

"Sounds good to me. I'll check with Nicole."

As he left the café and headed back to the market, Sam heard music coming from the other side of the square. Then he recognized the kinetic form of Princess Tawana, banging on a tambourine and grinding her hips in front of Les Jambalayas. The number ended just as Sam approached the band.

"Tawana!" he cried.

"Sam!" The singer rushed forward and greeted him with a big, sweaty hug. She was wearing a white cotton robe, nothing like her sequined satin stage gowns. "You a sight for sore eyes, boy. I was so worried about you when we saw you in Dover. You were in such a whole heap of trouble and all. Then I saw you on TV. Lord, the way that man talked to you. But you shut him up, boy, you sure did!"

"That's all blown over, Tawana. But, hey, what are you doing playing for coins in Le Vésinet? You guys are big stars."

"Used to be big stars, baby," she said, eyes sliding sidewise toward her trombone man. "Until some Evangelical newspaper found out Jean-Pierre here belonged to a Communist labor union and our American record company canceled our contract. We been blackballed. We out on the street again."

"That's terrible."

"Oh, I don't mind too much," she said, mopping her face with a red bandanna. "I still got a bunch of savings from our heyday. I never was in this for the money, anyhow. I just want to touch people's hearts and spread the message, you know what I'm sayin'?"

"I do, Tawana." Sam bent down and threw a five-euro note into the basket at her feet.

She winked at him, then closed her eyes and struck up a pulsing rhythm on her tambourine. The bass and banjo came in behind her. She spread her arms wide and began to sing in a loud, strong voice that echoed across the square without the aid of a microphone.

> *We gonna win the battle of Arma-ged-don,*
> *Arma-ged-don, Arma-ged-don,*
> *We gonna win the battle of Arma-ged-don,*
> *On that glorious Judgment Day.*
>
> *Oh, Jesus gonna lead us at Arma-ged-don,*
> *Arma-ged-don, Arma-ged-don,*
> *Jesus gonna lead us at Arma-ged-don,*
> *So you better kneel down and pray.*
>
> *Yes, you better kneel down and pray,*
> *Yes, you better kneel down and pray,*
> *You better kneel down and pray . . .*